STACY M. JONES

The Fuse

For Leo

Acknowledgement

The Fuse took a great deal of research as I knew nothing about bombs. I appreciate Leo, whose real first name is used in the book, for his time and expertise and his guidance in making the info accessible to me. Thank you also to the detectives, special agents, and forensics teams I've had the pleasure of working with through the years and the knowledge and expertise they have shared with me. Special thanks to 17 Studio Book Design for bringing my stories to life with amazing covers. Thank you to Dj Hendrickson for your insightful editing and Liza Wood for proofreading and revisions. Thank you to my readers who have truly made this series a success. I am enjoying sharing Kate's adventures with you.

CHAPTER 1

FBI Special Agent Kate Walsh reclined in the chaise lounge in the backyard behind her brownstone on Marlborough Street in Boston's Back Bay neighborhood. The yard, if one could even call it that, was a small square patch of grass Kate had lined with flowers. She had even planted an herb garden in one corner along with some tomatoes that her FBI partner and best friend, Agent Declan James, said would never grow. But grow they had, and she ended up with so many ripe, delicious tomatoes that Kate had dropped off several to her neighbors.

It had been a spectacular summer and respite from her work at the FBI. Kate planned to soak up the remaining summer rays before cool air blanketed the region, and they went back to work.

After their last case in California, taking down a cult, their boss, Martin Spade, who ran the special division that Kate and Declan called home, gave them a three-month vacation from work. That meant from mid-June to mid-September their time was their own. Spade promised not to call them in the middle of the night and tell them to pack and be at the airport within the hour for a case across the country. Spade had kept his promise.

While their last case had been a success, neither of them had walked out unscathed. Kate had some emotional baggage to shake off while Declan had to nurse physical injuries from being shot in the leg. More than a week in the hospital had turned into a month of physical therapy while Kate wrapped up all the paperwork in the case. After that, they had been free to take their three months off. Spade had provided them with plane tickets to anywhere in the world.

After almost no deliberation, they had chosen Fiji. The goal was to get as far off the beaten path as possible and spend as much time outdoors as they could. There had also been very little discussion about whether they'd take the trip together or separately. Who else would they go with?

Kate hadn't had a real relationship in so long she couldn't pinpoint the details of the last, and Declan was fresh out of a divorce, which also meant he was broke. He had been living with Kate since his separation and the divorce had him living with her for the foreseeable future. While he hadn't had kids with his ex, she had still taken him for a huge chunk of money.

Kate had been alone in the huge brownstone since a terrorist bombing ended her parents' lives when she was in college. Her father had been a U.S. ambassador after spending his career as a history professor at Harvard, Kate's alma mater. The brownstone was too big for Kate to be there alone, but selling it was never an option. There were too many memories. Besides, she couldn't imagine calling anywhere other than Boston her home. So, they were there together – working and living as friends and most definitely not having a relationship.

Just as Kate had started to drift off for an afternoon nap, Declan stuck his head out of the back door. "What do you say about a picnic lunch in Boston Common?"

Kate opened her eyes and took in the cloudless blue sky overhead. Her stomach growled at the mention of food. "Sounds good," she called to him. "I assume you already made lunch knowing I'd say yes."

He held up the wicker picnic basket and jiggled it. "All packed and ready to go. I grabbed a blanket out of the closet that we can spread out." Declan took a step out, holding onto the screen door to keep it open. "Do you want to go out this way or the front?"

While Kate wanted to have a picnic lunch at Boston Common, the act of getting out of the comfortable chaise and walking there was unappealing. "This way," she said, buying herself a few more precious seconds of doing absolutely nothing – something she'd become quite accustomed to over the last few months.

Kate had spent her thirty-six years going, going, and going. From undergrad to grad school to get her master's degree in forensic psychology with a specialization in forensic linguistics to the FBI academy. She had only been with the Bureau for a couple of years when she had been asked to join the elite unit run by Spade. Declan had been asked to join as well, mostly because he was already Kate's partner and no one else wanted to work with him. Going rogue had been his standard early on. Declan also happened to be one of the most eagle-eyed agents she'd ever worked with at the FBI. The evidence he could spot at a scene was beyond her abilities.

A shadow fell over Kate and she tipped her head up to see Declan standing there wearing shorts, a tee-shirt, and flip-flops. He had a Red Sox ball cap pulled low on his forehead and sunglasses on. Kate teased, "Are you running from the paparazzi?"

Declan laughed showing off a smile that made women weak at the knees. "Get up, lazy. You've been sitting out here for the last two hours. You also skipped a workout with me this morning. We are going back to work in a week."

"Right, in a week. Don't bother me until then." Kate pushed herself up from the chair. Declan had a few inches on her but both were strong and in shape. They had to be to do their jobs. Kate was naturally thin and Declan had been a college athlete. He maintained that muscle through the years. To most, they made an attractive couple.

It was a short walk, not even a full block, and then across Arlington Street into Boston's Public Garden. Boston Common was on the far side of the park across Charles Street. At the last minute, they decided to stop right near the pond in the Public Garden. Declan put the blanket down on the grass and then dropped to the ground and pulled items out of the basket.

Kate stood there watching him, wondering if she should help or let him continue. He seemed to have it all under control so she sat down cross-legged and watched him.

Declan had made turkey sandwiches stuffed with meat, cheese, lettuce, and tomatoes with the spicy mustard Kate liked. He also had grabbed plums and grapes from the fridge, a bag of chips, and the red velvet cupcakes she had made earlier that week. He had a thermos of what looked like sweet tea and cups.

She laughed. "How hungry are you?"

After Declan set the basket aside, he looked at the spread. "I'm starving, but I packed more than I realized. Maybe it's as bad to pack a picnic basket on an empty stomach as it is to go grocery shopping."

Kate twisted her long dark hair into a ponytail and then dug into the food, unwrapping one of the sandwiches and taking a huge mouth-watering bite. She groaned. "You make the best sandwiches."

"It's only good because someone else made them. I feel the same way when you cook." Declan took a bite of his sandwich and then smiled over at her. "I admit, I did well. It's got to be the tomatoes and gouda."

Kate paused for a moment, relishing the conversation. The fact that all they were talking about was who made the best turkey sandwich reminded her that this wouldn't last for long. She knew work would come back with a vengeance. As she looked over at Declan, he had a similar expression. "We've been avoiding work for too long. The vacation was great, but it might have been too much of a break."

Declan agreed. "I could retire right now and never look back. That's probably a bad sign."

Kate felt the same way. In reality, with the money her parents left her, she never had to work at all. She assumed she'd get bored after a while. "Tell me something crime-related, anything."

"There was a shooting in South Boston last night."

Kate shook her head. "When isn't there a shooting in South Boston? Something else, something interesting."

Declan shrugged and popped a grape in his mouth. "This isn't crime-related, but there was an explosion at Magnolia House at Dartmouth a few days ago."

"What's Magnolia House?"

Declan pulled his sunglasses up and eyed her. "You don't know what Magnolia House is?"

"No idea. Should I know?"

"I thought all of you Ivy League snobs knew about secret societies." He threw a grape at her that landed right on top of her sandwich. She plucked and popped it in her mouth. "I assumed you belonged to a secret society at Harvard and never told me – on account of it being a secret."

Declan often teased Kate for going to Harvard and joked that she was the far smarter of the two of them. Declan had held a 4.0 at Boston College for all four years. "I didn't join one of those societies. My father was…" Kate trailed off not sure even now after his death that she should talk about it.

"He was what, Kate?"

Kate swallowed, ignoring the lump in her throat thinking about her father. "He had been a Knights of Fire member. That's the oldest senior club on campus. It still only admits men."

"That's a fairly innocuous way of describing them." Declan eyed her suspiciously. "The Ivy League secret societies are notorious for their secrets and rituals and the number of powerful, wealthy, and connected people who come out of them. Presidents, members of Congress and the Supreme Court Justices, high-powered attorneys, CEOs, Olympians."

When Kate didn't say anything, Declan raised his eyes to hers. "Ambassadors."

Kate shrugged it off. "They are a little creepy which is why I never joined one. I could have if I had expressed any interest, which I never did. So, did anyone get hurt at Dartmouth?"

"Two students were killed and another five are in the hospital, one in critical condition."

Kate set her sandwich down and took a sip of tea, thinking she had to have misheard Declan at first. "What happened?"

"The news report said it was a gas line explosion. You know how old our infrastructure is up here in the Northeast."

"Why did you bring that up when I asked about crime?"

"Secret society. Maybe it wasn't a gas explosion. Who knows what kind of stuff they get up to in their houses," Declan said, taking another bite of his sandwich. He finished chewing and drank some sweet tea. "I haven't been following crime lately either. Spade better have something good for us because the idea of sitting in the field office in Boston day after day is unappealing."

Kate had never been one for desk work. "I'm sure the Boston office is better than being in the office with Spade." As soon as the man's name left her mouth, Kate's phone rang. She fished it out of her pocket then held it up for Declan to see. "I swear he has us bugged."

"See what he wants."

Kate answered and before saying anything else, Spade asked her to put it on speakerphone so Declan could listen in. "I'm outside, Spade, in the Public Garden." He told her to do it anyway.

Spade announced, "We need you in upstate New York. There was an explosion this morning at Cornell University. How far is Ithaca from you?"

"It's a little over five hours by car," Kate said, a sinking feeling filling her stomach. "Where on campus was the explosion? We were just talking about the gas line explosion at Dartmouth."

"That wasn't a gas line explosion," Spade corrected. "I was asking you how far it is because I think you should drive. After you leave Ithaca, I need you to double back to Hanover, New Hampshire, and speak to the authorities at Dartmouth. They believe it was a bomb."

"A bomb?" Kate asked, confusion in her voice.

"Where was the explosion?" Declan asked Kate's question that Spade hadn't answered.

There was a ruffle of papers and then Spade said, "At the Sword and Crown house. It's one of their senior societies or clubs or whatever they call themselves these days. They certainly aren't what we had in our day. My…" Spade trailed off and Kate and Declan shared a look. Neither were surprised that Spade had been a member. He had gone to Princeton before joining Army intelligence and finally the FBI. There might have been a stop with the CIA. No one was too sure of Spade's background. The man was a bit of an enigma.

Kate asked, "Why does New York want us so fast? Usually, the New York State Police do a good job on their own. They have a great bomb squad."

"They do, but they heard about the explosion in Dartmouth and don't want to play around. They want federal help immediately. The sooner you get there the better. They are still sifting through debris."

"Any confirmed deaths?"

"Four. Several more are in the hospital. This happened at five in the morning. Most of the students were still sleeping." Spade got quiet for a moment then barked an order to someone in his office. He got back on the line, his voice quieter now. "Kate, you know your way around an Ivy League school. You know how the parents are going to be. These are connected families, legacies. This needs to be handled with care. If there hadn't been the case in Dartmouth, the FBI wouldn't have been called. Call it a gut feeling but two secret societies on different Ivy League campuses – we've got a serial bomber on our hands."

Kate wasn't ready to go quite that far, but she understood why Spade had. "When are they expecting us?"

"Morning meeting at eight. You'll meet with New York State Police Investigator Mitchell Murphy, who is in charge of the investigation in Ithaca. From there, I'm sure he'll introduce you to whoever was on site from the bomb squad."

Kate stared down at her half-eaten sandwich. Their vacation was officially over. "We'll be there at eight tomorrow morning, Spade. You can count on us."

CHAPTER 2

Sword and Crown wasn't on Cornell University's campus. The long driveway was about one hundred feet away on Stewart Avenue overlooking the Fall Creek Gorge. Secluded in the woods, the house was only partially visible from the street. Thankfully, the bomb only impacted Sword and Crown and not any of the neighboring properties.

A tomb-like structure had been built in 1910 as the headquarters for Sword and Crown. It was where meetings, activities, and rituals were held. Later, in the 1930s, construction expanded the building to include areas for residences in the back. The bomb took out the residences and damaged the tomb-like structure.

Kate glanced down at the photograph that Investigator Murphy had provided her and Declan. They had met at his office at eight, but there wasn't anyone else there to meet with them. Murphy, who told them to drop the formality, wanted them to tour the bombing site first to get a feel for what they were working with before meeting any of the other team members.

Kate and Declan weren't going to complain. They always felt more comfortable getting the lay of the land ahead of meeting with other investigators. Seeing words on paper or hearing investigators talk about their findings never held the same value as firsthand accounts and being at the scene.

Not that there were any findings to go over. Most of what was found in the rubble was at the lab for processing. Based on initial findings, they believe a backpack filled with explosive material and triggered by a cellphone fuse caused the explosion. It was enough to take out the residential area, but the façade of the main building remained intact.

"What do you think?" Kate asked as they stood on the property surveying the damage.

The area was still too unstable for Declan to have full access, but he could see enough from their vantage point adjacent to the structure. "Whoever it was knew the area enough to know where to plant the bomb. They didn't go after the tomb-like structure but instead where the students lived."

Kate hadn't considered that until Declan said it. "You're right. If they wanted to destroy the main building that represents Sword and Crown, the bomb would have been placed in the front of or inside the tomb to destroy that. The bomber didn't go after that. He targeted the residences where Sword and Crown members were sleeping."

"It's more than that, Kate," Declan said, stepping closer to the destruction. "It was a maximum casualty event. The bomber chose a time of day when they knew people would be home and vulnerable."

Kate concluded, "The bomber isn't sending a message. He's going in for the kill."

"He?" Declan asked with eyebrows raised. "You couldn't have come up with a profile that easily."

"It's not that hard, Declan. Men tend to blow up things. We've seen it time and time again from terrorist organizations to lone bombers. What we are missing is the motive."

Declan couldn't argue the point. Everyone knew that bombers tended to be male. "Something feels different about this one to me. We need to keep an open mind, that's all I'm saying."

Kate glanced over at him. "When haven't I kept an open mind?"

"Don't look at me like that. It happens to both of us." Declan inched closer and then had to walk around the side to see it from a different angle. Murphy told them the area was too unstable and his team had already collected any evidence present. "Did they figure out where the bomb was placed? They have some yellow flags here. I don't know if that indicates where evidence was found or if it's significant for another reason."

Kate knew he was itching to start going through all of the evidence. Declan couldn't push the crime scene techs to move faster because they weren't with the FBI. Not that Declan was a bully, but he could smooth talk anyone to move his case up to the front of the line.

Kate stepped back from the structure to the grass. "Let's go back and talk to Murphy. We can see what's been processed and then see about speaking to some of the victims."

"Are you with the FBI?" a man called from the driveway.

Kate turned her head and saw that he was moving closer to them. "This is an active crime scene. Can I help you?" She stepped toward the man wearing a well-tailored gray suit. He had his dark hair slicked back and a watch on that would cost at least three months of Kate's salary – lawyer or parent, she guessed. Kate reached the driveway and extended her hand and introduced herself and pointed to Declan and introduced him. "Can I help you with something?"

"Terrance Becker," he said and shook Kate's hand, gripping it harder than most would. "My son is in the hospital. My flight landed an hour ago and I came right here."

Kate wasn't sure she understood him. "Your flight landed this morning and you came here instead of the hospital? How is your son doing?"

Terrance licked his lips and jabbed his finger toward the building. "Not everyone can be one of us. They are punishing us for who we are."

"We don't know the motive," Kate said, disliking the man already. "Were you a member here?"

"Hunt House at Yale. I wanted my son to go there, but he chose here." Terrance Becker spat the words. It was clear he had disdain for his son's choice of school. His eyes remained fixed on the scene.

"How is your son? Is it possible we can speak to him?"

"What?" He turned to her as if he hadn't heard what she said. "I want you to find whoever did this and then I want them prosecuted. Then, I'm going to sue them for everything they have and everything their family has." He looked Kate up and down, taking her in for the first time. "Why would the FBI send you? We need someone more experienced on this case."

Kate got this a lot. People expected FBI agents to look old, male, and grizzled by years of work. "I assure you that I'm experienced. I was asked to be involved in this case because of my experience. My partner, Agent James, and I are part of an elite specialized unit within the FBI."

Terrance didn't even bother to finish his conversation with Kate and didn't acknowledge what she had told him. Instead, he brushed past her and walked up the side of the house not crossing the yellow crime scene tape, and called for Declan, who when he saw the man made his way to the tape. They stood on either side of it.

Kate made her way to where they stood. "I was explaining our role with the FBI. You might want to give him your background."

Declan offered an overview of his background as well as Kate's background in profiling and then added, "I say this as humbly as possible, but the FBI only calls us into certain cases. You've got the best that the FBI has to offer."

Terrance turned his head slightly to look at Kate. "You're a profiler? I didn't know they let women do that."

Kate let out a surprised laugh. Before she could give him a verbal take down, Declan spoke up. "Agent Walsh is the best profiler the FBI has. If anyone will solve this case it's her."

"Well, she better," Terrance said, pointing between the two of them. "If you don't solve this case, I'll make sure you're demoted." Then he stalked off to the driveway and left in his rented Mercedes, pulling out of the driveway too fast.

Declan watched him drive down the road. "What was all that about?"

"I don't know," Kate said even though she did. "Let's chalk it up to a father whose son nearly died. Not that he cared much about that. He came here before he went to see his son in the hospital. I'm not a parent but that doesn't sit right with me."

"Me either," Declan said and then echoed Kate's feeling about the man. "We should go speak to Murphy. There's not much else we are going to see out here."

By the time they made it back to Murphy's office, stress had settled into Kate's shoulders. She wasn't a full hour into a new case and already she felt the knots coming back. They were directed to a conference room in the back of the New York State Police office. Murphy had set up poster-size images of evidence. He was putting up the last of the series as they entered.

Kate wasn't sure exactly what she was looking at – parts from a cellphone in one photo, then wires and metal pieces in another. Bombs were not her specialty.

Declan appraised the photos. "This is exactly what I was hoping for. I couldn't tell much by looking at the scene." He shook Murphy's hand. "You hear anything back from the labs or the autopsy results of the deceased?"

"Nothing yet. I expect it will be a few days." Murphy nodded at Kate and then gestured for them to sit. Murphy was well into his fifties and had a stocky build and bald head. The corners of his blue eyes crinkled when he smiled. He reminded Kate of a friend's father who went to every one of their soccer games and always brought extra snacks. There was a gentleness, competence, and kindness about him that made Kate glad he was lead on the case.

As he sat, Murphy asked, "You didn't get anything from the scene?"

Kate said to Murphy, "Declan made some astute observations about where the bomb was placed. It was clear that the bomber intended to kill rather than take out the front of the building – the symbol of Sword and Crown. Have there been any threats made against them?"

Murphy shook his head. "I interviewed a few of the survivors and no one had heard about any threats. Of course, it might come to light in the days ahead because most were too shaken up to be coherent when I spoke to them last night."

Kate understood that. There was always a balancing act for law enforcement, trying to get details when victims were injured. "We were thinking of going to the hospital today to interview those who are conscious."

"That's good. Today you might get more than I got yesterday." Murphy pointed up to the posters. "We know the bomb was placed in the back of the residential area. We assumed it was inside the residence but we don't have confirmation on that yet. No idea if they keep their doors locked. If not inside, then it was right up against the back wall."

"That was our assessment," Declan said and then broached the subject Kate was hoping to ignore, at least for now. "We ran into a father at the scene – Terrance Becker."

Murphy groaned. "He called this office twenty times yesterday."

"He went there before seeing his son at the hospital."

"Doesn't surprise me. Garrett Becker is his son. His parents are divorced and his mother, Debbie, is a sweet woman. I can understand why she left Terrance a long time ago." Murphy turned to Kate. "Forgive me, I shouldn't speak ill of people after a tragedy."

"I completely understand," Kate said, feeling at ease to disclose her interaction. "Terrance acted as if a woman shouldn't be on the case. I had a few choice words for him myself but figured that wouldn't be the best way to start the investigation. I held back."

Murphy grinned. "That was probably good. You don't need a fight on your hands before we even get started" He checked his watch. "The rest of my team should be here soon."

"Who are you bringing in?"

"Captain of the bomb squad – Leo Wallace. He's the best in the country and we are lucky enough to call him ours. He was a Navy Explosive Ordnance Disposal technician early in his career before retiring and working for the New York State Police. He's the go-to guy for explosives. I'll pull in the crime scene techs when the evidence is back. Right now, the team is us and Leo."

That was fine by Kate. While she relied on her team when needed, the smaller the team the better. Sometimes there were too many cooks in the kitchen and more voices only led them down rabbit holes that took them off track.

A few minutes into the discussion, there was a rap at the door. Leo Wallace announced himself and then said, "Sorry, I'm late. I was tracking down a lead."

Kate glanced over to see a man taking up most of the doorway. He had to have been at least six-four and well over two hundred pounds of muscle. Kate already knew he had nerves of steel to do the job he did.

After formal introductions, Leo sat down and rapped his knuckles against the tabletop. "By the evidence I'm seeing, we are looking at a professional bomb maker. This isn't this guy's first rodeo. I can't say for certain, but I'd bet money there will be more. This guy isn't done by a long shot."

Kate had suspected that but hearing it out of Leo's mouth solidified what Spade had suggested – they had a serial bomber on their hands.

CHAPTER 3

"What makes this bomb different from others?" Kate asked, hoping to understand more to profile the offender.

Leo had pushed the chair back so he was sitting hunched over with his arms on the table. His voice was much like the man himself – masculine and with an air of confidence and expertise. "At first, when we got to the scene, we thought it might have been several pipe bombs given the debris field. Through interviews, we found out that in the back corner kitchen, there was a small workbench, so what we were seeing were the nails and screws from the workbench being blown all over rather than a pipe bomb being packed with the usual materials. After further investigation, I determined it was C-4 packed into a backpack with a cellphone trigger."

Murphy pointed to the poster boards. "That's some of what you're looking at here."

Leo gave Murphy a thumbs-up. "As you probably know, C-4 is typically used in the military and demolition. It's also a terrorist's favorite bomb. In 1996, terrorists used C-4 to blow up the Khobar Towers U.S. military housing complex in Saudi Arabia. In 2000, terrorists used C-4 to attack the U.S.S. Cole, killing 17 sailors."

Kate knew the devastation from a C-4 bomb all too well. "C-4 was used in the U.S. Embassy bombing in Kenya."

"That's right," Leo said and then caught the solemn look on Kate's face. He raised his eyebrows in a question.

"My parents were killed in that bombing. My father was Ambassador Joseph Walsh."

"I'm sorry, Kate. I had no idea," Leo said. "I remember that well. We lost fourteen people in that Embassy and the terrorists were never caught."

Kate hadn't meant to suck all the air out of the room. "Thank you. It was a long time ago. I merely brought it up…" She didn't finish her thought because she wasn't sure why she brought it up. The conversation could have continued without that tidbit of her personal life.

"You brought it up because it was relevant, Kate," Murphy said, offering her a smile. Then he did Kate a favor and dropped the subject and got them back on track. "The bottom line is we know how destructive C-4 is and how uncommon it is for amateur bombers. It's not something some college kid is making in his dorm. RDX, the explosive component, is not commonly found and that's what was used in this bomb."

Leo thumped the table with his hand. "This is someone with bomb-making knowledge and access to materials. The bomb was sophisticated enough that we are looking at someone who is experienced and who has most likely done this before – even if only testing it out."

"I understand that," Declan said and then countered, "There are videos and recipes on the internet for making C-4. Isn't it possible that someone watched that and then made these bombs?"

"It's possible," Leo admitted. "Not probable. If that's what they did, then it's been years of practice for them. To be able to make a bomb that took out the back of the building but left the front mostly untouched took careful skill and planning. I stand by the statement that we aren't dealing with an amateur here. This is someone who knows what they are doing. If these were pipe bombs or unsophisticated, I'd be telling you something different. If I know anything, I know bombs and bomb makers."

"I concede that point," Declan said. "My only point was that we are talking about Ivy League schools with some of the brightest minds in the country. Half the kids in here could probably hack our government computers. Times are changing. We need to figure out if the threat is international or homegrown."

Murphy agreed with that. "I don't think we can rule out a student or faculty member for that matter. I'll concede the point to Kate, but I'd say that we aren't looking for international terrorists. I'd assume we are looking at homegrown terrorism."

"Correct," Kate said, echoing what he said. "This is homegrown – targeted. Someone has an agenda and they have started to carry it out. I agree with everything Leo said as well. My profiling work only goes so far. Leo knows bomb makers and those dynamics. Between the two of us, hopefully, we can narrow the field. Do we know if the bomb is similar to the one used in Dartmouth?"

"Exactly the same," Leo said, surprising Kate. He explained, "I don't just work with the New York State Police. Sometimes I consult with other jurisdictions and the police in Hanover called me when they figured out it wasn't a gas line explosion. They were looking for help, so I reviewed some of the evidence. We are looking at the same thing, even where the bomb was placed. The bomber targeted the back of the house with the residential areas. The bomb did slightly more damage because Magnolia House doesn't have as solid a structure in the front like Sword and Crown. It's a huge house and the main force of the explosion was in the back."

Kate and Declan hadn't been briefed about the explosion at Magnolia House because Spade hadn't been given the information before they arrived at Cornell. She explained that to Murphy and Leo. "Are there other similarities we should be aware of between the two?"

Murphy gestured with his hand when speaking. "There's the obvious that it's two Ivy League schools and two secret societies. Magnolia House is all women while Sword and Crown are men. Neither is co-ed. I asked about any threats to Magnolia House, but they are scrambling for answers in Hanover. They spent the first few days after the explosion going on the assumption it had been a gas line explosion. Once they ruled that out and a detective realized they were dealing with something far worse, they were already behind in the investigation."

"How many days between the two bombings?" Declan asked, pulling out his phone to take some notes.

"One week. Both bombings happened in the early hours of Monday mornings between five and five-thirty," Murphy explained. "The bomber waited until all the students were back from weekend trips and asleep in their beds before sunrise."

Declan looked up from his phone. "Witnesses?"

"None that we've found here at Cornell. I had officers canvassing the neighborhood, but no one saw anything before or after the explosion. Most of the people who live in the area were woken up by the blast and had no idea what was happening until they ran out of their homes. No one saw anyone suspicious or had any idea what had happened. Almost no one connected the two bombings."

Kate raised her eyes to him. "You said *almost* no one. Does that mean someone connected the cases right away?"

Murphy nodded. "A sociology professor. He teaches about deviance and crime. I'll have to dig out his statement for you because the details escape me at the moment. One of the local Ithaca police officers took the statement for us. I'm only remembering now because they mentioned it to me. There were no red flags about the guy, but the officer who took the statement hadn't heard about Dartmouth and had asked me if it was true. Is that concerning?"

"Not really, especially given the subjects he teaches. If he lives close by, he might be an additional person to interview." Kate looked to Declan to see if he had additional questions before she wanted to broach what could be a touchy subject.

Declan checked the note and then rested his phone on the table when he was done. "I don't think I have anything else right now. We'll have more questions as we continue. The evidence from the lab is going to be most interesting to me."

Leo sat back and folded his thick arms across his chest. "Me too, but I doubt we'll see anything surprising since we already discovered it was C-4. How can I best assist the FBI with this?"

"That's what I was going to address." Kate crossed her legs under the table and made sure to make eye contact with Murphy and then with Leo. "Most local police don't love the FBI coming in and taking over, so we were pleased that we were called in this early. As Leo said, we are dealing with someone who has made bombs before and will most likely continue. Right now, they are targeting Ivy League schools. I don't know if that will continue to be his target or if he'll target other universities or what else. We need to create a task force to work on these cases – all of the cases as one."

"You think a task force covering multiple states is possible?" Murphy asked, looking skeptical.

"We've done it before. It's not always welcome, but the cases where we have worked as a task force usually get solved faster."

"Usually get solved at all," Declan stressed, adding to what Kate said. "The FBI would run point on the task force and then we'd bring in local representatives like the both of you."

Before either of them could respond, Kate said, "I'm bringing this up now because we all agree there will be more bombings. Murphy, you were savvy enough to call us in early and we applaud that decision. More often than not local law enforcement won't call in the FBI until the last minute and then we are so far behind the learning curve. We have a real opportunity here to strike while the iron is hot so to speak. You are an essential part of our team and we want you to remain on the task force, in fact, help us lead it. The same for you, Leo. I'm impressed with your résumé and experience. I need your help to solve this case. Would you be willing not only to be on the task force but help with leadership on it?"

"I wouldn't have it any other way," Leo said and then looked to Murphy. "Are you in?"

"No question," he said and then turned to Kate. "I have to tell you when I called the FBI, I had no idea that things would go this smoothly. It's always a risk but you have more federal resources than we have and once I knew that Dartmouth was also a bomb, we were looking at a federal case. Better to request help than be assigned the help. What's the best plan of action?"

Kate might have been confident in how she spoke and approached them about a task force, but it hardly ever went as smoothly as it just did. She had no idea if the cops in Hanover at Dartmouth would be as receptive. "Would either of you be willing to call your colleagues in Hanover and see if they are on board with the task force and see if they can assign a representative?"

Leo raised his hand off the table. "I can give them a call. They were willing to loop me in so I can smooth it over with them. I don't think it will be an issue. They are already in over their heads and might not have someone to assign. I can take that on though."

Declan expressed his agreement with the decision. "I appreciate that. Sometimes it's better if another local reaches out. As Kate said, not everyone likes being a part of a team." He turned to Kate. "Anything else before we go?"

Murphy stood from the table. "You'll need a list of names of the victims in the hospital and the list of those who survived. The university is setting up counseling for them and providing other accommodations for now. The administration has rallied around them and is doing everything they can to help." He left the room and came back a few minutes later with a list. "I had an officer compile names, contact information, and locations where you can find them. All of these people have already been interviewed. Do you want to interview them fresh or see their current statements beforehand?"

Kate took the list from him. There were names of students and other people from the neighborhood. This would save them a good deal of time and energy. She glanced up at Murphy, thanking him. "I'd like to see their statements. That way we can see if there are any inconsistencies we need to address."

Kate handed the list to Declan who skimmed it. He looked to Leo. "Could you ask the cops covering the Dartmouth case if they could compile something like this for the task force? It's good we collectively keep track of who has been interviewed, by whom, when, and their statements."

Leo said he'd do that. As he stood, he reached his hand out to Declan and then to Kate. "As Murphy said, we never know what to expect when the FBI comes into a case. I'm going to enjoy working with you both. I'll call you as soon as we get crime scene info back."

Kate pushed in her chair and glanced over at Murphy, who had something on his mind. It was written all over his face. "What's up?" she asked, eyeing him.

"The media. Are we going public with the formation of a task force and any details related to the investigation? We need to decide what we are keeping from the public."

Kate knew that question would arise. She was hoping she'd have more time to interview people first. But Murphy was right – they needed to get in front of the story. "I'm comfortable with you being the spokesperson if you'd like. You've already done a press conference when the story broke. I think if we are all in agreement, we can say we suspect that the Cornell and Dartmouth bombings might be connected – although we are still assessing evidence and witnesses. You can mention that the FBI has been called in and we are forming a task force. I'd leave out any information about the kind of bomb used. Let's keep a lid on that for as long as we can."

Declan, Leo, and Murphy all agreed with that assessment. Declan added, "We appreciate you taking the lead with the media. Kate and I would rather be in the field and not in front of the camera if we can help it." He raised his eyes to hers and a smirk teased at his lips. "We were recently undercover and while not an experience Kate wants to try again, we never know where they will send us."

"Understood," Murphy said before letting Kate and Declan know he'd call with updates as soon as he received them. He asked them to wait while he grabbed the file with all the witness statements.

Kate left the meeting with a stack of witness statements they had to go through and her faith in collaboration with local law enforcement bolstered – at least for today.

CHAPTER 4

"What was that smirk about?" Kate asked, pulling into traffic and heading toward a local coffee shop. They could have stayed in Murphy's office and reviewed the statements but Kate wanted to get out in the community as quickly as possible, even if it meant taking a seat in a local coffee shop.

Declan sat in the passenger seat with the thick file folder on his lap, toying with the radio to find a local station. Kate had driven from Boston to Ithaca in her SUV because Declan was still recovering. He had been given clearance to drive but was more comfortable being able to stretch out. Kate was starting to think he was enjoying being chauffeured around.

"What smirk?" Declan asked, still fiddling with the radio.

Kate side-eyed him and noticed he was smirking again. "You know exactly what smirk. It's on your face right now. You were thinking about us undercover on the last case."

He stopped with the radio and angled his head, smiling now. "It's a memory seared into my brain. I'll never forget playing your husband." He glanced down her body and then bobbed his eyebrows up and down suggestively. "Along with everything else."

"Declan!" Kate screeched, trying not to laugh and encourage him. They had spent part of the vacation discussing the last case, acknowledging how close they had come to crossing the line between friendship and something more. They admitted their mutual attraction for each other and then decided that nothing could happen between them. Not only would they probably kill each other, but it would destroy their friendship, and more importantly, their working partnership. It didn't mean that Declan had stopped flirting or that Kate had stopped thinking about kissing him. Only, she wasn't going to admit that to him.

Declan broke into a big belly laugh, pleased with himself for eliciting a reaction from her. He pinched her side. "It's like you're a wind-up toy. All I have to do is turn the key to get the reaction I want. You're too easy, Kate." Then he paused. "Well, not *that* easy."

Kate hated that he knew her well enough to know all the buttons to push. "Focus on the case, please. That went well in there with Murphy and Leo. I'm glad they are going to be team players. It will make our work so much easier."

Declan agreed and stared out the passenger side window. "Did something strike you as odd about the professor knowing the cases were connected?"

"No," Kate said, slowing at the red light. She turned to look at him. "It was what I said. I was curious at first but given what he knows about crime, it's a natural connection."

"Even though the media was still saying the explosion at Dartmouth was from a gas line?"

"Yes. I think if it hadn't been another Ivy League school or if it hadn't been another secret society that it might raise suspicion. Those are two huge similarities, so a reasonable person might question them. Is it suspicious to you?" Kate accelerated and changed lanes.

"I don't know. He might know someone at Dartmouth who was suspicious about the official story and they shared their concern. They might know something we don't."

Kate hadn't considered that. She knew when her father was alive, he kept a pretty close relationship with other history professors at other universities. "We can ask." Kate took a right and pulled into the coffee shop parking lot and found a spot. She cut the engine and then sank back into the seat.

Declan didn't open his door. He remained there, watching her. "You know there's something with the media we didn't address."

Kate knew what he was going to say. "We suspect another bombing will happen next weekend. You're wondering if we should give a more specific warning?" Just as Declan could read her mind, she could read his.

"It's a fine line. We don't know for sure he will strike again, and if we make it public and acknowledge his pattern, then he could just as easily strike another day. It's not like we can stake out every secret society on every campus."

"It's not every campus." Kate considered how easily they could stake out the secret societies on Ivy League campuses at the very least. The logistics would be a nightmare and most universities might not even be willing to admit their students could be targeted. Still, though, Kate knew they had to do something. Even the statement she had advised Murphy to put out would ring alarm bells for parents.

Declan touched her arm. "Something is tumbling around your head?"

Kate explained to him her idea about putting extra patrols on Ivy League university campuses. "I don't know that anyone would be willing. If we make it public knowledge, we might also drive the bomber underground only to reemerge later. We could speak to the administrations at the universities and then connect with local law enforcement in these jurisdictions and ask for undercover patrols. It's one night and who knows what they might uncover that way."

"It's worth a shot. Are there eight Ivy League schools?"

"Yes." Kate rattled off the other six. "Brown University, Columbia

University, the University of Pennsylvania, Princeton University, and Yale University. And then Harvard."

"Do you think there is any relevance to the universities the bomber chose first – proximity to him, maybe? What about the years they were founded?"

"Definitely not the years they were founded. Dartmouth was second to last in 1769 and then Cornell in 1865. They were the last two but he didn't hit them in order even if he was going newest to oldest. I don't know if the order is significant or means anything." Kate looked over at him and what she was thinking could have remained unspoken, but she said the words. "We aren't going to know more unless he does it again."

That was the hardest part about serial crimes. The more the killer struck, the closer the cops got to figuring out the pattern, the killer's idiosyncrasies, and their personality. It meant that more people would have to die and be injured and Kate couldn't stand that thought.

Declan lifted the stack of files, not addressing what Kate said. "Let's go inside and review the statements. We can decide if we should call the other schools and what exactly we can tell them. Then, we interview the kids."

It was a full day ahead of them, but Kate was glad to be back at it even though she wore the stress of impending deaths like a cloak around her shoulders. Once in the shop, Declan handed her the stack of statements, which she took to a back table far away from other customers. Declan went to the counter to get them coffee and snacks.

Kate sat down and dropped the stack on the table and opened the file to read the first statement. Before she read, she counted them. There were close to thirty statements in all. There were statements from students in Sword and Crown and neighbors who had heard the explosion and were close by in the aftermath.

She split the pile and gave half to Declan. The first thing Kate read though was not a statement. It was Murphy's incident report, which he had also included. Kate was looking for a specific detail and found it halfway down the page. There had been twelve members of Sword and Crown at the residence the morning of the bombing. Four of them were deceased and others were in the hospital. Three had come away with only minor injuries and were now living in campus housing. The three who were the least injured were sharing a bedroom at the front of the building, which explained their minor injuries in comparison to the others. After seeing the devastation to the building, Kate thought it was nothing short of a miracle that any of them got out alive.

The statement didn't indicate if twelve were how many members had been "tapped" for that year's membership or if that was just who happened to be home at the time. Kate knew from her time at Harvard that most secret societies pick or "tap" juniors for membership and the senior class members put them through an initiation process. Then their senior year, they repeat the process all over again. Some societies had what was similar to Greek rush for sophomores as a chance for the society members to assess who was available for later membership.

Kate also knew that each society chose a specific number of members. She had been honest with Declan that she hadn't joined a secret society. That's not even what they were called at Harvard. They were known as Final Clubs. Many Ivy League universities had played down these societies calling them all sorts of things like Eating Clubs at Princeton. Others like Dartmouth seemed to embrace these societies. Kate had heard that there were fourteen different senior societies, five of which keep their membership secret. Nearly thirty percent of the student body were members.

Most societies, no matter what name they went by, were powerful. It was only in recent years that they had expanded their membership beyond white males. In the case of the earliest secret societies, it was Protestant white males. Now they were diverse and some co-ed, although several single-sex societies remained.

Just because Kate hadn't joined herself didn't mean that she didn't know someone who did. A guy she had been dating for a while at Harvard had been "tapped" for the prestigious Porcelain Club. The deeper he got involved with them, the wilder the tales of his involvement and initiation had been. She wasn't supposed to know half of what he had told her. But it didn't last. The deeper he got in, the more he pulled away and became more secretive. It was fine because he had started to become someone Kate didn't like much. The wildest thing she remembered him telling her was that if members didn't earn their first million by the time they turned forty, the club would give it to them.

Kate understood why people joined, especially if there was the promise of prestige and power later in life through their early connections. There was a reason why so many powerful people came out of these secret societies and it was early access to powerful people who helped them on their way. Kate saw nothing wrong with it. It was how the world worked. Even though her father had encouraged her, at heart Kate wasn't much of a joiner. She even struggled with her relationship with the FBI at times.

"You look like you're a million miles away." Declan handed her an iced mocha latte and a muffin. He placed his coffee on the table and sat down. "What are you thinking about?"

Kate didn't want to talk about her old boyfriend. "My time at Harvard. I was thinking about some of the classmates I knew who joined these kinds of societies and how they changed over time." She took a sip of her coffee, thanked him, and then raised her eyes to him. "Why didn't you ever join a fraternity?"

"Boston College doesn't have any, but they do have several clubs I never joined." Declan laughed. "I was too busy playing hockey and keeping up my grades. I was a scholarship kid. My parents couldn't afford to pay for college, so I was on my own. Luckily, my grades and my hockey skills were enough to get me nearly a full ride. The rest I needed student loans, which I'm still paying. Why do you ask?"

A smile teased at her lips. "You seem like someone who would have joined."

Declan tried not to smile. "You mean I was a womanizing drunk?"

"That's not true of all Greek life," Kate said and then laughed. "But yeah, I can imagine you as a character in *Animal House*."

"Never," he said, affronted. "Good Catholic boy like me? I was taught by the Jesuits. I was an altar boy!"

Kate rolled her eyes. He had been anything but a good Catholic boy when they met. His womanizing ways while they were in the academy were notorious. She pointed to his stack of statements. "Okay, altar boy, read the statements, so we can go to the hospital and start interviews."

They quieted down and buried their heads in witness statements. The officer who had taken the majority of the statements had done a great job with the level of detail he gathered and the questions he asked. Kate would have to remember to commend him for the job well-done. There was nothing that stood out to her as significant. As Murphy had indicated, no one heard or saw a thing before the explosion or after. Almost all the neighbors had called 911 and medical emergency crews and the fire department were on the scene quickly. Kate couldn't see where anyone had done anything wrong – not that she was specifically looking for that. But it was important for her to know if there were any early missteps in the case.

"I read Garrett Becker's statement," Declan said, pulling Kate's concentration away from a neighbor's account of that early morning. "He said that he woke up earlier than usual because he heard someone outside. He went to one of the empty bedrooms near the front of the residence to look out the side window at the driveway when the explosion happened. His roommate died. Garrett believes that had he been in bed during the explosion, he'd probably be dead too. He said he's sure that he saw something but he can't quite remember what. There's a note that the doctor said he might have a traumatic brain injury from the blast. They are still evaluating him."

"Is there a reason he didn't look out his bedroom window?"

"Doesn't say in the statement." Declan dropped Garrett's statement on top and inched the pile forward on the table. "I say we start with him. None of the other guys had anything to say other than the weekend had been normal, there were no known threats against them, and they had all been taken by surprise during the blast."

Kate hated that the one kid who had something to say was the son of the father she had hoped to never see again. "I read the same in these statements. These kids were taken completely off guard. They never saw it coming. The statements I read from the neighbors weren't much help either. I guess we should start with Garrett," she said, even though it was the last thing Kate wanted to do.

CHAPTER 5

"Debbie Becker," Garrett's mom said as she shook Kate's hand at the door to her son's hospital room. She stepped out into the hallway to speak to them. "Garrett has already spoken to another officer and then his father blasted through here demanding answers from him. He's fragile right now. The doctors are still evaluating him."

Kate explained why they were there. "We don't want to cause Garrett any stress and will make this as quick and as painless as possible. Were you here when Garrett gave his statement to the other officer?"

"I was but they asked me to wait outside. He asked me some questions after, but I don't know anything. I don't live around here and know nothing about Sword and Crown. I didn't want Garrett to join." She looked back toward the hospital room door and started to cry. Then she pulled it together quickly and turned back to them. "Garrett joined as a way to get closer to his father, but Terrance never knew how to be a good parent. He doesn't care what Garrett wants or is interested in. Terrance wants a son just like him and I'm bound and determined to ensure that Garrett is as different from his father as possible."

"We understand," Declan said.

Debbie offered a shy smile. "I'm sure you think I'm awful speaking like that, but if you knew my ex-husband you'd understand."

Kate put her hand on Debbie's. "I met Terrance this morning at the crime scene. Not the most pleasant or caring person I've ever met."

"Then you know," she said with relief in her voice. "Garrett is an only child. He's all I have. I don't understand what happened. They said there was a bomb, but who'd want to bomb a bunch of college students?" She looked at them with a pleading look on her face.

Everyone always asked *why* and Kate rarely had an answer, even sometimes after a case was solved. Damaged people cause damage. That was about all the *why* she would ever come up with. Even though Kate specialized in serial crime, the *why* of it was hard to explain. It wasn't like someone killing a cheating partner or killing someone they were robbing. It wasn't a crime of passion or greed or any of the usual motives. It was different and difficult to explain to people because it was so senseless. Even when a perpetrator gave a reason, it hardly ever made sense to the average person and certainly not to the people who were harmed by their actions.

With her voice clear and confident, Kate explained, "We don't understand the bomber's motive at this time. Our main goal right now is finding whoever is responsible so they cannot do this again and to bring them to justice for what they did to Garrett and his friends."

Debbie nodded as if she understood. "Let me go in first and tell him that you're here to speak with him." She turned and then angled her head to look back at them. "You know it's ironic. When Garrett was little, he wanted to be an FBI agent. That's all he ever talked about, but then his father convinced him to go another direction."

"It's not too late. He has more than enough time to change his mind again," Declan said, leaning against the wall to wait. When Debbie went into the room and closed the door behind her, he raised his eyebrows in a question to Kate. "What do you think?"

"I think Debbie is a good mom with a lot on her plate right now and has an ex-husband who will probably only cause stress and make the situation worse for them both."

"Let's hope he doesn't make the situation worse for us."

That was one of Kate's concerns. "If Terrance gets too bad, we'll have Spade handle it. I've never seen anyone get dressed down by Spade and want to go a second round. He has pull to the White House." Their boss ran in political circles and got their elite unit a higher budget than most fully staffed FBI field offices. Kate knew they also had very little oversight. Spade was a power player among Washington's inner circle. Kate was sure she didn't know half of how much pull Spade had among the top echelon of the FBI, Department of Justice, and maybe even the president. She wasn't sure she wanted to know.

A few moments later, Debbie cracked the door. "Garrett is awake and you can speak to him now. Please don't take long. He's been falling asleep so easily and the doctor said he needs all the rest he can get." She opened the door wide and stepped out. "I'm going to walk down to the cafeteria while you speak to him."

Kate appreciated that Debbie left on her own accord and she wouldn't have to ask her to leave. Declan stepped into the room first and Kate followed him. Garrett was in a private room and the bed was on the far wall adjacent to the window. Garrett had bandages on his face and up both arms. Kate couldn't see the rest of him under the covers.

He turned his head slightly to see out of the one eye that wasn't bandaged. "You really with the FBI?"

"We are," Declan said, taking a seat next to the bed. He introduced himself and Kate and then asked, "How are you feeling? You look like you're holding up considering all you've gone through. You must be pretty tough."

"Lucky is more like it." He paused and took a breath. "I know you probably want to know what I heard that made me get up and go into another room. I still don't remember. The doctor said my memory might never come back. I remember waking up and hearing a noise, a kind of scraping noise against the house. You know when a tree limb scrapes against the house."

Declan nodded. "I had a big old tree outside my bedroom as a kid. Used to wake me up all the time."

"It was like that, but then it got louder. My room didn't have any windows so I went to the front of the house to look out the study room window and that's when the explosion happened. I don't even know if I made it to the window, so I might not be remembering what I saw because I didn't see anything. Sorry about that."

Declan gently patted the bed next to him. "You don't need to apologize. It was a good thing you got up when you did. We know that your roommate was killed in the explosion. We're sorry for your loss. We know this is all a lot to deal with."

"It is," Garrett said and then grew quiet. He turned his head away as a tear rolled down his cheek. "That's why I want to remember. Someone killed my friends and tried to kill me and the others. If I can help, I want to help."

Kate moved around the side of the bed so he could see her better. "Garrett, the only way you can help us right now is getting better. That's all that's important. The more you try to force your brain to remember, the more elusive the memories can become. Do you remember everything days and months before the explosion?"

"Yeah. As far as I know, none of those memories are gone. Is that important?"

Kate smiled. "It's a good sign your brain is going to heal itself. Do you remember if there were any threats against anyone in the house or did anyone have issues with anyone?"

Garrett considered Kate's question. "We aren't the loudest guys on campus if you know what I mean. We are an exclusive society and we are secret, but we fly under the radar in comparison to some of the others. Not too many people are curious about us."

"Not creating a lot of enemies then," Declan said.

"Right. There was this one guy, Asher Bass. He was a legacy. His father and grandfather were Sword and Crown, but he wasn't voted in last year. He vowed revenge, but I don't think he'd do something like this. It was the class ahead of us who made the decision. None of us living at the house now were the ones who kept him out. His father called us and tried to get him admitted after the fact, but we can't break tradition like that."

Kate thought it was a potential lead. "Does Asher still go to school here?"

"Yeah, I saw him not even a week ago." Garrett's voice cracked as he spoke. He looked to the cup of water on the tray table and Declan got up and grabbed it for him, bringing the straw to his mouth for him to take a sip. He drank some water and then put his head back on the pillow.

"When I saw Asher, he told me that we were all losers and he was glad that he didn't get in. Asher went back and forth like that. One minute saying he was going to get revenge and the next acting like he didn't care. I'm sure it was hard for him. He came to Cornell expecting to be in Sword and Crown."

Declan put the water back and sat down. "Do you know why he wasn't admitted?"

"He'd been in trouble a few times for petty things. Once he was arrested off-campus for underage drinking, but his father got the charges dropped. He had failed a class or two as well. He just wasn't right for Sword and Crown. It was his fault he didn't get in."

Kate asked, "Do you know where we can find him?"

Garrett rattled off an address where Asher lived off-campus. "I don't think he'll talk to you. You might want to act like you're there to see if he can help."

Kate smiled. "That's a good instinct, Garrett. Your mom said that you had wanted to join the FBI."

"Still kind of do. My dad thinks I should do something more… " he trailed off and looked away from them. "Important, I guess. Something that makes more money."

"Money isn't everything, Garrett," Declan said. "I can tell you that you'll never find a more rewarding career. Just remember your dad can't live your life for you, but I'm sure you'll be successful at whatever you choose to do. There is a lot of time to decide."

After asking Garrett a few more questions that didn't yield much, they left with a promise to return to check on him. Declan gave Garrett his card with his direct cellphone number on it in case he wanted to talk about joining the FBI or remembered anything important.

Kate was glad they were able to finish up before Debbie got back. She left word with Garrett's nurse that they were done and would follow up with Debbie later. Kate and Declan went to interview a few more of the students who were in the hospital.

About ninety minutes later, they didn't have anything more than what had been in their statements. Two of the other young men mentioned similar descriptions of Asher's behavior when Kate asked about him. No one thought he'd bomb Sword and Crown. That seemed too far fetched.

As they were walking back to the car, Kate asked, "Do you think not being admitted to Sword and Crown would be reason enough to bomb it?"

Declan shook his head. "I can't see a student doing this. Even if he wanted revenge on Sword and Crown, why would he bomb Magnolia House at Dartmouth? We should speak to Asher, but I'd be surprised if it led to much of anything. Not to mention where is this kid getting C-4 or the know-how to make the bombs?"

"The internet like you said earlier." Kate had been thinking about the question Declan had asked Leo. He had been dismissive of the idea that anyone could see a video and make a bomb, but terrorists did it all the time. Before Declan could reiterate Leo's point, she told him her reasoning. "These are sophisticated and highly intelligent young men, most of whom have considerable wealth. If he wanted C-4, I'm sure he could figure out a way to buy the materials and make it. Not to mention, someone else could have made it for him. We don't know that there is only one person involved."

As if to reinforce Kate's train of thought, her cellphone rang at that moment. Spade. "You got something for us?" she asked as she answered.

"There's chatter online about the bombings. There's a group known as the Sisters of the Revolution. Have you heard of them?"

"No. Should I have?"

"Radical feminist group. They have staged sit-ins, shown up at rallies, broken into a few places, and even made threats against men in Congress."

Kate wasn't sure what Spade was saying. "You think a group of women are behind the bombings?" Her tone was full of disbelief and an edge of annoyance that he'd even suggest something so silly.

"I'm not saying they did it, Kate. I'm saying the online chatter from one of their members seems to be taking credit for it."

It sounded to Kate like a bluff. "Where would we find Sisters of the Revolution?"

"That's the thing, Kate. There's a chapter right on Cornell's campus."

Kate glanced over at Declan who was staring at her in anticipation as she absorbed the details from Spade. When she hung up, she said, "Looks like we need to go talk to some radical feminists."

She wasn't even sure what the term meant – wasn't any woman demanding equality deemed radical?

CHAPTER 6

Like Sword and Crown, Sisters of the Revolution wasn't technically on Cornell's campus as Spade had said. Kate found them on Kline Road, in an old sorority house that had been sold to the group in 2010. Even though he had balked at the idea, she had Declan drive while she gave him directions from the hospital. She also spent the time reading about them online. Until now, this wasn't a group that either of them had heard about, so the more information they could find before the interview the better.

"There seems to be some duality to their purpose," Kate said, reading their website. The group had a national website and then chapter websites – much like a fraternity or sorority. "They are focused on feminist causes and they do engage in a good deal of charity work."

Declan glanced over at her as she paused. "I heard a *but* in there."

Kate was trying to choose her words carefully. "There seems to be a militant arm among them. Several of their members have been arrested for protesting and harassing people on the street. There are arrests here for vandalism, destruction of property, and a slew of other mostly minor charges."

"There's nothing wrong with protesting, Kate. If that were true, you'd have to lump my hippie parents among them."

"It's not the protesting that concerns me. It's petty crimes and the sheer number of arrests of their members. Let's take Lily Cole,

Cornell's chapter president. She's been arrested close to twenty times for harassment, destruction of property, and vandalism. There are a few people who have orders of protection against her."

"You pulled her up in the system that fast?"

"No," Kate said, her voice growing loud. She thrust her phone toward Declan even though she knew he couldn't take his eyes off the road to look at it. "This is all in her bio on the chapter's website. She takes pride in these crimes. Lily has been kicked out of Cornell, but because the house isn't on Cornell property, she has remained as the de facto chapter president."

"Who is she harassing and vandalizing?"

"Mostly fraternity members and some sorority members. She blames women as much as she blames men for what she considers the oppression women face." Kate was struggling to decide how she was feeling. It was bumping up against her political and moral beliefs. She believed in equality for all – equal pay right on down the line. But she wasn't public on her stances. She hadn't even had most of those conversations with Declan. She had come across women like Lily before and they didn't like Kate. She worked in a man's world and her best friend was a man. It never sat well. She wasn't feminist enough, or at least, that's what she had been told.

"You're struggling," Declan said, turning right onto the street. "You're making those little humming noises when you're trying to work something out in your head."

Kate hadn't realized she was doing that. "I don't like labels, Declan. I know what women face. I know what I faced when I started in the FBI and even before that. I had professors tell me that I should pick a different career. Our leadership at the academy gave the handful of women in our class extra scrutiny. None of it was right. I know the inequalities in the system because I'm part of the system, Declan."

"I'm right there with you, Kate. So, what's the issue?"

"I'm not going to break windows to get my message heard. I'm not going to scream at a man who opens the door for me that I can do it myself."

"Has that happened?"

"I'm thinking of someone I knew in college." Kate flashed back to several run-ins she had in college and her heart began to race as if she was about to experience it again.

Declan put a hand on her arm. "Don't overthink it. There are extremes in everything and that's when there's usually trouble. Let's go in and figure out if they could be responsible, and if not, why they were taking credit for it on a message board. That's our only focus."

Kate knew he was right. "If Lily has been as destructive as she detailed in her bio, then who knows who might want to make her a scapegoat for this. For all we know, it's not them taking credit."

"Exactly, Kate, so there's no reason to stress about it now." When Kate indicated the house was coming up on the right, Declan slowed, put his turn signal on, and then parked on the side of the road just down from the house in front of a vacant lot where it looked like a house once stood. Now, it was a plot of overgrown grassy land.

He turned to Kate. "What's the approach for the interview? We have no idea how many young women will be in the home. Does Spade have confirmation that the posts came from this IP address?"

Kate had been so focused on other things she hadn't considered the plan of action. "No, Spade didn't say the IP address was confirmed just that the poster said they were from Sisters of the Revolution. I'm sure we can get the tech team on the IP address if needed. I don't want to mention Sisters of the Revolution taking credit right away. I want to hold that back and act like we are canvassing for information. Based on their responses, then we can get into it at some point."

"That makes sense especially since the IP address isn't confirmed. It could be anyone posting that."

Kate didn't disagree, but the information she saw about Lily Cole pricked her suspicions. She raised her eyebrows to him. "You ready?"

Declan flashed a grin. "Should I be afraid?"

"I'm not sure." Kate laughed because she wasn't sure how the young women would respond to either of them. "I have a feeling we are going to have to roll with this interview and go with their flow."

Declan didn't disagree. They got out of the car and walked down the road to a two-story white house. At the front door, Declan rapped his knuckles against the wood and a moment later, a young woman with long brown hair dressed in cuffed jeans, a tee-shirt, and flip-flops answered the door.

"Can I help you?"

Declan flashed his badge and introduced them. "We need to ask you a few questions. Are there others here with you?"

The young woman cast her eyes to Kate. "Do you speak or do you always let a man speak for you?"

Kate silently groaned. *Here we go.* She faltered for only a moment and then remembered she wasn't nineteen and unsure of herself. She was an FBI special agent in an elite unit. Kate locked eyes with the woman and smiled. "Declan's nicer than I am, so I thought he should start. But I'm happy to take the lead if that would make you more comfortable. Can we come in?"

"I'm the only one home. Everyone else is at class." She stepped out of the way and let them enter. They followed her through a grand foyer into a well-worn but clean family room. As she sat on the couch, she said, "I don't know anything about the bombing, if that's why you're here."

That didn't make Kate suspicious. It was probably all everyone on campus had been discussing. "When did you first become aware of the bombing?" It was right after she asked the question that Kate realized the young woman hadn't introduced herself. "Let's start with your name and your affiliation with Sisters of the Revolution."

"Do I have to answer your questions?"

"No, but it would make it easier for all of us if you did. The bombing killed four students and injured several more."

The young woman smirked, not showing any emotion for the loss of life. "Their loss doesn't mean I need to give up my rights."

"You're right in that you don't need to help us." Kate put her hands on her hips and looked down at the young woman. "You don't have to like us being here or help us. We are here hoping to make sure this doesn't happen again. For all we know, your house could be next." Kate turned to go and left Declan standing there.

"Kate," he said, calling after her but she didn't stop. She made it back to the front door when the young woman finally yelled for her to come back.

"Autumn Stewart," the young woman said when Kate returned. "I'm a junior and have been with Sisters of the Revolution for a year. I joined at the end of my freshman year but only moved into the house this semester. I was serious when I said I didn't know anything about the bombing."

Kate had learned much about Autumn in their small exchange. She gave in easily when someone stopped playing her game. Autumn was someone who could be easily broken in an interview. Kate walked across the room and sat down in a chair across from the couch. Declan did the same.

"When did you first become aware of the bombing?" she asked again.

"The morning it happened. We aren't that far away and we all woke up with the blast. It took us a little while to figure out what had happened."

Declan asked, "Were you surprised that someone attacked Sword and Crown?"

Autumn shook her head. "I wasn't surprised that someone attacked a secret society but I was surprised that it was them."

"What does that mean?"

"None of these secret societies are good, but there are worse ones on campus. There are bigger targets than them."

Targets. It wasn't a word the average college-aged student used and Kate picked it up right away. "Is this something you think, or is it something you've heard being discussed here in the house?"

Autumn lowered her eyes. "Discussed here, but it doesn't mean that I don't feel that way."

"What's the word around the house about who is responsible for this?"

"No one is sure."

"What about Lily Cole? What does she think about the bombings?"

"I can't speak for her." There was something about Autumn's expression that told Kate the young woman wanted to say more, so she and Declan remained quiet and let the silence fill the room. Like most people, Autumn felt the need to fill it. "Lily was happy it happened. If you looked at our website, you know Lily has a different approach than most of us."

Kate zeroed in on her. "Does that mean you haven't been arrested?"

Autumn shook her head. "I wouldn't mind if I got arrested for protesting something I believed in, but no, I'd never do some of the things that Lily has done. Most of the women in the house wouldn't either. Lily is a bit more extreme than the rest of us."

Declan looked at Kate and she knew what he wanted to ask. He was looking to her because he assumed it would sound better coming from a woman in this circumstance. Kate asked, "Do you think Lily is capable of the bombing?"

"What?" Autumn asked, her head snapping up not hiding her shock. "No, never..." She didn't finish her sentence.

"Is there something else, Autumn? We won't disclose what you've told us."

Autumn clasped her hands together and inched back on the couch. She bit her lower lip. "I don't think Lily is responsible, but she had an incident with members of Sword and Crown when she was a freshman three years ago. The people who were there then are gone. Lily still thought it needed to be eradicated. Not just them – all secret societies and fraternities and sororities."

Kate tried to show no emotion. "Do you know the details of what happened?"

"Lily was bullied and harassed by some seniors. A few of us thought she might have been sexually assaulted, but Lily said she wasn't. It was constant bullying and harassment for a year. The school did nothing to protect her. She never understood why they singled her out." Autumn reached up and tucked hair behind her ears. "Lily likes to say that Cornell kicked her out because of all the arrests. In truth, she quit because she couldn't stand being on campus with them. Even after those students graduated, it was like she had developed some anxiety about going back to certain buildings, so she dropped out."

Declan turned to her. "Is that when Lily started more extreme behavior like vandalism and harassment?"

Autumn nodded. "Lily said if those guys could get away with it, so could she. She got arrested though, which only proved her point that men can get away with anything."

"Where is Lily now?"

"We don't know," Autumn said quietly, staring down at her hands. "Right after the bombing, she packed her things and left."

"Was Lily here in the house last weekend?"

A flash of recognition came over Autumn's face and Kate was sure she had heard about the explosion at Dartmouth. "Lily was away for the weekend. We weren't sure where she went but she was back on

Monday afternoon."

"Autumn," Kate said loudly enough to draw the young woman's attention. "Would it be fair to say that you and possibly other young women here are concerned that Lily is involved in the bombings?"

Autumn sat still for several moments. When she did speak again, her voice was so soft that Kate could hardly hear her. "A few of us have had concerns, but none of us think she'd go that far."

Kate and Declan took turns asking a few more questions about Lily, Sisters of the Revolution, and other members. Autumn responded honestly and openly. The more the young woman spoke, the more comfortable with the interview she became. She didn't have any knowledge that Lily knew about bombs or could acquire the bomb-making material. There was nothing yet to tie Lily to the attacks. Autumn let Kate and Declan search Lily's old room but they found nothing suspicious.

By the end, Autumn had promised she'd call Kate if she heard from Lily or found out anything else. Kate never addressed Sisters of the Revolution taking credit online. There was no reason to show her hand that soon.

At the door, Kate asked one last question. "Magnolia House at Dartmouth was all women. If this is Lily, why would she attack other women?"

"Lily believes that it's mostly women who hold other women back. They are willingly being used as tools for the patriarchy. She'd hate a woman like you, Agent Walsh – working for men, partnering with a man. She'd see you as a traitor. Lily has a very all or nothing viewpoint."

Kate had assumed as much. "We'll be in touch. If Lily contacts you, let us know."

CHAPTER 7

"I believed her," Declan said as they made their way down the driveway toward the road. "I also believe that someone in that house probably knows where Lily is and has more information. Autumn seemed young and unsure of herself. Not someone I'd trust if I were planning a bombing."

Kate agreed with him on that. "We don't have enough to get a search warrant."

"When we come back, we should bring Murphy with us." Declan and Kate made it back to her car. Standing a few feet from the back bumper, Declan tossed the keys to Kate. "I hurt less when you drive."

"I'm not babying you anymore." She tossed the keys right back at him but Declan missed and the keys dropped to the ground. "It's not like you to miss a catch," she teased and walked right past him toward the passenger side as Declan bent to the ground to pick them up.

As Kate's hand touched the handle to pull open the car door, Declan screamed her name. It was unlike anything she had ever heard from him before. It was the sound of desperation and sheer terror.

"Run! Kate, run!" Declan screamed again.

Kate stood paralyzed by his intensity. Seconds later, Declan jerked her arm and dragged her back into the open field. "Run!" he shouted in her face.

She moved her legs as fast as she could, keeping up with him, sprinting to get away from her car. All at once, an explosion shot them forward, crashing them into the earth. Kate landed with a thud, her forehead smashing into the hard ground. Her cheeks and chin burned as they scraped along the grass and dirt.

She shook her head as her ears rang. Disoriented, Kate tried to push herself up but her body was weak and her senses on overload. She lowered herself back down and lay there. "Declan," she said, her voice sounding weak and not like her own. She sucked in sharp breaths as pain shot through her shoulder and left arm. "What happened?" He was lying next to her with his face turned away. "Declan," she called to him more frantically this time.

Slowly, he turned to face her. "There was a bomb under your car. I saw it when I went to pick up your keys."

If not for a missed catch, they'd be dead.

Kate had no words. The incessant ringing in her ears burned through her brain. "Are you okay?"

Declan pushed himself to a kneeling position and checked himself over. He had a gash over his right eye. He dabbed the blood with the corner of his sleeve. "I seem to be okay. Are you?"

Kate tried pushing herself up again and this time was successful. She rolled over onto her backside and brushed the dirt from the front of her pants. Her shoulder and arm still hurt but she figured it was just bruised from the impact. Sirens wailed in the distance as her SUV remained engulfed in flames. She and Declan shared a look. "I guess the bomber is still in Ithaca."

Declan chuckled. "That's what you think of right now? We were seconds from death. Your car is destroyed. We're going to need a new ride, new files, and you're going to have to call your insurance company and see if a bombing is covered. Not to mention, your insurance premium is going to skyrocket." He leaned over and gently turned her chin so they were facing each other. He tenderly brushed a spot on her cheek. "That looks like it hurts. You've got a grass and gravel burn."

She pointed above his eye. "You're going to need stitches."

As they helped each other stand, the fire department and the police arrived. Murphy pulled up moments later and spotted Kate and Declan in the field. He cut through an adjacent property and then through the tree line to meet them.

He looked over their injuries. "What happened?"

"Car bomb," Declan said and then explained how they were still alive. "If Kate hadn't thrown those keys back at me and I missed the catch, we'd be dead. The explosion was huge and meant to kill."

Murphy ran a hand over his bald head and cursed. "I can't believe someone went after you like that. Where were you?"

"Too much to go into right now," Kate said, her cheek starting to burn more. She winced as she touched the spot. "We'll fill you in later, but we haven't made much progress today."

Murphy pointed to Declan's head. "Let's get you two to the emergency room and we'll let the fire department put out your car and then Leo will do what he does best. In the meantime, we'll sort out getting you a new car to drive."

"I'll call my insurance company and they'll get me a rental. Just get us to the hospital if you can." Luckily, Kate had all the essentials with her – her phone and wallet. She didn't keep much in her SUV so she hadn't lost much – nothing of real value.

Later that afternoon, they sat in Murphy's office. Kate had a bandage over her cheek and Declan had a few stitches over his eye. Bruises had started to form on both of them. Aches had started to set in too. She had been right that her arm and shoulder were only bruised and would heal without much of a fuss. Kate felt like she had gone a few rounds in a boxing match. They were alive and that's all that mattered. A car rental company would be dropping off a new car at the police station within the hour.

Spade had been rendered speechless. The call to him from the emergency room had been one of the only times Kate and Declan had heard the man at a complete loss for words. They had been in danger before but never like this. It had been a direct attack on them.

"Do you think it was Lily Cole?" Murphy asked after they explained their earlier meeting with Autumn.

Kate wasn't sure. "I have no idea. She'd have to have some serious skills to set up the bomb in the short amount of time we were in the house. We were only there about forty-five minutes total."

"It means the bomber has been watching you."

Kate had already reasoned that and it sent a shudder down her spine when she realized. At the time, she had been sitting on the edge of the hospital bed as the nurse tended to her wounds. Kate realized they were once again a target in the investigation – the hunter had become the hunted.

"We've only been here one day and already we are attacked?" Declan asked, rhetorically. "Doesn't make a lot of sense to me, unless we were getting close and I don't feel close to knowing much. We don't even have a solid working suspect list."

Kate let Declan's words sink in. "It wasn't an attack to stop us from investigating. It was an attack to show they are smarter than we are – that we are vulnerable. It was a show of force and intelligence. The bomber wants us to know that they can get to us at any time."

"They? Are you not so sure it's a man now?" Declan asked. He wasn't saying it in a condescending *I told you so* kind of way. He was more curious that she had changed her language. "You said *him* earlier."

"Him. Her. Them. I don't know." Kate rested her head in her hand in frustration. "Murphy, do you know anything about Lily Cole?"

"Not as much as I'd like," he admitted. "I'm aware of Sisters of the Revolution. They have been on our radar for a while. They are a feminist group that came out of the sixties. They did a lot of good work politically and in activism on campus here. They have classified themselves radical feminists and their work certainly falls along those ideologies. They were instrumental in championing rape as an expression of patriarchal power, not sex seeking as it had been defined. They have taken on issues related to marriage, pay inequality, they championed for professors here to get tenure who had been denied for years even though they were more qualified than their male counterparts. Over their history here, there have been only a handful of minor incidences tied to the group itself. Most of the serious criminal activity has come from a handful of people. Sisters of the Revolution does not condone criminal activity. Getting arrested for peacefully protesting is one thing – some of the other activities are beyond their scope."

Declan seemed to understand. "What you're saying then is that, by and large, the group itself isn't the issue. It's a few members over the years who have taken things too far."

"Correct. Lily Cole is one of those people." Murphy sat back and crossed his arms. "If memory serves me, even their national organization asked them to take down Lily's biography from the website, which seems like it's promoting her misdeeds."

"That's exactly the impression I had when I saw it," Kate said. "I was surprised she put all of that out there for the world to see. Autumn said that Lily faced some bullying and harassment when she was a freshman. Do you remember anything about that?"

Murphy shook his head. "That wouldn't have been handled by the state police. I can make a call and see if the local police department has anything."

Kate wasn't sure if seeing the details would help with the case. She wasn't even sure that Lily was a suspect – certainly a person of interest at this point. "I don't know if it will be relevant but if you can get some information, I'd appreciate that."

"What's your plan now? It's going to be some time before Leo has anything back on the bomb that nearly killed you."

Kate expelled a breath and looked at Declan. He seemed as worn out as she felt. It had been a long day for the first day in an investigation. "We've got a lead on Asher Bass. We want to interview him next. That's where we were headed when Spade called us about Sisters of the Revolution. We'll need to interview their other members as well."

"You going to interview Asher today?"

Kate checked her watch. It was nearing six-thirty. She was tired, hungry, and in desperate need of a shower. Still, she might catch Asher home for the evening. "I think we'll try him and then head back to the hotel. I want to do some research tonight to get a jump on tomorrow."

As they stood to leave, Murphy raised his eyes to them. "I've got at least fifteen years on you both so forgive me for saying this. It's okay to take a break tonight. It's been a rough day. Declan, I know you're healing from some other injury. I can see the slight limp when you walk, and Kate, your parents died in a bombing. This has to bring up some issues for you both. Take the night to yourselves and settle in. You won't do anyone any good if you're exhausted and overwhelmed. I've got investigators out there talking to neighbors about the car bomb and Leo is doing all he can. Let us handle it for the night."

Normally, Kate would be annoyed that someone told her to slow down. Tonight, she was grateful for someone watching their backs. She thanked him. "I'm going to leave Asher until morning."

Declan nodded in agreement. "We appreciate it, Murphy. Call us the minute you hear anything back and if the investigators out there in the field get any solid leads."

Murphy assured them he would. As Kate and Declan walked outside, she got an alert on her phone that the rental car had arrived. She chuckled to herself. "I had forgotten we didn't have a way back to the hotel. Luckily, the car arrived."

Declan pointed to the front of the parking lot to the blue SUV. "I see the car and my heart starts to race. Do you think we'll ever get in a car again and not worry about a bomb?"

Declan had articulated the worry that had been in the back of Kate's mind since the bombing happened. "I hope it goes away eventually. But yes, it's going to be on my mind every time I open the car door and every time I start the ignition."

As they approached the car, Kate showed her identification to the rental agent who was dropping off the car. She signed a quick form, he handed over the keys, and they were on their way. Declan looked under the car just to be safe.

After driving a few blocks, Declan asked, "Were you telling Murphy the truth that we're done for the day and heading back to the hotel, or are we still going to track down Asher?"

Kate hadn't been sure. She wasn't driving in the direction of the hotel, but rather aimlessly driving down side streets until she made a decision. Night had already fallen and the streetlights overhead cast shadows on the cars that lined the road. As they passed each one, Kate expected it to explode. She had to shake it off if she was going to be able to continue on the case.

Kate flexed her fingers on the steering wheel. "I can't interview anyone tonight. I'm barely thinking straight. I'm paranoid that someone is out there watching us right now."

Declan touched her arm. "You're not paranoid, Kate. Someone tried to kill us earlier today. We were being watched. If it wasn't Lily, then it's safe to assume we had been watched for a good part of the day. Why choose that moment to bomb?"

Kate had already been considering why then. "There were probably cameras everywhere else we went today – the police station and the hospital. At the bombing site, the car wasn't out of our sight so they couldn't have done it then." She pulled over to the side of the road and put the car in park. "Or none of that is true and it's Lily or being made to look like it's Lily. I don't feel like I know anything for sure."

"Are we stopping for a reason?"

Kate didn't explain her reason for stopping and Declan didn't press. When she was ready to speak again, she asked, "What did you see when you bent down to pick up the keys?"

Declan and Kate had given their statements separately in the emergency room and hadn't discussed the incident in detail since it happened. This was the first Kate had asked the question. Declan ran a hand down his stubbled face. "I saw a wire, Kate. It was a wire that was out of place and something white like clay. I didn't see all of it, but instinct took over and I just knew."

"C-4 then."

"That's what I'm assuming. Leo will be able to tell us more. Someone was around to trigger it. I assume once they saw me drop to the ground to pick up the keys and scream for you, they knew I'd seen it. They were trying to kill us, Kate. That's all we need to know."

Kate swallowed hard. "Then what's to stop them from trying again? They could try at the hotel we are staying in. They could try the car again." She was starting to spin out. Her voice caught in her throat, her heartbeat pounded in her ears, and it was hard to catch her breath.

There wasn't much Declan could say to calm her down. "We checked into the hotel early this morning before anyone knew we were in town. Let's be extra aware of our surroundings on the drive back and reassess in the morning. It's the only way we will sleep tonight."

Kate nodded and put the car in drive. She practically held her breath all the way to the hotel.

CHAPTER 8

Kate sat in the living room area of the shared hotel suite. The space wasn't large but it afforded them their own sleeping areas with a middle living room area with a desk. They had ordered room service for breakfast, which they devoured. Kate sipped her remaining coffee while Declan finished getting ready.

Kate felt rested, albeit still sore. Her head was clearer too. Even though she had felt fear last night laying her head on the pillow, she had pushed it aside to allow her body to rest. Kate had willed herself to sleep and hadn't woken up once during the night. Declan said he slept the same.

She took another sip of coffee while she read news articles online about Sisters of the Revolution. The group as a whole had a good mission. The chapters did charitable work and were involved in local community initiatives. It seemed like what Murphy said was true – only a handful of their members took things too far and crossed the line into criminal activity.

Kate set her cup down on the desk and did another search on Lily Cole. She found the information she saw yesterday, but Kate wanted to dig further back. She added a date to the search, hoping to pull back news articles that included the harassment Lily said she experienced. Nothing came back. Whatever had happened hadn't made the news.

Kate sat back in the chair and took another sip of coffee. "Are you almost ready?" she called to Declan. She wasn't sure why he was always the last to get ready. They weren't sharing a bathroom, so he couldn't blame her for taking too long.

Declan walked out of the bathroom still tucking in his shirt. His hair stuck up in the back and he patted it down, trying to keep it in place. "I'm surprised we haven't heard from Murphy or Leo. I was sure one of them would have called with an update by now."

"They probably assumed we needed the sleep. We'll talk to them today."

Declan stopped at the desk mirror and tried one more time unsuccessfully to tame his hair. He finally gave up and ran a hand through it, allowing it to go every which way so the uncooperative strands looked intentional. He glanced down at Kate. "What's first on the agenda?"

"Asher Bass. I'm hoping to catch him before he heads to campus for class. I don't think anyone would be expecting the FBI to show up at seven in the morning." Kate finished her coffee and then pulled her things together. Declan stood by the door and watched her as if she were the one running late. She grabbed the Do Not Disturb sign from the dresser, playfully elbowed him in the gut, and slipped the sign on the door as they left.

Asher's street had a row of Craftsman-style houses, and his was the third one down the block. It had blue siding and white shutters and a few chairs on the porch. There was also a rug and potted plants hanging from chains. It looked well-kept for a house that was being rented to college students.

"You going to take the lead?" Kate asked as they got out of the car. She wasn't sure why but she assumed Asher might respond better to Declan.

"Got it covered," he assured her as they climbed the porch steps. Before he could knock, the door swung open and a tall young man with freckles and bright red hair answered the door. He had on gray sweatpants and a Cornell tee-shirt.

"I assume you're cops," the young man said, stepping aside and making a grand sweeping gesture with his hands welcoming them inside. "I'm Asher Bass and I assumed you'd be showing up at my door sooner rather than later."

"Why is that?" Declan asked as he walked past him into the house. He kept his hand on the butt of his gun as he flashed the badge on his chain. He introduced himself and Kate. "Is there anyone else here?"

"No. My father rents the entire house for me. My mother shows up once a month to plant flowers and make the place presentable as she calls it. Please, go into the living room. I expected the state police. I must be in trouble to warrant the FBI. I'm making coffee, do you want any?"

Kate and Declan declined but walked into the living room and checked out the space. It was nicer than any college living quarters Kate had seen. The brown leather furniture looked new, the television affixed to the wall was larger than any she'd seen in someone's home, and the place had a tidy vibe like nothing was ever out of place.

Asher left them standing in the living room for several moments before he returned with a cup of coffee and sat down in a leather straight-back chair. "Please, sit, let's talk. I assume you're here because of the bombings. Everyone on campus has been talking about it, as I'm sure you can imagine. It's the biggest thing to happen to Cornell in decades." His tone was even but lacked any sort of emotion that would normally be found when speaking about such a tragedy.

"You don't seem all that upset by the news," Kate said, watching his reaction.

He took a sip of coffee and shrugged. "I wouldn't say that I'm not upset, but there's not much I can do. It didn't hurt me or my friends. I wasn't a witness, so there's not even much I can say. Although, I understand why you're here."

"Why is that?" Declan asked, sharing a look with Kate. She could tell that he was feeling the same about Asher's demeanor. It was suspicious, to say the least. He had the removed emotion of someone jaded and much older.

Asher narrowed his eyes. "I assumed you would have heard by now. I was turned down by Sword and Crown and got angry about it. I said some unfortunate things that could have been taken as a threat. I think anyone in my circumstance would have been offended. It was a slap in the face to my whole family that I wasn't admitted. My father was the most disturbed by it."

Declan took a seat on the couch and Kate followed. This way they'd be at eye level with Asher. Declan leaned forward and rested his hands on his knees. "When you said your father was angry, do you mean angrier than you?"

"Yeah. My grandfather's class was the one who built the addition in the back of the house. He was the first class that lived in residence at Sword and Crown. They wanted their members to live together. It afforded them more bonding than being scattered across campus. Not only that but generations back, my great however many times grandfather was one of the founding members. I'm a legacy and I'm the first generation to be denied. My father was enraged. Wouldn't you be?"

"I would think it would depend on why I was denied," Declan said, staring over at him. "Our understanding is that you've gotten yourself into a little bit of trouble that your father has bailed you out of a few times. The members of Sword and Crown had the right not to take the risk on you."

Asher laughed loudly and shook his head. "Did you go to college, Agent James?"

Declan smirked. "All FBI agents go to college. Yes, I have a degree."

"From any school worth noting? I assume not since you're a government worker."

"Boston College," Declan said with pride.

Asher gestured with his hand. "See, that's what I mean. I'm Ivy League and unless you're Ivy League you're not going to understand. It's a whole different ball game when you're sitting on the top of the mountain. I don't expect you to get it. But yeah, I got in some trouble and my father bailed me as any good father would. The follies of youth." Asher shrugged like it was no big deal. "As I said, it's not your fault you don't understand. Ivy League is just different, man."

Kate cleared her throat. "Does Harvard count?"

Asher seemed confused by the question. "Does Harvard count for what? It's an Ivy League school."

"I'm aware," Kate said, evenly. "It's my alma mater."

Asher laughed. "There's no way you went to Harvard and then went as low class as to work for the FBI. No offense, but if you went to Harvard, you'd be much more successful."

Kate hated this kid. She couldn't even say something as benign as dislike. No, it was pure hate for everything this kid stood for and his behavior. Kate crossed her legs and plastered a stiff smile on her face. "Not everyone who goes to or graduated from an Ivy League school is as entitled and snobbish as you are. What I want to know is where you were on Sunday night into Monday morning?"

Asher didn't falter with Kate's dressing down. "I was here alone. I don't know how to make a bomb, Agent Walsh. Even if I did, I wouldn't waste my time attacking Sword and Crown. The guys living in that class haven't done anything to me. They weren't the ones who decided to keep me out. Yes, I directed some anger at them when they wouldn't change the rules, but it's not their fault. They are governed by more than a century of tradition."

"Is your father still *enraged*?" Declan asked, stressing the word.

Asher stared back at Declan in disbelief. "You think my father had something to do with this?"

"I'm asking if he's still angry."

"Of course he's still angry. But my father doesn't know anything about making bombs. My father got his retaliation on Sword and Crown. He cut them off financially."

Declan shifted his eyes. "Your father was paying money to Sword and Crown?"

Asher nodded. "My family paid the taxes on the property, for the utilities, and the upkeep and maintenance. When he came to learn that I hadn't been admitted, he called and threatened to cut off his financial support. It didn't matter. I wasn't let in. He cut off the money. I heard Sword and Crown has back taxes to pay. Who says they didn't blow up the place themselves? They were in danger of losing the property."

This was the first time Kate had heard that and she didn't even know if it was true. It would be easy enough to find out. For now, she remained focused. "Where do your parents live?"

"New York City. My father runs a hedge fund. If you still don't believe me, he was in London when the bombing occurred. He's still there. I'm sure you can get proof of that besides asking me."

Kate wasn't sure she had any reason to bother Asher's father. She asked him if he or his father had ever been to Dartmouth. Asher said he hadn't and, to his knowledge, neither had his father. Asher offered to call his father's secretary to confirm his trip, but Kate waved him off. "I don't think that will be necessary. Is there anyone who can confirm that you were at home Sunday night into Monday morning?"

Asher sipped his coffee. "Unfortunately, no. Had I realized I would need an alibi, I would have made sure to have had someone sleep over. You're going to have to take me at my word."

Kate asked him a few more questions that didn't produce much other than his same attitude of indifference and then she turned to

Declan. He asked a handful of questions and then got down to the final one. "Can Agent Walsh and I search your house?"

"No," Asher said, shaking his head. "I don't have anything to hide, but I know my rights. If you want to search, get a warrant."

"If you have nothing to hide, you wouldn't mind a search," Declan countered.

"I'm not that gullible." Asher set his cup down on a nearby table and stood. He waited for Kate and Declan to do the same. When they didn't move, he said, "If there's nothing else, I'll see you out."

Kate stood but she had a couple more questions. "Do you know Lily Cole?"

Asher blinked rapidly twice. "You think she had something to do with this?"

"I didn't say that. I'm only asking if you know her."

It took him a few beats, but Asher finally responded. "I know she's crazy. I know she has attacked fraternity members. She threw paint all over some sorority girls heading to one of their formals. She also broke windows at the Sigma Chi house. If you think she had something to do with the bombings, you might be on the right track."

Kate stepped toward him. "Do you know her personally or just the rumors?"

"She was in my sociology class sophomore year. She argued with the professor constantly until he kicked her out of class." Asher scrunched up his face. "Lily isn't easy to get to know. There's a wall of anger around her that no one is getting past. I held a door open for her once and she screamed at me that she wasn't incapable of opening the door herself. I didn't even think of it like that. I hold the door for anyone behind me, man or woman."

"Have you seen her recently?"

Asher shook his head. "Not so far this semester. Probably last spring sometime, but I can't recall when exactly."

Kate didn't have anything else. She followed Asher to the front door and as she crossed the threshold behind Declan, Asher called after them, "I'm glad you weren't too badly hurt when your car blew up. It would have been horrible if something happened to the two of you." There was no trace of emotion in his voice. It was almost jovial like he was taunting them.

Declan turned back. "How do you know about that?"

He gestured toward their injuries. "It's all over the internet. It made the morning news."

"I appreciate your concern," Kate said, matching the same lack of affect in his tone. She nudged Declan down the steps and when they got back to the car, she blew out a frustrated breath. "That went nowhere."

"He's got no alibi, Kate. He wouldn't let us search. He doesn't seem to care that anyone is dead. I'd say he remains on our suspect list."

Kate didn't have any reason to disagree but still, she thought Declan was off. Asher didn't seem to her like the kind of guy to get his hands dirty. "I hate that kid. He's everything wrong with rich Ivy League students, but I'm not sure he's good for this. We can keep him on the list for a lack of a more viable suspect."

CHAPTER 9

After spending most of the day running down potential leads that went nowhere and witnesses who didn't see anything, Kate and Declan made their way back to Murphy's office. It was only the second day of the investigation and they had already been attacked and the leads had dried up.

"We've got next to nothing," Declan said, slumping down in a conference room chair. He glanced in Kate's direction but her expression told him she agreed with him. "What are we going to do? I feel like we are going to sit around until the next bomb happens."

Kate didn't want to say they were already defeated. She wasn't going to wallow with Declan. "We haven't received a crime scene evidence report yet. Leo is examining the bomb that nearly killed us. There will be more leads to follow. Give it time."

Declan was usually more patient than Kate. She wondered what was going on with him. Although, coming as close to death as they had would be a damper on anyone's mood. She stared over at him until he smiled.

"Stop looking at me like that," he said.

"Like what?"

"Like you're worried about me. I'm fine." Declan pushed himself upright in the chair and put his hands on the table. "I'm just frustrated."

Kate was about to tell him that she felt the same when Murphy joined them. He slid a file folder on the table toward Kate. "Crime scene report?"

Murphy nodded as he sat down. "It doesn't tell us any more than what Leo told us already. C-4 and it was connected to a cellphone detonator. I've got some of my best hunting down where the bomber could be getting the materials to make C-4, particularly the RDX. If we can figure that out, maybe we can narrow our suspect pool."

Kate flipped open the report. "What about other evidence?"

"As you'll read, there wasn't much else. It blew the whole back of the residence apart. As Leo mentioned, there are remnants of a backpack which is what we believe the bomb was placed in. It was navy blue and the material was common for a backpack. We aren't able to tell brand yet, but even if we do, it could probably have been bought anywhere."

Kate scanned the documents one after the other. It was everything that Murphy was explaining to them. Nothing jumped out at her that he hadn't already indicated. She closed the file and slid it across the table to Declan. "This doesn't give us much more to go on."

"Did you find out anything today?" Murphy asked, looking hopeful.

"Not much. Asher Bass doesn't strike me as someone who'd build a bomb." Kate said the words and then grew quiet as she considered if that was how she felt. It would have been easier if she had felt like he could be a suspect. She conceded, "He doesn't have an alibi and also wouldn't let us search his residence without a search warrant. While that might say something to some, it doesn't tell me much. We don't even have enough to get a search warrant. I can't rule him out, but I don't have enough to consider him a person of interest even."

Kate and Murphy continued their conversation about potential suspects while Declan read over the report. A few minutes later, Murphy's administrative assistant popped her head in the doorway and told him he had an urgent call. He stood from the table to take the call in his office, but she advised that Kate and Declan might want to sit in.

"It's Harvey Bowman from the *New York Times*. He said he thinks he got a letter from the bomber. He saw the press conference and wants to speak with all of you." She left without saying anything else.

Murphy raised his eyes to Kate as he stood and leaned over the table to hit the blinking red light on the phone sitting in the center of the table. When the call was engaged, he said, "This is Investigator Murphy. I have FBI Agents Kate Walsh and Declan James here with me."

Harvey cleared his throat and then introduced himself. "I have an interesting letter here that I think you're going to want to see. I scanned in a copy and your assistant provided your email address. You should have it now."

Murphy scrolled through his email on his phone. He found the email, opened the documents, scanned the letter, and then handed it over to Kate. "It's not much of a letter. It's only a few lines."

Kate lowered her head to his phone. She read the simplistic print: *"Dear FBI, I am the one you seek. You think you can stop me but you can't. I showed you who is in control. You will not stop me. You cannot stop me. I will destroy all those who abuse their power. Get out of my way or this time I will kill you."* The note was signed *The Fuse*.

Kate's background in forensic linguistics came into play at times like this. She could often read a letter and understand important characteristics of the writer – gender, age, education level. There were so many hints and clues that Kate could understand, even what the writer was hiding or faking. This was short though and only gave so much away.

As she handed the cellphone to Declan for him to read, Kate inched closer to the table. "Harvey, this is Agent Walsh. When and how did you receive this letter?" He had only sent the letter and not the envelope or however it had been delivered.

"One of the administrative assistants opened it this morning thinking it was a letter to the editor. It was addressed to me on the outside but got sorted into the wrong pile. It was given to me after she had read it. It wasn't mailed. It was hand-delivered to the office."

That meant there had been many hands on the letter. "Where is the envelope now?"

"I have it here on my desk. Is it important?" he asked, confusion tinging his voice.

"Yes, it's important. It's what could contain some clues to the writer's identity. Please slip it into a baggie and preserve it for us. In the meantime, please snap a photo of it and email it to us now."

Declan raised his eyes to hers and mouthed, "He must not watch cop shows."

Kate smiled back, thinking the same thing. "What do you think?"

Declan shook his head and pointed to the phone. It was clear he didn't want to speak in front of the reporter. "Harvey, have you written any stories about the bombings that happened at Dartmouth and Cornell?"

"Yes, right after the cops said the explosion at Cornell was a bomb. My article came out before your latest press conference last night and asks the question if the Dartmouth bombing is connected." Harvey cleared his throat and then spoke quietly. "I think I'm the first reporter to say the cases must be connected. I also went to Columbia Journalism School, so I indicated that all Ivy League schools might be at risk."

It made sense to Kate why Harvey was targeted. She couldn't be angry with his reporting as it was only a matter of time before the media connected the cases. There had already been talk by local Ithaca reporters, but she hadn't realized that the theory had made national news yet. "When did your story run?"

"Yesterday morning online. This morning we received this letter. If they hadn't called themselves the Fuse, I might not have connected it at all. You know the fuse is the part of the bomb that initiates its function."

"Yes, we know what a fuse is," Declan said dryly. "Were you here in Ithaca for the press conference?"

"No. I watched it online." Harvey started to speak but his words tripped over themselves. He coughed and sputtered. "Do you think we have any reason to worry that the newspaper will be a target? We are all quite worried here at the office. Many of us are graduates of Ivy League schools."

Declan leaned forward. "Were any of you in secret societies?"

"What? No. Well, I wasn't. I can't speak for all of my colleagues. Do you think that matters? Should I ask around?" There was genuine fear in Harvey's voice.

He didn't seem to have the tough constitution that most reporters had. She wasn't sure if Declan was asking a legitimate question or winding the man up. "You should be fine," she said, weighing her words. "We don't know where the bomber will strike next. They seem to be targeting secret societies though and not newspapers. We are going to need to interview you and the person who opened the letter. Have you been able to trace how the letter entered the building?"

"Not yet. Do you think the bomber was here?"

That was the question running through Kate's head. She was sure by the look on Declan's and Murphy's faces that they were thinking the same. "We don't know. That's something we are going to need to find out. For now, bag up the letter and envelope as we asked and sit tight. Agent James and I might be down there ourselves to speak to you. If not, we'll let you know who we are sending. Please tell the staff to remain on high alert."

Harvey agreed to do as they asked and then he hung up. A moment later, a photo of the envelope came through to Murphy's phone. It was addressed like it had been sent through the mail with a stamp. What was missing was the postmark. The envelope had the same block-printed lettering as the letter. The bomber was trying to disguise their handwriting.

"What do you think?" Murphy asked Kate.

She studied the photo and then placed the phone on the table. "The bomber made their first contact. They want to engage with us. From this, I'd assume the writer is college-educated and they chose this print style to prevent any decent handwriting analysis. I can't tell if it's a man or woman through their word choices. I'd need more of a sample."

Murphy read a small section of the letter that seemed to refer to the bomb in Kate's car. "They are saying that if you keep investigating, they will kill you this time. Does that mean the last time, the intent wasn't to kill?"

Declan shook his head. "I don't understand planting a bomb if they didn't want to kill us. Surely, had we been in the car when it detonated, we'd be dead."

"Whoever this is, wants to toy with us," Kate said, trying to consider all the options as she spoke.

"Agreed," Murphy and Declan said in unison. It was clear to both of them that Kate wasn't done. Murphy encouraged her to talk through the rest of what she was thinking.

"I don't believe what they said in the letter. I think we were meant to die in that blast."

"Tell me why you think that," Murphy said and then waited.

Kate remained quiet for a moment, processing. She leaned on the table with her arms. "The bomber had no way of knowing that Declan would drop the keys and see the bomb under the car. If they wanted to simply scare us, they would have exploded the device as we were walking to the car, not wait until we were nearly getting inside. As Declan said, if we had been in that car when the bomb exploded, we'd be dead. I think they are covering for their failure by saying that. The bomber intended to kill us and failed and it's bothering them. To maintain their sense of control, they needed to reach out and prove that they had let us live – that it hadn't been a failure on their part."

Declan nodded along as she spoke. "They needed to prove they are smarter than us."

"Correct." Kate checked the time on the clock on the wall. It was 3:21 pm. "It's been roughly twenty-four hours since the bomber planted the bomb in my car and they are already engaging with us, trying to convince us they are in control. It tells me they are easily rattled when something doesn't go their way. They have a high need to prove themselves."

"What does it mean for the case?" Murphy asked.

"It means they are going to strike again – soon. Maybe even sooner than before."

Murphy shifted his eyes between Kate and Declan. "Is there anything we can do to stop them?"

Kate desperately wanted to say yes, but she knew the bomber was one step ahead of them. "We need to go to New York City and interview the newspaper staff."

Declan seconded that. "Do you think we should notify Colombia and Princeton? If we assume the bomber delivered that letter, they are in New York City. Colombia is right there and Princeton isn't far from there."

Murphy looked at Declan with skepticism. "Do you think they'd give themselves away like that?"

"They may not realize that they have. In the press conference, you didn't come out and say we thought they'd be targeting other Ivy League schools. The newspaper did, but we didn't admit to thinking there was a pattern," Kate explained.

"Is that a yes or no to calling Columbia and Princeton, Kate?" Declan asked.

She nodded her head. "I'll make those calls on the ride to New York City."

Murphy asked, "What do you want us to do in your absence?"

"Could you speak to other members of Sisters of the Revolution about Lily's whereabouts and see if they are willing to let you search the place? We don't have grounds right now for a search warrant, but I'm interested in what the members know about her and have to say." Kate turned to Declan to see if he had anything else to add.

"Run down any leads with the detective involved in the bombing in Dartmouth. That would be helpful too," Declan said. "If any more evidence comes in here or when Leo has the report about the car bomb, let us know."

"Certainly." Murphy stood and shook their hands as they rushed out of the office.

Kate had a sense of urgency to get to New York City. She didn't think she could prevent another bombing but being where the bomber had just been would hopefully take her one step closer to uncovering the truth and preventing more deaths.

CHAPTER 10

K ate paced the upper west side Manhattan hotel room as Declan watched her. He had changed into shorts and a tee-shirt and had already scarfed down a decent room service meal. Kate had picked at her food as she had grown frustrated with their inability to connect with anyone by the time they had arrived in New York City that evening.

Traffic had been snarled and Harvey Bowman had grown tired of waiting for them and allowed the staff to go home for the evening. He waited until nine then he left too, promising Kate they could all meet first thing in the morning. Kate had made the case for why it was so critical to speak to everyone that evening, but Harvey hadn't relented. He told Kate that he had talked to the *New York Times* staff who had been in contact with the letter and no one seemed to know how it ended up in the pile of incoming mail. The demands of an FBI agent didn't mean much. They were sidelined until morning.

As Kate had suspected, calling the college administrations hadn't done much of anything either. There was no direct threat made against the schools or any of their buildings, including clubs and societies. There was no reason for them to sound the alarm and put their students and faculty on high alert. Mostly, they didn't want to associate themselves with what they considered tragedy and scandal that had befallen the other Ivy League schools. It hadn't mattered how much Kate pleaded and even threatened that the colleges could be facing lawsuits if a bomb was detonated on their property while they stood by and did nothing. At that, both administrators had ended their calls with her.

Kate pounded her fist into the palm of her hand. "We can't just sit here all night and do nothing."

Declan clicked the television on and pointed. "We aren't doing nothing. It's the bottom of the eighth and the Red Sox are up by two against the Yankees. We can watch the end of the game. You can finish the food you barely touched and we can get a good night's rest. I'm in pain and laying low for the evening will probably do me good."

Hearing that Declan was in pain, Kate turned to him with worry in her eyes. "I hadn't even thought to ask if you were all right. You fell pretty hard with the blast yesterday and you're still in a healing process."

Declan sunk back into the couch and folded his hands behind his head. "I know, Kate. That's why you should come over here and massage me and make sure I'm feeling better." He tried to hide the smirk that was slowly spreading across his face. "No?"

His gray tee-shirt fit snug against his biceps and chest. She knew the contours of his body under the shirt and for a brief second, Kate let her mind wander. If she were dating him, she'd have massaged him and done anything else to make him feel better. But that wasn't what this was. Kate shook the thoughts from her head. "There will be no massages."

"You thought about it though. I can tell by the look on your face. You should give into temptation, Kate." Declan winked at her.

She ignored him. "While I'm up, I'll get you water and pain medication."

Declan shook his head. "It makes me sleepy and I want to see the end of the game." He patted the couch next to him for her to sit down.

"You've done all you can do for one night. Relax and we can start fresh in the morning."

Kate wavered, fighting the sense of responsibility to keep at it with the case. Declan was right that there wasn't anything more she could do tonight. It wasn't like she could track down each secret society connected to Columbia and knock on the door and tell the people inside that they were potentially the target of a bomber. She'd sound like she had lost her mind. Her professional credibility would be at stake. No, there was nothing more she could do.

Surrendering to the loss of control for the evening, Kate allowed Declan to reel her into the comfort of the couch and sat next to him. "I haven't watched baseball in a long time," she said as she sat and tucked her legs under her. She snatched a cold French fry from her plate.

Declan pointed to her half-eaten cheeseburger. "If it's cold, call and order another one. Spade was being cheap by not allowing us two rooms. We're lucky we got our own beds."

"I don't think it was Spade. The hotel wasn't going to comp two rooms at the federal rate for us. I looked on their website and the rooms go for close to five hundred for the night."

Declan glanced around the basic hotel room with two beds, a couch, a television, and a desk. The view from their thirtieth floor wasn't half-bad but not worth five hundred dollars. "Who'd spend that kind of money to stay here? It's not even in the most exciting part of the city."

Kate didn't know who'd spend that kind of money but she was too tired to care. As soon as Declan had given her permission to wind down for the night, her brain had taken the task seriously. She'd be lucky to finish off her cold food and make it to her bed. "When was the last time you went to a Red Sox game? We should go next season."

Declan turned to her. "I haven't gone in so long I can't remember. My ex-wife hated baseball."

"Your ex-wife? You mean Lauren?"

"I'm not speaking her name anymore. It's a new policy of mine and I'd appreciate it if you didn't say it either." Declan stared at the television screen. "I need to put all that behind me. I'm putting distance there. My therapist thinks it's a good idea."

"Your therapist?" Kate asked, not hiding the shock in her tone.

Declan nodded. "You know they sent me for an evaluation after getting shot. It wasn't as bad as I thought it would be. I've gone a few times. She's helping me work through a few things with my marriage."

He hadn't told her he was going to therapy. Not that Declan needed to tell her. It was just that Kate hadn't realized he was capable of keeping secrets from her. Declan was usually vocal about everything whether Kate wanted to know it or not. She rested her hand on his arm. "I'm glad you're talking to someone if it's helpful."

"She asked about you."

"About me?" Kate said, discomfort immediately setting in. She didn't like knowing Declan had spoken to his therapist about her. "What did she want to know?"

Declan still had his eyes trained on the television. "If we were sleeping together. She wanted to know the nature of our relationship. I guess I mentioned your name too many times and she was curious."

"Why would you talk about me?"

Declan finally turned his head and looked at her. "Why wouldn't I mention you? You're my partner and best friend. We also live together which she thought was super weird. I explained that it works for us. She got it in her head something more must be going on. She even wondered if it's why my marriage ended."

"Is it?" Kate hated to ask the question and she held her breath waiting for the response. Lauren had more than once accused them of cheating.

"Not directly."

Kate raised her eyebrows. "Indirectly?"

Declan nodded but remained quiet for several moments. It set Kate on edge. When he finally spoke, he was thoughtful and reflective. "When my ex first asked for a divorce, I didn't think it had anything to do with you, even though we both know how many times she accused us of having an affair. I was so adamant that we weren't that I overlooked why my marriage was failing. The truth is, she and I never had the connection that you and I share. I was never able to be myself with her the way I am with you. So, are you the cause? No. But our friendship has shown me that there is more out there for me. Particularly, if I'm going to have a relationship with a woman. You're not the cause but our relationship has shown me what I should be looking for in the best possible way."

Kate didn't know if that was necessarily true. She didn't know anything about relationships or how to make one work. She dismissed his praise. "It works between us because we are in the same line of work and we get it. I understand why your personal life can't be a priority and why you have a packed suitcase sitting in your closet for when the FBI tells you it's wheels up in an hour. I understand your work which is ninety percent of your life. Having a real relationship with me would be as bad as anyone else."

Declan chuckled and patted her on the leg before standing. "Take the compliment, Kate." He stood there and watched the final inning of the ballgame while Kate stared up at him. He had lost weight after the shooting – mostly muscle weight. Before the accident, his legs had been thick muscle, and now, they appeared smaller. He had been doing mostly cardio and working with the physical therapist to get mobility back. Kate was concerned about him now that she was sitting back and getting a good look at him.

"Are you done with physical therapy?" she asked.

He turned to look down at her. "Are you admiring my physique?"

"I'm noticing you've lost a good deal of muscle mass in your legs." She tried to hold back the smile as she added, "Even your upper body is a little smaller. I'm fairly certain I could take you in a fight."

"You could probably take me in a fight before I got shot." Declan looked down at his legs. "You're right. I need to get back in the gym now that I'm healed up. I probably need to dial back the cardio."

Kate stood and looped an arm around his back and leaned into him. "Processing your feelings with a therapist, not lifting weights, and saying sweet things to me about our friendship. I barely recognize you, Declan. Next, you're going to tell me you've taken up meditation and yoga. If you start talking about your guru, I'm getting a new partner."

Declan leaned his head down on hers. "No gurus but you didn't even notice that I scaled back drinking so much, too."

Kate had noticed that but she didn't want to draw attention to it or jinx him. It had been a good change that happened in the middle of their vacation after one night that had them both hungover the next morning. Kate didn't drink more than one or two normally and could go long stretches without touching alcohol at all. She could go the rest of her life without another drink if she was being honest with herself. Declan, though, she had often wondered if he was approaching the line of addiction.

After their hangovers had cleared, Declan stopped drinking on the trip. Even when they had arrived back in Boston, he had only an occasional beer while watching television. Kate had watched it play out cautiously and hoped he didn't go back to drinking more frequently.

"I noticed," she admitted, "but I didn't want to say anything. Is there a reason you stopped?"

"I stopped liking how I feel when I'm drunk." Declan ran a hand through his messy brown hair. "Nearly dying can have a life-shattering impact on you. I survived being shot and promised that if I made it through, I'd make some changes in my life." He held his arms wide. "These are the changes I'm making. Not the muscle loss but everything else – a kinder, gentler, more reflective, sober Declan."

Kate stared up at him with skepticism on her face. She wasn't sure she liked the sound of his plan other than the sober part. She had thought he was pretty terrific the way he was before the shooting. "Try not to lose too much of yourself in the process of finding your *new* self." She left him standing there and headed toward the bathroom.

Declan called after her. "Does that mean you thought I was perfect before?"

"Perfectly flawed but perfectly you," she shouted through the bathroom door. He didn't respond, which was good because Kate wasn't sure what else she could add. She was still dealing with her attraction toward him. It was hard to lock down those feelings now that they had bubbled to the surface.

Kate washed her face and brushed her teeth and got ready for bed. By the time she left the bathroom, Declan was standing by the large window overlooking the city. Kate watched him for a moment, fighting the urge to wrap her arms around him and lay her head against his back. "I'm going to bed," she said finally, her voice catching in her throat.

He turned and smiled. "I'm going too. I was looking out over the city and it struck me how complicated cases must be to work here. There are so many people and tourists. It must be like finding a needle in a haystack every single time."

"I never really liked New York City because it's too crowded," Kate said, pulling down the covers and climbing into bed. She undid her ponytail and let her dark hair fall over her shoulders as she sat up in bed. "I'm hoping to interview the newspaper staff, get a few more leads, and then run them to ground. I don't want to be here any longer than necessary."

Declan let the curtain fall closed and then he climbed into his bed. Before shutting off the bedside lamp, he said, "You said in the meeting with Murphy that the letter didn't give you any clue to gender. Is that true or were you avoiding the question?"

Kate remained quiet for a moment considering if she wanted to say aloud what she thought. Finally, when Declan urged her to speak her mind, she said, "It sounds like a woman to me. Some of the word choices hint that it could be a woman but I'm not sure. The letter was so short. I didn't want to say and lead us in the wrong direction. Let's say that given the note, I can't rule out that it's a woman."

Declan didn't press the issue further. Kate fell asleep wondering if everything she knew about profiling bombing suspects was being tipped on its head.

CHAPTER 11

Kate's phone rang seconds before Declan's. Neither woke up in time to answer. The bedside hotel phone ring echoed through the room and woke them fully. Kate sat upright and let her eyes adjust to the darkness. She reached for the phone. "Hello," she said as the word caught in her throat.

Spade's deep commanding voice came through the line. "Kate, there's been another bombing. Raven Hall on 116th street. The explosion took out the whole building and the two adjacent. Detectives from the New York Police Department are on the scene. Murphy and Leo are on their way from Ithaca. I insisted they be there. There's not much you can do right now but still get to the scene. The fire department is working to put out the blaze. They had to call in additional support to put out the fire. There are no known survivors."

No survivors. The words slammed into Kate's chest. She had known it was going to happen. She should have tried harder to warn them. "We're on it."

"I've emailed you information about Raven Hall. You'll want to review it before going to the scene. The address is in there, too, in case you forget." Spade let Kate absorb the information and then he told her to be prepared. "Kate, the media is going to be all over this. It's going to look like a failure on the part of the FBI for not stopping this guy."

"I tried to warn them," Kate said, knowing she'd had nothing to go on. It wasn't Columbia's fault – she didn't have the evidence to convince them. "I'll take care of the public relations issues."

"Kate," Spade said, letting his voice go quiet, "I hope you know this isn't your fault no matter what the media is going to say. The evidence hasn't been there. There was nothing you could do."

Kate didn't buy that. There was always more that could be done. Spade didn't like it when she was too hard on herself. "I know," she lied. Then she rushed him off the phone, explained what was happening to Declan, and got out of bed to get ready.

Kate threw on clothes, tied her hair up in a ponytail, and swiped enough makeup on her face to put color back in her cheeks. She read aloud the email from Spade as they descended in the elevator. "Raven Hall is Columbia's oldest secret society founded in 1822. It was founded as a literary society and then its activities grew more secretive with time. The building is six stories, from what's known as the basement crypt to residential floors and then top floor, which has a library, a bar, and a ballroom with a chandelier that was shipped in from France in 1902. All twenty members, only from the most elite families, live in the house. There is a housekeeper and a cook who live in residence."

"The bomber was right when they said they'd be attacking those in power," Declan said before hailing a cab outside of the hotel. They had their car parked in the hotel's parking garage but there would be nowhere for them to park at the scene and it was too far to walk.

Columbia was situated in the Morningside Heights neighborhood of Manhattan – just north of where they were staying. Kate continued to read the email to look for any important facts to share with Declan. So far, it was just an overview of Raven Hall. The one thing of note was that the building was not part of Columbia's campus and had no oversight from the administration.

That meant even if Kate had convinced Columbia's administration to issue a warning to all their societies the students at Raven Hall could have simply chosen not to heed the warnings and there'd be no repercussions from the university. Kate wasn't sure why she felt better but some weight had been lifted off her shoulders. Maybe she had done all she could.

The cab pulled to a stop three blocks from the scene. The road had been blocked off and a perimeter wall of NYPD uniformed officers held back traffic and interested people mulling around the streets. Even from that vantage point, Kate could see the billowing black smoke rising in the air a few blocks away.

Declan paid the cabbie and they flashed their badges at the perimeter. One of the young, uniformed cops said he'd radio to a detective that they were on their way. He shouted after them, "Don't go any closer than the firefighters allow. It's still an active scene."

It didn't take long for them to be stopped in their tracks. The street was filled with cop cars, a crime scene tech van, and a bomb squad armored vehicle. Several uniformed and plainclothes cops were held back not able to get closer to the scene.

From where they stood, Kate couldn't see the firetrucks, but she saw a group of firefighters walking shellshocked people, who were wearing their pajamas, down the middle of the closed-off street. Kate assumed it was people in nearby buildings who had been woken from a sound sleep by the explosion and then were forced to evacuate.

"Who is in charge here?" Kate asked the group of cops to her left. "I'm FBI Agent Kate Walsh and this is my partner, Agent Declan James. We need to speak to whoever is heading up the investigation. This case is connected to two others currently under federal jurisdiction."

Kate wasn't sure why she was being so forceful but she had heard good and bad things about NYPD – highly skilled but territorial. The last thing she needed right now was a fight or to have to call Spade to make sure they had access to what they needed.

A man slightly taller than Kate with a medium build and head of dark hair stepped forward with his hand extended. "I'm Det. Tony Crane with the NYPD. We were told to expect you. You probably could have slept through the night and met us in the morning." He gestured toward the crime scene. "As you can see, we aren't going to get anywhere near it tonight, not until the fire is out. I got word it's only about forty percent contained. We can't even get a search and rescue team in there to look for victims. At this point, we believe there will be significant casualties."

Declan shook Det. Crane's hand. "Do we know for sure that it's a bomb?"

"We don't know much of anything right now. There was some kind of explosion and witnesses and the fire crew confirmed that it originated in the Raven Hall building. Now whether it was a gas explosion or a bomb is still up for debate." Det. Crane locked his gaze on Declan. "Given the incidents at Dartmouth and Cornell we figured we needed to bring in the FBI right away. Before I could even make the call though, Martin Spade called my captain. I don't know how he heard about the explosion. It hadn't even made the news yet."

Declan nodded in understanding. "It's how Spade operates. He's one step ahead of everyone. We appreciate your willingness to call us right away."

"No reason not to. If this is a bomb and you have information about the other cases that can help solve this one, it benefits everyone." He paused for a moment and then said, "I was eager to call you in but surprised that you were already in the city. Was there a specific threat made against Columbia?"

Kate shook her head. "There's been no specific threats in any of the cases. It's obvious by now that there is a pattern. We thought there was a pattern on the day of the week the bombings happened, but that's not the case now."

Det. Crane raised his eyebrows. "The other two occurred in the early hours of Monday morning, correct?"

"Yes. That's correct," Kate said, surprised he knew that. "Have you been following the cases?"

"My daughter goes to Yale. Two explosions at Ivy League universities are concerning."

Declan asked, "Is she part of any secret society?"

"No. I cautioned her against such activities," Det. Crane said, leaving Kate to wonder why.

She didn't get a chance to ask a follow-up question because a firefighter was charging toward them. He explained that they were able to clear survivors from nearby buildings because it looked like the fire would spread beyond what they initially thought. When Kate asked if there were any survivors pulled out of Raven Hall, he told her that none came out and because of the explosion and resulting fire, it wasn't safe for anyone to go into the building. He told them it would be a total collapse. Kate asked if they had any idea what caused the explosion.

"Some kind of incendiary device. It wasn't a gas explosion. The gas company has ruled that out," he said and left as quickly as he joined them.

"That makes six buildings that have had to be evacuated," Det. Crane said, shaking his head. "Can we assume at this point it's a bomb?"

While Kate believed as soon as Spade had woken her from sound sleep that it had been a bomb, she never liked getting ahead of herself. "Let's not state anything as fact yet until we know for sure. We have members of our task force from the New York State Police joining us soon. One of them is a bomb expert."

"Captain Leo Wallace?" Det. Crane asked with hope in his eyes.

"Yes, he's worked both the Dartmouth and the Cornell cases so far and the bomb planted in my SUV."

"What?" Det. Crane said, acting as if he hadn't heard her correctly. "You were already targeted by this bomber?"

Declan explained to him what had happened and then pointed to Kate's cheek and the cut on his head. "Luckily, these were our only injuries. If I hadn't missed Kate's toss, we wouldn't have survived."

"Tiny little decisions can mean the difference between life and death," Det. Crane said quietly, looking off in the distance. It was clear to Kate the man had seen a lot during his career that weighed heavily on him now. He shook himself out of whatever had occupied his mind. "You never said what brought you to New York City. If it wasn't a specific threat, why are you here?"

Kate had forgotten they hadn't answered. "The bomber was angered by the fact that they hadn't killed us. They delivered a letter to the *New York Times* office and the reporter who received it called us. We want to interview their staff and pick up the letter in person. We believed at the time that the bomber might be here given the letter was hand-delivered. I tried to warn both Columbia and Princeton but we had no specific threat, so there was no action taken. Raven Hall is off-campus anyway and not under the jurisdiction of the university. I don't think there's much anyone could have done." She said the words but she was still having trouble believing it herself.

"Have you met with the reporter yet?"

"No. We only got to the city around nine last night. Everything is moving rather quickly with this case." Kate turned and looked down the street in the direction of Raven Hall. She still couldn't see anything other than a blocked-off street but she could imagine the scene – a blazing fire destroying centuries-old buildings, shellshocked people ripped from their homes, and firefighters risking their lives to put the fire out. Something was bothering her about it. There was something different about this one compared to the other two.

Kate turned back to Det. Crane. "I know the buildings are close together and that could account for the rapid fire spread, but I'm wondering if the bomb was larger than the others."

"Why?" Det. Crane asked.

"Because of the damage," Declan said, echoing her thoughts. "At Cornell, only the residential part of the building was destroyed. In Dartmouth, it was part of the house but not the entire house. Here, it looks like the bomb took the whole building down, causing the fire to spread rapidly to adjacent buildings. I think Kate's right to question if it was a larger bomb."

"There was less of a cooling-off period, too," Kate said, her stomach flipping at the implication. "It's possible the bomber is ramping up activity. This happens sometimes with serial killers. The thrill they had with the first and second kill suddenly doesn't bring the same pleasure, so they decrease the cooling-off period between murders. They have also been known to up the risk. That may be what's happening here."

Det. Crane looked like he wanted to say something but then didn't.

"Please don't hold back with us. If there's something to say, say it," Declan encouraged.

Det. Crane still didn't look like he wanted to share his thought, but he said it anyway. "I was curious if this was in retaliation for you not being killed."

He said aloud what Kate hadn't even wanted to consider. Leave it to a New Yorker to get right to the heart of it. "It's possible," she said quietly.

Det. Crane put his hand on her shoulder. "I'm not blaming you, Agent Walsh. You're not responsible for the actions of a sick mind. Understanding him is important."

Kate stepped out from under his touch. She didn't think he had meant it, but he came across as condescending. "Det. Crane, I appreciate your kind words. I don't know that I made myself clear when we arrived. Agent James and I are from a special unit within the FBI. I'm an expert in forensic profiling. So, yes, you are correct – understanding the bomber is the highest priority for catching them. We have also not ruled out that the bomber is a woman."

Det. Crane smirked. "Bombers are never women."

"That's not technically true," Kate corrected him and then held her hand up when he started to argue with her. "Traditionally, in the cases we see here in the United States, the bombers are men. Conflicts across the globe have seen female suicide bombers in growing numbers. Let's not forget this city's history. Weather Underground members were making bombs in a Greenwich Village townhouse when one of the bombs detonated. Three of them were women."

"I stand corrected," Det. Crane said, his cheeks reddening. "What's the plan now? How would you like to work with the NYPD?"

"Let's meet in the morning once Investigator Murphy and Captain Wallace arrive." They agreed on a time and place and then Kate and Declan left to go back to the hotel.

As they were leaving, Declan nudged her side. "Give Crane a break. I think he means well."

CHAPTER 12

The next morning at nine, Kate and Declan sat at a table in a conference room at the *New York Times* office. Harvey Bowman had directed them to the room and then left them waiting there. He insisted on getting his editor and a lawyer to sit in with them. While he had every right to do that, Kate didn't understand the cause. They didn't have any problem with the newspaper or the staff. They were simply there to gather more information.

It seemed the newspaper editor and lawyer felt the same because Harvey returned alone. He sat down across the table. "They think I can do this alone. If you need to speak with them, they are happy to join."

"You seem nervous, Harvey," Declan said, assessing him. He was in his early forties and had a receding hairline. Dark tuffs of hair stuck out from the sides of his head and his shirt was a bit rumpled. "Did you sleep last night?"

Harvey swallowed hard and shook his head. "I kept waiting for my building to blow up and then when I got the call that a bomb went off at Raven Hall, I thought about leaving the city altogether. I have kids, Agent James."

"We understand," Declan said and then turned to Kate.

She didn't know what to tell him. The likelihood the bomber would go after Harvey or the newspaper was low, but then again, she would have thought that about herself. Kate didn't have any words of advice for him. "You need to do whatever you want to protect your family. But I appreciate you sitting down with us this morning. We won't take up too much of your time."

Harvey slid the bagged envelope and letter across the table along with a sheet of paper with three names on it including Harvey's. "Everyone in the mail room wears gloves. There were three of us who touched the letter and envelope. I found out from my assistant that the envelope was not sealed. It came to us open like that. What do you want to know?"

Declan explained that a cop would be by later to take the prints of all those who touched the letter for comparison and then he got started with questions. "Have you figured out where the envelope first came into contact with the staff here?"

Harvey nodded. "It was brought up with the morning's mail. We assume someone snuck into the mail room and dropped it in the bin with the incoming mail. It was then sorted and brought to our floor. From there, it was sorted and brought to my assistant. Those are the three names mentioned."

"Are there cameras in the mail room?"

"No. It's connected to the alleyway that runs behind the building. The mail trucks pull up and unload, and then it's brought in and sorted. It's the same area for other supplies that come into the building. It's not widely monitored. From that area, you need a key to access the rest of the building. There are staff who work down there all day but they are busy. No one reported seeing anyone strange coming in yesterday morning."

Kate would have to see the area for herself, but it didn't sound like they had much to go on. "That's it? That's the only interaction anyone had with the letter?"

"That's all, Agent Walsh. I know it sounds rather boring but that's what happened. The letter was among the other mail that was delivered to our floor that day. You can speak to the person who delivered it if you like. The letter was in the middle of the pile, according to Lynn who sorted it on our floor. I'd be happy to have you speak to her."

Kate said she wanted to and Harvey got up from the table and left. When he did, she turned to Declan. "What do you think?"

He shrugged. "I figured this would be the way it would go. Whoever this bomber is they are smart. They didn't mail it and instead hand-delivered it right before the bombing. They drew us here."

"Do you think they didn't mail it because of timing?"

"I'd assume so. For whatever reason they wanted to give us the message before the next bomb went off, but not in enough time for us to do anything about it." Declan sat back and tipped his head back and let out a frustrated groan. "Maybe Det. Crane is right and it's payback for not killing us. The bomber is toying with us."

Kate couldn't disagree with him. The bomber was toying with them and winning. The report they saw on the morning news was that at least twenty-two people were assumed killed in the explosion. Leo and Murphy were at the scene now already working to figure out what had blown the building apart.

"This feels like a waste of time here." She nudged the bag with the letter and envelope. "Other than retrieving this."

Lynn was a small woman with a pixie cut of blond hair. She looked no more than twenty and smiled nervously at them as she sat. "Harvey said you wanted to speak to me."

"We had a few questions about the letter that was delivered to Harvey yesterday," Kate said.

Lynn pointed to the letter. "I didn't see the letter until I was about halfway through the pile. I noticed it right away because it was open and there was no postmark. We don't normally have hand-delivered mail in the sent mail piles. We don't get too much hand-delivered like that – hardly anything outside of couriers."

"The letter wasn't on the top?"

"No. It was in the middle. I had already sorted a good deal of mail for each of the journalists and departments on our floor before I came across it. When I did, I stopped what I was doing and took it right away to Abigail, Harvey's assistant."

That was interesting to Kate. "Was there a reason for that?"

"I know it sounds silly to admit but last weekend I watched the movie *Zodiac,* and that killer sent letters to the *San Francisco Chronicle.* It had the same weird block print writing." Lynn blushed as she was speaking. "Of course, I didn't think we were getting a letter from the Zodiac killer, but I was a bit freaked out by it and wanted to make sure Abigail saw it right away."

"That was a great movie," Declan said and smiled at her. "It was fortunate you had seen that and knew to handle the letter with care. Did you tell anyone else about it?"

"Only Abigail and then Harvey. We were in his office when he called you. We had read the letter together and then talked for a bit about what it could be connected to. Harvey had read about the bombings at the Ivy League schools and then tracked you down."

"Are you sure that the letter was brought up by the mail room? Would they have sorted and opened an envelope like that?" Kate asked.

"They have so much to sort down there, I'm sure they didn't even notice that the envelope was opened or was missing a postmark. All they focus on is who it's addressed to and throw it in a pile. It was mid-stack as I said, so, yes, I'm sure that's where it came from before it landed on my desk."

Kate couldn't argue with that and it didn't give her much of a lead. She thanked Harvey and Lynn for the information and said they'd head down to where the mail came into the building.

On the way down in the elevator, Declan said, "This proved not to be much of a lead after all."

"Let's see what they say downstairs."

"Do you trust Harvey and Lynn?"

"I trust what they told us is true about their experience. That said, I don't know that I believe Harvey did a decent enough job interviewing the staff downstairs. You also don't know the relationship between them. Maybe they don't like Harvey. Maybe he questioned them in a way that made them feel like they had done something wrong, so they lied about what happened."

Declan stood back and let Kate step out of the elevator before him. "Harvey doesn't seem like that intimidating of a guy. The first sign he might be caught up in a criminal case, he's ready to run for the hills. Did you ever check out what kind of reporting he does?"

"He's a general reporter but he does cover crime stories." Kate had been surprised to see that when she had done her research. He hadn't sounded like a confident man over the phone and that impression had been shored up by meeting him in person. Declan was right to think he wasn't intimidating. "It's our impression of him, but you never know what co-workers might think. They could have a different impression of him."

Kate and Declan followed the directions Harvey had given to the shipping and receiving area. Once off the elevator, they followed a narrow hall and then took a right. A metal door stopped them in their tracks. The door was locked as Harvey had explained it would be. Kate pressed the white button on the side of the door and waited. A moment later, a man came and let them into two large bays that had their doors opened to the afternoon breeze. The doors were similar to garage doors but much larger. Kate could see the narrow alley outside. It would be easy enough for someone to slip in but probably not unnoticed. She was surprised by the number of staff in this area. She counted at least twelve people.

"I'm Jon, the supervisor down here," he said extending his hand to Kate. "Mr. Wallace said you might have some questions for us."

It interested Kate that Harvey didn't go by his first name with the newspaper staff. She introduced herself and Declan. "We have a few questions about a letter that was received by Harvey yesterday morning."

"We don't know much about that. He asked us already."

"What's your relationship like with Harvey?" Kate continued to use the man's first name, hoping to level the playing field.

Jon wouldn't be so informal. "I don't know Mr. Wallace well, but he's one of the newspaper's long-time journalists. He's upper management. I've never spoken to him before today when he came down to question us."

It was as Kate had suspected. "Tell me, Jon, did you feel like you were free to tell Harvey the truth about what happened with the letter?"

Jon cast his eyes to the side. "I'm not sure what you mean, Agent Walsh."

Kate was sure he understood perfectly. "Harvey, Mr. Wallace as you call him, came to ask you about the letter that was hand-delivered to this receiving area. I would assume that if you or one of the employees here did something you considered wrong, you might want to protect that individual. I've met Harvey and he's not the least bit intimidating to me, but then again, my job doesn't depend on his impression of my work. My question is, did you avoid telling him the whole truth to protect you or someone that works down here?"

Kate paused but Jon didn't say a word. She urged, "I have no intention of telling him anything you tell me, but Agent James and I have to find the person who left that letter. That explosion at Raven Hall last night most likely killed everyone living there – the letter is connected to that and two other bombings at Ivy League schools."

Jon rubbed the back of his neck and didn't meet Kate's eyes. "We aren't supposed to accept anything that isn't officially delivered to us – you know from the postman or a shipping company. There was a young woman yesterday morning who walked back here through the open bay doors and tossed a letter on top of a stack of mail in the bins. She left without saying anything. She didn't think she'd been noticed at first. After she dropped the letter and raised her eyes, she saw me and smiled. I didn't think it would do any harm."

Declan asked, "Do you know if the letter she dropped is the one in question?"

Jon shrugged. "I'd have no way of knowing. I didn't go and look at what she dropped. It was just a letter. I assumed it would get sorted in the mail." He glanced up at Declan. "I didn't think it would do any harm. It was a small envelope. It's not like it was a box or even a large priority mail envelope. You can't fit a bomb in something that small."

"No," Declan said, agreeing before cautioning him. "But you can fit anthrax or another powdered chemical."

Jon argued, "That isn't what happened though."

"This time."

Kate didn't want to be combative with him. "Tell me about the girl that you saw."

Jon squinted as he recalled the details. "She was young, probably no more than twenty-five. She was of average height and thin. She had a ball cap on her head, so some of her face was shielded. There's one thing that stood out though – she had strands of purple hair sticking out from the cap."

"Purple?" Declan asked.

Jon nodded. "Obviously dyed. I don't know if she had her whole head that color or just a little. The hair I could see was purple."

Kate pulled out her phone and pulled up the photo of Lily from the website. She showed it to Jon. "Is this her?"

He leaned over to get a good look at her face. "I can't say for certain but I think so."

Kate turned her eyes to Declan who registered the same look as she felt. They had their first solid lead in the case. "Did she say anything to you?"

"No. I didn't see her come in and neither did anyone else. I noticed her when she was dropping a letter in the mail bin. She must have had time to look to see where she was putting it because it was right there with the incoming mail." He pointed to several stack bins right next to each other. "Not all of them are for incoming mail."

"Did you see where she went when she left?"

"To the right, back down the alley toward the street most likely. I didn't follow her out." Jon stepped back from them and then looked at the other people working. He gave Kate a pained look. "Are you going to tell Mr. Wallace I lied? I've worked here a long time and have a good salary and benefits. I can't lose this job."

Kate sympathized with him. "I'm not telling anyone anything. If you see that girl again, please call me." She handed him her business card and then left with Declan, considering the best approach for finding Lily before there was another bomb.

CHAPTER 13

Kate and Declan sat around the conference table in the New York State Police office in downtown Manhattan. She was surprised when Murphy called her earlier and told her that he found them some workspace and was already meeting with Det. Crane.

Leo was still at the scene, which Kate wanted to see. Murphy told them to come to the office first because there wasn't anything for them to do at the scene. The fire inspector and Leo were still assessing, and the recovery team and medical examiner were working to remove remains. It was a horrific gruesome scene but there wasn't anything they could do there.

Det. Crane followed Murphy into the conference room and dropped a stack of files on the table. "Before we start, let's drop the formality and call me Tony. I have a feeling we're going to be working together for a while on this case."

Kate liked that he had jumped right in. "What's all of that?"

Tony pulled a few files off the top and handed them to her. "I spent the early part of this morning pulling a profile for each of the students at Raven Hall. There's not much – Columbia is still working on more detailed profiles for me, but we have the basics to start. At this point, they are all presumed deceased along with the cook and house manager. I said housekeeper last night but I was wrong. There was a house manager who cleaned, paid bills, kept the students in line, and did a whole host of other things for them. The staff are presumed deceased, so that makes twenty-two people."

"It's the largest death toll so far," Declan said, leaning over Kate to look at the file she had opened. "Were all of the students seniors?"

"Yes, twenty of them are chosen each year and all of them live at Raven Hall."

Kate slid a file over to Declan and picked up another one and opened it. Tony had included a photo of each student and she was reminded again how young and full of life they had all been. "Do we have any confirmation that all of them were in Raven Hall last night?"

"No," Tony said. "We don't have confirmation of much of anything. I was told that everyone in the surrounding buildings was accounted for. That means we don't have casualties elsewhere from the fire spread. The death toll last night was projected to be much worse with the surrounding buildings ablaze. That's one bit of good news that everyone else got out."

Declan raised his head from the file. "What about all the parents? Have they been notified?"

"An official at Columbia is handling that. They have also set up a place where parents can meet. Many of them are traveling today to get here. I told the administration that we'd be over later today to address the families when we know more – if we know more. Right now, I assume we don't have much of an update." After they all agreed that addressing the university and the parents was going to be necessary, Tony looked at Kate. "Did you learn anything at the *New York Times?*"

Kate updated them about the young woman that was seen. "We have a positive identification on Lily Cole. I'm not sure how I feel about her as a lead suspect though."

"What do you mean?" Declan asked with surprise in his voice.

"Do I think Lily is capable of something like this? Possibly, but

I'm not sure how she's pulling it off logistically. To make bombs like this she needs a place to be. She'd have to be getting supplies and making bombs. Does she have that kind of privacy at the Sisters of the Revolution house? Doubtful unless all of them are involved. We should be able to get a search warrant now. Still logistically, it has problems. She bombs Dartmouth, a week later Cornell, and then a couple of days later my SUV. Then overnight she races to New York City, drops off this letter, and plants another bomb. I don't know that a young woman can pull all of this off alone."

Declan asked, "Do you think she has help?"

That hadn't been the direction of Kate's thinking. "I'm wondering if Lily is the help. Throwing things at frat brothers is a far cry from building bombs. I think we have to ask ourselves if it's a job for one person."

Kate's theory silenced the room. It was clear no one else had been thinking along the same lines. In truth, neither had Kate until she said it aloud. She added, "We have enough right now to start digging into Lily's background beyond what we know. We have to decide if we name her as a person of interest in the media and flush her out or keep the details close to the vest."

"There's value in both," Murphy said. Then he looked across the table at Kate. "Are you saying that you think it's a group that Lily is working with like a terror cell?"

"I don't know what I'm thinking," Kate said honestly. She shifted in her seat and crossed her legs. "At first, I considered that Lily might be doing this alone, but I had trouble making all the pieces fit. There's too much travel involved. As I said, the person would not only have to procure all these materials, which RDX is hard to come by, but they'd also have to store the materials and make the bombs. I can see Lily writing the letter, but I don't know that I see her as the bomb maker."

"Younger people than her have been radicalized," Tony countered.

"That's true," Kate said, wondering what the distinction was in her mind. Terrorism was terrorism but there was something different between religiously or racially radicalized and what they were dealing with here. "Let's think about some recent bombing cases and explore the differences to what we are seeing now."

Declan rested his arms on the table. "How recent?"

"Post-1980s. The seventies and earlier were filled with bombings. I read a statistic recently that said during eighteen months spanning 1971 and 1972, there were more than 2,500 domestic bombings."

"Are you serious?" Murphy asked, his mouth falling slightly open.

Tony smirked at him. "You're old enough to remember the seventies and before. Civil Rights, Weather Underground, pipe bombs, and pressure cooker bombs. It was a wild time and people forget how blasé we were about bombings back then."

Murphy shook his head as if he couldn't believe he had forgotten how bad it was back then. "I guess I forgot with time."

"We're old," Tony said and they both laughed. "What bombings do you want to consider, Kate?"

Kate had been thinking about the recent bombings that came to mind, "Let's consider the Unabomber, Oklahoma City, Boston, the Atlanta Olympics, and Utah."

Tony raised his eyebrows. "Utah?"

Declan explained, "Among the Mormons. There was a documentary on it on one of those streaming channels. They were hand-delivered bombs and two people died if I'm remembering correctly. Those bombs were small in size."

Kate gave an overview of each of those cases to catch everyone up to speed. Then she said, "Only the Unabomber, Atlanta, and Utah were true lone bombers. There were three people involved in Oklahoma City and the two brothers in Boston."

Tony was looking at something on his phone. He glanced up.

"The Atlanta bomber, Eric Rudolph, placed two additional bombs in Georgia and one in Birmingham, Alabama. He had dynamite and it looks like a radio-controlled nail bomb. He was a survivalist."

"Like Ted Kaczynski, the Unabomber," Murphy added.

Tony kept reading, "Mark Hofmann, the Utah bomber, was using the bombs to cover up forgeries. Seems like they all had different motives."

Kate confirmed all their information was correct. "We know the motive here. The bomber told us – they are exacting their revenge on elite students in Ivy League schools. There is a clear target, at least so far, and a clear motive. The question I keep coming back to is why use bombing as the method when it's so rare today and is so hard to pull off."

"Maximum destruction," Declan said almost as a question. He looked up at Kate and she encouraged him to continue with his train of thought. "Not only does it kill people but it destroys the building – sometimes very old buildings which house the secret society's activities."

"That's right," Murphy echoed. "The bomber isn't going to accomplish that in a mass shooting. He might not survive to get to the second and third locations. No other method of killing would afford that either. Even with something like poisoning, he can't ensure mass casualty and remain at a distance. It enables him to kill from location to location."

Declan tapped on the table. "That reinforces Kate's theory that the bomber is highly intelligent. There's logic in what they are doing and the method they are choosing. So, right now, we know they want power over those they consider in power, mass casualty and to target the building itself – the symbol of the secret society."

Tony added, "It's also a removed way of killing. The victims don't see the person so there's no identification."

"Other than when they drop off the bomb," Kate reminded him. "It's possible the person making the bombs isn't the one delivering them to the locations though."

"Why not go after people in real power?" Tony asked, interrupting. "Secret societies aren't powerful. These are college seniors who have barely made a mark in the world. There are banking institutions and sites of big business and even government buildings that hold the real seat of power."

Kate had considered all of this. "I believe the bomber has some connection to secret societies. Whether they were rejected from one or had issues with members while in college, I don't know. There are also vast conspiracy theories about secret societies and the power they potentially hold for their members."

Declan nodded along and then added, "The bombs are cutting the pipeline of the rich and powerful. Look at the damage already done. Not to mention, scaring other secret society members present and future. It's telling them they are no longer safe. Rich, powerful kids who think they have it all – and many times they do – learning, maybe for the first time in their lives, that they aren't so safe after all. Someone has power over them."

Kate snapped her fingers. "That's the core of the motive, Declan. The bomber is showing they are the one in control, the one in power now. I assume they feel that power was taken away at another time and this is their response."

They talked motive and planning a little bit more before Tony asked, "So, we get a warrant for Lily Cole and Sisters of the Revolution, and then what? How do we track her down without going public?"

Declan said, "We have to go public. Give her over to the media and mention she's a person of interest. Let the public help us find her." He saw the uncertain look on Kate's face and pushed harder. "Kate, if you truly believe that she is involved in some way, then she might turn herself in and help us. Even if she doesn't turn herself in, she'll be on the run and could make a mistake and slip up. Going public with some information now shows that they aren't in control as much as they think."

Kate was worried about what Tony had asked last night. "Declan, what if by identifying Lily they ramp up even more? This time it was a whole house that took out half a city block. If we push them, what will it be next time?"

"You can't be worried about that, Kate," Murphy said, standing from the table. It was clear he was getting antsy sitting for so long. "I think we show what we've got on Lily. Then see what they do next. Right now, we have nothing to go on. We are going to have to rattle some cages and shake some trees. This bomber has a plan. Let's see what they do when we show that we are hot on their trail."

Kate smiled up at him. "That might be overstating it." She was nervous that the case was out of their control. The bomber would strike again, but they couldn't do anything but wait for the next one. She conceded, "Okay, let's wait to see what Leo has to say and then we run with the story."

They decided to break because Murphy needed coffee. He asked Declan if he'd like some, so the two left the conference room together. When they were alone, Tony asked, "This probably isn't a fair question, but what do you think it's going to take to solve this case? It took seventeen years to catch the Unabomber. We can't withstand seventeen years of this."

"Those were mail bombs sent from a shack in the mountains. The person doing this will slip up. We already have clues in their choice of bomb-making material. Ever since Timothy McVeigh blew up the Alfred P. Murrah Federal Building in Oklahoma City, the government has worked hard to secure bomb-making materials. RDX is not easy to come by."

Tony breathed out hard. "I've seen a lot in this city. We need something to say to those families when we meet with them, something more than we have right now."

Kate agreed with him but she didn't have any more to add. As far as the families, she didn't have any more than what she told the families in Cornell. *They were doing all they could to find the person responsible.* It sounded hollow even to her.

CHAPTER 14

Leo arrived at one in the afternoon with an evidence bag in hand. He arrived long after Kate and Declan had ended their morning meeting with Tony and Murphy. For the hours following, Kate had sat with Declan going through the list of Raven Hall members. They had each done research online and hoped to find more about each student. Even when they had that information, nothing pointed to the bomber.

Kate hadn't realized until she saw Leo how much she was hoping that he'd shed some light on something they were missing. "I hope you have something for us. Were there any survivors?"

Leo looked to the floor and shook his head. "They recovered remains, but all are presumed deceased." He sat down in a chair at the table and laid the evidence bag on top, not explaining what was inside. Kate couldn't see from her vantage point. Whatever was contained within was small.

Leo started with an apology. "I haven't had time to provide a written detailed report but will submit that when I can. I wanted to speak to all of you and give you an update before that."

Kate texted Murphy and Tony to let them know Leo was back. Once they were in the room and seated, he explained, "This bomb was different than the others. The same C-4 was used but the bomb itself was significantly larger. They wanted to do more damage and they did. The other bombs were placed near the back of the buildings. This was placed dead center."

Kate didn't understand how that was possible. "Are you saying you believe the bomb was placed *inside* of Raven Hall?"

"Yes," Leo said with frustration. "We were finally able to determine that the other bombs were placed outside of the structures. That's what the blast evidence tells us. This bomb, we believe, was placed in the basement of Raven Hall dead center of the structure. It's why it decimated the entire place. No one stood a chance in there. It's also why the fire spread so rapidly to the adjacent buildings."

Kate's mind flooded with possibilities. "Someone had access. The doors weren't locked?"

"We don't know how they got in, Kate, but they got in. Unfortunately, everyone who knows the current goings-on at Raven Hall is deceased. We are flying blind on this one. We don't have a single witness."

Declan didn't seem to like the answer any more than Kate. "No one saw anything? A neighbor? A cabbie? Some random person walking down the street?"

Leo slid the evidence bag toward Declan. "Not even the person who had this stuck to their door. They saw and heard nothing but came out of their home this morning for work and this was there, pinned to their front door. They didn't know who to bring it to so they walked down to the scene and told one of the cops who gave it to me."

Declan picked it up and examined the contents from the outside. "What is it?"

"Note thumbtacked to the front door. It's from the bomber. The bomber takes credit for the bombs at the colleges, threatens the FBI, and promises more destruction. Claims no one can stop them. They are going to finish their mission and then fade away never to be seen or heard from again. It's signed *The Fuse*."

"That's how the other letter was signed," Declan said and gestured toward Kate to tell him about the *New York Times*.

Kate explained that it was Lily Cole who had dropped off the first letter. "It doesn't mean too much yet. We haven't found her. She's out there somewhere, but we've decided to use the public to help track her down. Hopefully, that will lead us to her and whoever she is working with."

Leo agreed with the decision. "You're sure it's more than one person?"

"We aren't sure of anything," Declan said. "Logistically, I think the consensus is that it's more than one person."

"That's good," Leo said. "I was going to suggest something similar but, Kate, you're the profiler and I didn't want to step on anyone's toes."

"Step away," Kate said with a smile. "Leo, don't hold anything back with us. If you have a theory based on what you're seeing at the scenes, tell us. Normally, Declan and I are much more active at the crime scenes. Given what we are working with here, we are relying on your expertise, and we are more than open to hearing anything you have to say."

Leo told Kate he appreciated it. "This is a brazen attack in the middle of Manhattan. This bomber got close to those they killed. They got into the house, found a spot that was going to do the most damage, and then left and detonated it. Given the note left a few blocks away, it's clear they stuck around and watched the destruction. I'm sure they hung around long enough to know the damage it did to adjacent buildings. It's clear they are pleased with themselves and they are getting more emboldened with each attack." Leo's anger and frustration were evident in each staccato syllable. He tugged at the collar of his shirt as if it had grown too tight in the last few minutes.

Kate wished she had words to make him feel better, but they were all feeling the same. "What about the bomb left in my SUV?"

"Same. Set to a cellphone detonator. We already determined the bomber was close by when that happened. This just confirms it." Leo cursed under his breath. "It's all the same signature so we know it's the same bomber."

"Signature?" Tony asked.

"Same bomb materials, same design, and detonator switch. That's typically what I call a signature. It tells me it's the same bomb maker. Given they are taking credit for it, we can assume we are on the right path." He turned to Murphy. "We haven't released any of the bomb specifics to the public yet, right?"

"No. I didn't think that we would. I assume you want that to stay among the team."

"Yeah. Exactly. That way if we get a copycat, we'll know it right away." Leo turned back to Kate. "What have we told the public about this bombing? I haven't heard much on the news, but obviously, I've been a little too busy to watch it closely."

"We were waiting for you to get back with more details before we held a press conference tonight. We also need to go to Colombia this evening and meet with the parents who want an update. Do we have anything else we can share with them at this time?"

No one had anything to offer. Giving the public the name Lily Cole was going to be big enough. As they continued going over the details of the case, Tony got a call on his cellphone. He stepped out of the conference room to take it. From her chair, Kate watched as his face lit up in surprise. She could see him ask the person on the other end of the line if they were sure and then he said he'd call them right back. When he was done, he ripped open the conference room door.

"We might have a break in the case. At the very least, there is one survivor from Raven Hall."

"How is that possible?" Leo asked, shock in his voice. "No one could have survived that blast."

"He didn't," Tony confirmed. He held up his cellphone. "That was one of the cops at the scene who called me. A young man got a frantic call from his parents and came rushing back. Finley Lloyd was supposed to be in that house. He was there for the house meeting and dinner and then left to go spend the night at his girlfriend's place in lower Manhattan. He was far enough away that he hadn't heard the explosion and they hadn't been watching the news. He slept in because he wasn't supposed to have a class until two this afternoon. He said he woke up to several voicemail messages from friends and family who couldn't believe that he was gone. Finley said he had no idea what was happening so he called his parents back and got the news. He rushed to Raven Hall not believing them. He's distraught and downstairs." Tony looked at Kate. "Do you want to interview him or would you like me to do that?"

Kate hadn't realized she was holding her breath as she listened. "I'll interview him, but you are all free to listen in and watch if you'd like. That way if you have additional questions, you can send them in with Declan as follow-up."

Murphy escorted Kate to an interview room. She grabbed a soda and a bag of chips for him from the kitchen. She didn't know what he liked but figured the gesture would be good enough for now. If there was anything to make him more comfortable, she was willing to do that. Before Kate got settled in the room, Declan came in.

He asked, "Are you treating him as a witness or a potential suspect?"

Kate hadn't considered him anything more than a potential background witness. It hadn't occurred to her to think of him as anything else. She explained that to Declan. "Is there a reason you're asking?"

"He's the only survivor, Kate." Declan stared at her wide-eyed. "I know it doesn't seem fair but right now, we need to be careful how we interact with this kid. What if we find out later that he's a person of interest?"

It wasn't like Declan to ever second-guess her when it came time to interview someone. She considered what he was saying but still chose to stick with her plan. "If it changes later, it changes and we can address it then. Right now, I want to make him as comfortable as possible and get as much information as we can."

Declan saluted her. "I was being cautious."

Kate glanced up at him. Declan hadn't been cautious a day in his life. "Are you feeling okay?"

"Fine," he said and left the interview room, leaving Kate to wonder why he had just lied to her.

She couldn't focus on Declan because Tony walked in with Finley Lloyd. "Agent Walsh, this is Finley. I told him that you had a few questions for him and he has some of his own."

Kate stood and shook the young man's hand. He was sheet white and his dark hair was a mess of untamed curls crowning his head. She assumed his rumpled shirt and jeans had been pulled from the floor earlier in the day. "I grabbed you a soda and some chips. I didn't know if you had eaten."

"I haven't," he said, staring back at her with vacant dark eyes. It was the look of trauma. He took a seat and opened the soda but didn't drink from it. "I don't understand what's going on."

Tony excused himself and Kate sat down at the table with Finley. She wanted to be gentle with him but at the same time, she couldn't mince words. "There was a bomb placed in the basement of Raven Hall. It detonated a little after two in the morning."

"The cop I spoke to said everyone was dead. My parents thought I was dead. My friends back home thought I was dead. I don't understand how something like this could happen."

His voice was monotone and had no emotion. He hadn't made eye contact with her yet either. "Finley, where are you from originally?"

"Seattle. My mother saw it on the morning news and called me around noon east coast time. I thought she was kidding. Then I thought it had to have been a mistake." He slumped lower in his chair and his bottom lip quivered. He was trying to fight back the tears. "I can't believe they are all dead. Who would do something like this?"

"Have you seen the news about the bombings at Cornell and Dartmouth?" Kate watched him closely to see if he had any kind of physical reaction to what she had told him, but there was nothing. He remained unmoved.

"I don't watch the news much. I haven't even been on social media. I got sick of it over the summer." He took a tentative sip of the soda and then set the can down, steadying it. "I spent the whole summer in Seattle. My girlfriend did a study abroad over the summer. We haven't seen each other much, so I've been spending a lot of time with her even though my focus should be on Raven Hall."

"It saved your life so don't be too hard on yourself," Kate said and kept her focus fixed on him.

He finally raised his eyes to hers. "I never even wanted to be in Raven Hall. Did you know that?"

Kate shook her head. "I don't know much about you at all, Finley. You were a name in a file until we got the good news you were alive. Is there a reason you joined?"

"My father and my grandfather and my great-grandfathers before them. I'm sixth-generation Raven Hall. It was expected of me and I joined. I didn't think not joining was an option." Finley pushed himself upright in the chair. "Can I be honest with you?"

"Please do," Kate said evenly.

"I think secret societies are stupid. The rituals and secrecy and having to live there. The meetings and all the other crap that goes along with it. It's the dumbest thing I've ever been involved in."

"Is that why you left last night?"

Finley nodded. "We had a house meeting to talk about an upcoming event – a masked ball if you can believe that. What year is it? I have to go to a stupid masked ball. I wasn't interested in it, but when you're in Raven Hall, you're part of the group – heck, you are the group. There's only twenty of us so we all have to be involved in everything." Finley pinched the bridge of his nose and recognition came over his face. He looked over at Kate. "Did you say there were other bombings at Dartmouth and Cornell? What was bombed?"

"Two other secret societies – Sword and Crown at Cornell and Magnolia House at Dartmouth."

Finley absorbed the information and closed his eyes. When he opened them again, his fist was clenched and he looked right at Kate. "I can understand why people hate us. I don't blame them for targeting us." Finley then asked for a break.

Kate didn't want to let him go. She wanted to force him to stay in the thick of it, but her instinct not to push him too hard won out. She turned her head slightly toward the mirror and a moment later Tony came in and walked him to the bathroom.

When she was alone, Declan stepped into the room. "What do you think?"

"There's rage under the trauma," she said, realizing now that Declan might have been right. She had been too quick to think of him as only a victim. When he returned, she'd have to try another approach.

CHAPTER 15

"I'm sorry, Agent Walsh," Finley said when he returned ten minutes later. He was markedly different, from his body language and the way he carried himself to the expression on his face. He sat upright. "I think I'm in shock. It's hard for me to believe that everyone I had dinner with last night is dead."

Kate wasn't sure about the change, but it was easier to speak to him now. He was far more engaged and actively listening. "Tell me about the house meeting last night."

"As I said, it was about that ball, which I thought was stupid. I said that and a few of the others agreed. It's tradition though so it's not like we weren't going to do it. A few of us were making jokes and laughing and not paying attention. Andy, the house manager, was getting annoyed with us because we weren't focusing on what we were supposed to be doing. He couldn't finish his work for the night until the meeting wrapped and dinner was done."

"Does Andy live there at Raven Hall full-time?"

Finley nodded. "Andy did a lot of things for us including paying the bills. Most people thought he cleaned the place, too. He didn't do that, but he oversaw the woman who came in once a week to clean. Most of us enjoyed having Andy around."

Kate opened her eyes wide. "There were people who didn't enjoy having Andy around?"

"He was kind of a stickler for tradition and that annoyed some of the guys. Even last year when I was brought in as a pledge, I can remember some of the guys complaining about Andy." Finley shrugged. "It went both ways though. I don't know that Andy liked most of us. He called us spoiled and entitled and said that as the years went on the groups of members got worse and worse in their entitlement. He went so far as telling one of the guys he wasn't a man and wasn't raised right."

"Sounds like things could get pretty heated at Raven Hall."

Finley scrunched up his nose. "If Andy is dead, I hate speaking badly of him. Is any of this important?"

Kate wasn't sure what was important or not. It was digging through it all to find the one string that led to something important. She was honest with Finley about that. "I don't know what bits of information are going to lead to finding the killer. How did the meeting go last night? Was there anything unusual?"

"We finished dinner and all had our assignments for working on the ball. Some of the guys went to watch television. Others went to do schoolwork and I left to go to my girlfriend's house. Everything seemed normal."

"Was it okay with other members that you left for the night?"

"Sure," Finley said. "I'm not confined to the house. Most of us have girlfriends. We do have a rule that no one but members can sleep over at Raven Hall. That means we have to go to our girlfriends'. I try not to do it every night. The whole point of being in Raven Hall is to spend our senior year bonding with our brothers and making the right connections. Andy helps with that too."

"What do you mean?"

"Take me for example. I want to go into criminal law. That's what I'm studying and I already got into Yale Law School. Andy helped me make connections with some trustees at Yale who helped with my interview process and acceptance. He also introduced me to big criminal defense firms where I'll probably get a job out of law school."

"It sounds like he helped you a lot."

Finley nodded. "When he's focused on the mentoring side of things, he's done a good deal for all of us." He paused for a moment and shook his head. "I can't believe he's gone. He could be annoying, but he was a good man who helped many of us."

Kate was trying to get a read on him, but overall, he seemed like a good kid. "You were here in Manhattan over the last two weeks?"

"At Raven Hall, my girlfriend's apartment, and classes. I can't afford to miss any classes. I haven't left Manhattan since I arrived in August."

That would be easy enough to check out. Kate's initial concern was receding now that Finley seemed to be engaging more. His anger seemed to have dissipated some too. "Have there been any threats against Raven Hall?"

Finley turned his head to the side and locked eyes with himself in the mirror. He ran a hand through his dark messy curls and then refocused his attention on Kate. "I didn't realize I was such a mess."

"You've had a devastating shock." Kate would come back around to the threats because there had been some. She could tell by the way he avoided the subject. Kate would allow him to think she was moving on. "Were you friends with most of the people in Raven Hall?"

"I wouldn't say friends, no. We all pledged together last semester. Most of the guys I hadn't met before then. I have a group of friends from Columbia that I see from time to time. That's one of the hardest parts about being in Raven Hall. All these strangers are now supposed to be my family and I'm supposed to let go of the friends I made over the last few years."

"I don't understand what you mean," Kate said, fibbing slightly. She had seen what he was talking about firsthand, but she wanted him to elaborate. "Is there a reason you couldn't keep up your friendships?"

Finley leaned back and stared at Kate. "How much do you know about secret societies? I mean really know, not the crap you see in movies and stuff."

"I graduated from Harvard, so I know a little. Not as much as you. I never wanted to be a part of one even when the opportunity presented itself." Kate shifted her eyes toward the mirror. She hadn't told Tony or Murphy about her college years and Declan only knew bits and pieces.

"You had the option of not joining?"

Kate nodded once. "I chose not to so I was shut out of that world. You can become more of an outsider than someone who is never even considered."

Finley smiled for the first time. "They don't like to be rejected. They like to do the rejecting. It's part of the game, the allure. Most people want in until they are in. Don't get me wrong, there is a lot of good that goes along with being a member – a lot of perks. My future is pretty much set. Being a Raven Hall member opens a lot of doors that would otherwise be closed even for someone who comes from a well-off family and has an Ivy League education. Being a part of any secret society is like becoming a member of all of them. There's a global network that has my back. But with any kind of power it corrupts over time, members see themselves as invincible."

"You seem to be talking about something or maybe someone specifically."

Finley waved her off. "You know the stories as well as I do. There are drug convictions and sexual assaults and a whole host of other criminal behavior swept under the rug when you're someone like me." Finley held his arms out wide. "I don't have to be responsible for my actions when I have a network of people willing to cover up my actions for me. Don't you know we are the future senators, congressmen, judges, lawyers, and people in power? We are a network that's going to make laws, enforce those laws, and change those laws to keep us in power and people like you beneath us. We'll give you just enough so that you think you are achieving, but at the slightest indication that one of you are taking power from us, we are going to break you like a twig." Finley's voice dripped sarcasm and anger and that hot rage Kate had seen before just beneath the surface.

Kate was sure something had happened to this young man that he wasn't telling her. His left eye twitched as he grew angrier. "You seem to hate the group that you're a part of and I'm not sure I understand why. You seem to detest the very power you've been given. But you also seem to understand the game of it all better than anyone your age. Please help me to understand what it is you're not saying. What's sitting right below the surface that's bubbling up when you talk about Raven Hall?"

Finley took another sip of soda and ripped open the bag of chips. He popped one in his mouth and crunched down hard. "I have a sister, Agent Walsh. Everly is three years older and also went to an Ivy League school until she was sexually assaulted on campus by a member of a secret society. The assault was filmed and shared on social media." Finley locked eyes with Kate. "Guess who got in trouble and expelled?"

"I'm guessing it wasn't the young man who assaulted her."

"Bingo!" Finley said and slapped his hand down on the table loud enough to make Kate jump in her seat. "I won't tell you the name of the school, although you can find that out, or the secret society and all that. Nothing can be done now – my parents and sister have tried. You'd think if my father cared about my sister. he wouldn't force me to become a part of the very system and network that destroyed her. Yet here we are. To answer your original question about my friends. No, I wasn't friends with the guys at Raven Hall. I despised them if you want to know the truth – not them individually but what the whole thing represented."

"It must have been hard then to be a part of Raven Hall."

Finley closed his eyes. "You have no idea. I guess the bomber did me a favor." As soon as the words were out of his mouth, his eyes flew open. "That isn't what I meant. Of course, the loss of life is terrible. I just…"

Kate understood what he meant. If she were in his shoes, she might be feeling the same thing. She couldn't fault him or judge him for those feelings. "Finley, I am sorry for what happened to your sister. The system isn't fair and it isn't just or right what happened to her."

"It is what it is at this point."

"You avoided the question about threats. Had there been threats against Raven Hall leading up to the bombing?"

Finley shifted and then moved again seeming not to be able to get comfortable. He finally slumped in his seat and rested his arms on the table. "There had been letters sent to us claiming that we either had to all quit being Raven Hall members and close down for good or face the consequences. No one took it seriously. I didn't take it seriously. It became a sort of joke."

"If that's all it is why are you uncomfortable speaking about it?"

Finley swallowed and then coughed. "The letters started after the first party of the semester when it was rumored that one of the Raven Hall members got aggressive with some women. It never rose to a sexual assault allegation but it was something we were dealing with. They were allegations but nothing had been substantiated so I'm hesitant to speak about it. I went to the three women myself to try to get them to tell me what had happened. They wouldn't tell me much. They assumed I was looking to cover it up. In the end, I wanted the member kicked out regardless of the outcome and I was outvoted by the rest of the members. No one sided with me."

Kate remained quiet while Finley took another sip of his drink and toyed with the can. When he stopped, he looked up. "They blamed me for sending those letters. The rest of them thought it was me because I had wanted the member out."

"Was it you?" Kate asked, watching his reaction to her question.

"No," he said with a disgusted laugh. "I didn't have enough of a backbone to do something like that. I'm a coward."

Kate didn't think he was a coward. "The person sending the letters is hiding. You came right out and confronted a whole group of people who didn't agree with you. You're not a coward, Finley. It sounds like you were the brave one in the group. Did you see the letters?"

"Yes. I saw two of the five that were dropped off."

That sparked Kate's interest. "They were dropped off at Raven Hall?"

"Yeah, they weren't mailed. The notes were pinned to the front door with a thumbtack."

Kate hoped Declan was paying attention. It was the same way the note was left last night after the bombing. She never thought a thumbtack might be evidence in a case but there was a first time for everything. Kate pulled out her phone and flicked to a photo of the letter from the New York Times and showed it to Finley. "Did the writing look anything like that?"

He leaned into the table to get a better look. "Exactly like that. We joked that we had a kid just learning how to write sending us threatening notes."

Kate tucked her phone away. "Was there ever any specific threat?"

"No. Just that we'd all pay for our crimes one way or another."

"Is that a direct quote?"

"Yes or close enough. That's why we thought it was tied back to the incident with the three women."

Kate could see why he thought that but she didn't think it was as small as one incident of aggressive behavior.

CHAPTER 16

"They'd all pay for their crimes one way or another," Kate said aloud in the elevator later that evening as they made their way back to the hotel room.

Declan glanced down at her. "How many times are you going to repeat it? You've said it at least thirty times since meeting with Finley."

Kate tapped at the side of her head near her temple. "There's something important in there that we haven't figured out yet. I keep saying it in the hopes that something jumps out at me." Kate yawned and covered her mouth. She couldn't wait to eat something and then get some sleep.

It had been a hectic afternoon. While Kate was interviewing Finley, Murphy had gotten a search warrant for Sisters of the Revolution. He had his team from the New York State Police spend the day searching the whole house and interviewing the women. The goal was to get it done before they went public with Lily's name that night. Much to their dismay, nothing had been found at the house and nothing of interest came from the interviews. If the other women were protecting Lily, they were doing a good job of it.

After meeting with Finley, Kate released him and told him they might follow up with more questions at a later date. None of them thought that he had anything to do with the bombing, especially after confirming with his girlfriend that he'd been with her all night. Even

Declan relaxed a little.

After that meeting, they had gone to the Raven Hall site and Declan was finally able to get a good look at the scene and do what he did best. Kate could tell that he was starting to get annoyed that they had been kept from it. While they both understood the caution involved, there was something to be said for seeing the scene firsthand. Leo had been right in that there was nothing left but charred rubble.

The recovery team had done their best to remove remains and now the medical examiner's office would be doing its best to go through DNA matches to confirm the victims. With the fire raging as hot as it did, some family members might never get a full confirmation that their loved one had been inside that building. There might be no remains to return to them. That was the worst-case scenario and one Kate hoped to avoid.

She had said as much when addressing the families in the auditorium space that Columbia had provided to meet with the families. There had been several questions that they simply couldn't answer. While normally fine with those kinds of death notifications and meetings with victims' families, Kate was glad that she had Declan, Tony, and Murphy as backup.

The families were right to be angry. She couldn't fault them for that. Kate and Declan took it personally that the case hadn't been solved yet. It's how they felt working any case. They lived and breathed each case as it came. It had always been like that. Kate assured the families that she would do everything she could to stop the bomber.

In truth, she knew they'd strike again and again until they were done.

After meeting with the families, Kate and Declan stayed in the background off-camera during the press conference that Murphy led. Leo stepped in and answered some questions about the bombs without giving away any of the details he wanted to keep private. Tony also spoke as the representative from the NYPD. Murphy did a good job speaking for all of them. When the media pressed why the FBI hadn't come out and made a statement yet, Murphy refocused them on the task force led by the FBI. Kate was happy with the way he handled himself. As Kate watched him, she realized that she and Declan could learn a thing or two from him in how he finessed the media.

The biggest bombshell of the night was that the task force had named Lily Cole as a person of interest. Murphy held up a photo of Lily Cole and indicated that the task force believed she had dropped off a note to the *New York Times* office related to the case. The media exploded with questions that Murphy tried to answer. A few he tossed to Tony who did his best. Overall, though, the task force had decided to share the bare minimum. When asked if the task force believed that Lily Cole had been responsible for the bombings, Murphy answered as honestly as possible – they didn't know. Finding and speaking to Lily was the highest priority for the task force and any tips could be called into the NYPD tip line that had been provided.

Harvey Wallace had been in the crowd of reporters and seemed more than a little annoyed that Kate and Declan hadn't disclosed the information about Lily to him while at his office. They hadn't even told him they had identified anyone. Kate assumed he had expected to get an exclusive on the story. No one was getting an exclusive on information that needed to be shared as broadly as possible. They didn't make any friends with that decision.

Now with all of that done, there was nothing more they could do other than head back to the hotel and get some rest. They were both hungry and tired and on edge waiting to hear if any tips came in about Lily. They were also anticipating the bomber's next move – would it be more letters or another bomb? They weren't sure.

Declan unknotted his tie and tugged it free of his shirt as soon as they were in the room. He kicked off his shoes and untucked his shirt from his pants. "I'm going to shower before getting room service. If you order something, get me a steak, vegetables, and baked potato."

At least his appetite hadn't diminished. Kate was still worried about him though. Some may have preferred risk-averse Declan, but she knew he was going against his instinct. More than anything, she worried that tempering his instinct would negatively impact the case. As the shower turned on, she called down for room service. She didn't want anything more than a grilled chicken salad. Kate wasn't even sure she could eat that much.

When she hung up the phone, she sat on the edge of the bed and kicked off her shoes. She reached for the shorts and tank she had thrown on the bed earlier and got undressed. The water was still running when she went to the bathroom door and knocked twice before pushing it open.

Before their last case, she would never have invaded Declan's privacy like this, but she was concerned about him. There was a wall that went waist high on the shower so she knew that she'd only see Declan from the chest up unless she walked into the bathroom and stood in front of the door.

Declan stood under the shower head and let the water fall down his back. His eyes were closed but he must have heard her. Without looking up, he smiled. "Please tell me it's my lucky night and you're joining me in here."

"No such luck, buddy." Kate leaned against the counter and smiled as he plastered a fake frown on his face. "I know I'm completely violating all the boundaries that we said we needed in place, but I'm worried about you."

"I'm worried about me too."

Kate was glad he was admitting that. "What's going on with you?"

"I'm not sure – depressed, in pain, feeling incompetent, terrified of making a mistake and getting one of us killed." Declan raised his eyes and met hers. "I've never second-guessed myself at any time during my career, even when everyone said I should be second-guessing my tactics. I missed all the signs in the last case and nearly got myself killed. This time, if I had caught those keys, we'd be dead, Kate. I can't get that out of my mind. Maybe I'm not cut out for this anymore."

Kate knew better than to debate with him. It wouldn't matter what she told him. She could have argued how good he was at his job until she was blue in the face. Once Declan got his mind set on something, it was hard to sway him. To be fair, she was the same way. But still, she needed to do something. "Is this why you've been so quiet and didn't push to be at the scene? Normally, you wouldn't have taken no for an answer."

"I didn't push to be at the scene because there wasn't much that I could do there. Leo had it under control with the medical examiner and fire investigator. I haven't said much because…" He trailed off and didn't finish his thought.

"What, Declan?" Kate pushed.

He shrugged. "I feel…in over my head. I've been having nightmares about being shot and I wake up in a sweat nearly every night. During the day, I feel paralyzed to make decisions, afraid I'll make the wrong one. I've been doing my best to press forward anyway. I didn't realize I was doing such a bad job faking it."

"No one noticed but me. That's only because we know each other so well." Kate pushed herself off the counter and walked toward the shower. "It sounds like you have post-traumatic stress from the shooting. Have you talked to your therapist about it?"

Declan shook his head. "You know I can't, Kate. You know they will put me on desk duty until I get my head right."

"Would that be such a bad thing?" She asked the question but already knew the response. Declan would never be able to sit at a desk from nine to five. He wasn't cut out for it and it would probably strain his mental health more than being in the field with her. "You can't go on like this, Declan."

"I'll sort it out. I was doing better but then there was the bomb in your SUV. It threw me for a loop. Set me back a little. That's all." He saw the concern on her face. "I promise, Kate. I'll talk to you more about it. I shouldn't have kept it to myself. There's been too much going on to focus on me."

"You have to focus on you, Declan, or you're not going to be any good for this case." Kate didn't want to make him feel worse. "I understand though. I've been there, right where you are. Just talk to me and we can work through it together."

Declan nodded and turned his back to her. He finished rinsing off and then shut off the water. "Can you grab the towel for me?"

Kate grabbed the towel to her right and walked to the shower and handed it to him. "Stop grinning like a fool. I've seen it all before. I really shouldn't be in here. I don't know what I was thinking."

Declan dried off and wrapped the towel around his waist. "You were so worried about me that you couldn't wait until I was done. Or you wanted a cheap thrill. I'll get naked anytime you want. All you have to do is ask."

"Don't make me regret being sweet to you. Dinner should be here soon." Kate turned and walked to the bathroom door. She looked over her shoulder at him. "Your scar is healing up nicely."

"I knew you were looking." Declan stepped out of the shower with the towel around his waist.

"There's nothing to see that I haven't already seen." Then Kate did something terribly unlike herself. She winked at him. "I can't say it's not impressive." Kate didn't think as bad as the last few days had been that some light flirting between them would do much harm.

A few minutes later, room service arrived. As Kate uncovered her salad and was pouring dressing on it, Declan came up behind her and wrapped his arms around her waist. He rested his chin on the top of her head and pulled her into him. "Hey, Kate," he whispered. "I appreciate you checking up on me in the way that you did. You always know how to say things to make me think rather than make me feel worse about the situation or myself. You understand me better than I understand myself sometimes."

Kate knew what he meant. She hadn't been confrontational or pushed him to talk if he wasn't ready. She allowed herself to be held by him and then turned in his arms until she was staring up into his seafoam green eyes – one of the sexiest qualities about him. "You'd do the same for me. You've always done the same for me." She bit at her lower lip remembering what it was like to kiss him – how thoroughly and tenderly he possessed her mouth.

Declan's hands slid down her back and rested just above her backside. He nudged her closer to him. They stood there like that for a moment, their gazes fixed on each other – unmoving, barely breathing. Then all at once he let go and cursed. "I want to kiss you, Kate, and I know that we can't do that."

Kate stepped back, realizing how close she had come to kissing him. "It's my fault. I shouldn't have walked into the bathroom while you were showering. I crossed the boundary we set." She shouldn't have admitted it but she did. "If it makes you feel any better, I wanted to kiss you, too. I nearly did."

Declan groaned. "That makes it a thousand times worse." He plopped down on the bed and then laid back and stared at the ceiling. "This feels like high school when you have a crush on your best friend but you know there's nothing you can do about it."

"You have a crush on me?" Kate asked, letting her voice go soft. She felt so childish saying the words but under the hard FBI exterior, she was still a woman who wanted him as much as he apparently wanted her.

Declan turned his head to the side and watched her. "Kate, I've always had a crush on you. I just tuck it away somewhere in my brain and never think about it. It's the only way I get through the day."

"Oh," she said in a rush of breath. This was a path they couldn't go down. They still had a serial bomber to stop. She reached for his hand and pulled him upright. "Your steak is getting cold."

Declan laughed. "That's all you have to say to my crush – *my steak is getting cold?*"

Kate didn't want to admit that she couldn't say what she was thinking. She laughed with him. "One of us has to be the adult and stop things before they get too far."

"You've always been better at being the adult." Declan got up off the bed, grabbed shorts and a tee-shirt, and went into the bathroom to change. When he came out, they ate and spent the rest of the night on the couch watching television – both of them avoiding the feeling of desire they knew was running like an electrical current between them.

CHAPTER 17

The next morning passed in a blur. It was a barrage of meetings and interviews. No potential witnesses had come forward. No one saw or heard anything, much like in the other cases. The statement about Lily Cole as a person of interest had done little the night before to garner more leads. There had been a handful of phone calls from people who knew her from Cornell but none of them could pinpoint her current location. A few of the callers had expressed surprise that she'd be considered a person of interest. They had said they knew she was radical in her approach, but they would never believe her capable of murder.

One of the callers, Lily's former chemistry professor at Cornell, had left his name and number with the hotline and had requested a callback. Murphy had given Kate the contact information and a quiet place to make the call while Declan went over a few more crime scene details with Leo, who had arrived at the office with some eight-by-eleven glossy photos.

Kate hoped the talk they had last night had done some good in raising his self-confidence. She needed Declan to do what he did best. No one had a better eye at a crime scene than he did.

Kate placed the call to Professor Steve Smith's office. It rang four times before he answered, and when he did, he was rushed and out of breath. After Kate identified herself, he apologized and said that he was in his attached lab working.

Kate outlined why she called. "You said in your message it was important that I call you back."

"Yes," Smith said, catching his breath. "I wanted to speak to you directly, Agent Walsh. I had wanted to speak to you before you left Cornell but understandably didn't get the chance. This is about Lily Cole."

"You were her chemistry professor?"

"I was but I was also her mentor, of sorts. She'd come to speak to me about a myriad of things. Lily was a troubled young woman. I think there was some abuse in her past. She alluded to it several times."

Kate jotted a few notes as he spoke. "Abuse? What do you mean exactly?"

"According to Lily, she grew up in a home where there was a good deal of domestic violence. She excelled in school and got out of there as quickly as she could." Professor Smith changed positions of the phone and it echoed through the line. "Agent Walsh, I don't know if you understand the impact of witnessing that kind of violence in the home. Lily's mother was hospitalized several times for the physical abuse she endured. Lily's two sisters were also abused. All three children were removed from the home at least twice and then allowed to go back in. I don't understand why because Lily said nothing had changed. She said her parents put on a show for the court and went to all the assigned counseling sessions and faked it until they got the kids back. Then they were at it again."

Professor Smith's information was confusing to Kate in some ways. "Was Lily also physically abused or was she a witness to it?"

"That was hard to determine. I would imagine if the father was that abusive to her mother, Lily did not get out unscathed. Her mother was an alcoholic and it sounded like some of the verbal and emotional abuse toward the girls came from both the mother and the father. I don't know specifics about physical abuse. Lily often complained that her mother had one job and that was to protect her children and she couldn't even be bothered to do that."

Kate knew domestic violence was more complex than that and a woman leaving wasn't as clear-cut as most people liked to believe. From Lily's perspective though, Kate could understand a child's reasoning. "Did Lily's mother ever leave her husband?"

"No. During my last conversation with Lily, she said her sisters are out of the home but her parents still refused any help."

That kind of abuse could damage a child in a myriad of ways. Kate wasn't sure about the connection he was making though. "How do you think that relates to the bombings?"

"I'm not sure that it does, but Lily was interested in bombs while here at Cornell."

Kate's mouth fell slightly open. It was the first confirmation she had heard. "How do you know that? From her chemistry classes?"

"No. She wrote a paper about the rise of female bombers in the seventies for one of her political science classes. In her research, she came to me and asked me questions about bomb-making. It seemed at the time like logical questions to ask when researching a paper of that nature." Professor Smith chastised himself under his breath. "That said, Agent Walsh, even after everything I've said that makes Lily look guilty, I'm having a hard time believing she is your suspect."

"Professor Smith, it's hard for people to believe the worst in people they know."

"That's not it."

"Then what is it?" Kate pressed.

"Lily was a terrible chemistry student. She failed my class miserably. I don't think she can make bombs." Professor Smith let a chuckle escape and then he apologized. "I'm not making light of the situation, Agent Walsh, it's just that Lily couldn't even pass a basic test with extra tutoring. How would she ever make a bomb, set it up, and detonate it? It makes absolutely no sense to me unless you know more about Lily than I do."

Professor Smith reinforced Kate's view that Lily wasn't acting alone. "Do you think she'd be swayed to help someone carry out a crime like this? Right now, we consider her a person of interest. If you saw the news, you know the bomber is leaving notes for us. There was one delivered to the *New York Times* taking credit for the bombings – including the one that nearly killed my partner, Agent James, and me. Someone at the *New York Times* office identified Lily from a photo as the person dropping off the note."

"Surely, that can't mean that Lily is the bomber. If she was, why would she give herself away like that?" Professor Smith reasoned.

"Maybe she didn't think that we'd follow her trail from Cornell to Manhattan," Kate suggested, not believing it herself. "People think they are going to get away with things all the time and are surprised by how the tiniest slipup will get them caught."

"That's probably true, but I stand by what I said. I can't believe that Lily is building those bombs. She doesn't have the technical capability to do that. She also doesn't have the resources." Professor Smith yelled to someone he'd be off the phone soon. To Kate, he said, "I have a meeting in a few minutes, Agent Walsh. I'd ask what kind of bombs are being made, but I suspect you are not disclosing that information to the public for good reason. It doesn't matter what kind of bombs they are. Lily isn't doing this – at least not alone."

"She's been arrested for a series of other crimes." When Professor Smith started to argue, Kate talked right over him. "I know most of them seem harmless to you – property crimes and such. It represents a pattern to me. Her crimes were increasing in severity. While I agree that it doesn't seem like Lily would be able to pull this off alone, it doesn't mean that she isn't involved."

Professor Smith remained quiet for several moments and then relented, having been at least partly swayed by Kate. "You've got me, Agent Walsh. I can't say with certainty that Lily isn't involved in this mess. For as much as Lily wants to be a leader and project herself as that, she has a follower personality. If the right person came along and their values aligned, she could be convinced. Because of her past, Lily has a lot of built-up anger bubbling at the surface."

That part Kate already knew, but it was good to hear someone else confirm it. "Do you have any idea where she is now?"

"No idea. I haven't seen her at all this semester. We talked by phone a few weeks ago. That was the last contact."

That frustrated Kate. "Do you have any way to reach her?"

"I've tried, Agent Walsh. When the bombing happened here at Cornell, I tried to call her cellphone, but it's been shut off. She must have a new number."

"What about her parents?"

"Hold on," Professor Smith said. Kate could hear typing on a keyboard. Professor Smith talked to himself as he searched for the content. "Here it is." He rattled off a phone number for Lily's parents and then cautioned, "These aren't good people, Agent Walsh. Even if they knew where to find Lily, they might not tell you. Even if they were willing to tell you, they might require payment for the information. I don't think Lily would confide in them. They'd be the last people she'd reach out to for help."

Kate noted the contact information and left it at that. "I appreciate the information. If you think of anything else, please let me know." She was about to hang up when she asked, "Professor Smith, you know the students there better than I do. Is there anyone you suspect of the bombing at Cornell? I'm sure you've taught some of the students who were Sword and Crown members. You must have some impression of what happened or heard speculation among the staff and students."

"I've heard all kinds of speculation from students to disgruntled parents and even angry professors who hate dealing with legacy students who refuse to do the work. We are supposed to pass them anyway. The entitlement is what gets us the most." Professor Smith mumbled something under his breath Kate couldn't hear and then spoke loudly. "Unfortunately, no I don't have any factual information to share. I would if I did. We all want to see this person caught and punished for what they have done. Most people I've spoken to believe it has to be someone from the outside. Maybe that's a feeling common for people who go through traumatic events like this. We simply can't believe that it's one of our own. It's tragic for all."

Kate offered her sympathies and thanked him again for the information. "If you think of anything else or hear anything from your colleagues, please give me a call." When the call ended, she called Lily's parents but ended up leaving a message. She was sure that she wouldn't get a call back.

As Kate sat there going over what Professor Smith told her, she remembered the other professor who had connected the two cases. She hadn't had a chance to call him. Kate scrolled through her phone for the note and called Professor Blair. He answered quickly and Kate asked a few questions about how and why he connected the two cases. It was as Kate had suspected – he had talked with a colleague at Dartmouth and compared notes. It was no more or less than that. Another dead end.

Murphy walked into the room and dropped a piece of paper on the desk as Kate wrapped up the call. "We got a tip this morning that a young woman matching Lily's description is hiding out at a house in Brooklyn. It's a drug house with addicts and homeless. It may be her. Do you want me to send someone down to check it out?"

Kate raised her eyes to look at him. "Do you think it's credible?"

"I don't have any reason to suspect it's not. I can send two uniformed cops down to check it out. They know the area better than we do."

Kate wasn't sure why but she wanted to check it out herself. She picked up the slip of paper and read off the address. "Is Declan around?"

"He just got back from meeting with Leo."

Kate stood from the table. "We'll go. I don't feel like sitting around the office and I know Declan won't feel like sitting around either." She saw the concerned look on Murphy's face but couldn't read what it meant. "Is there something wrong?"

He sat down in a chair. "I don't want us to waste too much time on Lily Cole. I thought about what you said. Maybe she's caught up in something bigger. I feel like we're missing something."

Kate understood his feeling as she felt it too. "Lily is all we have right now. I need to run it to ground. If it's nothing, it's nothing. The *New York Times* staff positively identified her."

"That's been bugging me." Murphy rubbed at the back of his neck. "I don't know that this bomber would write notes like this. I know some serial killers do – like the encrypted missives from the Zodiac killer and the Unabomber's manifesto. These notes, though. They don't say enough for me to believe them."

Kate slowly sat back in the chair, considering what Murphy said. "You think they are a fake?"

"I do." He locked eyes with Kate. "Think about what the notes are saying – it's not anything that couldn't be said after a bombing. There's no inside information."

"What about my SUV?"

"That made the news, right? The note said they could have killed you if they wanted to. It doesn't take someone there or the actual bomber to say that after the fact, knowing the bomb didn't kill you. They didn't say anything about when the bomb was detonated. You said yourself that the comment felt off."

That was true. Kate had felt maybe the bomber was compensating for not having killed them. She thought their ego had gotten the better of them. Now that Murphy said it and she mulled it over, he was right. "I hadn't given too much consideration to that. I was so focused on looking at the language they were using to find clues about their identity."

"We all get tunnel vision. I can see why you'd be focused on what you were. I think we need to take a step back." Murphy pointed to the address he had provided. "You still want to check it out?"

"I do. Let me see if I can find Lily and then we can meet this afternoon and reevaluate our strategy."

Murphy stood and headed for the door. Before he left though, he said, "I want to see if there have been any threats broadly against Ivy League secret societies, even ones that haven't been bombed yet. The bomber might be working their way up to their true intended target."

"You have been doing this a long time," Kate said, smiling as he left. They needed to broaden their scope and she was glad Murphy was there to remind her of it.

CHAPTER 18

"Tell me again why we are on the subway when Murphy said he could get us a car and a driver if we wanted," Declan said, holding tight to the metal pole in the second subway car from the last on the train to Brooklyn. His body swayed with the movement of the subway car. It wasn't a smooth ride by any stretch.

"I wanted to get out among the people," Kate said with a grin. She had imagined picking up chatter about the bombing, a nugget of information here and there that might prove useful. Instead, people had their faces buried in cellphones and books or had their headphones on, shutting out the rest of the world.

Declan pointed around the subway car. "It's New York City, Kate. The people don't care that some snobbish secret society got bombed. You're among the people and the people don't care. Look around."

Kate sighed and gripped the edge of her seat as the subway came to a stop. She glanced up at the sign. They had two more stops to go. "I don't know what I was thinking."

Declan smiled down at her. "You were thinking we have a crazed bomber on a mission and we have zero leads. You're grasping at straws and that's okay. You're even more shaken now that Murphy pointed out that the one lead we had – the notes – might not even be from the bomber."

Kate whipped her head around to see if anybody in their subway car had heard Declan speaking so openly about the case, but none of them had even glanced their way. She turned back to Declan, deflated. "That's exactly what I'm feeling."

"Something will turn up. It always does."

"You know. Even if it's not the bomber who is writing the notes, someone is and they might know more than they realize. There is a reason they are involving themselves in this."

Declan shrugged. "I wouldn't put too much hope into it, Kate. Let's just see what we see."

As the subway car came to a stop, Kate stood and Declan stepped behind her as they got off the subway car. They made their way through the subway station and out onto the streets of Brooklyn. This wasn't one of the gentrified neighborhoods shown on real estate reality television. This was the Brooklyn most people don't talk about.

The row houses had grown dilapidated enough that a few looked like they were barely still standing. Windows were boarded over. Trash littered the streets and the homeless sat encamped near the buildings. A woman in a short skirt barely covering her backside paced on a corner. Kate assumed either waiting for a dealer or her next customer. What she assumed was a drug deal happened across the street on another corner. The rest of the people hurried along the sidewalk to and from wherever they were going seemingly oblivious to the scene in front of them.

Kate and Declan looked out of place dressed in professional business attire. As they walked the two blocks to the address, a beat cop approached them. Kate noticed that he had spotted them as soon as they hit the street from the subway station, but he watched them traverse two blocks before approaching.

"How are you folks doing today?" he asked in a friendly tone as he gave them a once over.

Kate assumed he figured they were probably there to score some drugs. There was no reason to hide who they were or delay. She tugged the chain from around her neck and pulled her badge from the inside of her shirt while Declan pulled his badge and identification from his back pocket. "FBI Agents Kate Walsh and Declan James. We are searching for a young woman with a connection to the bombing that happened in Manhattan."

"Over here?" he asked, squinting his eyes from the sunlight.

Kate showed him the address. "The young woman's name is Lily Cole. We received a tip that she was staying here in a house with other homeless youth."

"I know most of the homeless kids around here. Got a photo of her?"

Kate pulled out her cellphone and scrolled through her photos until she found the school photo of Lily. "This is from last year. I don't know that she still looks like that. A witness said she had purple hair."

The cop peered down at the photo but shook his head. "She doesn't look familiar to me. Feel free to search but keep your wits about you. Danger lurks around every corner in some of those houses."

The cop let them pass but kept an eye on them as they walked to the building and then up the broken concrete steps. "I wouldn't want his job," Declan said as he reached for the door handle.

"I saw at least four crimes being committed while he's standing around watching the scene unfold." Kate wasn't sure why the cop wasn't doing anything about it. Then again, she hadn't ever worked a beat a day in her life.

"He can't arrest everyone, Kate. I'm sure he's there to keep the peace more than anything." He turned back to her before stepping into the brownstone. "He'd spend his day arresting everyone only to have them handed appearance tickets and be let out again. I'm sure he's choosing his arrests wisely. Let's give him the benefit of the doubt. He's out here every day."

Kate held her hands up. "I'm not really judging."

The smell in the house was the first thing that knocked Kate back. It was a mix of urine and body odor and death. She shook her head trying to free it from her nostrils. They walked through the darkened first floor. Declan got out his cellphone and hit the flashlight app and shone it around the space. It was empty except for one man curled up in a sleeping bag in a corner.

Declan circled back to the front door and took the stairs to the second floor and they did the same. It was on the third floor they found a young woman roughly Lily's age. She was sitting on the floor staring off across the room. She had a notebook opened in front of her and a pencil in her hand. She had drawn a beautiful landscape.

"That's amazing," Kate said, pointing down at the drawing. "Are you an artist?"

The young woman looked up at them and inched back, clearly afraid. Kate and Declan both flashed their badges. "We aren't here to hassle you," Declan said. "We are looking for someone. A young woman about your age."

Kate showed her the photo and the young woman shook her head. "Are you sure? Take another look. She might go by the name Lily."

The young woman looked back down at her notebook and then flipped back a few pages. She held up a drawing of a young woman staring out a window. Kate was sure it was Lily and that the window she was looking out of was in this building.

"She didn't call herself Lily," the young woman said, speaking for the first time. "She didn't tell me her name. She was only here for a night and then said she had a place to stay. She left and hasn't been back since."

"How long ago was that?"

"A few days. I lose track of time."

Kate needed more to go on than that. "Did she tell you anything about where she was going to stay?"

"Up on Central Park West but I didn't believe her. I figured she'd called home and was getting out of here."

Declan crouched down and asked, "Are you sure she said Central Park West?"

"I'm sure. That's why I didn't believe her."

They asked her a few more questions but she claimed she didn't know more. When they were done, the young woman looked around and then right back at Declan. "Who goes from here to Central Park West? She had to be lying. I didn't know why she was here. She told me she went to some rich Ivy League school but that she had to drop out and she was on the run."

"What else did she say?" Declan asked, keeping his focus on her.

"What does it matter if it's all lies?"

Kate stepped toward her. "It's not all lies. Lily went to Cornell and she is on the run. I know you might not want to get her in trouble, but we think Lily might be in danger." Kate was willing to lie to get information if she had to. "What's your name?"

"I know my rights and I don't have to tell you that if I don't want to."

"You're right," Declan said. "You don't have to tell us your name and you don't have to help us. But it's a lot better if you do. Do you sleep here?"

"Sometimes. It's a safe place from the streets."

Kate asked, "Where are you from?"

The young woman angled her head up to look at Kate. Her mouth was set in a firm line. "I'm not going back home. The streets are safer for me than my house."

Kate knew better than to tell her she understood. Instead, she said, "Maybe we can help you get into a shelter or something. You have a real gift for art. You'd probably do well if you returned to school."

"I can't go to school if I don't have an address. I don't have any money for tuition."

"There are programs," Declan said and then he didn't say more. It was clear the young woman wasn't going to allow them to help her. They couldn't force it on her. Declan pulled his wallet from his back pocket and pulled out two twenties. He handed them to her with a business card. "This is all the cash I have on me. Take it and get yourself something to eat. I don't know how long we are going to be here, but call me anytime if you need anything. I'll figure out a way to help you."

The young woman took it tentatively, still looking between them as if to ask what the catch was. "I don't know more than I told you."

"It's okay. I believe you," Declan said.

"What did she do? You said she might be in danger."

Declan nodded. "Have you heard about the bombings that have been happening at colleges? There was one in Manhattan the other night."

"I heard about it. She was a few days gone by then."

Kate did the mental math and Declan seemed to pick up on it too. He spoke aloud the words Kate thought. "Lily couldn't have been in Ithaca for the bombing or planted the bomb in your SUV if she was here in Manhattan."

"Whoa," the young woman said, scrambling to her feet. "Someone tried to kill you?" She had a worried look on her face as she glanced over Kate's shoulder. "I don't want any trouble here. If someone sees me talking to you, will they be after me?"

"No one knows we are here." Kate put her hand on the young woman's shoulder but she pulled away. "Are you sure you don't want to come with us?"

"I'm fine," she said, plopping back down on the floor and grabbing her sketchbook. She pulled it to her lap and opened it back up. She grabbed her pencil off the floor and went back to her sketch. She glanced up at them. "I'm here all the time alone. I can take care of myself."

Then she put her head back down and wouldn't look back up at Kate and Declan after that. She was done and it was her way of dismissing them. Kate reached for Declan's arm and tugged him back. They said goodbye to her and left the way they had come in. Another homeless guy was sitting on the first floor now. He moved something in his hand behind his back and turned his head. Kate felt no need to go over and see what he was doing. Declan saw it too and he kept walking toward the door.

Once they left the house and went down the broken concrete steps and hit the sidewalk, Declan grabbed Kate's arm. "Can we leave her there? She's no more than twenty, Kate."

It was a story as old as time. "I don't want to leave her there either, but she doesn't want help. There's not much we can do. You can't force someone in off the streets or to access services if they don't want them."

Declan wasn't buying that. "I'm going to speak to Tony when we get back. Maybe he can get them to send over a social worker or victim's advocate and they can help her."

Kate wasn't going to disappoint him by telling him that they weren't going to do much. She felt sorry for the young woman, but her mind was on Lily and who she might know on Central Park West.

CHAPTER 19

"We picked up some chatter on the message boards," Murphy said, standing from behind the desk when Kate and Declan entered the office that he was occupying for the time being. The large mahogany desk made the room feel cramped and closed off. There was barely room for the two chairs that sat across from it. Murphy pulled a stack of pages from the printer tray and handed half to Kate and the other half to Declan. "Let's go into the conference room to discuss what I've found."

"We got a lead on Lily," she said as they entered the conference room and sat down. "We've confirmed again she's been here in the city. The young woman we spoke to said she was headed to see someone on Central Park West."

Murphy stopped cold and pointed to the stack in Kate's hand. "There's mention of Central Park West in the chatter. A guy who has it out for secret societies. He believes it's the seat of power in America – a grooming ground so to speak and the crux of everything wrong with the country. He's a conspiracy theorist and believes that secret societies hold what he calls universal power that the rest of us can't tap into."

"Universal power through their connections or like a fountain of youth kind of thing?" Declan asked, skepticism in his voice. He pulled out a chair and sat, leaning back as he grabbed a stack of pages.

"Like any conspiracy theory, it's a bunch of jibber-jabber nonsense to me. The guy, Felix Poole, talks about universal power like the fountain of youth. There is an elixir, he claims, that on the night of initiation into a secret society, the members drink it, swear a blood oath, and then step into the process of being groomed for future leadership positions within the country."

Declan tried to hold back a smile. "Is that the guy's real name? I'd think if he was going to spill a bunch of nonsense like that online he'd hide his identity."

"He's got a website and everything." Murphy's expression matched Declan's. "Here's the kicker. He lives over on Central Park West. He's independently wealthy. Old family money or so he claims."

Kate flipped through the stack of printed pages until she found the chat conversations Murphy referenced. She skimmed over it, reading post after post that seemed to grow stranger as they went on. She saw exactly why Murphy had zeroed in on it. Felix both praised the bomber and then later down the chat hinted that the government may have planted the bombs to hide what they were doing within secret societies.

What Kate read into the chat more than anything was that Felix was toying with the other chat users. He'd reel them in with one theory and then guide them down another rabbit hole. He seemed adept at turning the conversation whichever way he wanted and his tone and style of writing indicated he took pleasure in it. He'd drop a little hint here or there and then watch the other users bounce with speculation and trying to figure out what he meant. Sometimes, he'd agree with them and other times, he'd back out of what he originally said and hint about something else. Kate wasn't sure Felix even believed the nonsense he was spewing.

After reading through the information and growing more frustrated, she slid the pages over to Declan. "No smoking gun but he taps into most of the common conspiracy theories out there including that 9/11 was an inside job. I can see why you zeroed in on him, Murphy. With his wealth, if it's real, he'd have the resources to pull off a bombing like this. Where does he live on Central Park West?"

"You're not going to believe this," Murphy said, smiling and letting them sit with the anticipation for a moment. "He lives in one of the last three remaining Gilded Age single-family row houses on the street." Murphy watched Kate's surprised reaction. "It's unbelievable that they are still standing, and from what I hear, in pristine shape. It sits right at the corner of Central Park West and 85th Street."

Unlike the other boroughs of New York City, there were few single-family houses left in Manhattan. Kate had read an article that stated there were only two-thousand single-family homes left and not all of them were row houses. The fact that Felix lived in a Gilded Age row house was a surprise to Kate. She owned a single-family Gilded Age row house in Boston's Back Bay, but the rarity of that in Manhattan drove home the point that Felix had money, or at the very least, came from money.

"Did you see anything credible in what he wrote that will give us a foot in the door?" Kate asked, taking one of the pages Declan had finished with and going over it again.

"Not much, but the fact that Lily was headed to Central Park West and she has a connection to the bombing gives us a little wiggle room. I didn't see anything that would give us a search warrant."

Declan expelled a breath loud enough that it got both of their attention. He dropped the pages on the table. "This guy looks as good as any of the others. He's completely out there in what he believes or what he's trying to convince others to believe. He's got the space to build these bombs and the money to pull it off. What else did you find, Murphy?"

"Nothing more about Felix." Murphy pointed to the stack of pages he had given Declan at the start. "I pulled more pages from that message board and found something strange. There's a mother whose son was killed at Brown University. He was killed while he was being initiated into Hunt House, which Brown claims has no affiliation with the university. That held up in court when the family sued them. They lost their case. She's been angry ever since, as you can imagine. She and her husband have been vocal advocates of exposing and shutting down secret societies."

Declan raised his eyebrows. "Do you think they'd be willing to kill other college-aged kids to prove their point?" His question dripped with sarcasm.

Kate agreed it was far-fetched. She had met many grieving parents and grief could do a lot of things, but she'd never seen it turn someone into a cold-blooded killer. "I'd tend to agree with Declan on this."

"I'd agree with you usually. Tess and Robert Hudson are a different story. Their son, Michael, was killed in a hazing incident. He climbed Hunt House's bell tower and fell to his death. They believe he was pushed. That was never proven. Hunt House members claim it was an accident and there was some speculation of suicide. The medical examiner ruled it an accidental death. Tess Hudson said in a recent post that every secret society should be destroyed."

Declan still wasn't buying it. "She might not have meant that literally. I can see why she'd want them to end, but I can't see a mom building and planting bombs and killing other students like her son."

"That's the catch," Murphy said, pointing. "She doesn't see the other students in secret societies like her son. She sees them as her son's killers. The poor woman can't get justice through the courts. Her writing gets increasingly angry and more erratic. The family has money. Do me a favor and read her writings and then tell me no. I know it might seem preposterous to even suggest, but I have a feeling you'll change your mind."

Kate reached for the pages Murphy referenced. If Declan wasn't going to read the pages she was, even if just to dispel Murphy's theory. She started out reading the posts wrestling with her mind to come around to the idea that a grieving mother would cause that kind of grief for others. As she read each post that grew from devastated at the loss of her son to anger that no one had been held accountable to downright violent, Kate grew so uncomfortable she had trouble not shifting in her seat as she read the words. *They should pay. They should all pay and feel the same pain I have right now. If they don't want to hold their children accountable, then I will.*

That was the last post and it was dated three months before the first bombing took place. She read the posts again and looked for any subtext behind what Tess Hudson was saying. What Kate was looking for was some indication that the woman could have committed the kind of horror that was unfolding now.

What struck Kate the most was that the anger in what Tess wrote wasn't just directed at Hunt House or even Brown University. It was directed at all Ivy League schools and secret societies much like what Felix was saying. If Kate were being honest with herself, while Felix rambled on about conspiracy theories, Tess had been harmed by the practices at secret societies and was equal to or possibly more of a threat than Felix.

Kate laid the papers on the table and then turned her head slowly to Murphy. He was staring at her intently, waiting for her response. "That was not what I expected at all. I assumed Tess was a normal mother consumed with grief. She is that – the writing was clear. It was so much more than that though – the rage and the threats. You don't normally see that in public."

"It took me by surprise." Murphy reached for the pages and handed them to Declan. "Read them," he said with a force not usually directed at an FBI agent.

Declan dutifully took them without a word of protest and read them while Kate and Murphy watched and judged his reaction. It was the same as Kate. She could read his face as it turned to sympathy for a grieving mother, surprise at the level of rage, and then to concern they had an active threat on their hands.

When he was done, Declan placed the pages on the table and laid his palms flat on top of them. He turned to Murphy. "How did you find all of this so quickly?"

"It was easier than you might think. A few quick searches on threats against secret societies lead me to the chat forums. It took some playing around with search terms. I didn't find anything at first, but I kept digging." Murphy jutted his chin toward the research. "Do we agree that Tess Hudson should be interviewed?"

"I'd like to do more research on her first," Kate said, hoping to find more about her before meeting the woman face to face. "Where in the country does she live?"

"Practically in your backyard." He leaned down and sifted through the pages until he found the one. He handed it to Kate. "Tess and Robert Hudson live in Lexington. I didn't bother printing anything other than the chatter on the message board, but there are pages and pages of links with news articles about her son's death and the legal battle that followed."

Declan folded his hands across his stomach. "If Tess is involved in this, then why didn't she start with Hunt House? That seems like it would be the most logical. She's in a battle with them and clearly by her own words wants them to take responsibility for what happened to her son. Why start with Magnolia House in Dartmouth – a secret society of women? It doesn't make a lot of sense to me."

It didn't make a lot of sense to Kate either, but at this point anything was possible. "There could be any number of reasons why," she speculated. "If they started with Hunt House, Tess might assume she'd be at the top of the suspect list immediately."

"What do you want to do then?"

Kate didn't have to think about it. "I want to go over to Central Park West and interview Felix if he's willing to speak to us and then head back to Boston."

"What do you want me to do?" Murphy asked, leaning against the wall. "I can stay here and keep going over all the evidence. I had my office send the info from Cornell here. Leo was able to grease some wheels with Hanover PD and they sent over everything they have regarding Magnolia House. It's the same as what we saw in Ithaca – no witnesses and not much to go on beyond what we already know. I'll let you know if I find anything more as I go through it all."

As Declan stood from the table, he asked, "Where's Tony?"

"He was heading over to the medical examiner's office today. They are still in the process of identifying remains. They have made a handful of identifications but other families are still waiting."

Kate was glad that Tony was handling that end of the investigation. She and Declan didn't have time to sit at the medical examiner's office waiting for details. She wanted to see the report when it was finalized – whenever that was. "Please tell Tony to call us if he finds anything. Let's schedule a video meeting after we speak to Tess." She stood from the table and as she passed by Murphy on the way out of the room, she put a hand on his arm. "If I haven't said it before, I appreciate all your help with this case."

He laid his hand over hers. "I'm glad we aren't in it alone." Murphy shook Declan's hand as he went out the door and then slapped him on the back for good measure.

CHAPTER 20

Kate steadied herself as she walked out of the police station. If there was one thing she truly hated on a professional and personal level it was dealing with conspiracy theorists. Their utter lack of logic hurt her brain. There was no rationalizing with them and rarely did two plus two equal four with them. It was always some half-cocked argument that made little or no sense. When challenged, they'd pivot and talk about something else or argue the point until the other person gave up.

"I need you to run point on this interview," Kate said, deciding it would be best for Declan to take the lead. "I'll hang back and observe for now. I can do that better when I'm not going head-to-head with him."

Declan turned the corner and checked his phone for the directions. They were close enough that they had decided to walk. "What makes you think it's going to be confrontational?"

"When isn't having a conversation with a conspiracy theorist confrontational?"

Declan laughed and threw his arm around her shoulders. "I can't believe you're still angry about the guy who tried to argue with you that the FBI killed JFK. I remember that night like it was yesterday. He got you steamed for sure. I couldn't believe you had humored that guy and had a conversation with him. Not that it was much conversation before it turned into a screaming match. For once, I wasn't the one getting kicked out of the bar. It was you!"

"I don't want to discuss that." Kate threw off his arm. She didn't want to remember that night. It was one of the only times she had lost her cool with someone to that degree and it was the dumbest argument. She couldn't remember the particulars of the guy's theory, but the feeling that it brought up was visceral. Even now, the total loss of control and embarrassment she felt for having allowed herself to get roped into the discussion washed over her. Kate had known going into the debate that night she wasn't going to win, but still, her headstrong nature didn't allow her to back down from it. Luckily, in her thirties, she had found some sense and a better way to navigate people like that. Kate figured it was better to let Declan take the lead with Felix.

Several blocks later, they arrived at the four-story, brick row house. Starting at the second floor was a rounded turret going all the way to a pointed peak at the top. The house sat adjacent to the sidewalk on one side and two more row houses were attached on the left. The row house right next to Felix's had an eye-catching yellow façade and museum-quality sandstone carvings including pairs of owls. It was truly a sight to behold. Kate was so taken with it that she didn't see the man standing in the window on the second floor of Felix's home.

Declan nudged her as he opened the wrought-iron gate and then grabbed her arm and pulled her along as he ascended the steps. "Some guy up there is watching us."

Kate glanced up but the man was gone. "New York City was the place to be in the Gilded Age. Lots of money, industry, and political influence. The homes were a status symbol with one person trying to outdo the next, particularly new money versus old. It had become a competition. Boston was a bit more subtle."

Declan teased. "Maybe I should be living in your servant's quarters."

"My house doesn't have servant's quarters. But I'm sure if you keep up your nonsense, I can create some." They walked up the few steps and stopped at iron gates that hid the front door behind them. "Is this open or locked?" Kate said as she gave the gate a push. Nothing happened and they both stepped back. There was no doorbell or anything to ring from where they were standing.

Declan ran his hand over the ornate gate and found a latch at waist level. He flipped it upright and then pushed one side of the door, swinging it open. At the front door, he lifted and dropped the brass door knocker twice.

Out of the corner of her mouth, Kate whispered, "If Lily is hiding somewhere in this house, we are never going to find her without a search warrant."

"Then let's hope we get along with Felix and convince him to let us search without one."

Before Kate could tell him that was never going to happen, a man pulled open the door. He wasn't more than five-foot-nine and wiry. He had a slim build and a tuff of dark hair on top of his head. Glasses too large for his face perched on his nose. He pushed them up and peered over Declan's shoulder. When he seemed to be satisfied it was just the two of them, he said, "I assume you're cops. I was expecting the whole force at my door." He looked both of them up and down and then waved them into the house, disappearing. He called over his shoulder. "You two I can handle."

Declan immediately put his hand on top of his gun. "What do you mean *handle* and why are you expecting the cops?" By that point, the man had moved into his home, leaving the door wide open for their entrance. Neither Kate nor Declan took a step inside. When the man didn't answer Declan's question, he barked, "Felix Poole, please come to the door."

"Good grief," the man said with a flare of drama as he came back to the door. "Okay, let's do this your way. I know why you're here to see me. It's uncivilized to stand in my doorway and talk. Besides, nosy Ms. Walters next door will get an earful and I don't want to listen to her run her mouth when you leave. Please come inside and I'll answer all your questions."

They made no move to follow him inside. Kate introduced herself and Declan and then asked, "Are you Felix Poole?"

His smile beamed. "The one and only." He paused and brought a finger to his chin. "Well, that might not be true. I might not be the only one. It might be a common name for all I know. But yes, I'm Felix Poole of the Manhattan Pooles. You might have read about my great-great-grandfather, George Poole. He was involved in the railroad and all that. He built this house. Can you believe I'm the only one left? Direct descendant. I might have cousins out there somewhere but who knows." He stepped back into the home and waved his hand to usher them in. "Could you please come in? I'd be happy to get this out of the way."

Declan took a step in and Kate followed right behind. "You still didn't say why you were expecting us."

Felix walked toward a grand formal living room with high-back chairs and leather sofas and one of the largest, most ornate fireplaces Kate had ever seen. "I wasn't expecting the FBI. Now, that's a surprise. I didn't know I was that important." He turned on his heels to face them. "Should I be worried? The FBI has done all kinds of nefarious things over its existence. Are you going to kill me? Is that why you're here? Please don't kill me. The house is a dreadful mess and I don't want that in the newspapers. Can you come back tomorrow after I've cleaned?"

"We aren't here to kill you, Felix, or debate the things the FBI has done," Declan said, his tone dry, indicating to Kate his patience was already wearing thin. "You alone here in the house?"

He pursed his lips. "Define alone."

"The absence of other people."

Felix waved his hand toward the ceiling. "There are countless of my dead relatives here in spirit form. Do they count?"

Declan blew out a breath like a bull about to charge. "No, Felix, they don't count. Alive people – living and breathing. Let me be more specific." He finally released his hand from the top of his gun and pulled his phone from his pocket. He found the photo of Lily and shoved it toward Felix. "Do you know this young woman? Is she here?"

Felix leaned in and squinted his eyes. "I'm not running a bed and breakfast if that's what you're asking."

Kate noted that he hadn't answered the question. She was trying to figure out if his behavior was an act, a question of his sanity, or maybe just some strange eccentricities. "Felix, we are looking for this young woman. Her name is Lily Cole and she is suspected to be staying here on Central Park West. Have you seen her?"

Felix put his hand on his chest. "You think this young woman is here with me? What would give you that idea?"

"We aren't at liberty to say," Declan said, putting away his phone. "Can we sit and talk? We have a few questions. You still haven't told us why you were expecting the cops. Have you done something illegal?"

Felix laughed, a high-pitched snort. "My gosh, no, Agent James. I figured you'd be coming to see me about my knowledge of secret societies since they are being targeted. You know, the bombings that have been happening. I thought you might need some background research. I'm an expert." He sat down on the edge of a chair and clasped his hands at his knees. "Why would you think I have done something wrong?"

Kate sat down on the brown leather couch. She didn't sit back but perched herself so she could turn her body to face Felix. Declan remained standing at the side of the room. "It's not that we believe you've done anything wrong. But we need to find Lily. She might be in danger and we must find her."

"Oh my," he said, dragging out the two words. "In danger? From whom?"

"The bomber," Declan said, letting the words hang there. When Felix didn't respond, he snapped, "Did you hear me?"

"I heard you, Agent James. I can't believe that a sweet girl like that would be working with a serial bomber." He raised his head and didn't bother hiding the smirk on his face. "Or do you suspect a sweet girl like that is the bomber? I've heard some silly theories but that would be the cherry on top."

Declan leaned against the wall and folded his arms across his chest. "You know her then?"

"No," Felix said. "But the photo you showed me was of a sweet young girl. It was an assumption on my part. What has she done?"

Kate knew he was toying with them. If he saw the news about the bombings, he knew they were looking for Lily and why. She'd play his game to a point. "We believe she might be working with the bomber."

"Why would you believe that?"

"As you might have seen on the news, Lily delivered a note to the *New York Times* office from the bomber."

Felix sat back and crossed his legs. He tipped his head to the side. "Aren't you more interested in what I know?"

"Do you know something about the bombings?"

Felix relaxed his shoulders and smiled, this time a genuine ear-to-ear grin. "I wondered when we were going to get around to this. I had been waiting since the first bombing. Now, you're here. Well, I'm just as nervous as a kid on his first day of school. The FBI here to ask me to help them solve their case. My followers are going to be stoked about this. Do you think after we talk we can do some photos for Instagram?"

Declan let out a low guttural growl that surprised even Kate. "Felix, buddy, you're starting to annoy me. Whatever this little thing that you're doing here is – knock it off. Answer the questions we ask or tell us you don't want to talk to us. This is wasting our time. There are not going to be any selfies or reports to your followers. This is a serious investigation in which there have been multiple deaths. We believe this bomber will strike again. Tell us what you know or I might consider bringing you in for obstruction of justice."

Felix turned his head away from Declan, disgust written all over his face. He didn't like being tested. "What do you think, Agent Walsh? Is that how you feel too or is your brute of a partner running the show?"

Kate stood and kept her eyes locked with his. "I wouldn't test Agent James, Felix. He isn't into playing games. We came here hoping you can help us, but so far all you're doing is sitting here putting on an act – and we know it's an act. You haven't answered one of our questions, provided no expert information, and claim not to know Lily. I think we're done here."

She turned away from Felix and walked toward the foyer, calling his bluff. Either he had no information or he wasn't going to share it. As Kate reached the door, he called out. "You're looking at the bombings all wrong."

Kate didn't want to turn around and give him the satisfaction but she did. "What does that mean?"

Felix was standing then and took a few steps toward her. "What it means is that you're probably looking at it like the bomber's goal is to kill those kids. Look deeper than that – find the one who isn't dead. That will solve it."

"The one who isn't dead?" Declan asked. "What's that supposed to mean?"

"The one who isn't dead has secrets to hide."

"The notes say it's revenge," Kate said, trying to make sense of what he was saying.

"It might be that too but look deeper and you'll find your answer."

Kate couldn't believe she was considering anything Felix was telling her. "Do you know this as fact or is this something you're speculating on?"

Felix stared at her, his eyes blinking rapidly. He pushed his glasses up his nose. "It's what I know to be true after studying secret societies for so long. They all have secrets to hide and they are willing to die and kill to keep them. Look for the one who didn't die – the outsider among the insiders."

"Yeah, we'll do that," Declan said as he brushed past Kate and walked out the front door without looking back. Kate knew he'd had enough and didn't believe anything Felix said.

Kate understood the feeling, but she handed Felix her card. "Call me if you think of anything else. When you see Lily, tell her it's important that we speak to her. I want to help her. Make sure you tell her that." Kate left hoping she had made her point.

CHAPTER 21

Kate assumed Declan would be halfway down the block by the time her feet hit the sidewalk, but as she exited Felix's home, she found him sitting on the last step of the stoop. "Are you okay?" she asked as she dropped down beside him. She glanced back to see if Felix was watching them, but the door was closed and they were alone.

Declan ran his hands down his thighs. "Nothing about what went on in there was okay, Kate. He's lying and we didn't even get to ask him anything important. There were a lot of ways that could have gone and I hadn't anticipated that." He turned his head slightly to look at her and his expression of exasperation said more than his words could ever say. He was angry with himself for some reason.

Kate hitched her thumb over her shoulder toward the house. "It didn't matter what we said in there, Felix was going to do what he did. That was a show for us." Declan sat up straight, resuming his normal posture. She said it again to reinforce her message and then added, "I think Lily is in the house. He refused to answer questions about her and steered the conversation elsewhere. He also wanted to know if she was in trouble and found it ridiculous that she'd be involved in the bombing. If he didn't know her, I doubt he'd jump to that conclusion so easily. They share a mutual disdain for secret societies, and let's be honest, he was pretty easy to find. I bet you she found the same chat room that Murphy found and contacted him. It's not like Felix tried to hide his identity."

Declan stretched his legs out in front of himself and leaned back on his hands. "How old would you say he is? He had some lines around his eyes and a few strands of gray in his hair, but overall, he didn't look older than us."

Kate had tried to gauge the same thing as they were talking to him. Mid-to-late thirties had been her guess as well. She was sure that Murphy had his birthday in the research, but as hard as she tried, she couldn't recall the detail. "Probably in his thirties. Does it matter? Lily is of age."

"No," Declan said, letting his voice drop. He glanced over his shoulder and inched closer to Kate. "In the hallway, there was a diploma from Princeton University. I noticed it when we first walked into the house."

Kate hadn't noticed it at all. The fact that Felix might have been a graduate of an Ivy League school didn't surprise her any. "He's more intelligent than he came across. Are you surprised he graduated from Princeton? You saw his writing. He's intelligent even if he doesn't direct it in a way that either of us would condone." She didn't like sitting right on Felix's step while talking about him. She grabbed Declan by the arm and stood. "Come on, let's get out of here and talk on the way back."

As they walked back toward the police station, Kate shielded her eyes from the sun. She should have brought sunglasses but had forgotten them at home. Thinking of home, worry filled her about the students at Harvard and the universities that hadn't been bombed yet. Kate knew it was coming but was unable to do anything about it.

Thoughtfully, Kate said, "We should put out a public official warning for the other universities that they could be targeted next." She quickened her pace as if wanting to create physical distance from what she had said. It could blow up in their faces. But honestly, they had few good options.

Declan reached for her arm to slow her down but she was too far ahead of him. "Kate, we talked about that after Cornell. Do you think it's going to make a difference? We've called the universities and issued warnings directly to them. You're ready to go public with it?" His tone wasn't one of disagreement but rather surprise. He had been calling for warnings all along no matter the storm it would create with faculty, students and parents.

Kate continued at her pace, forcing Declan to catch up with her. "I'm ready and it's something we have to do. It feels a bit like admitting defeat – like the bomber is one step ahead of us and we won't be able to stop the next bombing. But that's the truth, Declan. We aren't going to be able to stop it. An ounce of prevention is worth a pound of cure. There will be another bombing and probably soon. Let's call for a press conference tonight before we go back to Boston and interview Tess Hudson."

"I'll tell Murphy when we get back. He can issue it." Declan checked his watch. "We can probably make the six o'clock news. There is going to be bedlam, you know that. Some parents might pull their kids out of school. We are potentially unleashing mass chaos."

Kate knew that, but she also knew that if they issued an official warning, the universities would have no other choice but to put in extra security measures. They certainly wouldn't come out and downplay the situation the way they had over the phone. They'd be looking at significant liability.

"The chips are going to fall where they fall," Kate said evenly, resigned with the decision. "At least, we give the parents who want to protect their kids a fighting chance. I can't have any more deaths hanging over my head. We don't even have a viable suspect yet, and I'm starting to wonder if we ever will." Kate wasn't being dramatic for the sake of it. She allowed the words Felix had said to seep into her psyche. If this was about more than revenge, she had no idea what the motive might be.

"You don't have to justify it to me, Kate. I've been on board with it from the start. It might cause the bomber to go underground for a while, but if that happens, it gives us some breathing space to find more evidence. They aren't leaving many clues behind as it is. We need what we never get on these cases – more time."

"The one who didn't die," Kate said under her breath as they crossed the street to the police station. She said it twice more before Declan heard her.

He stopped cold in front of the police station blocking her from the door. He put his hands on her shoulders and looked down into her eyes. "Please tell me you don't believe that madman. He spouted nothing but nonsense."

"Maybe he didn't, Declan. I have a feeling he knows far more than we do about secret societies. If he went to Princeton, then maybe he knows from firsthand experience." It was clear Kate had a far different impression of Felix than Declan did. It was easy to dismiss the man as not being in his right mind, but there was something about him that Kate couldn't shake. His behavior had been an act, and she wondered what he was trying to hide.

Her mind raced with the possibilities. If they were leaving Manhattan to go back to Boston, she might not have an opportunity to interview Felix again. Kate watched as Declan's lips moved, but she was so far inside her head that she wasn't listening to him.

"I want to go back and talk to Felix alone," she said, interrupting him. "He knows more and this might be my only shot at it."

"You can't go in there alone, Kate." Declan had tried to hold her tighter but she stepped back out of his grasp. "We have no idea if he's involved or not. It isn't safe for you to go it alone. Let's research him online. I'll even explore his theory, but you're not going back there alone."

Kate didn't have a chance to argue her point. Murphy came running out of the police station with a phone in his hand and thrust it toward her. "Kate, he called. The bomber called!"

She lowered her eyes to the phone but didn't reach for it. "Is he on the phone now?"

"No. He called and asked to speak to you. I tried to engage him but he said he'd only speak to you. I've called you three times and then someone saw you both out here. He's going to call back in fifteen minutes." Murphy checked the time on his phone. "Make that eight minutes now."

Declan raised his eyebrows. "We need to get ready for the call. If you want to go back and speak to Felix, we can do that later before leaving for Boston."

He was right, of course. Kate would have to let going back to Felix's house drop for now. "Let me take it someplace quiet and then we can all listen in."

Murphy shook his head. "That's not going to work. He said just you and wouldn't talk on speakerphone. I tried to switch it over while I was on the call with him and he knew and hung up. When he called back, he said if I did it again, he'd blow up something."

"It's a man, then?" Declan asked.

"It could be a woman," Murphy said, confusing them both. "You'll hear, Kate. It's a mechanical voice, not a human voice. My overall impression was that the caller was a man, but I can't be certain."

Kate thought back to the letters. "How do you know it's real and not a prank?"

"He identified parts in the bomb – the particular brand of wires used. He also told me that you were parked next to a field and that Declan dropped your keys right before he blew up your car. We never made that bit of information public."

That was good enough for Kate. She and Declan followed Murphy into the police station, to the elevator, and up to the office he was using. It was a quiet enough space for Kate to take the call. She wasn't going to try to put him on speakerphone but she turned up the volume enough that she hoped they'd be able to hear him in real time. They also set up the phone so Kate could easily hit record as the call engaged.

Then they waited and waited. The tension in the room rose with each minute that passed. Murphy assured her that he would call. While she waited, Kate considered what she would say and what she hoped to get from him. As much as Kate hoped that she'd be in control on the call, she knew she had to remain loose and flexible.

When the ringing phone finally cut through the silence, they all jumped with a start. Kate hit record and then engaged the call. "Agent Kate Walsh," she said in a clipped formal tone.

"Agent Walsh, good, it's you," the mechanical voice said. "I don't enjoy my time being wasted."

"I was out of the office looking for you. You know my name, but what should I call you?"

"Fuse will do."

That was the name from the letter. "Does that mean you're the one sending the letters?"

"Whether I sent the letters or not, I like the name. I'm claiming it before some nitwit reporter calls me something else – something lame and ridiculous like they do."

"How does Lily factor into your plan?"

"No, Agent Walsh, I'm not falling for that. How do you cops say it – I can neither confirm nor deny that I know Lily."

Kate didn't know how long she would be given on the call and he surely wasn't going to identify himself, so she asked the next logical question. "Why are you blowing up secret societies?"

"Motive." He laughed. "Everyone always wants to know the motive and it's so rarely important."

"It's important to me."

"No, it's not. What's important to you is finding and stopping me. What's important to me is continuing my mission. I'd say our goals are incongruent."

"What is your mission?" Kate asked.

"I'm not that dumb. That's nearly the same question as motive."

Kate let the question drop. "Why are you calling me then? It's not to turn yourself in, so what do you want?"

"I want you to stop chasing me."

"That's not going to happen. I'm not going to stop until I catch you." She let her voice go deeper as she leaned her arms on the desk. "And I will catch you. Make no mistake about that. You might have thought that blowing up my SUV was going to stop us. It didn't. It only made us more determined." He let out a high-pitched mechanical laugh. It unnerved her but she shook it off. "What do you want?"

"I want you out of my way," he said when he finally stopped laughing. "I tried to kill you once and that didn't work out for me. It doesn't help that you don't have a family to threaten except that partner of yours. I might go after his family – yes, that's exactly what I'm going to do. Not that useless ex-wife of his or his criminal brothers. I don't think he'd care about that, but no, his parents. Back off or I'll blow up his family home or a car, maybe. Either way, they won't see it coming."

Kate swallowed hard and raised her eyes to Declan who had heard what he said. He frantically pulled out his cellphone and then left the room to make a call. They were used to their lives being at risk. It was all part of the job. Threats to their family were something neither would tolerate. Kate didn't want to give in to her fear or let him know that his words impacted them.

"Meet me," she suggested. "You want to have this fight with me, then meet me and we can work it out."

"The next time I see you will be right before I detonate the bomb that kills you. I can't wait to see that flash of terror in your eyes and then…bam! You're dead!" He screamed into the phone. He paused then, probably waiting for her reaction but Kate didn't give him one. She didn't fill the silence.

He spoke again, calmer now. "This is your last warning, Agent Walsh. Stop pursuing me or I kill your partner's family right before I kill the two of you. Let me work my artistry and it will be all over soon. I don't like going off-plan. I have a mission and I'm going to finish it. You're not going to stop me. The next target has already been selected and the bomb is already planted. All I have to do is detonate it. Do you want me to do that right now on the call with you, Agent Walsh? Would that excite you?"

"Don't!" Kate yelled and pushed up from the table. Her heart raced with the idea that someone else would die while she was engaged on the phone with the killer. She tried an old hostage negotiator task. "What can I get you for you to stop? What do you want? The FBI might be willing."

The call ended with no response from the bomber. Kate quickly rattled off the number to Murphy even though he had seen it when the call had engaged. "Is that the number he called you from before?"

"No. I'm running the number to see if we can get a hit on its location. You might want to check on Declan."

Kate handed Murphy the phone. "That's exactly what I'm going to do."

CHAPTER 22

Kate raced down the hall and spotted Declan through the wall of conference room windows. He had his back to her but the phone to his ear. The bomber was right in that she didn't have to worry about him harming anyone she cared about – she had no one except Declan close to her to lose. With her parents deceased and no siblings and no close extended family, the bomber couldn't do much damage to her in that regard.

Going after Declan's family was a close second. She wasn't particularly close to Declan's brothers, given their criminal past, but she cared for his parents, Eddie and Iris, as if they were her own family.

When Declan pulled the phone away from his ear and slumped down in a chair, Kate nudged open the half-closed door. "Did you get ahold of your mom?"

He turned to look at her and waved her in. Kate sat down next to him at the table. "I did. It took some convincing, but they are going to stay at a hotel for a few days outside of the city." Declan held up his phone. "I called my brother, too, and he promised me he'd make sure they go. He's going to tell the rest of the family to be on high alert. I don't know what else I can do."

"Not much else you can do," Kate said with concern and sympathy in her voice. "We are headed back to Boston soon and we can make sure they left."

"Should I call my ex? At least let her know what's going on."

"It's probably a good idea. Even though the divorce is final, I'm sure you'll feel guilty if something happened to her."

Declan raised his eyes, and with a teasing tone, asked, "If she gets blown up, does that mean I can stop paying alimony and get my house back?"

"Don't even joke about that."

"I don't know that she'll even take my call. Do you want to call her? That way, she might think I'm dead. That's the only reason you'd ever have to call her."

"What?" Kate asked, wondering why he'd think she'd ever call his ex, even if something happened to him. "Your mom can call her under those circumstances. She hates me and I don't think she'd even answer my call. Text her and tell her it's an emergency and ask her to call you. If she doesn't respond, text her and tell her what's going on."

Declan agreed that was probably the best plan. While he was texting his ex, Kate ran through the conversation with the bomber again. There was nothing that stuck out to her as significant. No words he used that gave her a clue into his identity. Kate stopped herself mid-thought and realized she was now calling the bomber *he*. Murphy had thought the same. There was something about the way the caller spoke that Kate thought she had been speaking to a man. It was the word choices and the cadence in the mechanical voice. Kate couldn't rule out that a woman was involved, but she'd bet a year's salary that the person on the other end of that phone had been a man.

He had spent the time researching Kate and Declan, too. He knew that she had no family and Declan had an ex and brothers. It meant that he probably knew where she lived. With the state of the internet, there was only so much hiding she could do. If someone wanted to get her address badly enough, they'd find a way. The home had been in her family for generations. The name Walsh was forever tied to the address.

When Declan finished texting, she said, "He's intelligent, most likely well-educated, white, and in his forties or early fifties. He has a good deal of money and the ability to move around freely. He's not constrained by a work schedule."

"You're sure now the bomber is a man?" Declan set his phone on the table and nudged it away. "That's what you thought initially and then convinced Tony it could be a woman. Do you know for sure?"

Kate considered the question and then slowly nodded. Even though it was a mechanical voice, she knew she had been talking to a man. "I'm sure. How did it go with your ex?"

"She doesn't care and won't change anything in her life to increase her safety. Then she blamed me for bringing this on her. She told me that if she died, I could live with the guilt."

"You did your best in letting her know. It's on her now, Declan. Let it go and let's hope the bomber doesn't go after her."

"I'm not sure I care anymore." He changed the subject quickly. "What do you want to do next? I'll go back with you so you can interview Felix." When Kate started to argue with him, he held his hand up to stop her. "There's no way I'm letting you go alone. I won't go in. I'll stand outside, sit on the stoop or even walk down the block. I'm not letting you go alone."

Kate took a moment to consider if going to see him again would matter. She had been thinking about what Felix said – consider the one who didn't die. "Garrett Becker," she said aloud and saw the confused expression on Declan's face. "Garrett, the young man at Sword and Crown who didn't die that night. He survived if only barely."

"Right, but there were a lot of other survivors between Magnolia House and Sword and Crown and there's Finley Llyod at Raven Hall even – the only survivor. You don't think Garrett had anything to do with the bomb, do you?"

Kate didn't trust anyone and couldn't rule him out. "We need someone to start going through all the backgrounds of survivors and the deceased. Maybe there is something in one of the student's backgrounds that will give us a hint as to who the bomber could be."

"That's a lot of time we don't have, Kate. I'll talk to Murphy and see if he has someone who he can put on it." He gave her a look that asked the question she still needed to answer.

"Yes, I want to speak to Felix again, especially after the call. I find it strange that he called within thirty minutes of us leaving Felix's house. Do you think he'd be so daring?"

Declan didn't know. "He was an odd duck, to say the least."

As the two of them walked out of the conference room to tell Murphy they were heading to interview Felix again, he came charging down the hallway.

"Here." He thrust a piece of paper toward Kate. "We got an address from the cellphone. Let's go get him."

Kate read the address half expecting it to be Felix's. It wasn't though. It was an address down in lower Manhattan on Church Street. She raised her eyes to Declan and then to Murphy who was now amped up to go and get the guy. "He's not going to be there. He's far too smart for that. It's a set-up, Murphy. We go in that building and I'm telling you, he's going to blow it."

Annoyed with being slowed down, Murphy barked, "What do you expect us to do then? We can't sit around here with a location on the guy and do nothing."

"We have to clear the building first," Declan said, stepping forward and taking charge. "We need to know more about the location before we go storming down there."

Kate pulled her cellphone from her pocket. She typed in the address and came back with a six-story building that was for sale. It looked from the information that the building had been cleared of tenants and would be a construction project for the buyer. Kate breathed a sigh of relief that no one else was in the building. She explained the information she found and then showed the photo from the real estate listing. "Let's call Leo and get the bomb squad in there. We can head there ourselves right now. Send in uniforms too and clear the area."

"You don't think he will blow it in the process?"

Kate wasn't sure but it was a risk they were going to have to take. "I think no matter what we do, he could detonate a bomb. Let's be as safe as possible and at least clear the area of civilians."

They all agreed on that. With a quick call to Tony, Murphy detailed the plan to the NYPD and got some uniformed cops on the way to the address. Murphy stressed that they shouldn't go anywhere near the building but to clear the area as quickly as they could. Declan, meanwhile, called Leo and updated him. Leo said he was on it and would bring together the bomb squad from the NYPD and New York State Police. It would be a joint effort.

Kate knew the whole thing was a set-up. She just didn't know the bomber's next move. She was sure that the bomber knew that by calling, the call would be traced. He was drawing them there. *What other choice did she have?*

Thirty minutes later, Kate and Declan stood at a far perimeter. The NYPD uniformed cops had done a good job of clearing the area, evacuating surrounding buildings, and setting up a wide enough perimeter away from the building in question. They had closed two whole blocks of Church Street going in both directions. Depending on the size of the bomb, Kate and Declan could still be standing in a blast zone, but they had refused to be pushed back any farther.

They stood with Tony and Murphy and watched as Leo manipulated the controller that navigated the tactical robot that was in the building seeking out explosives. The robot could travel over all sorts of terrain, manipulate objects with its robotic arm, and sample potentially contaminated areas. Its most important feature was that it was used to protect human life.

Leo called out as he cleared each floor. He had started in the basement as that's where the bomb at Raven Hall had been placed. When that was cleared, they all breathed a sigh of relief and then went back to holding their breaths as the robot went to the next floor.

Kate wasn't sure how long they had been standing there. She knew the bomber was watching them. She could feel his presence hovering over the scene. She had asked uniformed cops to search the adjacent areas. If the bomber was going to remote detonate, he'd be close by watching them. Kate looked out over the sea of bystanders, people who had been asked to leave their apartments and offices in the middle of the day. It was easy to see the people who hadn't been working, their casual wear standing out among men and women in business attire. All of them had the same look of strain and worry on their faces.

This area of lower Manhattan had been decimated when the World Trade Towers collapsed after a terrorist attack destroyed them. Kate assumed some were reliving the horror of that day as they stood there hoping there wouldn't be another explosion.

Kate's eyes landed on one woman whose face had gone pale and her eyes stared blankly at the building under investigation. She wiped a single tear that ran down her cheek and then lowered her eyes to the ground. She silently mouthed something as she stood there. Kate assumed it was a prayer. She averted her eyes so the woman could pray without being watched. If Kate had been religious at all, she might have said a prayer of her own. She was sure Declan's parents were doing enough praying for all of them. She imagined that as soon as Iris heard the news, she settled into her hotel and got out her rosary. Kate wished she had a stronger spiritual side, but years of seeing life-shattering destruction dulled any sense of faith her parents had instilled in her.

"He almost has the whole building cleared," Declan said, bumping her arm. "Are you listening?"

"What?" Kate said, looking up at him. She had heard him, but it took a moment for the words to register. "Cleared," she repeated more to herself. "The building is almost clear."

No sooner were the words out of Kate's mouth when the first shot rang out. Then a volley of shots from a high-powered semi-automatic rifle followed sending them all scrambling for safety.

CHAPTER 23

eclan's reflexes were faster than Kate's. He pivoted from where he stood, drew his weapon, and fired twice toward the third-floor window of the building directly behind them. Kate had reached for her service Glock but her fingers never reached it. She had been shoved back by Murphy to the brick wall of the building. Declan followed quickly after. They all spun around looking for Tony. He had been standing right near them when the initial shots were fired.

"Tony!" Kate called and then spotted him on the ground not far from where they had been standing. A puddle of blood formed under him and seeped out from each side. Kate started to run toward him but someone dragged her back as shots rang out again, preventing her from going out and dragging his body back to safety. "We can't just leave him there," she yelled to Declan and Murphy, who was already on a walkie-talkie calling in for support and medical assistance.

Declan ran along the brick building and headed for the front door. Kate followed him, trying her best to keep up. She made the mistake of turning her head toward the crowd and seeing several people including two uniformed cops on the ground motionless.

Kate stepped through the door behind Declan as a volley of shots rang out again. Her mind had no time to process what was happening. All she knew was they had to get to the shooter and stop them. Declan hit the stairs in the foyer and took them two at a time. Kate had her gun drawn covering their rear.

"Third floor, Kate. He's on the third floor." Declan didn't slow down. If anything, he picked up speed as the floor got closer. He turned the corner at the top of the stairs and headed for the front of the building. They had their vests on but that didn't prevent a head wound.

"Declan," Kate called but had nothing to say other than to caution him and that wasn't needed. As she got to the landing, motion in the stairwell above her caught her attention. As Declan hurried into one room, Kate locked her eyes on the stairwell above. She leaned into the banister and looked up as a shot came from above, missing her by inches. "He's heading upstairs!" she called to Declan before launching herself forward and running to the next set of stairs.

"Where? Where, Kate?" Declan screamed, coming up the stairs behind her, his face red and features tight.

Kate pointed to the ceiling. "He shot at me once from above and took off again up the stairs. There's probably roof access and he can jump from one building to the next." It was the only escape that Kate assumed he had. Declan brushed past her and climbed faster. She noticed his limp but he seemed to fight through it.

Declan made it to the top first and then to a smaller set of stairs in the back of the building that led to the roof access door. "Cover my back," he said to her as he kept his gun ready in front of him. He got right up to the door and put his shoulder into it. As the door creaked open, a shot rang out. Declan jumped back as the bullet pinged off the metal door. "He's out there."

Declan yelled for the shooter to surrender, telling him that cops were all around and there was no escape. There was no response, not even another shot. After a moment, Declan tried the door again, and this time it wasn't met with bullets. He swung it open farther and stepped out onto the roof. He kept a good shooting stance as he inched his way forward.

Kate followed him and once her feet hit the roof, she yelled directions for him to surrender as Declan had done before. It was met with silence and a frustrated groan from Declan.

"He's gone, Kate."

"No, he can't be gone, Declan." Kate didn't lower her gun as she scanned around the rooftop. There was a small table and two chairs but nothing else. She looked in every direction but saw no one. She expected to see the shooter jumping roofs and getting away. "He can't just vanish. Where is he?"

Declan leaned over with his hands on his knees, catching his breath – more out of shock and frustration than being winded. He righted himself and cursed a long string. "What just happened, Kate? What just happened?"

Kate didn't know. She struggled to find the words but nothing came. The bomber had drawn them there and opened fire on them. It was off his pattern and none of it made sense other than retaliation for still pursuing him.

"All clear here," a cop called from an adjacent building's roof. He must have had the same thought as Kate – he'd escape by jumping roofs.

"You didn't see anyone coming down the stairs while you were headed up?" Declan asked, walking to the edge where the two buildings nearly met.

"Nobody," the cop said, "the whole stairway was clear. Did you get eyes on him?"

"Only for a brief second when I opened the roof access door. He immediately shot at me and I had to pull back my position. I didn't see his face, but he was dressed all in black, AR-15 gun, and there was something silver on his wrist, a watch maybe. It's what I saw as I was closing the door. It glinted in the sun."

The cop nodded and then barked orders to his men to continue to search the surrounding buildings. "You going to search that building?"

Declan nodded. "We'll take care of it."

Kate had already begun to search the rooftop. It was sparse. Some rooftops in New York City have everything a backyard would have including hot tubs and outdoor grills. This rooftop didn't look like anyone came up here. Even the table and two chairs had rusted. Kate walked a grid on the roof looking for shell casings or any other debris the shooter might have left. She had just about given up hope of finding anything when she walked behind the brick chimney on the far part of the roof diagonal to the door. There she found it – the shooter's means of escape. A metal roof hatch.

"Declan, over here!" she called from her position. "I think I found out how he got away."

"What is it, Kate?" he asked after finishing up with the cop. His face was still red and a row of sweat formed at his hairline. When Kate pointed down at the hatch, he cursed.

Kate leaned over to pull open the hatch but her hand froze as Declan screamed for her to stop. She angled her head to look at him with her hand still hovering over the handle. "What?"

"He could have rigged it with explosives."

Kate righted herself, frustrated that they seemed stymied at every step. "In that short amount of time? How would that even be possible?" In truth, Kate knew he had enough time. He might have gone to the hatch quickly, but they had given him at least five minutes head start while they searched the roof and Declan spoke to the cop. It was more than enough time to rig a bomb to the hatch.

Declan remained steadfast. "I trust nothing at this point, Kate. Let's go back inside and search the back of the building for the other side of this hatch. There will be access from the inside."

As they headed back toward the door, shock and adrenaline started to wear off and Kate zeroed in on the sounds at the scene – people were still screaming, cries could be heard, and a siren wailed. In the heat of the moment, she had blocked out all of that. That was often the case. For her, the playlist of most intense gunbattles and traumatic events was often the hum of white noise. Some people didn't lose their sense of hearing like that, but Kate assumed she used whatever energy it took to listen in other areas.

Kate tugged on the back of his shirt. "Did you see that Tony was down? Murphy was calling in for help when we came inside the building."

"No," Declan said, shaking his head in disbelief. "I didn't see that. Was he hurt badly?" He opened the door, looked inside, and moved over to let Kate step in first.

She turned as they took the few steps down to the floor. "It looked like he was shot and had lost a good deal of blood. I don't know if he was alive or dead, Declan. There were several people down on the ground like that as we entered the building. I tried not to focus on it."

Declan came down the rest of the steps and then stepped in front of Kate, leading the way down the narrow hallway. He took a left down another hall, walking toward the back of the building. "What happened out there, Kate? I was prepared for an explosion not an ambush like that. I thought the cops had cleared these buildings?"

Kate didn't know and was trying to process it all as best she could. "The cops were supposed to clear this building. They said they did. It was inside the perimeter they had set up. This guy knows the area better than we do and he slipped in and out without being caught." Kate walked holding her gun by her side. She didn't want to holster it just yet. She followed Declan down the hall and they stopped when they reached a door that had been left slightly ajar.

Declan toed it open slightly, enough to see inside. He leaned to one side and then the other trying to get a better look. Then all at once, he shoved Kate back, cursing. "There's a bomb rigged to the hatch, Kate, just like I suspected. Let's get out of here."

Kate turned and took off in a sprint with Declan right behind her. As quickly as they had entered the building, they left. Kate kept waiting for an explosion to propel her forward and shatter her surroundings, but they reached the sidewalk without incident.

Kate burst through the door onto the street. Her eyes were assaulted with the carnage left behind from the shooting. She didn't know where to look, each place her gaze landed was more horrific than the last. There were several bodies on the ground with white sheets placed over them. Medics worked on other people and carried them on stretchers to waiting ambulances.

"Back!" Declan shouted coming out the door right behind her. "There's a bomb in this building. Back! We have to get back."

Medics working on those who had been shot scrambled to finish what they were doing and transport the injured to waiting ambulances. Uniformed cops frantically shoved people back and shouted for people to clear the area. Members of the bomb squad led by Leo ran to the building.

"Where is it?" Leo asked and then shouted orders to the squad behind him. Leo refocused his attention as Declan explained where the bomb could be found.

"Got it. We'll take care of it." Leo and his team suited up with protective gear and then entered the building alone as Kate and Declan moved back with the rest of the cops and civilians.

CHAPTER 24

Kate stood across the street far enough away from the building to be safe in case the bomb detonated. Declan stood next to her with his mouth slightly agape as he took in the scene for the first time. Kate had told him what to expect, but she could see now that words didn't do justice to seeing the scene firsthand. Declan started to say something and then stopped. He ran a hand down his face and turned away.

"I know," Kate said as they shared a silent moment. There was nothing else they could say. The destruction that the shooting caused exacerbated an already horrific situation. Every nerve-ending Kate had tingled with fear and apprehension. It also made her more determined than ever to make sure the killer paid. She was even okay pulling the trigger and making sure he paid with his life.

"Kate! Declan!" Murphy called from their right. He rushed toward them, shoving other cops aside with the walkie-talkie still in his hand. "We have sixteen people hit, seven deceased. I saw the bomb squad rushing into the building. What's going on?"

Declan updated him and they shared a moment of frustration and anger at what had occurred. "I nearly caught him but he fired at me on the roof and then disappeared. I didn't even get off a shot. Once Leo is done, we need to get back into that building and search the third-floor room."

Declan pointed across the street to the building that had brought them down there, the one Leo had been clearing when the shooting started. "What did Leo find? Was it rigged?"

"No. It was a set-up all along. Leo found a phone sitting on the floor at the top level of the building. There was a note that said, *Gotcha. The Fuse*. We were played, but there was still nothing else we could have done. We had to follow the lead down here. How were we supposed to know a serial bomber would turn into a mass shooter? That's not how it's usually played."

"It's not," Kate said, angry with herself. They were expecting a bombing and Fuse had pivoted and shot at them instead. He was one step ahead of them the whole time, and even with all her skill and experience, she felt out of her depth. "I didn't read the situation correctly. I can't seem to get a good profile on him. The notes seem like they are from a woman and then we got the lead on Lily, which we still don't have pinned down. Now, this," she said, gesturing with her hand toward the carnage. "I just don't know…"

Murphy put his hand on her shoulder to steady her. "Kate, no one expects you to do this on your own. You've got a whole team behind you and none of us were expecting this. I've been doing this job for twenty-five years and I've never seen anything like it. Cut yourself some slack." He turned to Declan. "You seem to be the only one who had eyes on him. Did you get any kind of description you can share?"

Declan gave Murphy the overview, which wasn't much. "It was a flash – a second or two if that. I couldn't pick him out of a lineup if you wanted me to. I got a better look at the gun than anything else." Declan ran a hand across his forehead, wiping the beads of sweat away. "What happened? I thought the building was cleared."

Murphy waved over a young cop who had been standing off to the side. Introductions were made and the young man explained, "We cleared that whole building. When we arrived, several people were home. We got the building superintendent to walk us through the place. We knocked on doors and then told the people who were home to leave. In the units where no one answered, he unlocked the doors and we double-checked to make sure they were clear. There were two units on the third floor that were vacant. We asked him to unlock those and we stepped in and saw they were empty and we left. In hindsight, someone could have been hiding but those doors were locked. I spoke to the building superintendent after the shooting and he had no idea how the person would have had access, but clearly, they did."

The young cop looked dismayed by the whole thing and Declan offered words of encouragement. "You did everything you were supposed to do. I don't think I would have searched an empty apartment. Hindsight is twenty-twenty. You were only supposed to get people out safely and that's what you did."

"I know. I feel awful like I could have stopped him."

"No," Kate said. "None of us could have. He would have found a way. If it wasn't that building, it would have been another."

When the officer walked away, Declan said, "He's going to need some counseling. We better make sure he speaks to someone."

"Maybe we can ask Tony…" Kate's hand flew to her mouth, upset with herself that with everything going on she hadn't asked about his status yet. "As I was headed into the building, I saw that he was shot. Did he make it?"

"He's at the hospital." Murphy lowered his head. "He lost a lot of blood. He took a hit to his abdomen. They aren't sure he'll make it. I sent a cop with him who is going to update me. I'll let you know as soon as I know anything."

"How many from law enforcement are injured or deceased?" Declan asked, letting his eyes focus on white sheets covering bodies lying in the road.

"Two deceased uniformed cops and five injured including Tony. This killer wasn't only after cops. He killed and injured civilians. This was a planned attack."

Kate had assumed as much. He lured them down here, and when their focus was on the building where they had suspected the bomb might be, he ambushed them. Kate didn't have to wonder about the motive. He had made himself clear on the phone – *stop chasing me*. This was the result of them refusing to comply with his order. He knew they'd track the phone to lower Manhattan. They were lucky more people hadn't been injured or killed. This attack was worth him nearly getting caught. He had been serious about his threat. Kate's heart rate quickened thinking about Declan's family and hoping they had already made it to safety.

Declan gestured toward the building. "Once Leo gives the all-clear, we need to search the place. I want a crime scene tech to go over everything. Kate and I touched the door to the roof, but they still might be able to pull off other prints." He hitched his jaw toward the scene. "There are countless shell casings that need to be collected and dusted for prints. We need to see if there are cameras down here too. Maybe we got lucky and got the guy on camera."

"Already on that. I'm waiting for the call back from the city to see where the nearest cameras are located. The media is also calling us for a briefing." Murphy zeroed in on Kate. "What do we want to say?"

There was a whole lot Kate wanted to say including issuing a dire public warning to the universities. If this didn't get their attention now, she wasn't sure what would. "This is a game-changer. I want to go public with everything we have so far, still holding back the bomb material info as we did in the beginning. This was a strike at the heart of law enforcement and we are going to strike back even harder."

"I agree," Murphy said. "I'll get a press conference together. The mayor's office wants to be briefed so I'll take care of that. Do you want to see the statement before I go live with it?"

Kate trusted him. "That's not necessary, but I'm sure Spade will want an FBI representative at the press conference. Let me connect with him and see what he wants to do. I also need to go back and interview Felix again before Declan and I leave for Boston."

"You're still going?" Murphy asked, drawing back with surprise in his voice.

Although he seemed uncertain about her going, Kate couldn't tell whether he thought it was a good idea or not. "Fuse is going to strike again. We need to follow every lead no matter where it takes us and right now, this is all we have. All we may end up doing is ruling out Robert and Tess Hudson, but it's at least a step forward. We need to catch him before he does any more damage."

Leo walked out of the building a moment later with his squad behind him – two of them carrying the container with the inactive bomb. His squad went to the truck and Leo came over to give them the all-clear. "We contained the bomb. Had you pulled open that latch on the roof it would have blown. We cleared the rest of the building and didn't find anything else, thankfully. You're free to go in and search. There's debris near the window he was shooting from and at least two shell casings on the roof."

Kate asked, "Once he came down that hatch, any idea where he went?"

Leo pointed back toward the building. "There's a back stairwell. Makes no sense to me why the hatch is there, probably a holdover from earlier in the building's history. It doesn't seem to have much use nowadays."

Declan turned to Kate and asked her if she was ready to search the building. She asked if Murphy would join them. He said he'd take care of the media and update the crime scene techs before they went in. He was still waiting for the additional medical examiner support as well. With Tony down, Murphy had assumed the role of coordinator and that was fine by Kate.

She said, "Call us if the crime scene techs find anything of value."

Murphy nodded his head in agreement. "Let me know if Felix tells you anything else. I don't think we have enough for a search warrant, but if you want some eyes on him, I can get an NYPD surveillance unit on him."

Kate thought that might be a good idea. They still hadn't found Lily and Kate was sure that Felix knew where she was. If she was hiding in that house and a surveillance team were on it, they might find her.

Kate followed Declan back into the building through the same door they had raced through when the shooting erupted. It was the first time Kate had a chance to get a good look around. Inside the front door were stairs to the left and an area with rows of mailboxes and a garbage can straight ahead. Two elevators sat side by side on the right. She hadn't noticed them before.

It was a six-story building and she assumed most people didn't take the stairs very often. The staircase had a black metal railing and was only wide enough for two people to go up and down. If someone was carrying something, they wouldn't have been able to pass at the same time.

"Let's head to the back and see that staircase and follow the path he might have gone to get out of the building," Declan said, pointing to the hall near the elevators. "I assume he went straight out the back so I'd like to see what we're dealing with here."

It was Declan's scene for him to do what he pleased. Kate gave no argument and followed him down the hallway that had four apartments, two doors on each side. The hall ended at a brown door with a square window in it. Declan pulled it open and they were in a back area of the building that looked significantly older than the front. Kate assumed the building's super probably swept and painted the front to keep up appearances. The back gave away the building's age. There were marks on the walls, some graffiti, and scuff marks on the old linoleum floor. Across from the set of stairs was a door that went outside.

Declan opened it and stepped out into a small alleyway. The smell of garbage and rotting beer cans wafted through the air. Kate scrunched up her nose as the smell hit her. There was a blue dumpster and a smaller green recycling bin sitting off to the left. A half-bent chain link fence separated the properties. The alleyway ran from north to south behind the neighboring buildings.

"He could have gone anywhere from here." Declan cursed several times, leaned back against the brick wall of the building, and slammed his foot into it. He balled up his fist. For a brief moment, Kate thought he might punch the wall, but he brought his temper under control after a moment and ran his hands roughly through his hair. "We're failing, Kate, and we don't fail."

There wasn't much she could say because they were failing. They had gotten so far behind, Kate wondered if they'd ever catch him. This was the first time in their career that Kate didn't have any words of encouragement or comfort for Declan. Words weren't needed because when they locked their eyes on each other that alone spoke volumes.

After a few beats, Declan pushed himself off the wall. "Let's catch him and make him pay."

CHAPTER 25

Two hours later, Kate stood on Felix's porch waiting for him to answer the door. Declan had insisted he come with her and waited down the block. They had decided to give the appearance that Kate was there alone.

The door creaked slowly open and Felix stood there with confusion on his face. "Did you want something else, Agent Walsh?"

"I'd like to speak to you again if you're amenable to that. We are about to leave Manhattan and I'd like to chat with you before I go. I don't know when I'll be back in the city." She waited for him to invite her inside, but he didn't budge. She broke his gaze and then looked him over. He had a bandage on his hand that wrapped around his palm and three fingers from his middle to his pinkie. "What happened there?"

He held it up for her to see better. "I was doing some work in the back of my home and cut it on some boards. I don't think I need stitches, but I cut it up pretty badly."

Kate wasn't sure she believed him. "Could I come in and talk to you?"

Felix leaned to the side to look beyond her. "Is your partner with you?"

"I'd like to speak to you alone if that's what you're asking." Kate stepped toward him, challenging him to let her inside. He moved out of the way and held the door open for her. She didn't wait for his offer to sit down. She went into the living room and took a seat where she had sat hours earlier. She would take a more direct approach with him this time.

Felix stood on the edge of the living room watching her. He didn't ask her to get up and didn't make a move to sit down.

Kate looked over at him. "The sooner we get this started, the faster I'll be gone. I'm sure you're not happy having to speak to the FBI twice in one day. I know I wouldn't be."

Felix hesitated for a moment longer and then slowly made his way into the room and sat down in the chair. "I'm not sure I can tell you any more than I told you earlier. I'm not the person you're looking for, Agent Walsh. I don't know what I can do to prove my innocence."

Of all the things Felix might have been, he wasn't innocent. Kate just didn't know what crimes he had committed yet. "You didn't tell me anything earlier besides a riddle that didn't make any sense. I'm here to allow you to start over with me. You're a highly intelligent man who knows more than the rest of us. I'd like you to enlighten me."

He furrowed his brow, not in anger but confusion. "What did your partner think of me? He didn't seem to like me much."

Kate observed him, calculating what answer would get her closer to the truth. She chose her words carefully. "Agent James didn't think you had much worth exploring. He was against me coming to speak to you at the start and he was definitely against me coming back. A big waste of time is how he phrased it. I have to be honest with you, Felix, you're more intelligent than you let on in that meeting. I think you wanted Agent James to think you weren't mentally up to the task. I don't think you believe half the stuff you spout online. I think you do it for the sheer enjoyment of getting a rise out of people – stirring the pot so to speak."

Felix had no response for several moments and then slowly a sly smile spread across his face. "You're perceptive, Agent Walsh. Your partner is like a big dumb jock. I'm sure he serves a purpose sometimes, but he didn't understand me. I acted how I assumed he wanted me to act. I gave him what he expected."

Felix sat back and crossed his legs. He smacked his lips. "I'm not going to tell you what I believe and what I put out there for all the fish to feed on. That can still be my little secret. What I will say is that I don't like secret societies. That much is true. They are a cancer in America. Breeding grounds for poor leadership, wealth, and privilege. I'm quite enjoying seeing them knocked down a peg or two."

His eyes lit up as he said the words and Kate believed that he was happy watching all the destruction. She didn't know if he had been the cause of it. "Do you own any guns, Felix?"

"Guns?" he asked as if he hadn't heard the question. When Kate repeated herself, he said, "I've never needed a gun."

"That doesn't answer my question, does it? Do you own any guns, yes or no? It's a simple question." Kate knew from a search he didn't own any legally.

"No, Agent Walsh. I've never owned any guns nor are there any in my home. My parents didn't own guns and my grandfather had a hunting rifle. He liked to go upstate hunting in the winter. My grandmother thought it was dreadful, but women didn't have much say back then, so she lived with it and cooked venison for him after the kill." Felix opened his eyes wide. "Is there a reason you'd ask that?"

Kate leaned forward and locked her gaze on him. He held eye contact while she spoke evenly and calmly. "Did you hear about what happened in lower Manhattan? The bomber, who calls himself Fuse, ambushed the cops and bystanders after he called the police to speak to me. We traced the call like he knew we would, and when the bomb squad was sweeping a location for explosives, we were ambushed. You wouldn't happen to know anything about that, would you?"

Felix had recognition in his expression that Kate couldn't place. "I had nothing to do with that, Agent Walsh. I'd never attack law enforcement and innocent bystanders. It sounds like you've got this guy on the run. Why else would he attack like that?"

"He wants me to stop chasing him and will do whatever he can to stop me." She tucked her hair behind her ears and gave him a stone-cold stare. "Felix, I'm going to tell you what I told him. I'm not going to stop until I catch him, and when I do, I'll bring him to justice along with anyone else who helped him. I don't care how I bring him to justice either. Do you understand what I mean?"

"That you'd kill him if you have a legal opportunity to do so."

"That's right. I probably shouldn't admit this to you, but he's tried to kill me twice. If the time comes and I'm put in a position where it's my life or my partner's life and his, I will take a kill shot and not think twice about it. I might sleep better for it."

Felix's eyes fluttered up and he swallowed hard. "Have you ever killed anyone before?"

"In the line of duty, yes, I have."

It was clear Felix didn't know what to make of her. He tilted his head to one side and then the other, watching her. Kate had been quieter and softer when they interviewed Felix earlier. That had been part of the plan. Kate could twist her personality as needed, depending on the best course of action to elicit the information she needed. The softer approach hadn't worked. Felix had taken center stage and put on a show for them. Now, it was Kate's time to unmask him.

Felix laid a hand on his chest. "What do you think I know?"

"I want to know who is helping him because I know he isn't doing this alone. He has help whether those people realize they are helping him or not." Kate was sure Fuse could be a lone gunman and bomber, but she had said it to watch Felix's reaction. She wasn't surprised when she saw a flicker of recognition. "That's right, Felix. I know this man had help. When I find those who helped him even in a small way, they will pay for the crimes. If you think he will protect those people, he won't."

Felix got up from the chair and went to the window at the end of the couch and looked out. He let out a breath and it was like watching all the air in a balloon deflate. His whole demeanor changed. "Agent Walsh," he said slowly, "I know you're hoping to get me to confess or slip up and say something you can use to find the person responsible for these actions. I don't know who it is."

Kate repositioned to look directly at him. "I hear a *but* in that statement."

Felix shifted his eyes to the side to focus on her. "As you know, I had been running a message board, but there was a second one that I shut down a few weeks ago. There were threats made that I didn't take seriously at the time. People say things on the internet. But the threats were what's happening now – bombs blowing up secret societies and their members being killed and injured."

Kate tried not to react – like a skittish horse, she needed to wait for him to come to her. When he remained quiet for a few moments longer, she asked, "I'm assuming I haven't seen the one you're talking about now."

"That's correct. People had to have permission to join. I vetted people who were interested in the topic. They mostly came from the message board you saw. I set it up for people who wanted more privacy and to speak more freely."

"About what?"

Felix turned away from her and stared out the window. "How to stop secret societies, fraternities and the like. It was meant as an educational forum at first, but then so many people joined who had either been hurt by these groups or their children had been hurt. It wasn't the typical kind of conspiracy stuff I normally post. These were real people who had real problems." He turned to look at Kate. "They made real threats."

"If you vetted the message board members then surely you have some names for me. You must have your suspicions about who could be doing this."

Felix remained quiet for an uncomfortably long time. Then he sat down on the edge of the couch near Kate. "I have a name for you but I don't know if this is the person that you're after. Robert Hudson. He lost his son in a hazing incident. His wife, Tess, might also be involved. She was always more vocal than he was, but he said he owns weapons, knows how to build bombs, and has the resources to pull off crimes like this. They live in Boston, I think. That's where his IP address came from, but people can mask that easily enough."

Kate gave no recognition that this was a name she already knew. "Have you spoken to Robert or Tess directly?"

"In person or on the phone, no. I've had several conversations with them over the message board but not in a few weeks. I didn't warn anyone I was shutting down the boards. I woke up one morning after a night of reading a lot of vitriol and threats of violence and shut it down." Felix cradled his injured hand with the other, possibly trying to garner some sympathy. "You have to understand, Agent Walsh, I didn't think the threats were serious. That's why I never called the police. I figured if I shut down the outlet for their threats, they might get past it. Sometimes dwelling on things for too long and having a forum with others egging you on can push people to do things they'd never otherwise think of doing. I thought I was doing the right thing shutting it down."

Kate wasn't going to let him off the hook. "When the bombings started, you didn't feel the need to call the police and share the information you had?"

"I don't know for sure that it was someone from my message board. I didn't feel like I had credible information anyone could do anything with," he said weakly. "I didn't think a mother and father would kill other children."

Kate understood what he was saying but it didn't excuse him. "Help me to understand why, when I gave you the opportunity earlier today to tell me what you knew, you said nothing other than some riddle about the person who didn't die. I still don't know what that means."

"It could still be him," Felix said under his breath.

Kate wasn't sure she had heard him correctly and asked him to repeat himself. When he said it again, she asked, "Who?"

Felix turned to Kate and his look burned through her. He was on the verge of telling her. He turned back to the window. "There was another guy on the private message board. He made threats and talked about bombs like Robert Hudson. He alluded to the person who didn't die."

Now it was finally making sense for Kate. "Does that guy have a name?"

"I never knew it and he only used a screen name. Sicherung. It's German, I believe. I was never able to locate him. His IP address kept changing. Eventually, I gave up."

Kate asked him to spell the screen name and when he did, she entered it into a translation app on her phone. When she saw the translation, her head snapped up. "Have you spoken with this person recently?"

"No. Not since the last night on the message board. It was his posts that got me the most concerned. Robert had a different screen name but for all I know they are the same person."

Felix looked back at Kate with an expression of guilt. "That private board was getting too aggressive even for me. It wasn't conspiracy anymore, these were threats."

With the message board gone, Kate had no idea if it could still be mined for data. "Can you access the message board that you shut down?"

"No. It's gone. I deleted the whole thing."

Kate stood and went to him. "Do you still have the computer that you used to access the message board?"

Felix pointed to the ceiling. "I have it upstairs in my office. Does that matter?"

Kate was forming a plan in her mind, but she couldn't execute it there. "Don't touch any of your electronics, got it?" When Felix readily agreed, Kate asked, "You said for all you know Sicherung and Robert Hudson are the same person. Why do you think that?"

Felix stared at her like he wasn't sure what to say. "It was just a feeling. Those two never directly interacted."

"Listen closely," Kate said, her voice stern. "You have two options right now. I know the one I'd pick if I were you. You can cooperate with FBI computer forensics or I can arrest you for obstruction of justice. Take your pick."

Felix didn't hesitate as genuine fear flashed in his eyes. "I'll cooperate."

"You just made your life a lot easier. An FBI computer forensics expert will be here soon. In the meantime, we'll be watching you." As Kate turned to leave, she remembered one more thing. Turning back, she said, "I know that you know Lily. I need to find her. Where is she and how is she involved?"

"She's not involved, not in the way you think." Felix licked his lips nervously and held up his injured hand. "She was here, but she left. After you came here today, she tried to leave. I wanted her to stay and confide in you because she wouldn't tell me what was happening. We struggled and she got the better of me." He raised his eyes to Kate. "That's the truth, Agent Walsh. I wish I knew where she went because I'm concerned for her safety. I think she knows who the bomber is."

Kate believed him. "Do you know anything about the notes that were sent?"

"I didn't know anything until you mentioned her name on the news, and when I asked her about it, she said she did what she had to do."

Kate still didn't understand one thing. "Why was she here?"

Felix rubbed his eye and sighed. "Lily and I met on the message board. She told me that she was supposed to meet someone in Manhattan, and when they didn't show up, she was staying in some drug house. I gave her a place to stay until she could sort it out. That was all, I swear to you. She crashed here, but I didn't see or speak to her much. She came and went as she wanted and never told me what she was doing. I regretted letting her stay almost as soon as she got here."

Kate would have to take him at his word. She was glad she came back. "FBI computer forensics will be here soon. Cooperate or else," she warned him again as she headed for the door and left.

CHAPTER 26

"Sicherung," Kate said, badly pronouncing the word as she met Declan a block from Felix's house. He had been watching from the corner, leaning casually against the metal pole of a street sign. As she approached, he stood upright and walked toward her.

"Come again?" Declan asked, his eyebrows raised.

Kate said the word slower the second time, still butchering the pronunciation. But that didn't matter as much as the English translation. "Fuse," she said with force after repeating the word in German again. "That's what the word means and it was the screen name of a guy who made threats about using bombs on Felix's private message board. Robert Hudson also made threats and said he knew how to make bombs. We've got two viable suspects – one known and the other unknown right now. For all we know, they are both Robert Hudson. We need to get FBI computer forensics in here. I don't want local. I want Ditch to handle this."

Declan made a sour face. "Last I heard he was on a job in Uzbekistan."

Kate wasn't deterred. They got pulled off one job and sent to another all the time. "I'm calling Spade. There's no one better than Ditch."

Ditch – Kevin Detrick at birth – was a thirty-seven-year-old hacker who had been arrested by the FBI. In addition to being wanted by the U.S. government, he was wanted by the Saudis, the Chinese, and the

Russians for a swath of international espionage, money laundering, and insider trading. He had made fools out of some of the most powerful leaders around the globe and they'd literally have Ditch's head if given the chance.

Spade had sprung him, and as they say, made him an offer he couldn't refuse. For the past two years Ditch had been the computer forensics expert on Spade's team. He was Spade's secret weapon. Kate wasn't sure what else he did for Spade, but if there was a computer forensics job to be done, Spade didn't need to send in a whole team – he sent in Ditch.

Kate wasn't sure how the man had gotten his nickname and she didn't care. At first, she had balked at the idea of working with a known criminal, but once she saw the results, she shut her mouth and let Ditch keep right on doing what he did best. Declan never had qualms about the man's background, but his interactions with Ditch were less than cordial.

Declan pointed back toward Felix's house as she called Spade. "There's an unmarked car down the road set up for surveillance. Do you want me to call them off?"

"Leave them for now." Kate started to call Spade but then stopped. "If you could, go get one of them and have them watch Felix and make sure he doesn't mess with his computer equipment. He shut down the message board but still has the laptop he used to access it. I need to make sure that between now and when Ditch arrives, he doesn't do anything to it. I already told Felix we'd be watching him and that FBI computer forensics were on their way. He agreed."

Declan agreed but looked at her skeptically. "It's not a quick flight from Uzbekistan. Don't you think someone in the FBI computer forensics here in Manhattan could handle this just as well?"

Kate ignored him, walked down the block, and called Spade. He answered with a sharp greeting as he always did and then softened his tone as he asked if she and Declan were all right after the events of the day.

Kate assured him they were fine and then she gave him a progress report. When she was done answering his questions, Kate told him what she needed. "We need Ditch here now." Before Spade could argue or tell her that his best asset was out of the country, she explained, "The message board is down now. It was deleted weeks ago. I need Ditch to take a deep dive on the computer that Felix has and see if he can hack the system somewhere somehow to resurrect this message board and scrub it for information." Kate wasn't even sure it was possible. She was anything but tech-savvy.

After Kate finished pleading her case, with a trace of sarcasm in his voice, Spade asked, "Can I respond now, Kate?"

Embarrassed that she had spoken over Spade, her cheeks warmed. "Sorry, sir. I wanted you to know how important it was that we have Ditch on this."

"You're in luck, Kate. Ditch arrived back on U.S. soil last night. I'll have him wheels up within the hour." As Kate thanked him profusely, Spade interrupted. "Make sure to meet him before you take off to Boston. Get him a steak and a bottle of Merlot as a thank you and he'll be as compliant as he gets. You know him, Kate. He likes his ego stroked."

"Got it, sir, and thank you." Kate hung up feeling for the first time that they might have a break in the case. She hurried back down the block to Declan who was walking toward her with one of the cops. He said hello to Kate and told her that he'd secure the property in question. He went up the stairs to Felix's house and was let in without hesitation or incident.

When Kate and Declan were alone, with excitement in her voice, she said, "We got him, Declan." She relayed Spade's message about what they needed to have in Ditch's hotel room for when he arrived.

Declan yawned and rolled his eyes. "Anything for the diva. The world has to roll out a red carpet for a man who should be doing life in a federal penitentiary. God forbid he should act grateful that we saved him from assassination."

Kate couldn't help but smile. Ditch may have been a genius hacker, but he was moodier than anyone Kate had ever met. He acted like he was a gift to women and in some ways, he was, with his blue eyes, chiseled jaw, swoop of dirty blond hair, and chiseled abs. He grew up in California and he was a bad boy surfer to his core. Declan thought it cliché. But Ditch was not only an attractive man but had the intelligence and charm to match.

"You don't have to be so jealous," Kate teased as they headed back to their hotel to check out.

"Not jealous," Declan said with his chin held high, not looking at her. "As I said, I don't understand why we have to cater to him. Spade kept him out of prison and he should be humble and happy the FBI is doing that much for him. What if I demanded a steak and wine to do my job?"

Kate couldn't argue with that. But Ditch had skills few had. "I don't like it much more than you do. Ditch has skills we need and there's a premium on that. If all I have to give him are steak and wine, it seems like a small price to pay to catch this killer."

"As long as that's all you have to give him."

"What's that supposed to mean?" Kate asked even though she knew exactly what he was hinting at. "I don't still have a crush on him if that's what you're trying to say."

Declan kept walking and hadn't turned to look at her, so Kate had a hard time seeing his expression. She didn't know if he was serious or teasing her. When he spoke next, she knew that he was trying to get a rise out of her. "So," he said, holding back a smile, "you admit you had a crush on him."

Kate realized then what she had admitted. She blushed. "For like five minutes. You better not say anything."

"He knows, Kate. Everyone knows." Declan looped his arm around her. "I forgive you. I know you have a crush on me now. We just need to make sure it's less obvious to everyone."

Kate shrugged off his arm and walked a bit faster, leaving Declan behind her.

"I was kidding, Kate. Are you okay?" he asked, catching up to her when they stopped at the corner and waited for the light to change so they could cross.

"I'm okay, but I can't focus on anything other than the case. It feels wrong to share a lighthearted moment with you when Tony is in the hospital fighting for his life and when so many people have already been murdered by this monster."

"Monster?" Declan asked, pulling back in surprise. "I've never heard you talk that way. You've always lectured me about using language like that."

It was true that Kate didn't like when other cops or FBI agents called killers monsters or similar language. Monsters were mythical and the kinds of people they were dealing with were human and could be caught and brought to justice. She didn't like dehumanizing human acts no matter how horrible they might be. This time was different. "I'm feeling what I think the rest of you have felt before when working on other cases. It's unimaginable to me that someone could create this kind of destruction and destroy so many lives and for what? Why would someone do something like this, Declan? It makes no sense to me."

It was Declan's turn not to have any words of encouragement for her. The reality was they were both feeling beat down by the case. "Let's get back to the hotel and get Ditch set up so he can do what he does best. Maybe all we need right now is another one of our team members."

Kate didn't want to talk about her foul mood. "How's your leg holding up? We've been walking a lot. I've seen you limping."

Declan tugged on his pant leg and pulled it up a little. "It's better than I thought it would be. I've got some swelling and it's starting to get a little stiff."

"I'll drive on the way back and you can put the seat up and prop it up with some ice."

They made it back to the hotel and cleaned their room, throwing clothes and other personal items into their suitcases. They took showers and dressed in fresh clothes for the trip home. By that time, Spade had called to tell her that Ditch had landed and was in a cab on his way to the hotel.

Kate ordered room service for him including a steak just the way he liked it and the bottle of wine he wanted. It would be delivered to his room after he checked in. That should satisfy him, at least for the time being.

Kate and Declan would check in with him before they left. She was hoping this was the last time they'd be in Manhattan on this case.

Declan brought their luggage to the car while Kate stopped in Ditch's room after he texted her and told her that he had arrived and thanked them for the steak and wine. She knocked on his door and he answered wearing ripped jeans, a Grateful Dead tee-shirt, and green Converse that had seen better days.

"Kate, you're looking lovely as always," Ditch said, pushing blond locks off his forehead. He bowed and made a sweeping gesture as if welcoming her into a castle. "Welcome to my new home. Spade said I'm going to be here for a while."

Ditch had already thrown his opened suitcase on the floor. Clothes spilled out every which way. A white sock missing its mate had escaped to the floor next to the mess. Kate assumed he hadn't folded anything neatly and instead jammed everything in there. His suitcase was in stark contrast to his cases of computer equipment which were stacked neatly near the desk.

Ditch plopped down on the bed with his knees spread wide. He patted his thigh. "Why don't you sit down and tell me what I need to do. Then we can catch up."

Kate leaned back against the dresser. "Declan will be meeting us in a few minutes to go over everything."

Ditch looked up at her through strands of hair that had fallen back over his forehead. "Does he still want to kick my butt? He's got a real dislike of me that I haven't figured out. It's not like he's a Boy Scout. Stories I've heard about him, you'd think he'd have an appreciation about my rise to infamy."

Kate ignored all of it. "We need your expertise, Ditch," she said, leveling a serious look at him. Then she launched into the details of the case and what she was hoping he could find. She finished with the most important. "We barely have any suspects, Ditch, and the ones we have identified were all on a now-defunct message board. I need you to find them for me. While you're at it, I also need you to work with Investigator Murphy from the New York State Police. He's looking to see if there is some street camera footage of the guy who ambushed us. You might be able to work your magic on that system and find what no one else can."

"That sounds easy enough. Is this Felix guy a suspect?"

"I'm not sure what he is," Kate said, hoping that he wasn't. "He's eccentric but Declan doesn't trust him as much as I do. Not that I trust him, I just don't get the sense he's our suspect. He might be involved in some way. There is a cop over there now. Just watch your back."

Before Ditch could respond, someone knocked on the door. He stuck his tongue out at Kate and grumbled Declan's name. "Oh, speak of the devil," he said as he answered the door. "Kate was just complaining that she has you instead of me for a partner."

Declan didn't walk much beyond the door. He stood in the narrow entranceway and locked eyes with Kate who shook her head and offered him a smile. Then he leveled a look of disgust at Ditch. "Are you caught up on the case? Kate and I need to head back to Boston."

"Ditch has everything he needs," Kate said, walking toward them.

"Not everything I need." He winked at her. Then he turned back to Declan. "You take care of my Katie for me."

No one called Kate that except for Declan – it was a sign of affection between close friends, a pet name no one else used. Declan's back stiffened and before he could say anything, Kate shoved him back toward the door, thanking Ditch for his help and ordering him to call them with updates.

Once they were outside the room and a few feet down the hall, Declan hissed, "I don't like that guy. And what was he wearing? He looked like he came from a frat party."

"I know. Luckily, we only work with him remotely."

CHAPTER 27

Catching the first hint of morning light, Kate and Declan stood on the steps of her brownstone. They had crashed at a local Boston hotel the night before, concerned Fuse might have figured out Kate's address and rigged the place with explosives. They had called a colleague with the Boston Police Department, Det. Harris Briggs, who they had worked with on a previous case.

"You're getting me out here way too early," Briggs said, shaking Kate's hand and then Declan's. He stood about Kate's height, athletic build, dark eyes, and skin tone. His black hair was cropped close to his head. Unlike the last time they'd seen him, he'd traded in a clean shave for a salt and pepper beard. He ran his hand across his furry chin. "I was doing some undercover work the last few weeks. Got the case closed and can't part with it quite yet."

"It's a good look for you," Kate said and then pointed to her brownstone and explained the case and why she was calling out the bomb squad so early. She handed him her house keys.

Briggs took the keys. "Let me explain what you told me to the bomb squad captain and then we can meet down the road and get some coffee. I want to hear more about the case. I've been following the national news and have been pushing Harvard's administration to enact better safety measures. As I'm sure you know, they have their own ideas, and it hasn't been easy to get them to take this as seriously as they should. The press conference on the news last night should have lit a fire under them. You called them all out publicly and they can't avoid it now."

"Part of the challenge," Declan started, "is that some of these secret societies are not technically connected to the universities. The administration doesn't have a lot of say in what happens with them. Even if the warning is issued, it's up to the students to decide what to do."

Through a frustrated breath, Briggs said, "Let's talk strategy and see how I can help you."

Kate was glad that they had Briggs's support. He had been an asset in the previous case. It was why she felt the need to caution him. "This isn't like other cases we have worked, Briggs. This killer who calls himself Fuse has tried to kill us three times already – a bomb was planted in my car, he shot at us after drawing us to a location, and then he planted a bomb on the hatch of a roof. I'm sure he lured us up there hoping we'd follow him to where he had rigged the bomb. During the ambush, two officers were killed and others were shot including one of our task force members."

Briggs's expression went from shock to concern to anger in a flash of a few seconds. "That reason alone makes me want to help you take him down. My goal is to stop him before he gets to our city."

There wasn't anything else for Kate to say. "We'll meet you at the coffee shop at the end of the block." The place didn't need to be specified. Everyone in the local neighborhood had simply called it *the coffee shop at the end of the block*. It served a good cheap breakfast and strong coffee. The same guy had been running the place since Kate was in grade school. Her father would wake her up early on Sunday mornings and they'd walk to the Boston Public Garden and feed the ducks and then they'd stop for breakfast. Now the coffee shop and the bar next door had become a staple of Kate's life when she was in

Boston. Breakfast, lunch, and dinner were feet from her door if she didn't feel like cooking, which was often enough.

As they walked the short block, Declan remained quiet. He had been this way on the drive back to Boston, which Kate chalked up to being tired and his leg sore. He had been that way overnight in the hotel, too. Kate hadn't wanted to go to the house at two in the morning when they had arrived for fear it might have been rigged with explosives. She wanted the bomb squad out there to sweep the place. While she might have been taking extra precautions that weren't necessary, Declan had agreed with her.

Kate waved to the staff behind the counter and slid into a booth in the far back corner where they'd have some privacy. Declan sat across from her and pulled an eight-by-eleven glossy two-sided menu from its holder. He lowered his head and read it over while Kate watched him. After a moment, he realized that she wasn't looking at her menu.

Declan raised his head. "What's up, Kate? I can feel your eyes on me. You've been this way since we left Manhattan. The whole car ride you kept looking over and checking on me and last night when we went to sleep too. I'm fine."

"Fine is an answer people give when they are most definitely not fine. If you don't want to talk about it, tell me that. Don't shut me out in the middle of an investigation." Kate reached for a menu and Declan trapped her hand in his and brought it back to the table. They were holding hands, both leaning into the table looking at each other with the intensity of lovers, not work partners.

"If you must know," Declan said as his lips turned up at the sides, "I've been feeling guilty that I don't feel bad if my ex-wife gets blown up. When he threatened my family, you were the first person that flashed in my mind, and then my parents and my brothers. My ex wasn't even a thought in my head until you said her name. I started to feel like a terrible person that I didn't care if anything bad happened to her. That's what I've been thinking about – that I must have something wrong with me not to care about someone I was married to, that I had taken vows to love forever. I was thinking about how you're more important to me than she ever was. Then I felt like crap about it."

Kate ran her tongue across her lips, unsure of how to respond to him. It was a natural part of a divorce, she guessed. She had never made a vow to anyone and couldn't even imagine getting married. Kate wasn't even sure she was capable of that kind of emotion. When she couldn't take the tension between them any longer, she finally said, "I don't think you should feel guilty, Declan. Although, I understand why you do. It's not like you wish her harm. My opinion on it..." Kate stopped herself and reframed, "Do you want my opinion?"

"Of course."

"You were emotionally out of that marriage long before you physically left. It was constant fights about your work, which she knew going in. She had no problem living off the financial gain from your employment, but she never wanted to make any sacrifices. When you told her what was happening, did she even once ask if you were safe or how you were doing?"

Declan furrowed his brow and shook his head. "She never asked if I was okay. But that's typical. No matter how work went for me or how tough the case might have been, she never wondered or inquired how I was dealing with everything. Even when I got shot and was in the hospital, all she wanted to know was if it was going to impact her alimony payment."

Kate winced, horrified that it had been that bad for Declan. "That's not okay. I know you weren't the best husband but you certainly weren't the worst either. You were more married to work than her but no one deserves to be treated that coldly. I can understand why you don't have a lot of emotion left for her." Kate had been trying hard not to say Lauren's name as he had asked. She nearly slipped up a time or two.

"So, you don't think I'm completely messed up?"

Kate chuckled and tugged her hand out of his. "You can confirm with your therapist but you're probably sane enough." When she watched his face fall, she said, "It's probably perfectly normal given the circumstances. You can't be that messed up, Declan. You care about me and your parents. If you weren't feeling anything for anyone, then I'd be worried."

"Good," he said, letting the conversation drop. "I'm not going to worry about it anymore. I'm going to eat everything on this menu. I'm starving!" He growled as he said it and Kate's stomach growled with him.

They waited until Briggs arrived to order. He wasn't that hungry and only ordered coffee and a bagel with cream cheese while Kate and Declan both ordered eggs, bacon, pancakes, and home fries. Kate tried to remember when she had last eaten and couldn't pinpoint it. It was no wonder they were both famished.

As they waited for their food, Briggs asked questions about the investigation, and Kate and Declan took turns providing the details of what they knew so far. Declan also gave him a rundown of the different investigative bodies involved.

When they were done, Briggs asked the question that had been present in Kate's mind. "Where do you think Fuse will strike next?"

"I don't have any idea," Kate explained, with frustration apparent in her voice and written on her face. When she thought about him striking again, a knot formed in her stomach. "There's been no pattern that we've been able to discern. Sure, he's striking Ivy League schools, but the order in which he is choosing them is not a pattern we've been able to figure out."

Briggs sat with that for a moment. "He's hit three schools so far and that leaves five. Is there any meaning in the schools he's chosen so far?"

"Nothing adds up on this case," Kate admitted. "From where the bombings have happened to the sites he hasn't chosen. If we catch the guy and we understand him better, it might all make sense then. But hindsight, you know?"

Declan asked, "Is there a pattern that you see?"

"No pattern at all. That's the frustrating part." Briggs stopped for a moment while the server dropped off their coffee. He took the time to drop a creamer and two sugars into his before stirring it with his spoon and taking a sip. "I wondered if there was a geographic pattern starting in New Hampshire first and then to Ithaca. But it would have made more sense had he dropped down to Pennsylvania and New Jersey to hit the University of Pennsylvania and Princeton before hitting Colombia in Manhattan. Then wind his way back to New Haven and Providence, Rhode Island then finish at Harvard. There's not even a pattern in years the institutions were founded."

"You see what we're dealing with then," Kate said.

Briggs took another sip of his coffee and leaned into the table. "What about all the conspiracy theories around secret societies. Is there anything that connects the ones that have been targeted?"

Kate took a sip of her coffee and considered the question. "We haven't explored that angle at all. There's a general conspiracy about what these secret societies are up to – new world order and that kind of thing. I haven't read or heard anything that connects the particular ones that were chosen."

"Maybe that's an avenue to explore."

"You think that could be valuable?" Declan asked with a bit of skepticism. Before Briggs could answer, Declan went on. "The reality is we have had little time to be running down unproven claims. What we need to be focused on is preventing the next attack by catching the killer."

"You need to see what he sees," Briggs said drinking more of his coffee. "You said yourself the killer is a planner, methodical, and on a mission. His words. What's his mission then? What's the ultimate goal? Why these particular secret societies? He had many to choose from at each university. What's the connection with the ones he picked?"

Kate didn't know the answer and neither did Declan. But she wasn't buying anything related to a conspiracy theory. If there was a connection among them, it was grounded in logic. "I think the motive is a little more solid. We've not ruled out that we might be dealing with someone who has a serious psychosis that includes delusions. If that's the case, then no motive will make sense to us."

Declan turned his head to Briggs. "We have a computer forensic expert speaking to a conspiracy theorist right now and trying to resurrect data from the message board he once had. There were a handful of people who had made threats and he shut it down. It's not that we haven't considered conspiracy theories, we haven't had many leads to follow."

Briggs nodded his head along. "I want to help, so let me run with that angle. Let me see if I can find a connection among the three."

Declan agreed. "If you'd like to help with that feel free. Right now, the more ground we can cover the better."

The conversation was interrupted by Kate's ringing cellphone. She pulled it from her pocket and checked the screen. "This is Murphy with the New York State Police, who has been working the cases with us. Let me step outside and take this." She slid out of the booth and left Briggs and Declan sitting at the table.

"It's Kate," she said as she engaged the call and opened the door to the shop. She moved to the sidewalk and then found a quiet area at the corner of the building where she couldn't be overheard. "Do you have news for us?"

"I don't know," Murphy said, his voice constrained. "I'm not sure if this means anything or not. Do you remember how we said there were twenty-one dead at Raven Hall after we realized Finley Lloyd was still alive? There were nineteen students and then two staff."

"I remember," Kate said.

"My team has been running some background on everyone as you asked. It seems Andy Novak had a few connections to secret societies and not just Raven Hall. He graduated from Yale and had been a member of Scroll & Dagger. He got into quite a bit of trouble when he was there and was kicked out. I don't know the details only that he was forced out. Since then, he's had several jobs, including being the house manager at a few secret societies. It seems it's a life he can't get away from even as a grown man."

"What's the point? Novak is dead."

"His remains haven't been found, Kate," Murphy said with inflection. "We can't confirm that he was in Raven Hall when it exploded."

CHAPTER 28

"Are you sure?" Kate asked, her head spinning with thoughts and her stomach churning. She reached for the wall of the building for support. She had so many questions that it was hard to process where to start. The cars on the street in front of her stopped at the red light. A man in the first car glanced in her direction. Kate watched as the dark-haired man in his mid-forties turned up his lips and smiled at her. She shrank back against the building realizing then how unprotected and exposed she was standing there on the street. She half expected him to raise a gun and fire at her out the open window.

"Kate, are you there?" Murphy said, snapping Kate out of her spiral.

Kate turned her head away from the man in the car. "I'm sorry. I'm standing outside a coffee shop and I suddenly realized how exposed we all are. I had the Boston PD bomb squad sweep my home for bombs this morning. We slept at a hotel last night."

Murphy, his voice low and quiet, said, "You'll feel safe again. Once this is all over, I promise you'll get back to normal."

Kate didn't know if that was true or not, but the reality was what she was feeling didn't matter. Her only focus had to be on the case. "Andy Novak. Tell me again what you were saying." She did her best to focus only on Murphy's words and shut out the fear that had bubbled up inside her.

Murphy started again. "I have the official report from the medical examiner. Twenty people have been accounted for in Raven Hall on the night of the bombing. Everyone who was there has been identified. There are no more unknown remains, Kate. We are missing Andy Novak."

Kate thought surely they had to be missing something. She didn't want to be morbid but the facts had to be stated. "Declan and I were at Raven Hall while it was on fire. It was one of the biggest blazes I've ever seen in person. Isn't it possible there wasn't enough left of him to identify?"

"Anything is possible, Kate," Murphy admitted. "But they were able to identify everyone else. All except for Andy Novak."

"Finley said that Andy was there that night. He was in the house before Finley left for his girlfriend's."

Murphy didn't counter that. "From what I can find, the man was a loner. He worked at Raven Hall and had no family to speak of except a sister in Oregon who I called. She hadn't spoken to him in at least ten years. She wanted nothing to do with me or the investigation. She said Andy never got over the fact that he got kicked out of Scroll & Dagger, which started as a literary society back in 1735, shortly after the school was started. During the Revolutionary War, the students in Scroll & Dagger were used as spies to pass notes to the Patriots about British troop movement. They also used the Yale newspaper to highlight Patriot causes and rally support. The first members of Scroll & Dagger were Patriots, Kate. And Novak couldn't get past not being a part of them. His sister said it had been a goal of his."

Her father had been an American history professor at Harvard. Kate had a strong command of American history as a result. She knew General Washington had used students at Yale and Harvard as spies and recruiters for the Patriot cause. Finding out that Scroll & Dagger had been used in this way wasn't a surprise. "While I appreciate the history lesson, what does this have to do with Andy Novak?"

Murphy mumbled something Kate didn't hear. Then he shouted at someone in his office and a door slammed shut, quieting the background noise echoing through the phone. "Sorry, it's a madhouse here. Novak's sister said that Andy wanted power and the one way he thought he'd get that was through Yale and Scroll & Dagger. He was obsessed with their history. He fancied himself like the Patriots. When he didn't get that, he became unhinged. That's the word she used. *Unhinged.* Once he was on the outside looking in, she said he vowed to destroy them."

It reminded Kate of a superhero movie at the moment when the bad guy becomes the supervillain. "Are you telling me that Novak was working at Raven Hall to tear it apart from the inside?"

"I don't know, Kate. All I know is what his sister told me and she wanted *nothing* to do with him." He stressed the word.

"What about his bomb-making ability? It would take someone with a bit of know-how to create the bombs that he has."

"I asked the sister about that and she said she wouldn't put anything past him. He is highly intelligent and highly motivated. I asked her about guns and she said that he's as obsessed with guns as he is with power. He had a whole arsenal of weapons. In the last conversation she had with him, Andy was going on and on about a new gun he had purchased. It was too much for her. She begged him to get help and then cut him off."

"Would she speak to me?" Kate asked, realizing Murphy hadn't even provided the woman's name.

"No. She told me to keep her out of it. Forget I had found her. We have enough, Kate. If his body isn't among the victims, then he looks like a good person of interest to me."

Kate had so many more questions. While she was excited by the possibility, she needed to slow Murphy down. "What about money? I can't imagine he was making that much at Raven Hall."

"Their family had money and millions were left to him and his sister after their parents' deaths. His mother passed a few years ago and his father years earlier. The sister said they were each left something like twenty million. There wasn't even any reason for him to be working at Raven Hall. Andy didn't have to work a day for the rest of his life if he didn't want to."

Kate felt like she was having Murphy convince her. It wasn't her intent. She needed to be sure and she was having trouble believing it could come together so easily. "What about where he built the bombs? Do you think he did that in the basement of Raven Hall and then drove the bombs to the other locations? Would he be able to pull that off with all the students around and in the middle of Manhattan? I can see building the bomb there that brought down Raven Hall, but what about the others?"

Murphy told her to hold on for a moment. Sounds of papers shuffling came through the phone and then he got back on the line. "How far is Andover from you?"

"Twenty-five miles north. Why?" Kate asked, her tone cautious and curious.

"Andy Novak has farmland in Andover and a pretty nice house if these real estate records are correct. His sister said she heard he bought the property a few years ago and that's where he goes during the summers and school breaks. She said it's remote enough that he could do just about anything on that property and no one would be the wiser."

Kate cursed loudly. "That's not far from Philipps Academy."

"What's that?"

"It's commonly known as Andover. It's a prep school and a feeder school for the Ivy Leagues."

"Is it important that he's close by it?"

"Depends on how early he wants to cut secret societies off at the knees. Several famous alumni who graduated from Andover went to Ivy League schools. Yale, in fact, and were in secret societies."

"Who?"

"George H.W. Bush, and George W. Bush both graduated from Andover. They both went to Yale and were members of one of the most famous and most secretive secret societies, Skull & Bones. President William Howard Taft and John Kerry were also Bonesmen, as they are known. Not to mention countless representatives and a handful of chief justices to the Supreme Court."

Murphy whistled loudly and long. "Are you kidding me?"

"Dead serious," Kate said and then took a breath. "Before we jump to conclusions, we need to prove that Novak was not in the house the night of the bombing. The only information we have puts him there."

"We don't know for sure, Kate, but you'd think he might have called us or come forward at this point. He's had enough time to see this on the news, be as horrified as the rest of us, and come forward. That hasn't happened."

"He could have seen it as an opportunity to fake his death," Kate countered, knowing she was pushing the boundaries of reality.

"Right and maybe the Easter Bunny is hiding out with Santa Claus," Murphy said with a little laugh. "Is there a reason you don't want to look at Andy Novak? He hits all the marks for me. I'd say we finally have our first solid lead."

"I'm not dismissing him. I'm trying to keep my hope in check," Kate admitted, realizing that was the resistance she felt. She couldn't take another letdown. "I agree that we need to look into Andy Novak and I'm sure Declan will agree."

Kate paused for a moment and looked into the coffee shop, wishing that Declan had been on the call with her. She wasn't able to put Murphy on speakerphone in the middle of the shop. Relaying the information would have to be good enough. As she turned back to the street, she considered Novak's actions. "Do you think Novak will go after Scroll & Dagger?" Kate asked, considering the reasons why Andy might not have targeted them first.

"Wouldn't you think it was likely considering their rejection is possibly what set all of this in motion? Do you want me to call Yale or do you want to do that?"

"You can call Yale if you'd like, but make sure you get every record on him that they are willing to give. We aren't going to get any search warrants or arrest warrants on Novak yet. We have nothing yet, only that his remains weren't recovered in a blazing fire. It's nothing to go on."

"Roger that," Murphy said and barked orders to someone in the office to get him the Yale administration number. Then to Kate, he said, "You don't sound like yourself."

Murphy had accurately picked up that something else was bothering Kate. She was stuck on what Briggs had identified. "Even if this is Novak, we still don't know why he's choosing the secret societies that he is. There are upwards of a dozen at each school. Why the ones he chose?"

"Does it matter, Kate? At the end of the day, he chose the ones he did."

It did matter if they were going to stop him. She told Murphy as much.

"I don't know, Kate," he replied a moment later. "Maybe the ones he chose have historical ties like Scroll & Dagger."

"It's possible. I don't know anything about their histories. I'd have to research."

They tabled the *why* for now. Kate and Murphy made a plan for tackling the next part of the investigation. He'd go and interview the only survivor at Raven Hall, Finley Lloyd, and see what else the young man had to say about his former house manager. Kate still had Tess and Robert Hudson to interview.

Before she hung up, Kate asked, "How's Tony doing? Declan and I have been worried about him."

"He pulled through surgery and the doctors gave him a high chance of survival, which is a blessing. He's still in intensive care. They are taking it day by day."

That was about as good an outcome as could be expected given Tony's injuries. "I'll be in touch when I know more," Kate promised and hung up. She stared down the street toward her house. There were several police cars parked in front and the bomb squad truck. Earlier that morning, she had alerted her neighbors next to her and across the street. Most of them were headed to work and wouldn't be home anyway. She had wanted to evacuate the whole street, but the Boston PD denied that request, given she had no real evidence her house had been rigged with explosives. The lackadaisical way Boston PD moved in and out of her home now, she assumed all was clear.

Kate's sense of relief was short-lived. She turned to walk back into the coffee shop and saw that most in the shop including Declan and Briggs had gotten up from their tables and were standing at the front counter watching the television overhead. Kate couldn't quite make out what was on the screen, but she knew it had to be big. Tentatively she walked inside.

Kate made it a few feet and then angled her head up to see the television. The news was covering a bombing. For a second, Kate thought they might be showing what had taken place in New York City. She scanned the footage for something familiar before the shot panned to one of the talking heads interviewing someone at the scene. Kate realized then that this was new footage of something that had just happened.

Declan turned to her as if feeling her right behind him. "University of Pennsylvania and Princeton," he said loud enough for her to hear him above the crowd. He pushed his way back through the other shop patrons. When he got to Kate, he put a hand on her shoulder and leaned down in her ear. "Let's go outside and get some fresh air."

Even though Kate had only just come back into the shop, she allowed Declan to guide her. Once on the street, he waited until she caught her breath, even though she hadn't realized that her breathing had been labored. She put a hand up to her chest. "I'm okay," Kate said even though she wasn't sure that was the truth. "Two in one day?"

Declan nodded. "Two more secret societies – one at the University of Pennsylvania and the other at Princeton. U of Penn happened this morning around four and then Princeton at five-thirty. There's only about an hour's driving distance between them. They don't think there are any survivors at either location. They are estimating another twenty-four dead between the two places."

"Murphy thinks he found a suspect," Kate said softly, realizing she was in too much shock to say anything else.

CHAPTER 29

Declan and Briggs followed Kate back to her house after the bomb squad gave the all-clear. Sitting in her living room, Kate gave Declan and Briggs an overview of her call with Murphy. She detailed all the circumstantial evidence about Andy Novak. Neither Declan nor Briggs seemed to disagree that he should be considered a potential person of interest. Declan had the same reservations Kate had when first hearing the news. He had asked nearly the same questions that she had asked Murphy. After Kate passed along to him the information that had been provided to her, he agreed Novak should be high on the list of persons of interest. Not that it was a very long list.

"That brings me to Tess and Robert Hudson," Kate continued. "We need to interview them and either clear them or find out their involvement. We are also waiting for Ditch to confirm the locations of the IP addresses on the message board."

Declan looked at Kate. "What was it that Felix guy told you – look at the one who didn't die. Is that what he said?"

Not that Kate had forgotten that information, but it had been pushed to the back of her mind as the more pertinent information was added. "That's what he said. We don't know anything more about the person who said that though. Ditch is still working."

Briggs looked between them both. "I can get a SWAT team together to go to the property in Andover. We are going to have to notify the locals."

Kate wasn't sure how she wanted to approach this. On the one hand, Fuse had ambushed the police before. There was a good chance that if it was him, his property might be a landmine of explosives. On the other hand, he might be so cocky that he'd never think someone would catch him. The approach was a toss-up and she relayed her fears to Declan and Briggs.

"Let's stake out the place first, Kate," Declan said and then turned to Briggs who agreed with him. "Let's keep SWAT on standby. If he's there, we can approach it as a notification – like we only want information on some of the students at Raven Hall. For all we know, he has a family. Did the sister say anything about that?"

"Based on what Murphy said, it didn't sound like Novak had a family," Kate said, but nothing had been confirmed. She told Briggs that she wanted to go alone with Declan to Andover. "Briggs, it might be a good idea to call some of the parents of the Raven Hall students to find out if they have any information about Andy Novak. They might have had some interaction with him in the lead up to the bombing."

"Sure," Briggs said with a look of disappointment. "Are you sure you don't need my help in Andover?"

Kate swallowed hard and saw the expression on his face. "I don't want to put you in the line of fire." She explained what had happened with Tony. "I'd rather Declan and I go it alone for now with the SWAT team. I don't have time to do all this research on Novak and I think it could be incredibly helpful to see if anyone had suspicions about him and his connections to the other bombing sites."

Briggs nodded and smiled up at her. "I wasn't discounting the importance of the research. I'm worried about the two of you going alone to Andover."

"We'll be fine," Declan assured him. "With SWAT on standby that's more than enough."

Briggs stood and told them that he'd contact them immediately if he found anything important. Before heading out the door, he told them to be safe and that he'd be in his office if they needed anything.

"I think he's disappointed we didn't want him in on the action," Declan said, following Kate down the hall toward the kitchen.

She pulled a glass from the cabinet and hit the button for ice on the front of the fridge. After a few cubes landed in the glass, Kate hit the button for water and filled her glass. On top of being sleep deprived, she was dehydrated too. She finished half the glass in one gulp and then looked up at Declan, who leaned against the center island. "I'm sure he's disappointed. But disappointed is better than dead."

Declan clicked his tongue. "Maybe we should ask Spade for a raise – hazard pay."

"Good luck with that." Kate leaned against the other counter, finished off her water, then refilled her glass. As she lowered the glass from her lips, she asked, "What's the best course of action here?"

"We should pay the Hudsons a visit first and give Briggs some time to do some background research on Novak. Once we know more, then we have Briggs contact SWAT and head to Andover. If this is our guy, he wasn't at this house recently. He went from Manhattan to U of Penn and then Princeton. I assume he made some bombs ahead of time to take with him."

That didn't make a lot of sense to Kate. "You're telling me this guy had bombs and weapons at Raven Hall. Then he leaves Raven Hall and detonates a bomb that kills everyone, lays low in Manhattan, ambushes us, and then flees to Pennsylvania and New Jersey? Where did he spend the night? Where was he assembling the bombs or storing them?"

Declan acknowledged that it would be a feat for most people. "Maybe Novak isn't Fuse."

Kate shook her head. "It feels like he could be Fuse. When Murphy started telling me about his background, it all fit for me."

"Where does Lily Cole fit into all of this?"

"That's still an unknown. We don't have any connection between her and Novak established, except if it's through Felix."

Declan raised his eyebrows. "The message boards."

Kate toyed with the glass in her hand as she tried to make the pieces fit together on the solid facts in the case so far. "Felix admitted to knowing Lily. Felix also might know Novak if he's the one who calls himself Fuse in German on the site."

"Should we check in with Ditch?"

Kate checked her watch. It was nearing ten in the morning. Ditch was good, but she wasn't sure that he was that fast. Still, before going to speak to Tess and Robert Hudson, it couldn't hurt. "Let's give him a call."

Declan grabbed his cellphone from the counter next to him and punched in the number. When it started to ring, he put it on speakerphone. "We are calling for an update," he said when Ditch answered. His tone was even but flat with no emotion and no trace of friendliness.

"I'm here, too," Kate said.

Ditch cooed and told her how good it was to hear her voice. Then he disappointed them. "I don't have much of anything yet. Felix was nice enough to let me in and give me his laptop, but it's going to take me time to resurrect the message board. I left a message with the hosting company, but Felix did a good job of scrubbing the data."

"Does that mean there's no hope of its recovery?"

"Oh, sweetie, there's always hope when I'm involved."

Kate ignored the term of endearment and Declan's eyes that were burning a hole in her forehead. "Do you need anything from us?"

"Not much either of you can do, but I'll be in touch as soon as I know anything." Ditch remained quiet for several moments and Declan nearly hung up on him until he coughed once and said, "Declan, you take care of my girl."

Declan ended the call without saying anything else. He tossed his phone across the counter. "Am I missing something here? Did you sleep with him?"

Kate would have been offended by the accusation but she saw the hurt on Declan's face and recognized his anger for what it was. "He's trying to throw you off your game, Declan. Of course, I didn't sleep with him. You know better than anyone I don't mix pleasure and business."

Kate put her glass in the sink and turned to head back into the living room. As she passed Declan, he reached for her, wrapping one arm around her back, and pulled her close to him. He leaned down and kissed her sweetly on the forehead. "I'm being a jerk and I'm sorry." They stayed like that for a few beats and then Declan said quietly, "Anyone but him, Kate. Anyone but him."

Kate playfully shoved him away. "You're being ridiculous. He's attractive but he's also a criminal and that would compromise my entire career."

Declan's broad smile revealed the hint of a dimple that only showed when he was truly happy. "That's what keeps you from being involved with someone – criminal activity? I've still got a chance then."

She leveled a no-nonsense look at him. "Can we please get to work? The Hudsons live in Lexington, so it's a short drive away. Do we want to take the rental or your SUV?" Kate still had the rental car and she'd have to make a car purchase shortly because her insurance company was only going to let her keep the rental for so long. She'd had the bomb squad sweep Declan's SUV which was parked in the small driveway at the back of her house.

"Let's take the rental. If Fuse is going to try to blow us up again, there's no point in both of us losing our rides." Declan headed for the back while Kate walked through the downstairs to the front of the house and double-checked the lock on the front door. Then she engaged the alarm. She didn't remember if she had set it while they were away. Kate didn't always feel the need for it, but now, she wondered if she'd ever leave and not set it.

The ride to Lexington took forty-five minutes instead of the normal twenty-five because of a backup on I-95. Declan had found a more scenic less traffic-filled route. The city living of Boston gave way to rural farmlands and two-story colonial houses with flower-filled landscaping. Even though it was still a few weeks before Halloween, most homes had pumpkins and colorful mums on porches and scarecrows in yards. Kate always enjoyed the whole vibe of fall in New England.

She read off directions to him as they navigated long, winding roads until they reached Maple Street. It was clear from the home that was set back on several acres that Robert and Tess Hudson had considerable wealth. Kate didn't need to look up the value of the property to know it was in the millions. She hit the button to lower the window and took in a breath of fresh country air. Kate imagined she could retire like this if she ever had the desire to sell her brownstone, which still seemed unthinkable to her.

There was a tan Lexus SUV in the driveway, but otherwise, the property was quiet. Declan stopped on the road in front of the home and they slipped bulletproof vests over their heads, unclasped their guns, and got themselves mentally ready.

Kate messaged the SWAT supervisor who was down the block on standby. Then they shared a look and Declan pulled up the long incline of the driveway and parked behind the Lexus. Kate's feet barely hit the concrete of the driveway when the front door pulled open and a wide-eyed woman with a mane of short tussled blond hair scurried out the front door. She got a look at Kate's vest, the gun in her hand, and the badge dangling from a chain around her neck and pulled up short.

"Are you here about Robert?" she asked through sniffled short breaths. "Do you know something? Is he dead?" When Kate didn't respond, she took a few tentative steps toward Kate. "Please, whatever it is, tell me the truth. I've been going crazy here worried out of my mind."

Kate flashed her badge. "Are you Tess Hudson?"

"Yes, Robert's wife."

"Are you alone here?"

Tess glanced back at the house and then to Kate, seeming confused by the question. "Yes, I told the cops when I called 911 that I was concerned for Robert's mental state and worried he might do something to hurt someone. I told the local cop the same when he came out and took my statement."

"How long ago was that?" Declan asked, stepping around the car.

"About a week ago. I haven't heard from him or the cops since. I assume since you're the FBI that it's bad." Tess couldn't hold back the tears any longer. "What's he done?"

Kate moved toward her, the gun in her hand at her side. "Let's go inside and talk, ma'am. There's a lot we need to straighten out."

CHAPTER 30

Tess Hudson led Kate and Declan through a large open foyer with a winding staircase to the second floor. The home had wide wood plank floors common for colonial homes and was decorated in a primitive style of that era. Kate felt almost as if she was taking a step back in time walking through the house. Other than the modern amenities like electricity and indoor plumbing, the house could have been a replica of one from 1776.

Once in a formal sitting room, Tess began to openly sob. She grabbed a tissue from the holder on an end table and blew her nose. "I'm so sorry. Our family has had so much tragedy and this is just unimaginable. We believed that someone was responsible for our son's death, but we would have never imagined something like this. I don't understand. Robert doesn't understand." She was speaking so rapidly and crying in between that it was hard for Kate to follow what the woman was saying.

"Let's sit down and talk," Kate said and then formally introduced herself and Declan. "We weren't contacted by the local police station and we don't know anything about Robert. We didn't know he was missing. We came to speak to you about another matter. Start from the beginning."

Tess blew her nose again and then sniffled back more tears. She blew out a breath and then went to the fireplace mantle and pulled down a photo of a young man playing lacrosse. He was posed after the game with a bright smile across his face. She handed the photo to Kate. "This is my son in his senior year of high school. We were so excited when he got into Brown. Michael had wanted to go there since he was a kid and first visited the campus with his uncle, who is an alumnus. He was an excellent student and was headed to law school." Tess choked back the words and dropped her head, too emotionally distressed to continue.

Kate would say the words she couldn't. "We know that Michael was killed during his initiation into Hunt House."

Tess snapped her head up. "Did you apprehend his killer?"

Declan shook his head. "No. We aren't investigating that case. We are here to speak to you about some things you said on the message board. You know there have been bombings at secret societies like Hunt House."

Tess pulled back in surprise. "Why would you want to speak to me about that?"

There was something they were missing. The air of confusion hung in the air around them. Kate could feel the energy and distance between them even though she could reach out and physically touch Tess. "You made threats on a message board against all secret societies. As you might have seen on the news, several of them have been bombed. Students like your son are dead." Kate tried to add up the death toll in her head but fell short. "The bomber also ambushed the police and bystanders."

Tess held her hand to her heart. "I've seen the news. It's terrible but what does that have to do with me?"

"You made threats, Tess," Declan said, trying to cut through the confusion. "We are here because you and your husband are persons of interest in this case."

"You think I had something to do with this?" Tess asked, her mouth forming an oval and her eyes wide. "I'd never do something like that and neither would my husband. We were on those message boards trying to draw out my son's killer. And now my husband has gone after him."

"You're not involved in the bombings?" Kate asked again, not believing she was being so direct with someone.

"Of course not," Tess said, the tears coming again. She took a few steps backward and sat down in a chair near the fireplace. It took her a minute to compose herself but when she did, her voice was clear and strong. "After we lost the lawsuit against Brown, we considered going after Hunt House and the students directly. Then we got a visit from one of Michael's friends who told us that no one had been with Michael the night he died. It hadn't been part of any hazing ritual at Hunt House. No one was sure what happened."

Kate holstered her gun and Declan did the same. She was sure they were face to face with a confused, grieving mother, not a killer. "Did you believe what Michael's friend said? I'm sure you wondered if he was lying so you wouldn't sue them."

"That's right. Neither Robert nor I believed him, at first. Robert questioned him at length. No one at Hunt House believed Michael's fall from the bell tower was a suicide or an accident. They were all as stumped as we were. They hadn't been able to speak to us because of the lawsuit against Brown. As time passed, we were able to get past some of our anger and realized that Michael would have told us had there been hazing. He would have shared with us had he been unhappy. He was a happy-go-lucky kid. The only person bothering him was the house manager at Hunt House and Michael shared that with us. He said the guy singled him out, but it was minor things – not cleaning up the kitchen well enough, leaving his laundry for too long in the dryer. I chalked it up to Michael being a twenty-one-year-old kid. It was harmless stuff until it wasn't."

Alarm bells went off for Kate at the mention of *house manager* given Andy Novak. "What does that mean, until it wasn't? Did something happen between them?"

"No one knows why Michael went up to the bell tower, but one of the pledges told me that the house manager wanted the bell tower cleaned. None of the boys had been given the task. Later, the pledge wondered if Michael had been assigned the job and hadn't fallen but had been pushed by the house manager, who promptly quit the day after Michael's death. He left no forwarding information on his whereabouts. It was a strange thing that made them all wonder. Of course, we didn't find that out until a year after Michael's death and we can't find this man now."

Declan glanced over at Kate and then asked, "What's his name?"

"Russell Whitlock," Tess said. "We saw a photo of him and my husband thought he looked familiar, but he couldn't figure it out. We have been desperate to find him." Tess stood from the chair and asked Kate and Declan to wait a moment while she retrieved something she thought they should see.

When Tess was gone, Kate turned to Declan. "Are you getting the same feeling as I am?"

"That Michael Hudson might be Fuse's first victim?"

Kate nodded slowly. "There's still a part of this story we are missing."

"A big part of the story," Declan echoed and then turned his attention back to Tess when she entered the room. She was holding a piece of paper in her trembling hands. She held it out to Declan who lowered his head to read it. He read the note aloud. *"You took something I wanted and now I've taken something from you. We're even."*

Declan handed the note to Kate so she could read it. It was typewritten rather than handwritten. She read the words over twice and then raised her eyes to Tess. "Does this have any meaning for you?"

"Not to me or my husband, but it set us on a path of exploring what this could be about. It didn't reference Michael's name, but we assumed that's what the note writer meant. We never did find the real meaning of it. Another dead end in the search for justice."

"We can get back to the note," Kate said, wanting to table that for now. "First help me to understand what you were doing on the message boards. You made some frightening threats against secret societies. You came across as completely unhinged."

"I know," Tess said and averted her eyes. "It was my husband's idea. See after we got that note, we remembered what Michael's friend had told us about the house manager so he started looking for Russell Whitlock. Robert couldn't find anyone by that name who matched the description we were given. We had never met the man ourselves. One of the young men in the pledge class told us that they found out that before he disappeared, Russell was posting on a message board about conspiracy theories and speaking out against secret societies. My husband got on there and started doing the same under my name, thinking a woman might gain someone's trust. We were searching for any information that would lead us to this guy."

It didn't make sense to Kate. "That's a dangerous game you were playing, especially using your name. Plus, if this man had killed your son, he knew your names. He would never have engaged with you."

Tess looked at Kate as if she had turned the world upside down. "Neither of us thought of that. We were desperate. My husband wanted to find him and scare him. He purposefully made threats and made us sound armed, and well…dangerous. I don't know exactly what he was trying to do. His reasoning at that point wasn't sound. It didn't make a lot of sense to me. I was dealing with my grief and Robert didn't want to go to counseling with me. He was singularly focused on trying to root out Russell."

Declan's expression said he was as confused as Kate. "How was posting this threatening stuff going to draw him out? I'm not sure I see the connection."

Tess held her hand to her head. "At first, I was willing to have Robert do whatever made him feel better and that message board seemed to do that. He thought he was doing something to bring our son's killer to justice. Then he got sucked into it and all reasoning was lost."

Kate assessed her body language as she spoke – hands open, relaxed back in her chair, legs uncrossed, comfortable eye contact. Tess wasn't lying. "Please tell me more about Robert's interactions on this message board."

Tess remained quiet for a moment as if absorbing the question and finding the words to explain. "As I said, Robert went onto the message board, hoping to draw out the person who killed our son. He was hoping to find information about Russell Whitlock or engage with him directly. But in the end, Robert started to believe some of the things he was reading. He started to hate secret societies, which didn't make any sense because he had been a member of one at Yale."

Declan lurched forward slightly at the mention of Yale. "What secret society was he in?"

"Scroll & Dagger," Tess explained, oblivious to the panic on Kate's face. "Robert had been quite proud of it. That's why when Michael said he was interested in Hunt House at Brown, Robert was all for it. Michael wanted to do it on his own without his father's help. Robert had offered to make some calls to grease the wheels for his acceptance, but Michael told his father not to. If he was going to be admitted, he wanted to do it on his own merit."

Kate slowed her breathing which had ramped up in hearing what couldn't be a coincidence. "Do you know what year Robert was a part of Scroll & Dagger?"

Tess rattled off the year and it matched the same time Andy Novak would have been a member. "Do you know if your husband knows

Andy Novak?" Kate asked, holding her breath while waiting for the response.

"I don't know any of their names. My husband rarely speaks of them," Tess said. "But one of the men in his class did offer to help him go after the killer. That's who Robert is supposed to be with now, but he's missing. I don't even know the man's name, so it's not like I can contact him."

Declan ran his hands down his thighs. Kate knew it was a sure sign he was ready to jump from his seat and do something, anything to stop the two men.

Kate shot Declan a look to slow down. They still had work to do here. "Did your husband take guns with him? He mentioned guns and threats on the online forum."

Tess bit her lower lip and shook her head. "It was all made up. I don't think my husband has shot a gun in his life. I don't even know if he's held one. Please tell me what's happening. I can see the looks on your faces and it's more worrying than before you arrived."

"We believe a man from your husband's pledge class at Scroll & Dagger might be responsible for these bombings." Kate watched the woman's face contort with recognition.

"And you think Robert is helping him?"

"We don't know, but that's what we are here to find out," Kate said and inched forward on the seat. "Do you know anything about the man your husband went to see?"

"Nothing. It was a part of my husband's life he didn't talk about." Tess clutched her hand to her throat. "He told me it was better if I didn't know."

"Is there any way you think Robert is partnering with the man committing these crimes?"

Tess shook her head and started to cry again. "My husband is suffering but he'd never kill kids, especially going after students

Michael's age. It's unthinkable."

"Does your husband know anything about bomb-making?"

"No," Tess said firmly.

Kate asked a few more questions and then Declan asked a few of his own. They were trying to pin down Robert's potential involvement. It seemed from what Tess said that he was just a grieving father who had gone after the man he thought killed his child and was duped by the killer. Every time they uncovered one bit of information that should have gotten them closer to solving the case, it only brought up more questions.

After the questioning was done, Tess allowed them to search her house, but they found nothing of interest – no weapons or chemicals or anything that would indicate that Tess or Robert Hudson was involved in the bombings.

As Kate waited for Declan to finish his search on the second floor, she scanned the photos on Robert's bookshelf in his office. Her eyes were drawn to one in particular. It was a group of men standing with arms looped over each other's shoulders dressed in khaki pants, shirts, ties, and blue blazers with a gold crest on the pocket. They were smiling like the rest of the world wasn't in on their joke. There were ten young men in the photo.

Even though the men were close to thirty years younger than they were now, Kate wasn't surprised when she saw Andy Novak with the smug smile of someone who thought he was right where he was destined to be. It confirmed everything she thought. But that wasn't all Kate saw in the photo. As her eyes scanned over the rest of the faces, the man on Andy's left caught Kate's attention. His face was strikingly familiar. She peered in closer to get a better look. It came to her all at once. Kate gasped audibly and her hand flew to cover her mouth.

CHAPTER 31

After Kate's discovery, she needed to show Declan what she found, but she needed more information first. She grabbed the photo from the bookshelf and found Tess in the kitchen nursing a cup of tea. She thrust the photo towards her, startling the woman who nearly dropped her cup. "Is this your husband's pledge class?"

With her hand shaking from being startled, Tess set the cup on the table and turned to Kate. She took the photo, peered down at it, and confirmed that it was. She ran a finger over the photo of her husband. "Robert was so proud of his pledge class. That is until they had to remove one of the members. Robert never said who but the decision had been a hard one for all of them. But it was tarnishing their legacy."

"Do you know that man's name?"

Tess shook her head and tried to hand the photo back to Kate, who wouldn't take it. "As I said, Agent Walsh, this was a part of my husband's life he kept secret. I never got names or any information."

Kate pointed to the familiar man in the photo. "Do you know him?"

Tess shook her head and let out a frustrated sigh. "Agent Walsh, it's a secret society, and even though this photo has sat on my mantel my entire marriage, I don't know any of the men in it. My husband would not disclose their names to me. He said it wasn't important. The only contact I knew my husband to have with them was a weekend retreat once a summer."

"I need to take a photo of this photo," Kate said as she took the photo back from Tess and undid the latch on the back of the frame. She tugged out the photo and laid it flat on the table. Then she snapped a few pictures with her phone of the whole group shot and then several more, zeroing in on each of the men's faces.

After Kate put the photo back in the frame, Tess asked, "Am I in danger?"

Kate didn't know the answer. "We'll give you police protection. You can remain in your home with an officer here with you or we can move you to a safe location. It's up to you."

Tess considered her options and opted to stay in her home with police protection. "I want to be here if Robert comes back."

Kate understood the reasoning, but she couldn't comment. She had no idea of Robert's involvement or if his life was in danger. Either way, she couldn't assure Tess that Robert would ever be coming home. "I promise to provide you with any updates that I can." That was about all Kate could promise Tess and she seemed to accept it.

Tess shook Kate's hand. "I don't know how to thank you. I promise you, Agent Walsh, my husband might not be in his right mind and consumed with guilt, but he would not kill other people's children. He'd never put other families through what we have been through."

"I hope you're right," Kate said evenly and then headed toward the front door. She met Declan on the porch. "I found something. Let's get to the car and I'll tell you there." As they walked to the car, a state police officer pulled up the driveway. Kate had called for protection and they had arrived faster than she expected. She briefed the officer quickly before he made his way to the house.

Once they were in the car, Kate handed her phone to Declan. "Take a look at those photos and tell me what you see."

Declan scrolled his finger over each photo and took his time studying them. He pointed out Andy first and then stared down at it just like Kate had. He pointed. "That guy. Who is that? He's familiar to me."

"Keep scrolling. I have a close-up photo with his face."

Declan kept going until he found the photo Kate mentioned. He brought the phone close to his eyes and studied it for several moments. "Terrance Becker."

"That's what I thought. His son, Garrett, was nearly killed in the bombing at Cornell. I'd bet money Andy Novak was posing as Russell Whitlock to get close to Michael." Kate took her phone back and then scrolled to the image of the note that Tess had shown them. She read it aloud to Declan. *"You took something I wanted and now I've taken something from you. We're even."*

Declan quickly caught on to what Kate had been thinking. "Novak is going after children from the men in his pledge class. He's seeking revenge for being kicked out." Declan looked over at Kate. "Can someone hold a grudge for that long? It's been close to thirty years."

Kate would have liked to say Andy Novak would be an anomaly but some people never let a slight go. If that turns to rage and there's no healthy outlet for those emotions, mixed with some psychopathy – it's a recipe for exactly what they were dealing with now. "We need to identify each of those men and see if they have children and where those children are right now. It's only a working theory, but it's more than we've had so far."

Declan started the car. "Are we heading to Novak's property in Andover?"

"I don't think he's there, but we have to rule it out." Kate called the SWAT commander first and updated them that they were heading to Andover now that all was cleared at the Hudsons' home. The SWAT commander assured Kate that they'd meet them there and be on standby should they need their assistance.

Next, Kate called Murphy and Briggs and connected them on a three-way call. Kate introduced one to the other and explained she needed their help. She updated them about what they found at the Hudson home and her new working theory.

"I'm going to text you a photo of the pledge class. We need to confirm the identities of these men and cross-reference with the students in the societies that have been bombed. If my theory holds, we need to reach out and warn them. We also need to find a way to confirm that Russell Whitlock and Andy Novak are the same man."

"It's a big jump, Kate," Briggs said with caution in his voice. "It's a lot of speculation on your part without any solid evidence to back it up."

"It is," Kate admitted, appreciating his grounding presence. "That's why we need to find the evidence. We already identified Andy Novak as a person of interest. We know he has been working in secret societies as a house manager. Now we know he has connections to two fathers connected to this case. I don't believe in coincidences. There's something here. I'm sure of it. We just need to prove it and go after Andy Novak."

"And Robert Hudson," Murphy added.

"He's an unknown right now. Tess is sure that he's not involved. For all we know, Robert may end up being another victim. Either way, we need to tread lightly until we have more information. Don't let the media get ahold of Robert's name as a person of interest."

"Understood."

As Kate finished up the call, she said, "Murphy, the easiest way to get the names of the men in that photo is to connect with Terrance Becker. If he's willing, he could help confirm their identities. As you know, when Declan and I met with him at the bombing site, he was less than helpful. We need to be careful not to disclose too much information because I could easily see him going after Novak himself or straight to the media."

"No problem, Kate. I have his contact information and can set up a meeting with him."

"I appreciate that. If he wants to speak to me directly, I can do that too. We are heading to Novak's farm right now. I'll be in touch when we learn more. Briggs, we can meet up when we are back in Boston this afternoon."

After the call ended, Declan started the car and looked over at Kate. "Do you feel like you're making a huge leap without a net under you?"

Kate hadn't thought about it in that way, but it was akin to what she was doing. She rarely went after suspects based only on circumstantial evidence. She didn't have much else to work with though. "I know it's a leap. If I was the kind of investigator who went on intuition, that's what I'd be saying now. You know I don't think in those terms, but I believe we are after the right person."

"I agree with you." Declan set the GPS and then pulled out of the driveway heading for Novak's property in Andover.

They had two schools left that hadn't been hit yet – Yale and Harvard.

Kate looked down at her cellphone in her lap and decided to appeal directly. She found the number for Yale administration on the website and then placed the call. She ended up with the secretary to the president of the university. Kate insisted that she be able to speak with him immediately. When the woman balked, Kate said more sternly, "If there is a bombing at Yale, then I'll be more than happy to mention your name on the news as the person who stood in the way of the FBI warning the president of the university. Are you okay with that?"

Kate was promptly put on hold without another word of deterrence. Moments later, the call was engaged again.

"Agent Walsh, I can't imagine what is so important that you are willing to drag me out of a meeting with an important donor no less."

President Christopher Byrne mumbled something about bad timing and how everyone thought they were important. "This is terribly inconvenient and then you strong-armed my secretary. I have a good mind to call your supervisor."

Kate ignored his threat, and if he thought he'd get anywhere with Spade, she'd have paid to listen in on that call. "Scroll & Dagger. We need to issue a warning to them along with every other secret society you have on campus."

"Let me stop you right there, Agent Walsh. That's what you have wrong. These organizations are not on our campus nor are they sanctioned by Yale."

"But they are your students. Parents don't know the difference between being sanctioned by Yale or not. They pay you large sums of money to educate their children. You may make a distinction, but trust me, if something happens, the parents of the dead students will not."

"Must you be so extreme?" President Byrne said. His voice had a hint of disgust. "I don't know where you went to college or if you did, but there are ways things are done in the Ivy League."

"Harvard graduate and my father was a Harvard professor, President Byrne. I'm more than acquainted with it. The primary suspect in these bombings has a connection to Yale. He was kicked out of Yale and Scroll & Dagger. You'd be wise to heed my warnings, if not only for the safety of your students but for your reputation as well. I know that you haven't been in your position for very long – two years if I read that correctly."

There was silence on the other end of the phone. Kate waited so he could process what she had told him. Finally, with his voice quieter now and his tone even, he asked, "You believe the person responsible for these heinous acts went to college here?"

"Does that surprise you?"

"It's shocking," President Byrne said and covered the phone as he told the person in his office that he'd have to reschedule the meeting. Kate could still hear him speaking even though his voice was muffled. She waited while he took care of whatever he needed to do to appropriately focus on the risk at hand. When he got back on the call, he had one question, "What should I do? It's not like we can evacuate the whole school."

"No, but you should tell the secret societies to quietly evacuate. Maybe you can set them up temporarily in dorms or a local hotel – something, anything until we can make some headway on this case. And it needs to be now, President Byrne. There were two more bombings and we only have two schools left. Yale and Harvard."

"All of them?" he shouted the question.

"All of them. We don't know what one could be hit."

"I'll do the best I can. I can't promise the students are going to go and I can't force them. You understand that, right? I can't force them."

Kate pivoted to her other reason for calling. "Does the school keep a record of secret society membership?"

President Byrne coughed and sputtered. "Not officially, no."

She didn't have time to play games. "Unofficially, is there a record?"

"Yes."

"Great, then I need you to go through the pledge class for Scroll & Dagger." Kate rattled off the year. "What I need is the names of each of those students and any current addresses you have on them. Then I want to know if any of them currently have children in your school – most specifically if they are part of any secret society."

"Slow down, Agent Walsh. I can't give you that information. There are protocols in place."

Kate knew that but she was also hoping he'd be willing to work around it. "We have lives at stake here. What I can tell you is that someone in that pledge class is a person of interest in this case. I believe that he might be going after the children of those members. One is already dead and another barely missed being killed in an explosion. For all I know right now, others are dead."

"Let me call you back," President Byrne said, defeated. Then the call went dead.

Kate hoped she had scared him enough to get what she needed.

CHAPTER 32

Andy Novak's property was a wasteland of overgrown grass. The two-story Cape Cod-style house sat far back from the road. It was painted bright barn red and had white shutters on all the windows and needed a good paint job. A white picket fence lined the perimeter of the vast property. A large barn sat off to the right of the house and a rusted tractor that looked like it had once been painted green was next to the barn.

"Doesn't look like anyone has been home in a while," Declan remarked as he pulled down the side road next to the house. They still hadn't seen an entrance to the property yet.

Kate stared out the front window assessing the property. Up ahead was a break in the fence and a dirt road that ran perpendicular to the house. Kate pointed where she wanted Declan to turn and he followed the curve of the road and then made a right into the property.

He slowed the car down to a crawl and then inched it forward. "Trip wire," he said as he noted how Kate was staring at him.

Kate pointed up toward the house. "There's mail in the mailbox. The mailman would have been killed if there was a tripwire. Put some gas on it. I can walk faster than this." Even though Kate barked that order, her stomach still dropped thinking that they could hit an IED at any moment. She had been trained for a lot of things, but she didn't have the nerves for this.

Declan white-knuckled the steering wheel as they shot forward down the dirt road. Dust kicked up around the tires, but they made it unharmed. Declan delivered them safely to the front door and cut the engine. "When am I going to stop feeling like the world around me is going to explode?"

Kate wished she knew the answer. "Months from now, I assume. I hope it's not never."

They had their protective vests on and both had their guns out and at their sides. He was the faster shot. Kate was more accurate. The last time they had gone to the range together flashed in Kate's mind. She avoided the memory to halt herself from smiling. Declan had grown frustrated with her accuracy. He was among the top in his class on the range, but Kate was just a tad better.

Declan took the two steps up onto the porch, the boards creaking under his weight. He checked the window first but the blinds were closed and he couldn't see in. "Here goes nothing," he said to Kate.

With his fist raised in the air to knock, someone said hello from behind them. Declan turned with his gun and aimed. Kate did the same. "Identify yourself!" he shouted, louder than he needed.

The elderly man shot his hands in the air. "Don't shoot me for heaven's sake!"

Neither of them lowered their gun. "Who are you?" Kate asked again, realizing the man might not have heard Declan.

He didn't lower his hands but hitched his thumb in the direction behind him. "I'm Stan. I live across the field there. You see that field? It hasn't been mowed in a few weeks. I always have to pester Andy about getting it done because he's making the neighborhood look bad, but he tells me he's too busy. This time, it's out of control, but I've hardly seen Andy around."

Kate lowered her gun and Declan did the same. "When was the last time you saw Andy?"

Stan screwed up his facial features in thought. "A few days ago – give or take. He was in a big rush to get out of here. Barely had time to speak to me. He's been like that over the last few weeks. Gets back here and leaves again. Sometimes a day later and sometimes a few times hours later."

Kate stepped off the porch. "What are you doing over here now?"

Stan lowered his hands and looped his right thumb in the belt loop of his faded dusty jeans. "I know Andy left here and I haven't seen anyone else around. But I've been hearing some yelling coming from the house. I don't have a key and I wasn't even sure I heard what I heard. I didn't want to call the cops and seem like a crazy old man. Figured with you two over here, might as well tell you."

Declan didn't holster his gun as Kate had. He stepped toward the edge of the porch landing. "How'd you know we were cops?"

"Didn't, until I got up close to you. I thought you were someone who knew Andy. I was going to mention the lawn, see if Andy was okay, and ask about the yelling coming from the house. Now that I see you're cops, I figured it would be best to mention the yelling first off. I swear I'm not just hearing things. My wife thinks I'm hearing things cause she didn't hear any yelling, but I swear I heard it."

"How long ago was the last time you heard yelling?"

"This morning. I just can't figure out where on the property it's coming from. I assumed the house."

Kate didn't see another house in sight. She didn't even know where Stan had come from. "Where do you live?"

Stan pointed to behind the house. "I'm right in the back of his property. He's got more land in front and on the side than in the back. My side yard bumps his property line. Then I own all those fields across the street. My family has had all this property for more than one hundred years. We sold this plot about fifty years ago, but I'm regretting it now with the way Andy treats it. But I suppose, right now, the yelling is more important than the grass."

Technically they had probable cause to go in if someone in there was in distress. Kate didn't want to do that. She hadn't heard the yelling and she wanted a search warrant in case there was evidence relating to the case. There was no way she wanted to risk evidence being thrown out for improper procedure. She glanced over at Declan. "What do you think?"

"Let me knock and see if I get a response." Declan pounded three times on the front door, called out, and then they waited. Nothing but the breeze blowing answered. Declan turned to say something to Kate but stopped and cocked his head to the side, like a dog who heard a noise. "I heard something."

"See, I told you I wasn't hearing things," Stan said, giving Kate a look that he had told her so.

Kate shushed him and listened but she heard nothing.

"FBI! Yell again if you need assistance!" Declan yelled and then knocked even louder this time.

Off in the distance, a muffled voice called, "Help me!" It was faint and Kate wasn't even sure she had heard it until the person said it again and again.

Kate stepped toward the door. "I can hear someone, but where is it coming from?"

"I'm not sure," Declan said and then looked back at her. "What do you want to do, Kate? We have probable cause to go in there." Declan stood poised to knock down the door if he had to.

Kate shook her head. "Let's call in the bomb squad and they can go in first. If Andy is holding someone hostage in there, I bet something is rigged with explosives."

Stan took several steps back. "Bombs! Hostages!"

Kate closed the distance to Stan while Declan made the call to the awaiting SWAT commander and Briggs.

Kate pushed Stan even farther back from the house right up to the edge of the tall grass. "What do you know about Andy Novak?"

"Not much of anything. He bought this house and property from the previous owner. He's not here all the time. I've questioned why he even owns it if he's never going to be here. He said he likes to have a place to come home to."

"Have you been in the home?"

Stan shook his head. "Andy is protective about his house. I haven't been in there since the previous owner was here. We had a much better relationship. Andy is a bit odd if you ask me."

"Odd, how?"

"Besides the coming and going so frequently, he isn't very nice. Kind of guy who's got a chip on his shoulder. You can't even have a conversation with him." Stan looked poised to say something else, but he held back.

"If there is something else, you need to tell us. It's important. If you're worried about getting him in trouble, trust me, there's nothing you can say that will cause him any more trouble than he's already in right now."

Stan stared up at the house and remained silent for a few more moments. Then he locked his gaze on Kate. "I'm not against guns. I've got a few hunting rifles and a Glock for protection, not that I need it out here. Worst this town ever sees is a little ruckus from the kids at the prep school. Andy's got some high-powered weapons in there and a lot of them. I've seen him bringing them in. I didn't say anything to him and I minded my business, but…something just didn't sit right with me. I can't even place what it is. Just seems off."

Kate had heard this from neighbors before in different cases. The need to mind their own business usually won out. Not that there was much Stan could have done. "Did you tell anyone your concerns?"

"My son and my wife. There's a neighbor down the road I've spoken to as well. He was in my yard and he saw Andy moving some guns into the house one day. We both shared a look and I could kind of tell he felt the same thing as me." Stan opened his eyes wide and had a guilty look on his face. "Should I have told someone else?"

"Not if Andy didn't do anything. There was no one to tell. You didn't do anything wrong," Kate assured him. "It's good to know about the weapons."

Declan got off the phone and walked to them. "Bomb squad and SWAT are on their way. I called Briggs first who immediately called in a favor and got a warrant from a local judge. We are cleared for going into the house."

Stan squinted at the house. "Do you think Andy has something to do with the bombs at those universities?"

Kate's ears pricked up at that. "Why would you think Andy was involved?"

Stan took a breath. "Well, I know he worked at a few Ivy League schools. We heard some rumors that he kept getting fired. Andy told my wife once that he had a job in Manhattan at another school, and my wife and I joked about how long that one was gonna last. Then after that, when he is home, I see him bringing in a lot of guns and other materials into the house. I don't know what other materials. It was dark out and I can't see too good too far, but he pulled up during the daylight and then waited till nighttime to bring it in. Now you have all these bombings." Stan pinched the bridge of his nose. "I didn't notice it but my wife did. She said isn't it funny that Andy is home and then a day later there is another bombing. He's always home right before and then gone the day of the bombing. My wife is like that, notices things other people don't."

"That's perceptive of both of you," Kate said, already knowing that Stan and his wife would be called to the witness stand should this ever go to court. She heard the SWAT and bomb squad trucks before she saw them pulling into the driveway. "Stan, it's safer for you if you head home now. How close is your house to Andy's?"

He had caught her meaning and smiled down at Kate and patted her hand. "Maybe I'll take my wife out for coffee. We have a little shop in the square that we both enjoy. It's probably best if I do that now."

"Thank you, Stan. We'll be in touch."

Stan nodded and thanked Kate and then shook Declan's hand as he made his way down the driveway past all the other law enforcement personnel gearing up to enter the house. When he got to the road, he looked back once and gave Kate a little wave before he put his head down and continued his walk.

Kate turned to Declan. "It was good Stan came over here. I learned things that will be helpful if I get the opportunity to interview Novak later."

Kate wasn't sure Declan heard her. His line of sight was locked on the house and he was itching to get in there with the bomb squad and SWAT. She touched his arm to get his attention and he turned to her. "I know there is someone in there, probably hurt, and waiting to go in is killing me. I want to run in there and get them out." Declan would have to wait.

They were pushed back into the tall grass as the bomb squad commander and his team climbed the front porch steps in full tactical gear to breach the front door. One of the guys had a battering ram and had the front door off its hinges in seconds flat. No explosion.

The SWAT commander came over and stood near Kate and Declan. He had his walkie out and was listening in as the bomb squad went through the home, clearing each room of any explosives. With each room cleared, Kate breathed a little clearer.

What seemed like an eternity later, they breached a basement door. "There's someone down here!" one of them shouted, his voice cracking over the walkie. It was followed by a string of curses and muffled sounds and the yelp of a man obviously in pain and in need of help.

When they could finally hear a clear assessment of what the bomb squad saw, it sent shivers down Kate's spine. There was a man attached to a chain with a trip wire explosive on it. If he moved too far or tried to get free it would blow. The bomb squad barked directions to the man while they got to work dismantling the bomb.

Kate's heartbeat pounded loudly in her ears, drowning out all other sounds. She wanted desperately to know what the bomb squad was doing, but they had gone nearly silent as they worked. The only sounds that came through the walkie were technical terms as the team worked together. The SWAT commander pushed them several more steps back from their current position as they waited to see if the man would live or die.

CHAPTER 33

By the time the bomb squad escorted the man out of the home, Kate had a pool of sweat at her back that made her shirt cling to her. Declan's jaw had been set so firmly Kate was sure it was going to hurt once he unclenched and started to speak again.

The man the bomb squad escorted out was covered in dried blood and his face had been badly beaten. He had his arm thrown over the shoulder of one of the officers as he limped down the front steps.

"Did you call for medical assistance?" Kate asked Declan as she gave the man a once over from afar. She wanted to assume it was Robert Hudson, but his face was so badly beaten that she couldn't make a positive identification.

"No," Declan said, drawing Kate's attention back to him. "I will." He stepped away to make the call while Kate went to attend to the man herself.

He had been deposited at the side of the house in one of two outdoor chairs. There was a small round table that separated them. He slumped forward resting his head on his hands. Kate held back giving him a moment to himself before she approached. He groaned softly as he moved his body in the chair, trying to find the most comfortable position. The hem of his shirt in the back rode up, revealing a patchwork of bruises on his back. Kate was afraid of what the rest of the shirt might be covering.

"I'm FBI Agent Kate Walsh," she said, coming around to stand in front of him. "Medical assistance is on its way. Can you tell me your name?" Kate wasn't sure if he had a head injury or what other injuries besides the bruising he might have sustained. Blood caked nearly every inch of his face.

He tried to speak but it only came out as a strained cough. Kate gestured to Declan to find and bring him over some water. He raised his head fully off his arms. "Robert Hudson. I came to Andy because he told me he'd help me find my son's killer. He's the one who killed him. Then he tried to kill me."

Kate didn't correct him, but she knew that Andy hadn't *tried* to kill Robert. If Andy had wanted Robert dead, he'd be dead. He wanted to torture Robert. There was a marked difference. "I spoke to your wife earlier, so I have a little bit of the backstory. Can you tell me what happened when you arrived here?"

"I will," Robert said slowly, struggling to speak. "There's something more important. Andy is going to kidnap a boy at Yale then bring him to one of the secret societies at Harvard and kill him there. He wanted two of the sons together, and the one at Yale isn't in a secret society. He's going to take him from his dorm or apartment. I don't know their names. I tried everything I could to get their names, but he wouldn't tell me. All I know is what I told you."

Kate wasn't sure which part surprised her more. "Why would he tell you this?"

Robert tried to raise his shoulders to shrug but he didn't quite get there. "I think he figured I'd be dead by the time he did it and it wouldn't matter. He told me all about the secret societies that he bombed. He even bragged that he had staged his death."

"When did you figure out Andy was posing as Russell Whitlock?"

"As soon as I got here. Andy's changed quite a bit over the years. He's heavier, has a thick beard, and his whole posture is different. Had

I zeroed in on his eyes, I might have known. They haven't changed. But I haven't seen him since we were kids in college. I even saw a photo of Russell, but I didn't put two and two together until I got here and saw Andy. I don't know why I didn't suspect it when he reached out to me after all these years."

"Did he say why he was going by another name?"

"He had been turned down by a few secret societies because he had earned himself a poor reputation. It was easier to create a fake identity."

"Did he disclose any of the other names he used?"

"No." Robert winced in pain and sat back in the chair. He put a hand to his ribs and tried to take a deep breath but couldn't. "I think he broke my ribs. Once he opened the door to let me in the house, Andy attacked me and then chained me up with that bomb. When he attacked me, it was like he was...I don't know outside his body or something. His eyes..." Robert shook his head as if trying to rid himself of the memory. Then he held his ribs again and groaned.

Kate knew he was in pain, but she also knew that once medical arrived, she wouldn't be able to speak to him and he had critical information that could save someone else. Kate would cut to the point and try to make this as painless as possible for Robert. "I know Andy and you were in Scroll & Dagger together at Yale. We believe he's going after children of men in your pledge class. Knowing that, do any of them have twins?"

Robert stared up at her through one swollen eye. The other was closed tight because of the swelling. "Is that what Andy is doing? He never said why he was bombing those places or what his motive was. As soon as he told me he killed Michael, I realized he was getting back at me for what I had to do when we were in school together. It's sick. Michael had nothing to do with it. Andy didn't give us any choice but to vote him out." Robert sat back in the chair still holding his side.

"Are you sure he's going after the others in our pledge class?"

"It's what I suspect. Terrance Becker's son, Garrett, was in the house that was bombed at Cornell. I know that Terrance was in your pledge class. The theory is an assumption on my part, but I have some detectives running down leads for me. Is there anyone in your pledge class who has twin sons?"

"David Rivers. He has two sons – Liam and Conner. I don't know where they go to school. I'm not even sure how old they are. It's been a few years since I've spoken to David. He hasn't attended our summer retreats."

That was enough to go on for Kate. She texted the information to Murphy. Then she looked back up at Robert. "Could you go through your pledge class for me and tell me who has college-aged children and where they go to school if you know?"

"I'll do my best." Robert slowly went through the list of his pledge class. Of the nine members of the pledge class, seven of them had children. Robert couldn't remember their ages, some he assumed were college age. He didn't know where any of them were attending school.

Robert wasn't done going through the list. He looked up at Kate and rattled off a name. "We have kids the same age. He has a daughter at Dartmouth who I know pledged Magnolia House. He texted me and told me how proud he was that she had followed in his footsteps and what amazing connections she'd make. He was so proud of her. Was Magnolia House one of the places bombed?"

"I'm afraid so," Kate said. It was all she had needed to confirm her theory. Now all they needed was to find the twins. "Is there anything else you can tell me about Andy or what he told you? Is he working with anyone?"

"He didn't mention an accomplice. I don't think he'd be working with anyone. He was always a bit of a loner." Robert took a breath that pained him. "I don't think he wanted to be a loner. Andy always wanted to be the center of attention. He never had the social skills to pull that off though."

Before Kate could ask her next question, Declan handed Robert a bottle of water. While Robert drank big gulps quenching his thirst, Kate gave Declan an overview of the information she had gathered. "It sounds like Novak has an end goal at Harvard. I updated Murphy who is going to try to find the twins."

"How long ago did Andy leave?" Declan asked.

"I'm not sure. I passed out for a while and then I woke up and yelled for help and passed out again. I don't know how long I've been out."

Kate drew his attention to her. "Did you see Andy making any bombs?"

"I didn't see it, no. But he told me that down there in his basement is where he made them. There were bomb-making materials all around – at least that's what he told me they were. I couldn't even begin to know what was in that basement."

Declan pointed to the front yard. "The bomb squad has an update for us about that."

Kate asked Robert a few more questions and then gave him her cellphone so he could call his wife and let her know he was okay. Robert got out a few words and then was filled with emotion and unable to speak – the pain in his ribs and swell of emotion too much for him. Kate spoke to Tess for a few minutes and gave her a brief update on Robert's condition. She promised she'd call back when the medics arrived and she knew what hospital he was being taken to in the area.

Sirens wailed in the background as Kate hung up. She told Robert how sorry she was about his son and thanked him for the information he was able to provide as the ambulance, with its lights flashing, pulled up the driveway. "I'll need to speak to you more later, but you need to take care of yourself first. I have Tess in protective custody, but we will make sure she gets to the hospital. I want both of you under protective custody until we can capture Andy Novak."

"If you need anything else from me, I'm willing to cooperate in whatever way I can."

Kate thanked him and then she and Declan got out of the way of the medics. As they walked away, Kate asked, "What did the bomb squad find in the basement?"

Declan held back for a second but the look on his face told Kate it was big. Then he said, "Enough RDX to blow up a small city. Plus, other bomb-making materials. We've got it all, Kate. Everything down there could be used in court to prosecute him. Was he really that cocky to think no one would ever connect the bombings to him and find this place?"

"He's supposed to be dead, remember? I think he believed no one would figure out that he didn't die in that explosion. He lured Robert up here with the intent to torture him. I bet he assumed Robert would move his leg and try to leave and end up killing himself, taking all the evidence with him. I don't know how he was going to account for Robert being at his house or the explosion, but he was already declared dead. We'd be left with a lot of questions, but it's not like we'd be going after a dead guy."

Declan cursed under his breath. "He's a sick guy, Kate. Do you think he's going to kill himself at the end of this or disappear?"

Kate knew that if cornered, based on his profile, he'd kill himself. There was no way he'd let the cops take him alive and he'd be too proud to ever let the cops kill him. He'd try to take everyone with him when he went, killing as many as possible in the process. That was the most dangerous part of all of it. She explained that to Declan and added, "I don't think he wants to die. He'll try to get away if he can. It's up to us to stop him."

"What's the plan?" Declan asked the question but Kate didn't answer because the bomb squad commander came over to them and explained the kinds of evidence they had found in the basement – old cellphones, switches, fuses, and RDX among other items. There was also a whole cache of weapons, ammunition, and tactical gear.

The commander's final words were chilling. "I don't know what else he had planned, but it was more than bombing some schools. We left everything in place down there except for the RDX which we have secured." He handed Declan an evidence bag with a handwritten page. "We don't normally take evidence out of scenes. We leave that for the crime scene investigators, but we figured you'd want to see this right away. We photographed where we found it before it was bagged."

Declan examined the contents of the bag. "What is this? I see the names of the governor and a few state senators and some federal representatives in Washington on here."

"I assumed it was a hit list, which is why we brought it up with us."

"We appreciate that," Declan said before handing the bag to Kate. Declan shook the man's hand. "Thanks for getting here so quickly and securing the RDX. We have Leo Wallace with the New York State Police running down some leads about where he got the RDX. Was there anything identifying a source?"

The commander shook his head. "We'll figure it out. There are only a handful of places to get RDX in that quantity. You'll know as soon as I know." The guy left to go back to his squad. The SWAT team had left as well, leaving Kate and Declan waiting for a crime scene team. As they waited, Declan said, "I told Briggs not to bother coming up and that we'd meet him back at the office. Sharon Esposito, with the FBI forensics unit in Boston, is on her way with the crime scene team. You remember her from our previous Boston case, right?"

"The woman you have a crush on and who called me your work wife?" Kate said, trying to hide her teasing smile. When Declan nodded, Kate said, "I remember her. Let's get gloves on and examine the hit list before heading back."

CHAPTER 34

After Sharon and her team of crime scene techs arrived, Kate and Declan gave her the overview and then left to go back to Boston as quickly as they could. On the way, Kate placed a call to the governor's office and briefed his security detail about the threats that had been made against him. Kate sent a photo of Andy Novak and then explained that he had used aliases in the past. He was known to be armed and extremely dangerous. The head of security asked Kate if they planned to alert the public and show a photo of Andy. They hadn't made that decision yet but assured him she'd call back as soon as she knew.

When Declan pulled the car into a parking space at the Boston PD, he cut the engine and leaned back in his seat. "Let's call Spade before we go inside and meet with Briggs and the rest of the team. I want Spade updated on this every step of the way."

Kate agreed and punched in the phone number. They didn't have to wait long. Spade picked up after one ring. She got him up-to-date with all the latest developments. "We are in the process of deciding the next actions to take, most specifically if we should go public with Andy Novak's name and photo. Murphy is tracking down Liam and Conner Rivers, but we don't have an update on that yet."

"Either way, go public," Spade said and then explained his reasoning. "Even if Novak has already kidnapped these kids, then we get more eyes on the lookout for him. If he hasn't done it yet, then maybe we can stop him. Either way, we need him apprehended now. Put a BOLO out on him and call every news station you can. You can let Murphy take the lead with the media for the task force as he has been doing. In the meantime, get word to the parents of these two young men and explain what's happening and get every secret society at Harvard evacuated. If you get any bit of resistance, call me back."

Kate disengaged the call and left the phone in her lap. "Sounds like a plan to me."

Declan excitedly thumped the steering wheel. "That's why I wanted you to call him. I figured we'd get resistance at Harvard and I wanted to hear from Spade that he'd clear the way for us. It's always better if we have Spade for backup."

Kate understood the reasoning and she fully agreed with him. She could only hope with what had already occurred there'd be no resistance at all. Even though it had been years since Kate had been a student, the alumni magazine kept her apprised of all the current information. She already knew Harvard's president by name without having to look it up.

She glanced over at Declan. "President Lawrence Marsh has been with Harvard for several years and in higher education his entire career. I'd hope he'd take threats like this seriously. Although, I am surprised that they haven't already evacuated."

Declan had his hand on the door. "You want to sit in the car and call him or you want to do it upstairs in the office?" His phone rang before Kate could answer. He pulled it from his pocket and said, "It's Murphy." He engaged the call and then hit speakerphone. "Kate and I are here. We are sitting outside of the Boston PD."

"I'm glad I caught you," Murphy said, slightly out of breath. A door slammed, a chair squeaked, and then he continued. "There are too many moving pieces right now to keep up with. First and foremost, we have Lily Cole. She was caught at the bus station trying to leave Manhattan. We are holding her but we don't have much to keep her for long. Do you want to interview her, Kate, or do you want me to handle that?"

Kate's excitement swelled. They had caught the elusive Lily Cole. "I can't come back to Manhattan right now, but get her in an interrogation room and set up remote access. I can interview her that way. We don't even know that she'll be compliant or speak to us."

"She's fairly shaken up, Kate. She hasn't admitted to anything, but I'd bet my last dollar that she's willing to talk. I'll get the interview set up for you within the hour."

"What are you holding her for right now?" Declan asked.

"Conspiracy to commit murder," Murphy said with a sigh. "Given we assume she wrote and distributed those letters it was enough to hold her. I don't think there's any judge in the world that will let that charge stick without more evidence to support it. I don't even think you'd get past a preliminary hearing."

Kate agreed and was surprised they had even gotten that far. "Has Lily said anything about where she was headed or the letters?"

"No. She hasn't asked for an attorney either. When asked if she'd like to make a phone call, she said she had no one to call. That she had no family to help her. That was it and then she went into the cell and didn't say anything else. We told her we were bringing in the FBI to question her and that she should think long and hard about what she wanted to do in this situation. I told her that she had an opportunity to help the FBI if she chose. I didn't even get as much as a change in facial expression. She's a tough cookie, but I still get the feeling she's willing to talk with the right person interviewing her."

Declan gave Kate a sideways glance. "You have a way with girls her age. Maybe she'll tell you more about Novak and where he is right now."

"That's if she's working with him," Kate said then moved on in the conversation. They could sit there and speculate all day about Lily, but it was easier to just get in front of her. "What about Novak's pledge class? Did you find the other members and confirm if they have college-aged children? Robert Hudson gave me information that I can share if you need it."

Murphy rattled off a few names. "Ultimately, your theory must be correct, Kate. Each house that's been hit so far has a child from one of the members of his pledge class. He's killed four of them and injured two others. We have been unable to track down Liam and Conner Rivers. We have local cops heading to Yale and Harvard to search for them, but right now we have no confirmation on their whereabouts. We have been unable to reach David Rivers or his wife, Melinda. We spoke to a housekeeper who said that they are traveling in Europe. We've left messages, but so far, there has been no return call."

"All right," Kate said, frustrated that none of that was good news. "I'm about to call Harvard's president. Let me see if I can get some confirmation about…" She trailed off realizing she had no idea which twin went to Harvard.

Murphy seemed to read her mind. "Liam is at Harvard and Conner is at Yale."

"Thank you," Kate said then gave Murphy a quick rundown of all the evidence they had found at Novak's house. "Robert and Tess Hudson will make good witnesses when the time comes. If the time comes, I should say."

"Kate, what's the worst-case scenario here? That hit list is fairly extensive. Let's say we don't stop him from killing Liam and Conner and he escapes Boston. What will he do then?"

Kate didn't even want to think of it, and by the look on Declan's face, he didn't want to contemplate it either. The question needed to be answered though. They couldn't ignore what was at stake in an investigation that already had the highest stakes of any she'd been on in a long time. "If he feels too pinned down in Boston, he will move down his hit list. I'd speculate Washington D.C. That area has the largest number on his hit list. I don't think Novak will stop unless we stop him or he finishes his list. We have to get to him first." Kate hated that he had gotten as far as he had.

"I assume someone will be watching Novak's house once the crime scene techs are done?" Murphy asked and Kate looked to Declan to answer. With so much else she had to focus on, that was a detail she hadn't planned.

"Taken care of," Declan said. "I have two FBI agents who are going to keep watch and they will rotate out to fresh agents every few hours. If Novak heads back to home base, he's going to be in for a surprise and then in custody. I told them to take him dead or alive and I don't even care if that's my call or not."

"I know we've put a lot on your plate, Murphy, but we need one more favor," Kate said. "We spoke to Spade and we are all in agreement that we need to go public with Andy Novak and his photo and mention the hit list. We want him to know that we saved Robert Hudson – although don't mention him by name – and that we found his stash of weapons and bomb-making material. We don't just need every law enforcement agency to be on the lookout for him, we need every citizen. We need to stress that no one should try to apprehend him themselves because he's considered armed and dangerous."

"Don't you think that will drive him underground," Murphy said with a hint of skepticism in his voice.

"It might," Kate conceded, "but the alternative is much worse. If we drive him underground then we save a few lives and have longer to hunt for him. We can't risk not getting public support in helping to catch him."

Murphy agreed. "I'll get a BOLO out and call the news stations."

They spoke for a few more minutes and then when Murphy was just about to hang up, he gave them a glimmer of hope with some good news. "Tony woke up about an hour ago. The officer called me and told me that he was able to speak a few sentences. He has movement in all his limbs and no apparent head trauma. He has been upgraded from critical to stable condition. He's not out of the woods yet, but it's favorable progress."

"That's the best news we've heard in days," Declan said, excitement in his voice.

When the call ended, Kate turned to Declan. "I can't help but feel the worst is still in front of us."

Declan laid a hand over hers. "We've made progress today, Kate. Enjoy the win."

Kate couldn't summon up the same level of positivity. "If you want to go in and speak to Briggs and update him, I'll call President Marsh and hopefully see if I can find Liam Rivers in the process."

Declan got out of the car leaving her alone to process how she'd approach this. She was anticipating a fight as she had with Yale. That's why she was shocked when her call was sent right through to President Marsh and he couldn't have been happier to hear from her.

"Agent Walsh, I've been expecting your call. Don't worry, I won't give you any trouble like some other universities. You name it and I'm going to get it done for you."

She had been rendered speechless for a moment. "Thank you, President Marsh. I can't tell you how happy I am to hear that. Specific intelligence has come to light that Andy Novak, our primary suspect, is going to kidnap a student at Yale and then bring him to his twin brother at Harvard and kill them both by blowing up a secret society. As you are aware from recent events, this isn't an idle threat."

"Do you have the two students secured?" he asked, interrupting Kate.

"No. We are searching for them now. We have local cops out to both Yale and Harvard trying to track these students down. We also have placed calls to their parents and we have been unable to reach anyone. My understanding is they are traveling in Europe."

"What's the student's name here at Harvard?" When Kate told him, he barked an order to someone either in his office or just outside to go and find this student. When he got back on the line, he asked, "What's next?"

"You need to evacuate all your secret societies as quietly as you can. I don't know if that's going to be possible, but I have no idea which one he'll hit. Liam Rivers is in a secret society, but there's no guarantee that's the one Novak will go after."

"I'm on it, but one question. Why as quietly as possible?"

"I would assume Novak might be watching. Ideally, we'd like to come to Harvard's campus and put cops on each secret society building and try to flush him out without putting students in danger. If he knows there are no students inside, he might change his game plan."

"That makes total sense to me, Agent Walsh. We will give you anything you need. I can set up a meeting with our head of security if you'd like me to do that."

"Yes, that would..." Kate didn't get to finish her sentence because there was a rush of conversation heard through the phone. There was someone in President Marsh's office and they sounded panicked. "Send him in. Send him in. For heaven's sake why wasn't he brought to me sooner," he shouted at the person.

"Are you there, Agent Walsh?" President Marsh said, his voice constrained. "I have dreadful news. Liam's housemate has been trying to meet with me all morning. He's gone, Agent Walsh. Novak may have already got him."

"Stay there and keep the student there. My partner and I will be right over." Kate's breath caught in her throat as she gripped the door handle. She raced to find Declan.

CHAPTER 35

Kate and Declan arrived at President Marsh's office slightly out of breath. After putting the interview with Lily on hold and finding Declan, they beelined directly to Harvard's campus. Kate told him everything that had transpired on the phone call and the student who claimed Liam Rivers was missing. Kate didn't know any more than that. The only saving grace was that President Marsh was going to do everything he could to keep his students safe.

Kate and Declan were immediately ushered into the president's office where they came face-to-face with a pale panicked student. President Marsh, a short bald man with a stocky build and kind brown eyes, stood over the young man who was sitting on the couch and clutching a bottle of water. When he saw Kate and Declan, he rushed to them, looking thankful to hand the situation over to more capable hands.

He gripped Kate's hand in his, which was damp with perspiration. "I'm so glad that you arrived. I've made some calls to security who were dispatched to evacuate the students as best we can. We don't keep a running list of what students are in these societies or living in the houses, so we are unable to contact students directly. We are doing everything we can. Do you want to meet with the head of the security team?"

Kate turned to Declan. "Could you do that while I speak to…" Kate hadn't been told the young man's name.

"Scott Kinney," President Marsh said, glancing over at the young man. "He's been in quite a state. He hasn't even been able to tell me what's happened, just that Liam Rivers is missing and that he found a note with threats made. He said it freaked him out given all the bombings that have happened. He said he called the other members of the society and warned them all."

Kate hated to displace the president of Harvard, but that's exactly what she was going to do. "Do you mind if I use your office while I speak to him alone?"

"Certainly," President Marsh said and then went to Declan and told him that he'd escort him to the security office. They headed out taking the secretary with them. The door was pulled closed behind them.

Once Kate was alone, she went over to the couch and sat down. "Scott, I'm Agent Walsh with the FBI. I've been investigating this case since the bombing at Cornell. We have a whole task force involved with law enforcement in different states. Earlier today, we found out about specific threats against Liam and his brother, Conner. I need you to tell me everything you know so we can find Liam as quickly as possible. He is in grave danger." Kate didn't want to upset the young man any more than he already was, but he had to know the seriousness of the situation.

Scott looked up at Kate with dark round eyes and thick eyelashes. He had a firm jaw and a tussle of dark hair that reminded her of Declan's when they were in their early twenties. His build was similar to Declan's as well. He handed Kate the note he had in his hand. "I didn't know what to do with this."

The paper was crumbled and Kate resisted the urge to flatten it out. The more she could preserve the evidence the better. She shouldn't have been touching it with her bare hands, but she didn't have much of a choice at the moment. The note was simple enough: *Don't go to the cops or Liam will die. He is a sacrificial lamb.* The note didn't surprise Kate, but she could see how a young college student would find the note terrifying.

"Where did you find this?"

"It was tacked to the back door of our house with a knife." Scott sat up straighter. "A knife from the butcher block in our kitchen. It means this creep was in our house. I have no idea what else he did while he was inside."

Kate had a few ideas but she didn't want to alarm him. "President Marsh said that the house has been evacuated of all its members. Is that true?"

Scott nodded and wrung his hands. "With all the other bombings, we didn't want to take any chances. There were only a few of us home anyway when I found this note. I thought it was a joke, so I called Liam but couldn't reach him. His cellphone didn't even ring, just went to voicemail, and he always has it on. Then I called his girlfriend and she said that she hadn't talked to him since he left her apartment last night. He was supposed to call her when he got back to the house and he didn't. She assumed he fell asleep when he got back and forgot. Liam's housemate said he never came back last night."

When thinking about Liam's actions the night before, Kate realized she didn't even know the name of the society where he was a member. "What is the name of your society?"

Scott hesitated to tell her but then thought better of it. "Knights of Fire."

"I'm familiar with it," Kate said and saw the shocked expression on Scott's face. "I'm a Harvard alumnus and so was my father. He taught history here, and when he was in college, he was a member of Knights of Fire."

"I had no idea." Scott blew out a breath and his shoulders relaxed. He sat back on the couch and his body seemed to sink in instead of being as rigid as when Kate first sat down. "Can you tell me what's going on? What is going to happen to Liam?"

"As I said, he and his brother are at risk right now. We believe the same person who is blowing up secret societies has taken Liam and his brother. We know that he plans to bomb a house at Harvard and kill both of them in the process. We need to search Knights of Fire. Can you make that happen for us?"

"I can let you in the main living room area, but that's probably it."

"That's not good enough," Kate insisted. "We need to bring a bomb squad in and search the whole place. For all we know, when he stabbed the knife into your door with the note, he also planted a bomb in the building."

Scott pulled back in fear. "You think he planted a bomb?"

"That's typically what he's been doing. That's why it's so important we get a bomb squad to go over every inch of that house."

Scott turned his head away from Kate. There was something he didn't want to tell her.

"Scott, whatever it is, I need to know. I'm not just trying to save Liam's life. I'm trying to prevent another attack. No one is safe to go back into your house now or for the foreseeable future with Andy Novak on the loose."

Scott turned his head sharply toward Kate. "Andy Novak?" he asked with a catch in his voice.

Kate leaned toward him with interest. "Do you know that name?"

Scott swallowed hard as what was left of his color drained. "He applied for a job with us over the summer. He said he'd been working with Raven Hall in Manhattan, but that he was looking for a change. When we asked for a reference, he refused to give it and got irate with us. He said that we should be able to offer the job as house manager without speaking to references. Andy insisted that his word alone is what we should use to make the decision."

Scott brushed the hair off his forehead. "What Andy didn't know was that I knew a guy at Raven Hall, and I called him to ask what he thought of Andy. I'm pretty sure I wasn't supposed to do that – employment law and all. But if we were considering him for employment, I wanted to know if the guy was a creep or a thief. Our house manager has access to our bank account. The guy I knew warned me not to hire him and even suggested that they were in the process of trying to get rid of him. They had to go through their board to do that and it might take some time. I didn't tell Andy that we called Raven Hall, but we told him we were hiring someone else."

Kate wasn't surprised that Novak had contact with some of his victims before the attacks. "Do you happen to know what they were specifically concerned about at Raven Hall?"

Scott took a sip of water and then rested the bottle on his lap. "He had bought several guns and left them in the basement of Raven Hall. It was more than that though. He also had a habit of interrupting house meetings, and the members felt like he was trying to be a part of them rather than overseeing the house responsibilities, which he was hired to do. One of the members was also concerned because Andy had called his uncle who was in the military and asked some strange questions."

"What kind of questions?"

"He never told me," Scott said, disappointing Kate. He seemed oblivious to her shift in mood as he continued, "My friend said that his uncle encouraged them to fire Andy and cut off all contact. My friend agreed with his uncle and that was the final nail in the coffin, so to speak. They met when school resumed this semester and decided to fire Andy the first week of October. They were in the process of lining up his replacement, but Andy was already searching for other jobs over the summer. Maybe someone tipped him off."

Kate had so many questions, but she was torn between gathering information about Novak and finding Liam and Conner. "What was Novak's response to not getting the job with Knights of Fire?"

"I expected him to scream and yell, but he didn't have any response at all. That was more disturbing, to be honest with you." Scott flipped through an email app on his phone. "We sent Andy and other candidates an email to thank them for interviewing but that another candidate had been chosen. We all kind of held our breath waiting for Andy to flip out."

It all sounded fairly routine to Kate, but she couldn't help but feel like she was missing something. "It sounds like you had a few people interview for the job. Why did Andy stand out during the interview process?"

"Because of his experience," Scott said and then shifted his body so he was facing Kate. "Andy had gone on and on in his interview about how much he wanted to be a part of Knights of Fire. He said that he had worked for other organizations similar to ours, including Raven Hall. But when the time came to review his references and get information about him other than through his direct responses, he balked. That's not normal. You know what I mean?"

Kate did understand and she understood why Novak didn't want to share the information. "Was Liam involved in the interview process with Andy? Had they met?"

Scott nodded. "They had met. Andy came in to interview twice with us and Liam was involved both times. He initially liked Andy, but then later when Andy started to get weird, he changed his mind. Andy never knew that. He got a rejection letter from Knights of Fire, not any individual member."

"Did Andy take any sort of interest in Liam, more so than the other members?"

Scott looked past Kate as if he were trying to recall. "He might have. I remember Andy had asked about our parents and if they approved of us being a part of Knights of Fire. Then he asked what our parents did for work. When Liam started speaking about his father, Andy asked a few more questions directly to him. He didn't do that with anyone else. I don't remember what those questions are now. I kind of tuned it out and didn't think anything of it at the time."

"Run me through the timeline of when you last saw Liam."

Scott opened the calendar app on his phone. "I keep track of house stuff here," he said, explaining what he was looking at. "I saw Liam last night at our house dinner at six. Liam left right after that for his girlfriend's place. He told me he wasn't going to spend the night because he had some studying to do when he got back. When he didn't return, I didn't think much about it. I figured he spent the night anyway and put off studying."

"How did Liam get to his girlfriend's house?"

"He takes the subway usually. There's little parking on her street so it's easier than driving."

Kate hadn't realized Liam had a vehicle. "Do you know if Liam's car is on campus still or at the house?"

"It's parked in the lot at the house. That was the first thing I checked. I thought maybe he had come back and got his car and went out again. I got scared when I saw it parked there. That and the note sent me over here right away."

Kate asked a few more questions to try to pin down Liam's typical movements, but all seemed fairly routine. "I'm going to need to see Liam's car when I bring the bomb squad over. You seemed to have an issue with a search of the house. Why is that?"

Scott's expression told Kate he had hoped she had forgotten about that earlier. "We have a ritual room where things are private and hidden. We aren't supposed to show anyone that."

Kate couldn't believe that even in the face of a potential bomb, he was still worried about keeping their secrets. "None of that matters now," she said, sharply. "The bomb squad has to go through every inch of the place to ensure your safety and the safety of your other members."

Scott remained quiet for several moments then resigned himself. "Then I should probably tell you about the drugs."

CHAPTER 36

urphy was holding a press conference making a public plea to help find Andy Novak as the Boston PD bomb squad unit went through every inch of the Knights of Fire house. Kate and Declan stood back at a safe distance and used Kate's laptop to watch Murphy's live statement being streamed on a local news station's website. The statement was solid, information factual, and Murphy's voice compelling in the action he needed citizens to take in helping with the location and ultimate capture of Andy Novak.

Murphy provided photos of Novak and enough information to lay out the case against him without giving away the entirety of their whole case. There was no denying that Murphy was a compelling speaker and a good media spokesperson for the task force. After he made the statement, Murphy handled the media questions like a pro.

"At least this is something we don't have to worry about on this case," Kate said, closing the website as the press conference wrapped. "Now, all we have to do is hope someone knows something and calls the hotline with information." She wasn't sure Declan was listening to her. He was focused on the Knights of Fire house. She bumped her elbow into his side until he looked down at her. "Did you get much information from the head of security?"

"No. They were able to clear all the houses and get the students to safety. We can say that we at least kept students safe at one Ivy League school, except for Liam and Conner. We confirmed they are both missing now. Their parents are still unreachable." Declan gestured toward the house. "Was Scott seriously worried that they'd get busted for drugs in the middle of all of this happening?"

"He was," Kate said, still not feeling right about how it played out. Before Knights of Fire would allow the bomb squad in, Kate had placed a call to Carmen Langston, Suffolk County's District Attorney, and secured immunity for the members for any drugs that might be found. There would be no way to tell who owned the drugs and it wasn't an investigation they were willing to dive into given everything else that had been happening. Scott promised her they weren't selling but had a stash of cocaine and ecstasy for personal use. If they had any more than the quantities specified, Langston promised she'd go after them and the immunity wouldn't hold.

Kate explained that to Declan and then said, "Let's hope Scott was accurate about what they had."

Declan glanced over at her. "I hate to even ask this, but have you heard anything from Ditch? I'm surprised he's taking this long."

Kate was surprised, too, but Felix had said he dumped the whole message board. "It might be taking him time to find the data. I haven't heard, but Ditch will call me when he knows anything."

Declan ran a hand through his hair, leaving strands sticking up in places. "Where do we go from here, Kate? We know who's doing this, we even know why, but we don't even have one lead where he might be."

"I don't understand how this guy can completely disappear like this," Kate said, even though that wasn't technically true. Andy Novak had remained in the small secret society circle since college, biding his time until he struck. Given the information she had learned from Scott, Kate believed that the prospect of getting fired at Raven Hall and a lack of future work in a secret society had probably caused him to snap. He had successfully killed Michael and Kate believed that had emboldened him to carry out his plan. If he couldn't be among them, then he'd tear down the whole structure both literally and figuratively.

"He's out there someplace, Kate. We need to find the first clue that leads us there." Declan checked his phone. "What time are you interviewing Lily?"

"At three. We pushed it back to give me a chance to interview Scott and come over here and check out the scene." Kate glanced around. "Not that there was much of a reason for me to be here. Nothing is happening."

"Do you think Novak will change his plan now that he knows we are on to him? We've stopped him from killing anyone else in secret societies at Harvard."

Kate thought back to all the bomb-making materials he had left in his house in Andover. "He has no choice but to change it up. Once Novak sees the press conference today and understands that we know he has Liam and Conner and that we found his bomb-making workshop, it's going to be a game-changer for him. He didn't expect we'd find that. With as much money as Novak has, I suspect he might have more property. Could you do some property searches while I interview Lily?"

"That's a good idea. If he's not able to blow up one of these houses, he's going to do something."

Just as they were getting ready to leave, the bomb squad commander walked out of the house with Det. Briggs, who had insisted on suiting up and going into the house with them. When they reached Kate and Declan, Briggs said, "All clear. Didn't even find the drugs Scott said were in the house. One of the members must have cleared them out when they left. Looks like he confessed to the stash for nothing. We'll go to the next house and clear that, too."

There were twelve houses in all that the bomb squad had to search.

It would take hours upon hours of their time, but Briggs insisted it was the only way for them to ensure safety. Kate didn't want to remind him that if Novak wasn't caught, he would easily slip back in and plant a bomb later. If it was what Briggs needed right now to feel like he was accomplishing something, then Kate was all for it. The reality was, without more leads, there wasn't much else for him to do.

Briggs had told Kate to use his office for whatever they needed, so that's where Kate and Declan headed after leaving the Knights of Fire house. Declan took a laptop and headed for a conference room while Kate texted Murphy to tell him she was all queued up for the interview with Lily. Her right palm itched with anticipation. She had been chasing Lily for as long as they had been chasing the bomber. Speaking to the young woman was either going to prove enlightening or a total waste of time. Kate wasn't sure, but she had to know.

Kate had the video chat app open on her laptop and a few seconds later, a young woman's face flashed on the screen. Her hair had been dyed a deep purple and was tucked behind her ears as it lay limp across her shoulder. Her face was free of makeup and she appeared younger than the photo Kate had seen on the Sisters of the Revolution website. Lily's face was drawn and she licked her lips nervously as she got her first look at Kate.

"You're younger than I thought you'd be," Lily said, speaking first. Her gaze roamed over Kate's image and then she looked away.

"I was thinking the same thing about you." Kate adjusted in her chair and relaxed her posture. "I'm not the enemy here, Lily. I want to speak to you because I think you got caught up in something that you didn't mean to and I'm your way out."

"I want to speak to a lawyer."

That was the worst thing Lily could have said. "If you mean that, then I have to shut down this interview right now," Kate responded sternly with disappointment on her face. As soon as Lily lawyered up, an interview would be shut down. "I'm happy to make sure you have a lawyer, but it means I can't help you from this point. Is that what you want?"

When Lily didn't respond, Kate tried another tactic. "After learning so much about you from one of your sisters at the Sisters of the Revolution house, I'm surprised you'd be helping a man commit these crimes. Not only a man but a former secret society member. He's been in that world longer than you've been alive. You were helping someone you called an enemy, Lily, and I want to understand why."

Lily focused on Kate, her eyes blinking rapidly and her hardened facial features turning soft. "I don't understand what you mean."

"What's confused you?"

"You said I was helping a man and I wasn't helping a man."

Kate paused and recalculated her approach. "You were helping someone then? Did you think it was a woman?" When Lily didn't respond, Kate laid out the whole case they had on Andy Novak. When she finished, Lily's face contorted in shock. Kate sat silent for a moment, allowing her words sink in and letting Lily feel the weight of it.

When recognition hit Lily's face that she had been duped, Kate had a moment of feeling bad for the young woman. "I can see that you don't know what you've gotten yourself into, but I'd like to understand your story, Lily. If you help me, then I'm sure I can help you. If you want that lawyer, we can stop and I'll call one for you. I'd rather we speak right now, and I can help you figure out your next best course of action."

With a slight nod of her head, Lily wanted to continue. "I never blew anything up. I didn't know any of the plans. All I did was deliver the note to the New York Times and one of the houses near the bomb site."

It was an admission of guilt but not of anything significant. "Who did you think you were working with?"

"A woman named Abby – another sister with Sisters of the Revolution in New York City. That's how she presented herself online. She said that we had to stop them. That too many things had gone wrong in our country and that secret societies were a pipeline." Lily furrowed her brow. "She said we had to cut the head off the snake and she needed my help."

Kate couldn't help but notice how closely the names Andy and Abby were to each other. She grabbed a notepad from the desk and the pen sitting next to it. She'd take handwritten notes even though she was recording the interview. "You met this person on the internet? Did you ever meet them in person?"

Lily shook her head. "We only spoke online. First, we met on a message board, then Abby messaged me privately and asked if we could chat off the board. She asked me to download a secure text messaging app." Lily mentioned the name of it and Kate knew that the messages were encrypted. There'd be no hope of recovering them for later evidence. That was the whole point of the app. The FBI had been dealing with this app for the past few years.

"When you were talking on the app, did you ever exchange phone numbers or email?"

"No. I had asked Abby if we could do that and she said it wasn't safe for us. That we could only talk on the encrypted app."

"Weren't you afraid that you were being duped? This person could have been anyone."

Lily shifted in her seat, pushing her shoulders back. It was the posturing of someone saying that they weren't a dupe and they knew exactly what they were doing. "I'm not stupid, Agent Walsh. I asked this person for a photo and other clarifying details just like they asked of me. And when she sent the photo, I went to the Sisters of the Revolution website and her LinkedIn page and her story checked out."

"Let me ask you something, Lily. Were you the first person to mention Sisters of the Revolution?"

Lily eyed her suspiciously. "Yes," she said slowly. "I mentioned it on the message board before Abby asked me to speak off of there. That's how she knew that I'd be friendly to her cause."

Kate could see the connections that Lily had missed. She didn't want the young woman to feel stupid, but it had to be pointed out. "Did it occur to you if you could find information about Abby on the Sisters of the Revolution website and her LinkedIn page that the bomber you call Fuse could as well?"

"What do you mean, Agent Walsh?"

Kate leaned her arms on the table and stared into her laptop screen. "I mean that you had said you were with Sisters of the Revolution on the message board before this Abby person brought it up. A quick website search will tell me what you're all about. Another website search will bring me to any of the chapters' websites where I can pull photos, get people's names, and then go to social media and also pull photos. Was there anything this person told you that wasn't also accessible online that you could verify?"

Lily shifted her eyes away from the screen. Kate couldn't tell if she was looking at something on the table or if it was just occurring to her that she had set herself up. When she looked back at Kate, she said, "I'm in serious trouble, aren't I?"

CHAPTER 37

After Lily walked Kate through her activity on the message board and then on the app, Kate pivoted to the most important details. "When did you first find out Abby's plan?"

"I didn't, not really," Lily said, slumping in her seat. "She had told me that she was going to get rid of secret societies and I asked her how. She said by scaring them into closing. It wasn't until the first bombing that I understood what she was going to do. Then when I didn't go to the cops with the information I knew, she said that I was involved now and that if I told anyone I'd be the one blamed. She assured me no one would ever catch her unless I spilled the details. If I did that, she'd kill me."

Kate believed that the threat had been made. "Where were you the weekend of the Magnolia House bombing?"

"In Hanover," Lily said softly. "We were supposed to meet but Abby didn't show. She told me she was running late and I didn't have anywhere else to go so I slept at the bus station. When I heard about the bombing, I knew what she had done. I got out of there."

Kate tried not to show any reaction to the news. "What about the Sword and Crown bombing at Cornell?"

Lily looked down at the table. "I was at the Sisters of the Revolution house. I figured then the cops would suspect it was me if they knew I had been in both cities during the bombings, so I left immediately. I hadn't been attending classes at Cornell this semester, but I was still staying at the house. I was broke and one of my sisters gave me money for bus fare. Abby demanded that I come to Manhattan and I was too afraid to say no. I told her I was on my way and she gave me an address in Brooklyn to meet her. That turned out to be an abandoned house."

Kate wanted to get to that, but she had one important question first. "Did you know that someone tried to kill my partner and me in front of your house?"

Lily shook her head. "I only knew about that later when they said it on the news. I wouldn't have been okay with that. Not that I was okay with anything that was happening. After the first bombing at Dartmouth, I had asked Abby why she had killed people and she said it was an accident and that the bomb went off at the wrong time. She said it wouldn't happen again. She said the goal was to get rid of where they met and did their rituals, not kill people."

Kate didn't believe that for a second. "Four women were killed at Magnolia house. What was your response after Cornell when more people were killed?"

"I was scared," Lily said, her voice filled with fear.

"So afraid that you were willing to meet with Abby?"

Lily argued, "I thought I could stop her." When Kate didn't respond, she went on. "Agent Walsh, I know what it's like to be so angry that you're willing to do things you wouldn't normally do to get retribution or even justice. I figured something had happened to Abby to make her this angry, and I figured if I could talk to her maybe I could talk her out of what she was doing."

Kate wasn't sure she believed her. "You said a moment ago that Abby threatened you. Help me to understand why you wanted to meet with a person you had never met before, that you knew had already killed students in two separate bombings, and threatened you. It makes no sense to me that you'd willingly go meet this person." When Lily didn't say anything, Kate pushed again, this time harder. "If you want me to help you, I said you have to help me. Telling me obvious lies that don't make any sense doesn't help me. You can sit in prison for a long time for all I care." She pushed her chair back like she was going to stand and end the interview. Kate wasn't bluffing. She had two young men's lives hanging in the balance and had no time to waste on lies.

All at once, Lily blurted, "Abby told me if I didn't come to Manhattan, she was going to blame the bombings on me. She said there was proof that I was in Hanover during the Magnolia House bombing. She said that she'd call the hotline and leak a tip that it was me, and since I had gotten in trouble before, the cops would believe it was me."

When Kate pulled her chair back in and resumed her attentive position, Lily continued. "The other stuff I said is true. Abby was making me meet her, but I thought I could talk her out of doing what she was doing. I didn't lie about that. But going to Manhattan wasn't a choice."

That was closer to the truth. "What happened when you got to Manhattan?"

"I told you I went to the address and there was no one there but a bunch of homeless people and drug addicts. I didn't feel safe there, but I had no money to go anywhere else. I stayed until Abby told me what she wanted me to do. She sent a message via the app and I copied it onto the paper and dropped it off at the *New York Times*. Then when Raven Hall was destroyed, I attached another note to a neighbor's door. I got freaked out after that and deleted the app. I hid out at a friend's house."

"You left notes even though you were already afraid that Abby was going to blame you? Before doing that, you hadn't been involved at all? Help me to understand your actions."

Lily stared off into space and then when a few moments passed, she shrugged. "I can't explain them. I was afraid of doing and then of not doing it. I didn't feel like I had any good options. But the friend whose house I was staying at reminded me Abby didn't know where I was and that if I deleted the app, she couldn't track me. That's what I did."

"Felix Poole," Kate said and watched Lily's reaction. By the look on the young woman's face, Kate knew that she had been in the house at least one of the two times she'd been there to interview Felix. "Was he hiding you?"

Lily wouldn't meet Kate's eyes. "He said he'd protect me. Felix didn't know who was responsible for the bombings, but when he found out that I was the one who wrote the notes when you put my face all over the news, he showed me how to delete the app and then later tried to kick me out. I guess he got freaked out too with me being there."

"Tried?" Kate asked, eyebrows raised.

"We got into a fight and I hurt his hand. I left after that. You had already been there and I figured you'd be back."

At least Felix had told the truth about that. Kate asked a few more questions about Felix, but there was no sign that he was involved in anything other than not having good sense and running a message board as he had. When she was done asking about Felix, she changed tone, pushing harder. "Lily, how did you feel about the bombings? You seemed to agree with them if I'm understanding you correctly."

Lily took a moment to respond, seeming to measure her words carefully. "I'm going to say it again so you understand, Agent Walsh. I had nothing to do with the bombings other than the notes, which Abby told me to do. I had no prior knowledge that any of the bombings were going to take place. Abby didn't tell me her plans ahead of time. After I dropped off the note and saw what she did to Raven Hall and all those people she killed, I cut off all contact and have been hiding out ever since. I don't agree with the bombings and wish I had never gotten involved."

"I believe you were being set up, especially being the one to write and deliver the notes. That alone puts a target on your back with law enforcement," Kate said honestly. "Given that, was there more Abby wanted you to do?"

Lily took a breath and let it out slowly. "At first, Abby wanted me to visit her in Boston, but I couldn't get there when she wanted me to. Then she wanted me to meet her at her house someplace north of Boston. She said she had another house near the beach in Cape Cod. If I couldn't make it from Ithaca to Boston, I sure wasn't making it to Cape Cod. I could tell she was getting annoyed with me especially after she felt like I agreed with her that secret societies needed to be stopped. That's why I tried so hard to get to Hanover. After the bombing, I think she was trying to blame me."

"Did you ever discuss bombings with her?"

"Not really, just after the fact. By the time she killed someone in the first bombing, Abby had changed and was threatening me. She said that I had to do something to be involved. I was glad that it was just dropping off the notes. As I said, when I saw what she did to Raven Hall, I got off the grid and stopped communicating with her."

"Did Abby give you an address for her house in Cape Cod? What area of the Cape?"

Lily shook her head. "We were supposed to meet at a restaurant in Hyannis near a bus stop and then she'd drive me from there. I wasn't able to make it in time."

"Did Abby tell you about her final plans or why she was doing any of this?"

"She didn't tell me about any plans," Lily said with a slight edge of annoyance. Kate knew she had answered that question a few times now, but Kate had to rule it out. "I don't know what more she has planned. I haven't communicated with her since I dropped off the last note. That was the last thing I did and the last time I had communication with her."

If Lily's story held, Kate wasn't sure what she'd be charged with. It would be something minor in comparison to the crimes that had been committed. Kate asked a few questions about the bombs and bomb-making materials, but Lily didn't know anything at all. Kate believed her.

"When am I going to be set free?" Lily asked.

"I don't know," Kate said, answering as honestly as possible. "I'm willing to speak to the prosecutor assigned on your behalf for cooperating." None of that mattered to Kate right now. Lily was in federal custody and that was probably the best place for her until Andy Novak was caught.

Now came the hardest part. Kate asked, "Do you know a man by the name of Andy Novak?"

Lily shook her head. "I've never heard of him before. Should I have?"

"He is the bomber that you've been corresponding with. I assume he's presented himself as a woman and a Sister of the Revolution to gain your trust. My guess is either he thought he might need some help and then changed his mind or wanted a scapegoat if the bombing went south."

Lily started to cry and she wiped the tears from her eyes. "I'm so sorry," she said.

Kate didn't have much sympathy for her or any more questions. "Lily, we believe Andy Novak has kidnapped Liam and Conner Rivers and plans to kill them. We have not been able to reach their parents, David and Melina Rivers. We are doing everything we can. Are those names you've ever heard?"

Lily squinted. "Liam Rivers who attends Harvard, and his father, David, who went to Yale?"

Kate wasn't sure how Lily might have known them. "Yes," she said cautiously, wondering what she had walked into.

"I haven't seen Liam in years, but I met him when I was in high school. His father went to college with my uncle."

Kate reached for her phone and scrolled through the photos until she found the one at Robert's house of his pledge class. When she found the photo she wanted, Kate enlarged it and turned the screen so Lily could see it. "Is your uncle any of the men in this photo?"

Lily stared at the screen. "My Uncle Mark is the third guy in on the left."

Kate asked the question she already knew the answer to. "Does your uncle have any children?"

"No. He never got married, but we were close growing up on account of how abusive my parents were. It was my uncle who helped me get into Cornell."

Kate couldn't help but feel that Lily sitting in protective custody was luckier than she realized. She had so many questions running through her head but none that Lily would be able to answer. Kate leaned on the desk and locked her gaze on the young woman. "Lily, if you think of anything else I need to know or anything you think might be able to help me find Liam and Conner Rivers, please let me know. The more cooperative you are the more lenient the prosecutor will be with you."

"What's going to happen to me?"

"Being in federal custody is the safest place for you right now." Kate finished up the interview and then was about to close the video chat when she remembered one important question that Lily should be able to answer. "What was Abby's screen name on the message board?"

"I don't know how to pronounce it or what it means, but it was in German."

Kate ended the video chat quickly now that she knew for sure what user was Fuse. This meant that Ditch could run an IP search for that user's name if he had been able to access the data. She pushed the chair back so hard it made a loud scraping noise on the floor. She stood in the middle of the office not sure what she should do first. She wanted to call Declan, but another call was more important.

By the time Ditch answered, Kate shouted, "Tell me you found something." Before he could answer, more calmly, she asked, "Is there an IP address in Cape Cod?"

CHAPTER 38

"I'm only just now getting into the message board, Kate. When Felix wiped it, he scrubbed it good. He admitted to me that he didn't want law enforcement to be able to trace it back to him, so this wasn't your normal data dump."

"You're in then?" Kate asked, not caring about the rest of what he was saying. The one drawback of Ditch was that he could get too down in the weeds with what he was doing instead of just cutting to the chase and giving Kate the information she needed.

"I'm in, but I haven't been able to run any searches or get IP addresses for the membership yet. That's going to take some time."

"We don't have time," Kate said frustrated. "I know the screen name in German is Fuse. That's who we are after. I need you to focus on running IP searches for that address only right now. And run all of them that you can find. For all we know, he was posting as he was moving locations. We know for sure that he was living in Manhattan and had a house in Andover. I just heard that there might be a third location in the Cape."

"I'll do my best, Katie, but you know my magic fingers need time to work." He chuckled. "Speaking of that, you know I like to take my time, right? You and I could…"

Kate couldn't believe he was being suggestive with her right then while she was desperately trying to save the lives of two college students. "Not now, Ditch! Actually, not ever, and stop calling me Katie, especially in front of Declan. I'm fairly sure if you do it again, I'm not going to be able to stop him from pounding you into the pavement."

Ditch laughed again and it infuriated Kate. "You two should just do it already. We all know you want each other. Declan is too much of a little boy to make a move. You need a real man, Kate."

"What I need is for you to do your job. Call me back if you find anything." With that, Kate ended the call. She was about to call Murphy in the hopes that he might be able to connect with Andy's sister, but Declan threw open the door and startled her. She dropped her phone on the ground and when she stood upright again, Kate saw how red his face was. Beads of sweat had started to form at his hairline. "What's going on?"

Declan took a few steps toward her, shaking a piece of paper in his hands. "I found it, Kate. Andy Novak has another address – on Dale Avenue in Hyannis. He had it buried under a dummy corporation. It's not listed under his name which is why we hadn't found it initially."

"Dale Avenue?" Kate asked, not sure she had heard him correctly. When Declan confirmed, her hand flew to her mouth. "That's right near the Kennedy Compound. Marchant Avenue intersects with Dale, which is a fairly short road. What is he planning to do?"

"Slow down, Kate. We don't know that he's there."

"We do," Kate said, reaching for the notes she had taken during the interview. "Lily admitted she wrote the notes dictated to her by Novak, but she didn't know it was him. Lily thought she was dealing with another woman in Sisters of the Revolution named Abby. She claims she didn't know anyone would be killed. Get this, Declan. Her uncle was in the pledge class with Novak. He didn't have any children. I assume he specifically targeted Lily and either wanted her as his fall guy or possibly, he wanted to kill her. He kept asking her to meet up places, but she wasn't able to get there. I don't think Lily has any idea how close to death she got. After she dropped the note at the *New York Times* and saw what he did at Raven Hall, she left the last note at the neighbor's house and stopped communicating with him. She deleted the app and everything. But here's the thing – one of the places he wanted to meet up with Lily was Cape Cod. This has to be it, Declan. It has to be."

Declan's mouth set in a firm line as he considered what they should do. "Let me call the FBI office here. They can chopper us in. Otherwise, it's a nearly two-hour drive. In the meantime, let's get Boston State Police involved. They have a SWAT team and a bomb squad and can at least clear the neighborhood and do an initial assessment for us. I don't know what more we can do without eyes on the place. We can't send in local cops to handle this."

Kate agreed to the plan and called Briggs, who was still working with the Boston PD bomb squad to clear Harvard secret societies. Once he was briefed, Briggs took the role of liaising with the Boston State Police while Declan called the FBI field office for transportation support. Briggs said he'd catch a ride with the state police chopper.

While they were all doing that, Kate called Spade and updated him. He was as shocked as she was. At the end of the call, Kate spoke her fears aloud. "If he wanted to kill these kids, he would have already done it. He could have blown up Knights of Fire or killed Conner in his dorm. I have a feeling Novak has something bigger than that planned."

Almost as if on cue, the other line rang with Murphy's name and phone number appearing on the screen. She told Spade she needed to take it and would call him back if it was important. She assumed it was about Lily, but was rendered speechless by what Murphy said. So much so that Kate needed him to repeat it.

"Fuse went to the media, Kate. I got a call from the *New York Times* reporter. He's going to hold a press conference on his own – streaming live inside a house with two hostages. I assume that's going to be Liam and Conner Rivers. The reporter told me that Fuse, which is what he's insisting on being called, has already called all the major networks and newspapers. He gave them an address in Hyannis where they should go and wait. What do you want to do?"

Kate cursed so loudly Declan popped his head back into the office to see if she was okay. "We just found out about that address when you called. We are headed to Hyannis right now. Murphy, the house is not far from the Kennedy Compound."

Murphy whistled. "When Fuse goes big, he really goes big. How did you figure it out?"

"Lily mentioned an address in the Cape and Declan found another property listed for Novak that he had hidden under a corporation. He was hiding that property for a reason. This has to be it. Did he confirm his identity, other than calling himself Fuse?"

"Only Fuse. A reporter I spoke to asked him to confirm that he was Andy Novak and the reporter said he screamed that he was only to be called Fuse and then hung up. What do you need me to do? It might take me a while to get up to the Cape."

Kate wanted Murphy there. He was the only calming presence in this case for her. "Get to the Cape when you can. You've been on this case since the beginning. You might as well be there at the end, too. Bring Leo if he's around. Boston State Police might want his assistance. Call the media on your way and see if they plan to stream Fuse or what they are going to do."

Kate wasn't sure if it was something in her voice or Murphy's innate intuition on the case, but at the end of the call, he said, "You've got this, Kate. This guy has knocked us all for a loop, but you've got it. Now go save those two kids and take him down."

It was the pep talk Kate needed.

When the chopper landed in Hyannis, a state police officer was there waiting to drive them to Dale Avenue. On the way, he updated Kate and Declan about the scene, which had grown more chaotic by the minute. Media had filled the neighborhood, with a mix of residents who were angry as much as they were terrified. The officer assured Kate that the media was being kept far back from the house.

He also explained that, thankfully, there was no one in residence on the Kennedy Compound today. He looked at Kate in the rearview mirror as he spoke. "The whole area has been cleared and the only home of interest now is a two-story simple Craftsman. It's got a wide enclosed sun porch on the front that blocks a clean line of sight into the front windows and the front door. There's a deck off the back, too. So far, SWAT hasn't approached. The hostage negotiator was hoping to make some headway with the guy but so far nothing."

Kate knew Fuse wasn't going to negotiate or be taken alive. Their only goal was to save Liam and Conner and stop Fuse.

The officer apologized for dropping them off so far from the scene. The road was a mass of people, four and five people deep up to the police barricade. Kate and Declan made their way through the crowd, flashed their FBI credentials to the cops standing guard, then moved through the barricade with ease. Once on the other side, the road opened up and was lined with police cars.

They were so far from the home, they had about a half-mile walk until they reached the perimeter the Boston State Police had set up back from the house. Kate saw then how difficult the situation they were dealing with was. The logistics were a nightmare – no sight lines into the home, and no good areas to breach.

Briggs, who had arrived shortly before them, catching a lift with the state police, pointed toward the house. "There is a small beach and the ocean on the other side. We've got two crews in the water on boats but no clean line of sight into the home. Do we have any confirmation that Fuse is Andy Novak, other than this being an address that comes back to him?"

"That's it," Declan said. "It's all we have right now but seems good enough for me." He hitched his jaw toward the house. "We need to make contact and make sure he's in there."

Briggs pointed to a man in full SWAT gear up toward the front of the line of cops. "Believe it or not the house has a landline. Fuse won't answer."

This was Kate's cue. If anyone was going to make contact with Fuse, it was going to be her. "Get me that number and we can get this started."

CHAPTER 39

The phone rang six times and Kate held her breath waiting for it to be answered. The line went dead and she tried it again. Nothing. Frustrated, she turned to walk back to Declan when her phone rang from an unknown number. It had to be him.

"Fuse, this is Agent Walsh," she said, engaging the call. "You have all of our attention now."

"Good, Agent Walsh. That is what I intended." He snickered. "I can't believe you showed up. You've got some guts I'll give you that. How many times have I nearly killed you and your partner?"

"Three and each time we survived. Imagine that, Andy Novak."

"Don't call me that name!" he shouted and then cursed at Kate. "You are to only address me as Fuse. Do you understand?"

Kate steadied herself. "I understand. Can you confirm that Liam and Conner Rivers are with you?"

"I can do you one better. I'm texting you a link right now."

Kate pulled her phone back from her face and waited for a text message to come through. When it arrived, she clicked the link that brought her to a website. In the middle of a screen was a blacked-out video. She hit the play button and the video sprang to life.

Liam and Conner were sitting in chairs but neither looked tied to them. There was a bomb below them and it looked to Kate like the chair seats acted as a trigger plate. Kate wasn't sure how the bomb worked and it would take an expert to tell her that. She also wasn't sure from the photos she had seen which brother was which. They were identical and now both had been badly beaten, so their faces were bloodied and nearly indistinguishable.

Kate forwarded the link to Declan so that they could watch the video while she remained on the phone. A loud murmur of noise rose behind them. Kate assumed the media finally realized the video that they had all been waiting for was finally live and they were all salivating over it.

Declan took his phone and went to find the bomb squad commander to get as much information about the bomb as possible. Kate figured she'd go right to the source.

Kate held the phone to her ear "How does that bomb work?"

"I'm glad you asked. It's genius. I can't even believe that I made it." He said it like he wanted praise from Kate, which she wasn't going to give. She remained quiet until he answered her question. "If Liam gets up, he has thirty seconds to get out of the house and take cover before the whole house blows up and kills his brother. If Conner gets up, the same thing. Now if both of them try to get up, it will detonate. Let's see which brother saves himself first."

This man was sick. He had pitted brother against brother in a fight for survival. There was someone noticeably absent from the video. "Where are you while all this is taking place?"

"You don't need to worry about that."

"I know why you're doing this," Kate said. "You're killing the children of men in your pledge class at Scroll & Dagger. You started with Michael Hudson."

Fuse let out a maniacal cackle. "You don't know anything."

He said the words but Kate was sure she heard a hint of surprise in his voice. "We found Robert, too. Alive. At your house in Andover. He identified you and we found all your bomb-making material. We know everything, Fuse. You should give yourself up now."

That revelation was met with deafening silence. A beat later, undeterred, Fuse said, "It's almost time for me to go live and tell the world my story." The call ended and Kate was left standing holding the phone with her focus glued on the house. They had to find a way to disable the bomb and get the boys out of there.

Kate marched over to Declan. "Fuse isn't in there." She explained that he hadn't answered the house phone but had called her back from an unknown number. Then she detailed how the bomb worked. "He's not in that house. He's around here somewhere watching this spectacle, but he's not in that house. He plans to escape this."

"Can we go in and rescue the boys then?" Declan asked, looking down at Kate.

She shook her head. "Absolutely not. He's close and he's watching, Declan. If we go anywhere near that house, I'm sure he will detonate the bomb."

"We can't just sit here and wait for them to die," he barked back at her.

Kate shared his frustration and didn't take it personally. "We have to figure something out." She turned to the bomb squad commander. "What can you tell me about that bomb?"

The bomb commander started rattling off technical terminology that Kate struggled to understand. When it got right down to it, he said, "I've never seen a bomb quite that sophisticated before and I'm not sure how we would dismantle it without killing someone in the process."

Kate rolled her eyes toward the sky and cursed loudly. "We need Leo."

"Leo Wallace?" he asked with hope in his voice.

"Yes, he's been on this case since the start."

The commander nodded his head. "That's exactly who we need."

Kate stepped off to the side and placed a call to Murphy. It rang a few times and then went to voicemail. She left him a detailed message and then called Leo directly. He picked up almost immediately. There was so much background noise Kate couldn't hear him though. It almost sounded like the rhythmic blades of a helicopter.

"We need you here!" she shouted into the phone. "Murphy has all of the details."

All at once, the noise dissipated and Kate could hear him. "We're here, Kate. Murphy got us a ride with the New York State Police chopper. We'll be there in ten minutes or so they tell me."

Kate was so happy she could have kissed the man. She got him up to speed as he drove toward her location. "The bomb squad commander with the Boston State Police said he's never seen a bomb quite like this."

"That's because it's probably military-grade," Leo said and then added, "About six months ago, a whole lot of RDX went missing from an Army base in Maryland. I have a contact there who has never heard of Andy Novak, but they suspected someone on base sold some RDX to a military contractor. You want to bet that was Andy Novak?"

Kate was sure it was, especially given they already knew how easily he changed up his identity. "Did they find the person who sold it to him?"

"No, it's an ongoing military investigation. I also found out that Novak's uncle was an explosive ordnance disposal specialist and I'm sure taught Novak a few tricks of the trade, probably without realizing his nephew was going to grow up to be a serial bomber."

"Do you think you'll be able to disarm it?"

"I've never seen a bomb I couldn't disarm, Kate. Figure out a way for me to get in there and I'll take care of it," Leo said with an air of confidence and no doubt in his voice. "We are just pulling up."

They ended their call and Kate explained to Declan that Murphy and Leo were making their way through the crowd now and what Leo said about the RDX. "I feel better with them here."

"We need to find a way into that house."

"I'm sure Novak has it rigged. We know there are cameras and he will see if we go in and probably detonate the bomb. What we need to do is find him, distract him, cut the power to the video, and give Leo time to disarm the bomb."

Declan smiled down at her. "Is that all?" He snapped his fingers. "Just like that."

Kate knew he was kidding, but she wasn't. If they had any shot of saving Liam and Conner that's how it was going to need to go. It would be a nearly simultaneous effort to stop him. Before Kate could organize her thoughts and come up with a plan, her phone rang again.

She scrambled to engage the call. "Hello."

"Agent Walsh, I don't know what you're planning out there, but don't do anything stupid. If you think I won't protect my plan, remember Manhattan. You've escaped from me a few times, Agent Walsh. Trust me, if I wanted you dead, you'd be dead. I'd be careful you don't cause me to strike out again. I've got you surrounded." The phone went dead.

Kate's eyes darted around the area and panic set in. "We need to clear the area!"

"What is it, Kate?" Murphy asked from her left. She was suddenly surrounded by Declan, Briggs, Murphy, and Leo.

As calmly as she could, Kate explained, "Fuse called me again and reminded me of what happened in Manhattan. We are all sitting ducks out here and so is the media. We are far enough away from the house if the bomb detonates, but we don't know what else he has planned. He could have IEDs all over this area and we wouldn't know it."

Kate had expected to see panic all over their faces but instead, it was steady resolve. "We aren't going anywhere, Kate," Leo said sternly.

"He has two college kids in that house and I'm going to get them out alive." Briggs agreed.

Murphy said, "Kate, he might just be trying to distract you, to shake you up, and get you off your game. We know he's armed. We know there could be bombs and he could shoot at us again, but we need to see this through to the end."

Declan put a hand on her shoulder. "We're going to stop him, here and now. This ends today."

Kate nodded, feeling every muscle tense and then loosen. They were right. They had all witnessed what Fuse was capable of and were there anyway. "Okay, let's find him."

That was easier said than done. They gathered a group of Boston State Police who were securing the area and told them to search for cameras and then go find the homeowners they had displaced and do a house-by-house search for Fuse. Kate was sure he was either close by and watching them or he had cameras rigged and was watching them from a distance farther away. Either way, he had eyes on them and was in a position of power. She needed to turn the tables.

They got about thirty minutes into the search when a rolling thunder of voices started up again from where the media and onlookers stood. Declan looked down at his phone and then held it up for her to see. "Fuse is going live."

A hush fell over the crowd as the video started. The video didn't show the man's face, only his shoulders down to his hands that rested on a large mahogany desk. There was nothing distinctive about him. He wore a black short-sleeve tight tee-shirt that showed off the definition of arm and chest muscles. He wore no watch or ring or had any birthmarks or even distinctive freckles.

His voice was clear and strong. "I started with a mission and I'm nearly done with this part of it. When I am finished, I will disappear to continue my work elsewhere. No more should our country be led by a small select group of people whose destinies have been pre-determined at birth. Generation after generation the same voices and faces dominate business and politics while the rest struggle to be heard and survive. I am doing this for the common man – every man. I have been wronged and justice will prevail." Fuse launched into a long-winded diatribe of conspiracy theories about secret societies and how everything he had done and will do will be to destroy what he called the pipeline to Washington and Wall Street.

As Kate watched the video, her eyes drifted to his side. Behind him, there was something on the wall, but she couldn't quite make out what it was. She could see a small hint of color every time he raised his arm. If he lowered his arm, it would disappear behind him. When he raised his arm again, the image reappeared. There were only flashes of it, but it was familiar to her.

Kate pointed to the screen. "What's that right there? Every time he moves his arm you can see it." Kate was no longer paying any attention to what Fuse was saying. She was focused only on the image.

Declan peered down for several seconds and then softly he said, "It looks like a blue background with a yellow bird's foot."

As soon as Declan said it, Kate saw the image more clearly. She could finally make out the full image. Her brain put the pieces together as it flashed and disappeared again as she wracked her brain for what the image represented. She was nearly there when off to the right of her Murphy yelled.

"It's the presidential seal!" Murphy rushed to Kate's side holding his phone out to her. "It's the eagle with thirteen arrows from the presidential seal."

Kate whipped around and stared directly at the Kennedy Compound. John F. Kennedy used the compound as a base for his successful 1960 U.S. presidential campaign and later as a summer White House and presidential retreat. He had been photographed working there on numerous occasions. Kate grabbed Murphy's arm. "Is there a fortified bunker or safe room on the compound?"

"I don't know," Murphy said and then turned to Briggs who shrugged. "How is it even possible he'd get in there?"

Kate pointed to a small marina visible from where they stood. "I only know this from being up in this area on summer vacations, but while the gate in front of the driveway is locked, the Kennedys don't have a private beach of their own. It's shared with this neighborhood. You technically need a pass but no one ever checks because no one is ever back here. All you have to do is unlatch the gate, walk into the marina area, and step onto the beach. From there, you just walk up the back hill to their property. I'm sure it wasn't that accessible when JFK was president, but that's how I've always known it to be. I'm surprised an alarm didn't trip, but with Fuse anything is possible."

"Who would know about the layout of the compound then?" Murphy asked.

Kate stepped to the side and called her boss. Her heart was racing so loudly it pounded in her ears and she cursed each time the phone rang without him answering it. When he finally answered, Kate asked, "Does the Kennedy Compound have a fortified bunker or safe room anywhere?"

Spade hesitated, and he never hesitated. "Why?"

Kate didn't have time for this. "Fuse is in there. I can see part of the presidential seal behind him on the video. He's in there, Spade, holed up and spewing his nonsensical conspiracies to the world while he's got two kids strapped to a bomb in his nearby house."

Spade, who heard Kate's tone even if he couldn't see the stress on her face that caused lines across her forehead, explained, "In the main house, there's a safe room where JFK worked. It's in the back right corner of the house. There are no windows and no discernable door. The room does not officially exist in the home's architectural plans.

It was an add-on. The wall is the door, but it's only accessible by a push-plate by the family room fireplace." Spade gave Kate explicit instructions on how to find the trigger mechanism for the hidden doorway and a basic layout of the room.

Kate didn't question how he knew this, but Spade knew all, so it wasn't surprising. "Declan and I are going in. If we don't come out alive…"

"Don't even say it, Kate." Spade paused and then wished her well. "Do what has to be done."

Kate knew exactly what that meant. She ended the call and then turned to Declan. "You ready?" She leveled him a look and he nodded once. They'd both go in and only fate and good training would determine if they both walked out alive.

CHAPTER 40

Kate and Declan took the beach route to enter the home, hoping that if Fuse had put up cameras, he might not have covered that ground since it was far less tree-lined. Briggs and Murphy had wanted to come with them but Kate needed them to assist Leo in getting inside the home. The bomb squad was there as backup for them all. They had little time to plan but made the best of the time they were afforded.

They belly crawled up the slope of the beach and lay in the overgrown grassy dunes as they assessed the main house on the compound. It was one of three homes on the property. All three buildings were white clapboard structures typical of Cape Cod architecture. From their position, they stared right into the sunroom of the home.

Kate doubted Fuse had time to rig the home with explosives. Being neighbors of the Kennedys, she was sure Fuse had heard about the home's interior or possibly even been inside. In 2012, the main house was donated by the Kennedy family to the Edward M. Kennedy Institute for the United States Senate. Ethel Kennedy now lived in one of the other houses on the compound. No one was present on the property tonight. For that, Kate was thankful.

Only a small light shone beyond the sun porch. The sun was setting low to the west and small LED lights that lit the pathway from the beach to the house had turned on, guiding them to the back door.

"You ready?" Declan asked her, his voice heavy and deep.

"Ready." Kate wasn't sure what compelled her, but before she leaped from her position and ran toward the back of the house, she turned her head enough to plant a single lingering kiss on his lips. "Please don't die," she whispered.

"You either," he said, kissing her back.

They counted to three and together they shot up from their position and ran toward the back of the house like their lives depended on it. Vests on and guns at the ready. They had probably only a minute to accomplish their task if all went well. They were counting on the element of surprise and Fuse's distraction of his ranting speech, which he was still giving as Kate and Declan left for their mission.

Declan tried the sun porch door and found it locked. As quietly as he could, he knocked out a pane of glass with a rock from the nearby garden, reached in, and turned the handle. Declan stepped in first and Kate followed behind, watching their backs. They paused only a moment to see if there'd be a response from inside the home. When there was none, they proceeded.

They moved swiftly through the first floor of the home. Kate felt the weight of history on her. An image of Jackie Kennedy in her pink Chanel suit with the president's blood on the front flashed in Kate's mind. Then another image of Jackie here in the home as she tried to recover from the loss. Kate had always wanted to see inside this home, but this was not how she had ever envisioned it.

They only had one chance to get this right. Kate zeroed in on the task at hand, pushing all other thoughts to the side. They made their footfalls as soft as possible as they went through the rooms, clearing each space as they went.

When they found the small hallway Spade described, Declan followed it to the end while Kate stood at the entrance to the family room. He turned when he got in position and looked at Kate one last time. They shared a look only two long-term partners could share – a rush of emotion and fear and a silent prayer that it would all be over soon and they'd both live to tell the tale.

They offered each other a smile and then Kate ducked into the family room and headed straight for the fireplace. Her breath caught in her throat when she found the push-plate. She hesitated for only a second. She placed her palm on it and pushed hard. Kate rushed out of the room to cover Declan. By the time she made it back to the hall, the shots came – one and then rapidly three more. Kate's eyes slammed shut and her body rocked forward with each shot, worried it was Declan on the receiving end. The night she found him bloodied and shot flashed in her mind.

Kate held her breath as she ran down the hall with her gun in front of her. She paused at the half-open doorway and then lunged in ready to shoot. She exhaled when she saw Declan standing hunched over the far end of a desk.

He angled his head to look at her. "Threat is neutralized. He had a vest on and I thought at first it was a bomb, but the first shot didn't kill him. It took a few more."

Kate rushed to him and stared down at the man Declan had killed. There was a pool of blood seeping into the cream-colored carpet and his face had been obliterated from the gunshots. There were no words she could say. They had this planned at the start. Once they knew where Fuse was hiding out, they decided that the only way to neutralize him would be to shoot him before he could reach for a detonator or fire back.

Kate whipped around and turned to the camera. The live feed had covered it all. She walked across the room to the phone set up on a tripod and ended the video feed without saying a word to the stunned viewers who had just witnessed Fuse's death.

"Are you okay?" she asked, returning to Declan. She put a hand on his back and he turned around finally, looping an arm around her shoulder. She stared up at his face and couldn't read his expression.

Declan closed his eyes. "I wasn't sure until I pulled the trigger that I'd be able to do it. I kept worrying that I would freeze or have a flashback from the night I was shot. I can't tell you how I feel to know I can still do my job. I'm sorry I wasn't more help on this one."

"Declan, you stopped him. You're the one who found the house and went in and stopped him. We all owe you a debt of gratitude." She nudged him in the belly just below his vest. "I'm not going to do all the paperwork that killing him on a live stream is going to entail. That's all on you."

Declan's laugh cut some of the tension in the room. "I can't believe we are in the same room where JFK worked."

Kate couldn't believe it either. She couldn't believe that a dead guy's brains were now soaking into the carpet. She looked back toward the camera and the chair that Fuse sat in while he spoke to the live audience. The presidential seal was right behind the desk. It was only by sheer luck that a small corner of the seal was visible in the video. If Kate believed in miracles, she'd have called it that.

"Liam and Conner," Declan said suddenly, bringing them right back to the risk they still faced.

As the words left Declan's mouth, Murphy and Briggs shouted their names from inside the house.

"We're in here, down the hall," Kate shouted back. "Have you heard from Leo?" she asked as Murphy crossed the threshold. The front of his shirt was torn and there was a streak of mud down the side of his cheek.

"We got him in through a basement window. As soon as Declan shot Fuse, Leo breached the room and started working on the bomb. Both boys are fine. They will need medical attention. Fuse roughed them up pretty badly when he kidnapped them. Conner positively identified him as Andy Novak. He said that his father had talked at great length about how he had gotten Andy Novak kicked out of his pledge class. It was a story the father told many times. Conner had seen photos of him and recognized him this many years later. Novak didn't explain why he was kidnapping them, but they knew it was him."

Kate didn't have any doubts that it was Andy Novak. The medical examiner would have to do DNA testing to rule it officially, but she wasn't worried about that now. There was so much left to do even though the case was officially over. There would be a tally of the death toll from Fuse's rampage, meetings with the universities and parents, and official statements to be released from all the law enforcement agencies involved. The amount of work to close the case would be overwhelming, not to mention working out a deal for Lily Cole, which Kate was adamant about. The young woman was troubled, but she wasn't a killer.

There'd be many lingering questions about the whys and hows and even probably conspiracy theories ranging around this for years to come. Kate couldn't think about all that now because her phone was ringing. All eyes turned to her.

"Spade," Kate said as she answered, stepping to the side of the room. "Declan killed him. It's over and Leo saved Liam and Conner."

"I know. I'd take the time to tell you both it was a job well done, but you've been requested."

"Requested? By whom?"

"The Secret Service," Spade said and let the words linger without explanation.

Kate didn't understand what the Secret Service had to do with this case. The Kennedy Compound was no longer an active presidential location. "Please don't leave me in suspense like that."

"You and Declan need to head back to Boston and pack your bags and then head back to the Cape. Take the ferry over to Martha's Vineyard. This is not public yet, but two senators have been killed."

"What?" Kate asked, her mind reeling. "Was it Fuse?"

"No, this isn't related," Spade assured her. "I'll give you all the details later, but suffice it to say there was an off-the-record, back-channel meeting between seven senators from both sides of the aisle and the vice president on Martha's Vineyard. Two senators are now dead. The rest, including the vice president, have been sequestered in the home in a remote part of the island. I'll give you the rest of the details later."

Kate's mind reeled. "I assume I shouldn't say anything to the rest of the team."

"Keep it all confidential for now. The public will know soon enough." Spade went to end the call but had one more dire warning for her. "Bring some wet weather gear. You probably haven't been watching the news but there's a Category 3 hurricane heading up the coast. Prediction right now is that it will move out to sea, but the European track has it heading right for the island."

Kate felt like she'd just been punched in the gut. "Understood," was all she could say, and then she ended the call. She looked around the room at the mess they were leaving behind. She did not doubt that Murphy and Briggs could handle it. She approached Declan and put a hand on his back.

"We need to go. We have another case."

"Already?" Murphy said, raising his eyebrows in a question.

Kate trusted both Briggs and Murphy, but she couldn't spill the details, not that she knew too much. "Unofficially, all I can say is we are being summoned to Martha's Vineyard by the Secret Service, not related to the president. Officially, I said nothing at all and you'll have to wait for it to hit the news."

Briggs and Murphy understood and promised to wrap up the case in their absence. Before they left, Murphy shook their hands and then pulled Kate in for a hug, which she was more than happy to give him. "Don't be a stranger, kid," he said and then released her. Kate was sure she had made a friend for life.

Once they were outside and had dodged the throngs of media still reporting and were headed for the car that would take them back to the helicopter, Kate gave Declan the details of what Spade said about the case. "I don't even know who the senators are or what kind of meeting they were having, but I assume since they are sequestered, they are all suspects."

Declan cursed. "I hate politics, Katie. I hate hurricanes about the same. But I've never had a bad trip to Martha's Vineyard." He smiled down at her. "Where are we staying?"

"I guess my house," Kate said, revealing a secret. Before he could react, she added, "It was my grandparents, and since I rarely get a vacation, I'm never there. I have a caretaker though."

Declan reached up and tugged at her hair. "I can think of worse places for a case. Do I get my own bedroom or are we going to share?"

"You get your own room and you better behave yourself with the Secret Service watching."

"You know me, best behavior."

Kate did know him and that's what had her worried. She felt like they were being thrown into the lion's den. "We are both going to have to be on our best behavior or our careers could be on the line." They had handled a lot of cases in their careers but their work rarely crossed politics. This could either be career-ending or career-making for them.

Kate was ready and she hoped Declan was, too.

About the Author

Stacy M. Jones was born and raised in Troy, New York, and currently lives in Little Rock, Arkansas. She is a full-time writer and holds masters' degrees in journalism and in forensic psychology. She currently has three series available for readers: paranormal cozy mystery Harper & Hattie Magical Mystery Series, the hard-boiled PI Riley Sullivan Mystery Series and the FBI Agent Kate Walsh Thriller Series. To access Stacy's Mystery Readers Club with three free novellas, one for each series, visit StacyMJones.com.

You can connect with me on:

- http://www.stacymjones.com
- https://twitter.com/SMJonesWriter
- https://www.facebook.com/StacyMJonesWriter
- https://www.bookbub.com/profile/stacy-m-jones
- https://www.goodreads.com/StacyMJonesWriter

Subscribe to my newsletter:

✉ http://www.stacymjones.com

Also by Stacy M. Jones

Watch for FBI Kate Walsh Thriller Series Book 5 - DEAD SENATE –
Early 2023

Access the Free Mystery Readers' Club Starter Library
PI Riley Sullivan Mystery Series novella "The 1922 Club Murder"
FBI Agent Kate Walsh Thriller Series novella "The Curators"
Harper & Hattie Mystery Series novella "Harper's Folly"

Sign up for the starter library along with launch-day pricing, special
behind-the-scenes access, and extra content not available anywhere
else. Hit subscribe at http://www.stacymjones.com/

**Please leave a review for The Fuse. Reviews help more readers
find my books. Thank you!**

Other books by Stacy M. Jones by series and order to date:

FBI Agent Kate Walsh Thriller Series
The Curators
The Founders
Miami Ripper
Mad Jack
The Fuse

PI Riley Sullivan Mystery Series
The 1922 Club Murder
Deadly Sins
The Bone Harvest

Missing Time Murders
We Last Saw Jane
Boston Underground
The Night Game
Harbor Cove Murders

Harper & Hattie Magical Mystery Series
Harper's Folly
Saints & Sinners Ball
Secrets to Tell
Rule of Three
The Forever Curse
The Witches Code
The Sinister Sisters
Scandal Knocks Twice

www.ingramcontent.com/pod-product-compliance
Lightning Source LLC
Chambersburg PA
CBHW021228310726
48971CB00006B/1733